UTOPIA 58

UTOPIA 58

DANIEL ARENSON

CHAPTER ONE

It was a cold dawn in days of war, and KB209 walked through the crumbling metropolis toward the rally.

Many others walked with him. White robes rustled, whispering like the gray sea beyond the power plants. White masks stared ahead, broad and blank like mannequin faces. KB209 himself wore the equagarb. He was the same as everyone else. He was no better than his comrades. He was equal. The pain always reminded him.

The citizens marched down the road, one by one, line by line, snaking like a white river through canyons of concrete and rust. All around them, the industrial complex rumbled and screeched and belched fumes. Factories loomed, their dark windows peering like serpentine eyes. Balcony railings leaked rusty tears, staining cement faces. Everywhere the chimneys pumped smoke. Gears turned. Pistons chugged and hammers rose and fell. Even over the constant ringing in his ears, KB209 could hear this song of industry. Smog hid the sky, and the scent of searing metal filled his nostrils.

The smell comforted him. Everywhere they were building weapons. Guns and bullets. Shells and missiles. Airplanes and tanks. The enemy was nearer every day. But Father protected him. Father was good.

"Do you reckon he'll be there today?"

The words came from BOT76. The comrade leaned closer, white robes swishing. Xer mask filtered xer voice. It emerged deep, distorted, and metallic, hiding any hint of age or gender.

"At the rally," BOT76 added. "They say Father will finally visit City5801."

"Father will visit when he deems us worthy," KB209 said. His mask too had a voicebox, giving him the exact same voice. A robotic voice. Mechanical like the gears, pistons, and chains clanging inside the factories. "Hush. Walk quietly. Some among us might be mute. They cannot speak. Dare you flaunt your voice?"

BOT76 gulped behind xer mask. Xe said no more.

KB209 had never seen his comrade's face. He didn't know if BOT76 was male, female, old, or young, whether xer skin was pale or dark, xer face fair or foul. He had never heard BOT76's true voice, though they had been comrades for years. They were the same. They were equal.

They kept walking. The road stretched on. They walked past textile factories, great halls where seamstresses sat at assembly lines, sewing uniforms for the troops. Around a soup kitchen where hundreds lined up, holding bowls, waiting for the Father's charity of cabbage soup. Under the towering white cranes where the bodies of dissidents hung, swaying in the cold wind.

It was a hard walk. It had been years since the surgeons had shortened KB209's legs, but they still hurt. Every step shot bolts of pain through his bones. His legs were disproportionately short below the knees now. But he was exactly 5'8". Like his comrades. Like all peoplekind. He was the same. He was equal.

A memory rose, unbidden. Himself as a young person. Growing fast, growing tall. Until a day when the doctors measured him. When they *tsk*ed their tongues behind their masks.

"I don't want the surgery," he had told them.

"You're too tall," a doctor replied. "That's hardly fair, is it? You would have an unjust advantage over your comrades. You don't want to oppress them, do you?"

KB209 trembled. "I won't. I promise."

A nurse stroked KB209's mask. "It won't hurt."

They had lied, of course. They had used no anesthetic. After all, throughout history, most patients had no access to drugs. Would it be fair for KB209 to enjoy painless surgery while others had suffered?

So they had cut his legs open. Sawed out chunks of bone. Bolted him back together. All while he screamed. For a few years—painful recovery. Then when he had grown some more, they had again taken their saws, and—

KB209 found himself trembling as he walked. Not just with pain. With rage. Horrible rage, a burning inferno. It was unfair! Why had they hurt him? Why did the pain still linger? He could have walked stooped over. Or others could have worn platform shoes to match his height. They should not have done this! They—

His mindcap activated.

A smooth voice spoke in his head.

"Forbidden thoughts detected."

And the pain came.

The electricity flowed from his mindcap, pounding his skull, rattling his brain. KB209 bit down on a scream. He trembled as the bolts slammed into his head. Stronger. Stronger. Searing. Burning.

"Enough," he whispered. "Please."

He reached under his hood. He clawed at the metal mindcap, but its screws were embedded into his skull. The electricity was still flowing.

I'm glad I'm the same height as everyone, he thought, biting his lip so hard he tasted blood. *I'm glad I'm only 5'8". It was unfair for me to be tall. Unfair to those born shorter. I'm no better than anyone. I'm the same. I'm equal. I'm sorry for ever being tall.*

The electricity stopped.

The pain ended.

KB209 gasped for breath.

As he kept walking, tears flowed behind his mask. He was so grateful for his mindcap. For reminding him. For keeping his monstrous side at bay. For keeping his thoughts pure.

He clutched the Iron Quelis that hung on a chain around his neck. An equal sign with a star in the middle. Symbol of equalism. Of all that was just and right. He gripped it so hard it nearly tore his white gloves. It hurt. But pain was good. Pain kept him on the equal path.

They kept walking. One by one. Line by line. Thousands of blank masks. Heading onward through the smog.

They were passing by barracks now. The concrete fortresses lined the roads, covered with barbed wire. Equalizers in white armor stood on the roadsides, manned the gates, and aimed rifles from the rooftops. They served in the Equapol, the People's Equality Police Force. The equalizers wore no masks, and instead helmets hid xer faces.

KB209 vaguely remembered the equalizers dragging him away long ago. Beating him. Shoving him into a train car.

The ringing in his ears made it hard to remember. They had measured his intelligence long ago. The same doctors who had fixed his legs. His IQ had been 115, they had said. Too smart. Unfair. Cruel. How could he be smarter than others, oppress them with his advantage? So the doctors had tweaked his mindcap. Made it forever ring. The song still sang in his ears. Even now, so many years later. No pattern to it. No end. Ringing, whistling, chirping, making it so hard to think, to focus, to remember. His IQ was now 100. Average. He was the same. He was equal. He was good to peoplekind.

KB209 was glad to have lost his intelligence, to be just like his comrades. But he wished he still had more of those memories. Not just of the doctors. Of himself.

His mind felt like a dark empty chasm. Where had he come from? His childhood was gone. Had he ever been a child at all? Did he have a true name? Had there ever been a life before the People's Party? Before equalism?

Did we wear masks then? he wondered. *Did we breathe clean air, and have parents, and—*

A zap again.

KB209 gritted his teeth.

The Party had always ruled. It had been there since the beginning, and it would be there forever. Equalism was good. Equalism was eternal. Father protected him. And the pain ended.

The line passed by rubble now, the ruins of bombed factories. Bricks rose in hills, and pipes and gears lay rusting under the smoggy sky. A few stray dogs roamed the desolation, ribs visible, fur patchy with mange. An orphan sat atop the bricks, not wearing equagarb, face visible to all. A boy, KB209 thought. Disgust rose in him.

A boy! How dared this child flaunt his gender. His face. His skin color. He was crying. So thin and hungry. Perhaps a victim of the war, his school gone to rubble. The urchin ran toward the crowd of comrades, palm held out. Begging for food. He was speaking, saying something, but the ringing in KB209's ears grew louder, censoring the forbidden words, words spoken without a distorting voicebox.

For a moment, a strange emotion filled KB209. Something soft and sad like melting snow. Pity?

He looked at this boy.

It's not his fault. He's hungry. He has no robes or mask. He—

The electricity bolted.

Disgust. Disgust rose in KB209, washing over all other feelings. Wretched waif!

"How dare you show off your face!" he said. "Do you think you're better than us? Do you think you're special? You are the same!" KB209 turned toward a group of equalizers on the roadside. "An enemy! A bigot!"

The equalizers approached. Their white ceramic armor clattered. Their visors hid their faces. They grabbed the boy and dragged him off. He screamed, but an equalizer slapped a palm over his mouth.

Another memory pounded through KB209. Himself—a young man, not much older than a boy. Dragged off by the police. Sent to a reeducation camp in the snowy mountains. The pain. The pain of it! The whips and shocks. The hooks holding his eyes open. The endless propaganda reels, tests, beatings …

He pushed the memory aside before his mindcap could jolt him. No. That had never happened. That was the enemy placing false memories in his mind. That was treason. Equalism was good. Equalism was just. Equalism was forever, and the Father protected him.

Past the rubble, they finally reached ArenaT671. The largest structure in City58OI.

The dome soared from the snowy piles of rubble, many stories tall. Its surface was raw concrete, same as any apartment block. All buildings in this city looked similar. Boxy. Gray. Equal. Even official Party buildings did not boast of their status. Banners draped across the arena walls, displaying white *quelii* on gray fields—equal signs with stars in their centers. More equalizers surrounded the arena, staring through the holes in their helmets, guns raised.

Another memory, fainter this time. Himself as a child. Coming here to see a game. Players kicking a ball. Crowds cheering. A blurry figure at his side, and a comforting hand on his shoulder. But there hadn't been a game here in years, maybe decades. Games were deemed too competitive, for how could one team claim to be superior to another?

ArenaT671 now served a new purpose. A noble purpose. For fifty-seven hours, every cycle, it was empty. And on the fifty-eighth hour, they came here. Crowds of comrades. For the rally. For the affirmation of faith and justice.

"He'll be here this time," BOT76 said. "Father will come. I can feel it."

BOT76 had suffered no electrical shocks during the long trek here. Xe never did. Xer thoughts were always so pure. KB209 envied xer. But then he crushed that feeling too. Envy was forbidden, a sinful feeling, a desire to be more than one's humble self. He could only hope to someday be as equal as his comrade.

They entered the arena. Whenever he came here, KB209 was struck by the beauty of this equality. Fifty-eight thousand comrades—all equal. Everyone exactly 5'8", their legs surgically shortened or lengthened with rods. Everyone with the same body—breasts amputated, fat sucked through tubes, bones broken and reformed. Everyone in white robes, hiding pale skin, youth, or grace, signs of cruel privilege. Blank masks, staring ahead. Metal mindcaps, buzzing, keeping thoughts pure.

Beauty. It was beauty.

KB209 stared at this wonder, and his tears flowed.

He climbed the tiers of concrete seats, making his way toward his assigned spot. The tiers rapidly filled, the people moving in orderly lines. The equalizers stood guard, guns raised and ready.

"I am popped up!" BOT76 said. "I love me a good rally. I spend all fifty-seven waiting for it. Nothing like some good old patriotism to make your heart beat, eh?"

"Some people have heart irregularities," KB209 reminded xer. He grew tired of listening to his comrade talk. The ringing was so loud today, and words made it worse.

BOT76 swallowed. "You're right, I … I'm sorry." Xe trembled and clutched the Iron Quelis that hung around xer neck.

"I meant no privilege. I hurt those with heart disease. I repent." Xe gripped the quelis tighter, and blood dripped from xer palm. "I repent!"

The tiers were almost full now. Fifty-eight thousand people. Yet the seat to KB209's left was still empty. Where was his usual left comrade, the laconic 76TY7?

Cold sweat dripped down KB209's back. At the last rally, 76TY7 had been xer typical dour self. Quiet. Barely cheering with the others. The equalizers had detained xer after the rally. Charged with not cheering loudly enough. KB209 had dared to hope his comrade would get away with a night in jail, maybe a public whipping. But if 76TY7 wasn't here today …

The memories again.

The reeducation camp.

The burning metal and—

No. No! Not the pain again. KB209 clawed at his mindcap. Equalism was good. Equalism was just. Equalism was forever, and the Father protected him.

Finally, a figure climbed the tiers toward them. Clad in white robes. Blank mask hiding the face. KB209 stared, and a sliver of hope filled him.

Yet when the person came nearer, he could read the tag stitched onto the robes. It was not his laconic friend. It was a new comrade. Xer name was patched onto the white fabric: LE905.

KB209 looked at xer. Trying to judge. To guess. Male? Female? Young or old? If she was female, was she pretty? KB209 had once seen a photo of his mother. At least, of the woman who had donated her egg to the labs. He had found her medical records, seen her unmasked face. Grainy, black and white, so beautiful. Did LE905 have such a face?

He looked away, clenched his fists, and tried to hide the pain of electricity pounding his skull.

Music began to blare from the arena's speakers. Shostakovitch. It was always Shostakovitch, for Father deemed all other composers inferior. The Eighth Symphony today, a favorite of the Party. The notes soared, triumphant. Backs straightened and chins rose across the theater.

The rally began.

Equalizers formed a ring around the concrete arena, and the screens descended.

Each monitor was huge, larger than a house. Fifty-eight of them descended on cables, making sure every comrade could see.

Fifty-eight was perhaps excessive. Even three or four would have been enough. But fifty-eight was the Numerus Sanctus. The holy number. There were fifty-eight cities in Isonomia, this great nation. There were fifty-eight schools in each city. Fifty-eight floors in the concrete buildings where the proletariat lived and toiled.

On fifty-eight screens, the Numerus Sanctus appeared.

The music softened.

A figure appeared on the monitors.

Like all comrades, he wore robes and a mask. But they were not white. This equagarb was golden, the robes woven of finest muslin, the mask forged of pure gold.

Comrades cried out in awe.

"Father! Father, protect us!"

KB209 shed tears. He cried out with them.

"Father! Father!"

The Father was one of them. He showed no skin, no face, no age nor race. Yet he was so beautiful. First among equals. The only male in a genderless land. Protector of them all.

He was not here in the flesh. It was only a recording, of course. A video on the monitors, and not even a live one. Just the same recording they saw every rally. But that didn't matter. They all knew: the spirit of the Father was with them.

The symphony ended with an abrupt, jarring note.

A voice boomed from speakers. The voice of the Father. Deep and resonant, yet soothing. Stern but kind. So loud that waves of bass vibrated through the concrete tiers.

"There have been fifty-seven utopias!" The Father announced. "Fifty-seven failed experiments."

The Father began to recite them. KB209 called out their names with his leader. With fifty-eight thousand other comrades.

"The Soviet Union. The Khmer Rouge. Jonestown. The People's Republic of China. The People's Republic of North Korea …"

The list went on. They kept reciting. All regimes from ancient history. How long ago had they risen and fallen? KB209 didn't know. Yet he could taste antiquity with every syllable.

Finally they reached the fifty-seventh failure. A regime called the North American Collective.

Silence fell for a moment, then the voice from the speakers boomed again.

"We are Isonomia! We are Utopia 58. We are the utopia that worked!"

It was the same speech every fifty-eight hours. KB209 had lost count of how many rallies he had attended. Yet today he cheered as loudly as ever. He cheered with everyone else.

Comrade 76TY7 had not cheered loudly enough last rally. Xe had disappeared. KB209 would never be so treasonous.

The Father's image faded. The monitors now showed the ocean. Gray, polluted waves, coated with a film of plastic, foam, and oil. The camera panned over this sea of trash, moving toward a distant land. A realm far in the Orient. A place where the sun was too hot, the air too dry, where sand instead of snow covered the streets.

A city. They viewed a wretched city of sandstone, copper, and palm trees. The most vile place in this world.

The Father's voice emerged from the speakers.

"Behold Zion! Behold the land of sin!"

Across the arena, the people booed. Their voices rose so loudly that throats tore. KB209 jeered with them, jeered as loudly as his polluted lungs would allow. All around him, his comrades were shouting, voices distorted by the voiceboxes in their masks. A cacophony of metallic screeches and rumbles like the city factories.

Equalizers patrolled among the comrades, recording the volume of the cries. One comrade was not loud enough. KB209 saw the equalizers dragging xer away. He looked back at the monitors. At the wicked land of aggression. And he kept booing.

The video zoomed in on a palace. A palace with gilded domes and walls of marble. Nobles appeared on screen, displaying their pale skin with impunity. Showing it off. Their bodies were obese, soft, pampered. Makeup defiled their faces. They bathed in luxurious pools. They ambled through gardens of plenty. They dined in glittering halls, fattening themselves on feasts.

"Behold the Zionites!" boomed Father's voice. "Behold how they hoard wealth. Behold inequality!"

The boos shook the arena.

The cameras panned out, moving away from the palace, revealing the slums of Zion. Mile after mile of shantytowns. Millions of Zionites lived in the wretchedness, clad only in loincloths, their skin draped across jutting bones. An old man crawled on the ground, sipping from puddles. A child wept in a corner, trying to suckle from the dry breast of his mother. Another mother was cooking her own baby over a campfire.

"The workers of Zion live in misery!" boomed the Father. "While their leaders grow fat on their labor. Behold the sins of inequality! Behold the decadence of our enemy! The Zionites would turn our glorious empire into such a hive of depravity. We must defend our fatherland! We must defeat the Zionites!"

"Kill them!" shouted a comrade several tiers down.

"Bomb their cities!" roared another comrade.

Beside KB209, BOT76 raised his fist. "Kill every last rat!"

At KB209's other side, his new comrade—LE905—screamed. "Burn the Zionites! Burn the bigots!"

The chant caught on. "Burn the bigots! Burn the bigots!"

The cries continued for a long while. The video of the slums ended. Now the monitors showed the figure of a man.

Of the Great Enemy.

Of him. The anti-Father. Standing twenty feet tall.

Bialik.

"Behold the enemy of equality!" boomed the speakers.

It was the same video of Bialik they saw in all the rallies. A hunchback. Eyes beady and glittering. Beard black. Nose beaked. His robes were embroidered with jewels, and slaves languished at his feet. His clawed hands clutched a goblet of blood. He drank greedily, spilling red rivulets into his beard.

KB209 stared in disgust. That wretched man! That ape! That vampire! Flaunting his gender, his wealth, his obesity! Abusing those beneath him! Threatening the glory of Isonomia! Hatred. Pure, hot, searing hatred filled KB209. Last rally, he had not felt enough hatred. His head still pounded from the electrical shocks. Today his wrath was purer.

Across the arena, the voices of the comrades rose to a frenzied howl. Comrades were trying to reach the monitors, to tear them apart, and the equalizers held them back.

"Show him your disdain!" cried the recorded voice of the Father. "Throw him your shoes!"

Caught in the fervor, KB209 removed his shoes. He hurled one at the nearest monitor.

"Pig!" he shouted.

Beside him, BOT76 tossed a shoe of xer own. "Murderer!"

LE905 hurled xer shoe with great force, scoring a direct hit. Xer shoe thumped onto the monitor, hitting Bialik in the eye.

"Bigot!" xe cried.

"Bigot!" KB209 shouted with xer, tossing his second shoe. Across the arena, thousands of shoes flew, peppering the monitors, hitting the vile creature in the video. Bialik kept guzzling blood, then tossed his cup aside and licked his sharp teeth.

"Die, pig!" LE905 was screaming. "Die! Zionite swine! Die!"

KB209 looked at xer, impressed by xer fervor.

A flash of color caught his eye.

He looked down at LE905's feet.

He gasped.

In a world of gray concrete, dark metal, and white equagarb, there it was.

Color. Vibrant red. Nail polish on LE905's toenails.

KB209 lost his breath.

Nail polish.

His head spun. Everything else around him vanished. The roaring mob. The brutal arena. The anti-Father on the monitors. The shoes that still flew. The voices that cried out.

He saw nothing but those toenails. That red. Not a red like the blood the Zionites drank. Red like apples. Like flowers. Like things he could barely remember, faded echoes of a past lost under decades of pain and sound.

KB209 had seen comrades cheer too meekly. He had seen comrades fall during the long marches. But he had never seen an act of such brazen defiance.

Those toenails. That was rebellion.

He wanted to cry out. To call the equalizers. To scream.

LE905 was a rebel! Xe stood out from the crowd! Xe was different, not equal!

She's female, he thought. *She's a sinner. She flaunts her gender! Her individuality!*

He had to turn her in. To be a patriot. To crush her bigotry, her oppression. How dared she wear the symbol of equalism while exposing beauty, femininity!

He saw an equalizer a tier down. KB209 was going to call out. To doom this traitor to the reeducation camps.

The apples were sweet. They crunched in my mouth.

I remember red anemones in a field.

The red breast of a cardinal.

A woman's kiss.

The mindcap was shocking him. The bolts slammed into his skull with a fury. But KB209's heart was pounding hard, and adrenaline flooded him. He stayed on his feet.

He looked at LE905. She was looking at him. Their eyes met through the holes in their masks.

She was a woman. And she had blue eyes.

They only made eye contact for a second, but it seemed like eons to KB209. An idyllic summer of lost childhood. A youth of love in a field of flowers. A second that became an era of his life more vibrant, real, and meaningful than the decades before it.

Then she looked away, and it tore out his soul.

She knelt and lifted shoes, two among thousands that littered the tiers. It didn't matter which ones she chose. All comrades had the same size feet, the toes surgically reshaped to fit the standard shoe. KB209's own toes had been shortened, the tips sawed off, leaving no toenails.

LE905 placed her new shoes on. And she vanished in the crowd.

The rally was over.

"Ah, shame!" said BOT76. He elbowed KB209 in the ribs. "I was sure the Father would visit us this time. I mean, videos are great. Splendid videos! But I was hoping we'd see him in the flesh. Ah well, maybe next time, eh, comrade?"

BOT76 had been saying this for years. Every rally, the Father was said to visit another arena in another city. In all his years coming to this arena, KB209 had never seen the Father appear in person.

"Maybe next time," KB209 said. "If we distinguish ourselves. If we prove ourselves the most equal."

BOT76 nodded enthusiastically. "I think we stand a chance now. We shouted extra loud today. Splendid shouting! Lots of hits with the shoes. That new comrade—xe hit that vile Bialik right in the eye! Super splendid. The Father will hear how pure our hatred is. He'll visit us next rally. Mark my words, KB! In fifty-seven hours, you'll see."

KB209 was barely listening. He was thinking of a woman with blue eyes. Of red nail polish. Of an act of rebellious beauty.

"Come on, comrade." BOT76 slung an arm around him. "Let's spend an hour in the milkbars. Some fermented breast milk will do ya good."

KB209 blinked. "Work. Must work. From each according to xer ability, to each according to xer needs."

BOT76 slapped him on the back. "Ah, you work too hard." Xe grimaced, earning xer first mindcap-shock of the day. "I mean—splendid idea, comrade. For the good of equality! With our toil, we worship the Father."

Both comrades found discarded shoes. The crowd was trailing out of the arena, heading to the factories and ministries where they toiled. They built weapons. They mined underground. They attached themselves to pumps, letting the machines harvest their milk. Some, like KB209, taught the sacred truths. The proletariat toiled all day, every day. Leisure was laziness, and there was a war going on. They all did their part. Soldiers fought.

Comrades toiled. All for equalism. All to defeat the Zionites. All for the grace and glory of the Father.

Outside on the road, BOT76 slapped KB209 on the back again. "See you in fifty-seven hours, comrade. Next rally should be a good one." He winked through his mask. "I'm off to sneak in a pint of breast milk before work."

KB209 did not join his comrade. The ringing was so loud in his ears. He could barely think. He knew that anything he drank or ate would taste like lead.

The truthhall, his place of toil, was only a few blocks from the arena. But KB209 took a circuitous route. He walked down the stone canyons, trapped between the cliffs of concrete and leaking rust. He passed by towering gears and pistons. He walked through the shadows of factories that belched out fetid clouds. Between the buildings, he saw the ocean. Gray, polluted, churning like bad milk.

Somewhere beyond the water—a desert land of sin. The land that caused all this pain. That stole their food, forcing the comrades to live on rations. That flaunted inequality. That all good, equal comrades fought to destroy.

A land of color instead of white and gray. A land of wealth and poverty instead of unity.

A land of red flowers.

A land of memory.

Red—like a smile from a bygone era. Like a nearly-forgotten kiss. Like toenails on a blue-eyed woman.

"Forbidden thoughts detected," intoned his mindcap.

It shocked KB209, and his teeth ached and threatened to fall from his gums, and piss ran down his leg. But KB209 thought of her. Of her blue eyes. Of an eternal second. Of a memory he refused to lose.

She is a female. LE905 is a woman. And I am a man.

At that thought, the electric bolts became too painful to bear. The mindcap thrummed, the screws tightening, the agony searing. KB209 filled his heart with nothing but love for the Father. With devotion to equalism. With hatred for the wretched Bialik. And there was no more pain. There was only comfort and goodness. Because equalism was good. And equalism was just. And the Father protected him.

He turned away from the gray sea. He walked toward the towering truthhall, prepared to toil for his beloved Father.

CHAPTER TWO

The truthhall rose before him, a Brutalist monument of concrete and steel.

Turrets rose toward the smoggy sky, splotched with bird droppings. Fences surrounded the complex, topped with barbed wire. Windows silently screamed, filled with bars like rusty teeth, drooling rusty rivulets. Equalizers, their white armor polished, stood atop the roof and towers, machine guns in hands.

There were fifty-eight truthhalls in City58OI. This one, Truthhall Y6W, was ranked last. This was where KB209 served his Father.

He approached the checkpoint. Equalizers stared through opaque visors, faceless, heartless, and patted him down. He passed under a barbed wire arch into a cement courtyard.

The pupils were already there, waiting for the school day to begin. They stood in formation. Line by line. Every child the same height. Their shoes had soles of different thickness, equalizing their heights. In a few years, once their adult height was reached, they would go under knife and saw, achieving true equality of stature.

The pupils wore their equagarb. White robes. Blank white masks. Their metal caps buzzed, bolted into their shaved heads. They stood perfectly still, not even brushing off the flies. Barely breathing. Patriotism. Hatred. Discipline. These were the three pillars all equal children stood upon.

As KB209 walked between them, one pupil turned xer head slightly.

KB209 froze, wincing. Perhaps the pupil was struggling with an itch. Perhaps just curious to see xer teacher walk by. Whatever the reason, the head had moved. Just the slightest of movements. But it was enough. It broke the entire formation.

An equalizer stepped forward, grabbed the child, and dragged xer to a corner.

The electrocution began. The prod slammed into the child again and again, and the screams rose. Piss and blood trickled across the asphalt.

Under his mask, KB209 grimaced. But he kept walking. He himself had endured much discipline as a pupil. It made one harder, stronger. Made the hate purer. He knew what all authoritarians knew. Obedience could only be injected into the cracks of a broken soul. Blind obedience could only be instilled into a soul shattered and reformed.

He approached the rack by the wall. He picked up a childprod of his own—a heavy metal rod with a buzzing tip. Armed, KB209 took position at the head of the yard, standing among the other teachers.

There were fifty-eight of them. Important comrades—but no more important than anyone else. They were educators. Punishers. Those who broke and molded young, degenerate minds into adults who would seek justice and equality. KB209's childprod crackled in his hand. It was broken, he thought. The handle often sparked, shocking him. He dared not complain. Pain kept him on the straight path.

The principal stood at their head. No taller or shorter, no wider nor slimmer, no different than anyone else. Yet the first among them. The quelis that hung around xer neck was not simple iron like the one KB209 wore. It was painted crimson, denoting xer status.

The principal turned to stare at KB209. Through the holes in xer mask, xer eyes were hard.

KB209 winced. He had nearly been late. He knew that displeased his principal. After the rally, he had wandered for too long in the city. He had been lost in thoughts of the woman. A female. A rebel with red tocnails.

Focus, he told himself. *Focus on your duty. Do not fail the Father.*

Banners unfurled across the concrete walls of the truthall, revealing white quelii on black fields. The banners framed a towering mural of the Father, golden and splendorous, arms wide open.

Speakers crackled to life. Shostakovitch began to blare out, grainy and skipping every few notes. The educators and pupils all saluted their painted Father. They chanted together.

"I, a comrade of Isonomia, solemnly pledge to forever defend equalism. I am no better than my peers. I will never oppress the weak. I will never flaunt superiority. I will never offend the Father nor my comrades.

"I vow to forever serve the Father, my great protector, and to serve Isonomia, my great fatherland. I vow to forever fight bigotry and inequality, wherever these scourges may rise. I vow to forever fight the Zionites, and to not rest until their evil is cleansed from peoplekind. I will give all my strength, and my life if need be, for the just cause of equalism and the siblinghood of all comrades.

"Equalism is good! Equalism is just! Equalism is eternal, and the Father protects me.

"If I break this solemn oath, then let the stern punishment of Isonomian law, and the universal hatred and contempt of the equal comrades, fall upon me."

The pledge ended. The speakers fell silent. The school day began.

The children marched in orderly lines, entering the concrete building. KB209 led his fifty-eight pupils, and around them, the other units marched in perfect precision. The footfalls formed a flawless beat.

The corridors displayed proud murals of Isonomian history. One mural depicted the Father leading the first comrades in revolution, toppling the old decadent regime, a dystopia of capitalism, inequality, and lust. In another mural, the Father led the White Army in war, smiting the Zionites, casting them back from the borders of Isonomia. Other murals depicted the great works of the fatherland: comrades building weapons in factories, digging in mines, or serving in the Equapol, the People's Equality Police.

The largest mural depicted children in a crowd, listening to their elders speak. A few children were whispering to equalizers, informing on rebels in their midst. Words appeared above the mural: *Zionite spies and rebels fill the fatherland. Listen. Inform. Protect!*

She had red nail polish on her toes.

KB209 had seen pupils walk out of step. He had seen adults dragged to reeducation for hating too meekly. But he had never seen such red, blazing, brazen rebellion.

Who was LE905? He needed to see her again. To look at those toenails. To talk to her. To gaze for an eternal second into her blue eyes.

He looked back at the mural.

Inform. Protect!

A chill ran down his spine. He needed to stop this foolishness. To turn her in. After class, he would approach the equalizers. He would inform on the rebel. He had vowed to serve his Father, after all. To fight the enemies of Isonomia.

He led his pupils into the classroom. They took their seats, and KB209 stood behind his metal desk. He placed his childprod on the tabletop, letting it crackle and intimidate any pupil who harbored thoughts of defiance. KB209 didn't like using the instrument, not like his fellow teachers. The others used their childprods with relish. KB209 preferred to frighten, not torture. Fear was more powerful than pain.

"Good morning, class!"

They stood at attention and saluted. "Good morning, Mux KB209!"

Mux was his title among them. The Father had wisely abolished titles such as *mister*, *miss*, or *missus*. Titles that assumed one's gender or marital status, that reeked of inequality. KB209 was their mux, their teacher, their master.

He knew that all tasks were equal. That all work served the Father. Yet KB209 couldn't help the treasonous thought from rising now and then: that his job was the most important among the comrades. His job was not to mold weapons or tools—but minds. In the war of ideology, the mind was mightier than any gun.

He opened a book on the desk. Across the classroom, the fifty-eight pupils opened their own textbooks.

KB209 knew a little about education in pre-equalism days. Most of the old subjects had been abolished. There was no more math, of course. How could one truly claim that one number was larger, more worthy than another? How could one truly say that one number was smaller, worth less? All things were equal, all numbers were the same, and mathematics offended the Father. Only the Numerus Sanctus, the holy number fifty-eight, was worthy.

There was no more science either. The old physics was full of lies. Everyone today knew that the Father himself controlled the world, not forces of nature. Every child knew that Earth was flat, and that the stars were angels who shone for the Father.

The old biology was heretical. The comrades had burned those books. The bigoted biologists had claimed that humanity was divided into two genders, male and female. And worse: that there were differences between the sexes, that men were taller and stronger, that women could grow children in their bodies while men could not. Filthy lies! All humans were equal. There were no genders. There were no humans stronger, taller, more fertile than others. Babies were created in labs, grown in vats, genderless and pure, formed to serve equality.

Truly, the past had been a barbarous time, and schools had brainwashed their children with filth.

But she is female, KB209 thought. *The woman with red nail polish. And I am male. And—*

An electric shock silenced him. He gritted his teeth, thankful for his mask and hood that hid his pain.

"Class!" he said. "Open your textbooks to page fifty-eight! And we will continue our lessons."

All pages in their books were numbered fifty-eight, of course. Thankfully they had bookmarks.

"Today we will learn the story of G45I, Martyr #58," KB209 said.

Every day, they studied the tale of another martyr or hero, role models for the children. There were several hundred martyrs—KB209 wasn't sure how many, because he knew no number other than fifty-eight. They were all number fifty-eight. They were all equal in their martyrdom. Though secretly, most teachers considered G45I their favorite.

KB209 spoke, recounting the tale.

"G45I was born with the name Peter. It was in the days before the Father, in his wisdom, removed our offensive names, assigning us names of equality. It was before Father removed our genders, back when children were born like animals to males and females. Peter was born in a village of hardworking comrades who grew crops for the White Army. Though he lived in a time of savagery, Peter was noble and a devout equalist. Many nights, he gave his dinner to the soldiers marching by his village, preferring to go hungry. To him, a meal was nothing. He did all that he could to help our brave soldiers defeat the Zionites.

"One night, when Peter was too hungry to sleep, he wandered toward the family barn, hoping to milk the cows to provide more sustenance to the soldiers. But in the barn, Peter saw his father speaking in hushed whispers to cloaked figures. Peter hid behind bales of hay and listened.

"His biological father was plotting to keep more food for himself and his family. To falsify records of their produce. To betray the soldiers. Treason against the True Father!"

KB209 stared at his class. The masks stared back at him, white and blank. Hate-meters were embedded into their skullcaps, still showing green.

"Treason!" KB209 repeated, slamming his fist on the desk.

"Treason!" the class repeated, pounding their own desks.

Their hate-meters edged up, the green turning yellow. Their rage was building.

KB209 knew the principal would be monitoring. The mindcaps were all connected to the central computer. The principal lurked high in xer office, always watching, measuring the hate.

KB209 continued the tale.

"Peter was tempted to say nothing. To do nothing. To return to bed. To collaborate against the Father!"

KB209 pounded his desk again. The hate-meters edged up, yellow turning orange.

"Traitor, traitor!" the pupils chanted.

KB209 continued. "But Peter's love for equalism was strong. He ran from the barn, ran through the fields, ran all the way to the nearest police station. He informed on his father. He brought the equalizers home. Peter's father was arrested for treachery!"

The children roared in approval. On their mindcaps, their patriot-meters were inching up.

"Peter's father was sentenced to fifty-eight years of forced labor. He still toils there today. Broken and penitent."

"He deserves no mercy!" shouted one child.

"I hope he suffers!" cried another child.

KB209 nodded. Good. Very good. Some hate-meters were almost red now. The principal would approve.

He kept reading from the book.

"Justice was served to Peter's father. But not to Peter himself. His own mother, incensed over her husband's arrest, turned upon her very son. She raised a knife—and she stabbed the boy again and again, murdering him in their own home."

"No!" the children cried.

"She's a traitor!"

"Kill her!"

Some children leaped onto their desks. They shook their fists in rage. They were using the old pronouns, the gendered pronouns—words to signify their disgust. More hate-meters rose from orange to red.

"The Father himself heard of this vile murder," KB209 said. "He was a young revolutionary then, forging our nation. He captured Peter's mother, and he tied her to a pole in the town square. There he electrocuted her for days on end. Keeping her alive and screaming. All while the comrades watched and sang for his glory. They say she still hangs on the pole, still screams for the Father, begging for mercy. This, the Father decreed, would be the punishment to any traitor. Justice was restored!"

The children all saluted, fists raised.

"Justice!" they chanted.

"We cannot bring Peter back from the dead. But we can remember his sacrifice. We have given him a new name. An equal name. We will always remember G45I, Martyr #58." He gestured at a photograph of the martyr that hung on the wall, masked and robed. He looked back at the children. "Someday, maybe you too will find a traitor. Maybe you too will inform to the police. Maybe you too will become a hero of Isonomia."

He checked their meters. The patriotism was reading quite high. That was good. But half the class had only achieved orange hatred.

KB209 gave it one more attempt. "Remember that your enemies, the Zionites and traitors, crave inequality! They crave oppression! They are bigots, and we will fight them!"

Simple words. KB209 often used them. Sometimes simple fury was the best. He squeezed a little more hatred from his classroom.

He sighed. It was hard today. In the past, KB209 had been able to raise everyone to red. But lately—too many insidious thoughts had been filling his mind. Doubts. Memories.

A beautiful woman, smiling with red lips. A field of flowers. A name. Legs that could walk and run with no pain.

Questions about a world before. About a world beyond the gray sea.

And now this new memory. This woman with red toenails.

How can I teach my class to hunt traitors when I myself am treacherous?

Oddly, the mindcap was allowing these thoughts. No electrical bolts hurt him. He understood why. The mindcap was leading him toward the inevitable conclusion.

He had to act. Right now. He should go straight to the police. He should tell them everything. About his doubts and memories. They could reeducate him. About LE905. They could crush her rebelliousness.

But he remained still. He forced those thoughts away.

I must see her again. At the next rally. To be sure I have her. To be sure we can catch her. I'll wait.

When the class ended, KB209 took the children out to the courtyard. They ran across the asphalt, playing soccer, as guards watched from their towers. There was no actual ball. They kept no score. They would tolerate no competition within the truthhall walls. If a child imagined xerself scoring a goal, who was to say xe did not? Every child was a winner. Every child was equal. They ran, kicking at nothing, a game of perfect equality.

"KT209!"

A shadow fell.

The voice rumbled.

KB209 turned to see the principal. A lump filled his throat.

The principal was the same height as him, of course. 5'8". But somehow xe seemed taller, imposing, that red quelis around xer neck giving xer an air of authority.

"Yes, mux!" KB209 said. The principal had gotten his name wrong. But he dared not correct xer. "Splendid weather today, isn't it, mux? You can almost see the sun through the smog."

The principal stared. Eyes dark and hard.

"KT209, come with me." Xer voice emerged robotic, emotionless, and KB209 thought it wasn't only the voicebox.

He followed the principal indoors, leaving the children to continue their game. As they walked down the corridors, the principal spoke.

"KT209, our truthhall rankings are slipping. Third from last for discipline, down from fourth last year. Dead last when it comes to patriotism and hatred. This is intolerable! Do you know what happens to the truthhall with the poorest ranking?"

KB209 knew. "The children are sent to the mines."

"To the mines!" the principal said. "All our work—down the mineshaft. Pupils who could have become generals, ministers, propagandists—mere miners! Our school's reputation would never recover."

KB209 gulped. "I taught them about Peter the martyr today. They did well. They—"

"Your class is pathetic!" the principal said. "It's *your* classroom that drags our truthhall down. That sinks our hatred average to dead last."

KB209 suppressed a shudder. "In the next period, we'll get into social injustice. I'll show them the reels of Zion. I'll—"

"That won't be enough," the principal said. "Here now, I want you to see something. Come with me."

They walked down the hallway. A scream rose ahead, followed by enraged shrieks. The two comrades approached a classroom. They stared through a window into a room. Class was in session.

"Ah, see here!" said the principal. "Mux U76A8—now there's an educator for you. Top of our school!"

KB209 watched the class, throat tight.

Inside the classroom, U76A8 pointed a gloved finger at a trembling pupil. "There xe is!" the teacher rumbled. "The traitor!"

The child cowered. "I'm sorry, mux! I didn't mean to drink my chocolate milk so soon. I was thirsty and—"

"And you thought you could drink before everyone else!" roared the teacher. "You thought you could flaunt your fancy drink, flavored and sweetened, while your fellow pupils brought only unflavored breast milk to drink. You are not equal!"

"I am equal!" the child said.

"You are a traitor to the Father. A bigot, a bigot!" The teacher raised his arms, seeming in a trance. "What do we do to bigots!"

"Kill them!" shouted a pupil.

"Rip off their heads!" shouted another.

"Justice for bigots!" chanted another child. "Justice for bigots!"

"Deliver your justice!" cried U76A8.

The children swarmed over their cowering comrade. They ripped off the white robes, revealing the child's nakedness. They tore off the mask, exposing a pale face, cheeks wet with tears.

A girl, KB209 thought. *A young girl.*

The other children tore into her. They were like piranhas on a drowning cow. Fingernails ripped through skin and flesh. Teeth sank deep. Blood sprayed. The girl screamed and screamed until the children tore out her throat.

KB209 looked away, feeling queasy.

The principal was staring at him. For a long moment, xe stared—hard, silent.

"What happened to you, KB209?" xe finally said. "You used to have fire in your belly. You used to rant, rave, pound the tabletops so hard you broke them. You used to whip pupils into a frenzy—or whip them bloody if they were meek. At your class this morning?" The principal shook xer head. "Half your pupils didn't even rank past orange for hate."

What *had* happened to him?

KB209 had been treacherous once, yes. He had rebelled that one time, long ago. But they had sent him to the reeducation camp. They had cured him. Restored his patriotism, his hatred, his discipline. He loved the Father with all his heart now.

And yet, even now, he was thinking of himself as a he. A male. A person with a gender. A man who had lost his name. Who had lost his past.

"I haven't been myself lately," KB209 said. "The mindcap, it's been acting up."

It was shocking him right now. It was still ringing in his ears.

The principal grabbed him by the collar. Xe stared, eyes bloodshot.

"I don't care what you're going through, comrade. I care about this truthhall. I care about Isonomia and the Father. Sort yourself out. Or by the Father, you won't just end up in the mines. You'll be sent right back to that reeducation camp in the mountains."

KB209 shivered. Images flashed in his mind.

Iron rods—beating him.

Chains—binding him.

Guards—laughing, burning him, making him crawl.

The smell—the horrible smell of his searing flesh, dripping blood, waste on the floor.

He didn't know how long he had been there. He didn't know how long ago it was. There was little left but images, smells, sounds. He had emerged from the camp purified, filled with love.

"I love the Father!" KB209 said. "With all my soul."

"To hell with love." The principal released him. "Get back to your pupils and raise your levels of hate."

KB209 returned to the asphalt courtyard. He stood for a moment, watching his pupils kick the air.

For the first time, he wondered. Could one of those children be his own? KB209 had been born biologically. Impure. Squeezed out the womb of a female. That was the old way. For decades now, babies were formed in test tubes. Grown in vats. Brought from the lab here to the truthhalls.

Like all good comrades, KB209 had donated his cells. He had given sperm. Today males were castrated at birth. Cells were harvested from the rest of their bodies for cloning future generations. No more comrades were created using the old animal ways. But KB209 was old enough to retain the sinful biology.

Are any of you my blood? he thought, watching them play. *The girl who drank chocolate milk, who was torn apart—was she my daughter?*

Again he remembered that kind face from his memory. The face of his mother.

He wanted to find her. To see her again. What had happened to her? He tried to remember. But the ringing was so loud.

My mother had red lips.

The mindcap burned.

The woman had red toenails.

The pain burned the visions away, leaving him in a world of gray.

He returned to his classroom. And he pounded on the tabletop. And he riled up his pupils. He taught them to hate, and he yearned for a woman's love.

CHAPTER THREE

He walked down the dark streets. It was time to go home. And it filled KB209 with dread.

The sun was setting, a blood-red stain beyond the veil of smog. Ocher light dripped over crumbling towers of concrete. A crow circled overhead. The sour smell of cabbage soup wafted from countless windows in countless apartment blocks. Electricity was limited at night because of the war. The apartments were dark and cold, but floodlights still operated on the street corners, illuminating murals of the Father. The Father was never in darkness.

The city was harsh, austere, a great machine of stone and metal. But clean. Remarkably clean. KB209 had watched many reels from Zion, seen the wretchedness of the shantytowns, the filth that rolled across their roads, the beggars and vagrants and squatters. There was no homelessness in Isonomia. There was no trash. The asphalt was spotless. There was rust, lots of rust, and rubble too. But that was because of the Zionites. Because of the war. Rust of metal, dust from stone, but no filth from peoplekind.

Speakers thrummed on poles, announcing that curfew was near. The soup kitchens were closing, dispersing those last few citizens who had stood in line all day, hoping for a meal. A few Party members swayed down the road, arms slung across one another's shoulders, singing a drunken song. Workers limped home, covered with soot and sweat, prepared for a short night before another grueling day in the factories. Police cars rumbled by. Barely any vehicles but police cars traveled the roads these days, what with the gas shortages. Soon, once the sun set, it would be the Equapol's domain.

A stray dog wandered the street toward KB209. It was a miserable beast, fur mangy, ribs pushing against the skin like demons trying to break free. The cur's tongue drooped. It must have been living on the streets for years. The animal whimpered, begging for food. KB209 had not eaten all day. He had no food to share. But he approached the mutt, hoping to comfort it with a pat. He reached toward it.

A bullet streaked.

The dog fell dead, a hole in its head. Blood pooled.

An equalizer approached, holding a smoking rifle.

"I'm sorry to have startled you, comrade," the equalizer said. "We always have a problem with the mutts when the weather is warm enough."

KB209 looked at his hand, which was frozen in midair, still reaching toward the dog. Blood speckled his gloved fingers.

He looked at the equalizer. All people were equal, but the equalizers seemed larger in their bulky ceramic armor, their helmets thick and heavy.

KB209 wanted to rail. To chastise the policeperson. To tell xer the mutt had done nothing wrong. That he, KB209, could have taken the animal home, fed it, sheltered it.

But he knew the penalty for arguing with an equalizer. His death would be slow, agonizing, and public.

"Thank you for your service, Mux Equalizer," he said. "Hail the Father!"

The equalizer raised a fist in salute. "Hail the Father! Have a good evening, mux. Return home quickly now. Curfew is near. Stay safe. Stay equal. Father will protect you."

KB209 walked between the buildings as the sun set. The buildings loomed alongside, seeming to close in, to trap him.

KB209 felt like the dog. Ragged and hungry, lost in a labyrinth of cement and steel. Perhaps he had always been lost.

He wondered where the dog had come from. Had it once lived in lands beyond the city? Lands where trees and flowers grew? Many years ago, when they had taken him to the reeducation camp, KB209 had peered through cracks in the train car. He had sought nature, signs of a lush world beyond the city walls. He had seen nothing but the desolation of war. Plains of ash, factories pumping smoke, thin farmers toiling in fields of thin crops.

But KB209 remembered flowers. An older memory. An echo of childhood. He had seen them, vibrant and red, a memory that all the pain and electricity and ringing could not erase. He wondered if the dog had come from such a land. A place with flowers and sunlight. That had been many years ago. Another lifetime. He wondered whether the only place with flowers and sunlight now was Zion. Whether the cruel Bialik hoarded these things, had stolen their beauty from the world.

I wonder if the dog had a name, KB209 thought. *Peter the martyr had a name. I wonder if I ever had a name. If my mother had given me one. I wonder if I was born in City5801. I wonder if I came from a land of flowers.*

The curfew was only moments away. The sun was touching the horizon. Soon the equalizers would be shooting not just dogs but people too, any of those who remained outdoors.

KB209 wanted to keep walking. To pass by his apartment building and just keep going. To avoid the despair waiting in his home. To walk past more and more buildings, free for once from the trap. To walk until he found a milkbar, and then walk some more until he passed by new streets, new truthhalls, then walk onward until he reached fields of ash and gray seas, and beyond them—a land of flowers. A land called Zion.

The mindcap screeched.

Electricity thrashed him.

KB209 screamed.

The cap thrummed, buzzed, threatened to crack his skull. He had never felt such pain. Not since the reeducation camp.

He fell to his knees, clawing at the mindcap, fingernails digging into his scalp. The screws tightened. The damn voice intoned in his ears.

"Treacherous thoughts detected! Treacherous thoughts detected! You have ten seconds to cease treason or the People's Police will be alerted."

He lay on the asphalt, bleeding from his nose, clawing at his ears.

"I love the Father," he whispered hoarsely, tasting blood. "I love equality. I hate the Zionites! I will destroy them. I will kill Bialik! I hate, I hate, I hate!"

The pain ended. KB209 lay on the ground, gasping for air, trembling.

Curfew was beginning. He looked around, waiting for the equalizers to run toward him. He knew they would not kill him. That mercy was reserved for dogs. They would take him back to that place in the mountains. That place of snow and barbed wire, of hunger and blood and electricity.

KB209 struggled to his feet, tears on his cheeks. He adjusted his mask, hiding his face.

I won't go back there. I never will! I am equal. I am just. The Father protects me.

The sun was a sliver on the horizon. KB209 ran.

He was a block away when the sun vanished.

Darkness cloaked the city.

KB209 froze. A police car rumbled down the road, and he pressed himself against the wall, willing himself to vanish. He dared not even breathe.

The car rolled onward.

KB209 breathed out in relief. He inched along the sidewalk, careful to keep his shoes silent on the asphalt. His building rose ahead, a concrete rectangle, fifty-eight stories tall. It was the same as every other building, as the countless that filled this city. It was home.

He kept inching forward. Only one building now separated him from home. A mural of the Father covered its facade, lit with floodlights. KB209 froze for a moment, hidden in the shadows. To get home, he would have to pass through the light.

He steeled himself, then ran.

He burst into the light. It blinded him. He kept running, feeling so small by the towering painted Father. An ant below a god. He raced, seeing only white light, but he was almost there, he—

"Whoa! You there!" The sound of a rifle cocking. "Halt!"

KB209 froze.

His heart stopped.

"Turn toward me, citizen! Hands in the air!"

KB209 turned slowly, hands raised, and placed his back to the wall. A police car idled before him, headlights bathing KB209. An equalizer was walking toward him, rifle in hand.

KB209 wanted to run. Not run away—but run forward. Attack the equalizer. Have xer shoot him, kill him on the street like the dog. The pain would end. The mindcap had never let KB209 kill himself. He had tried multiple times, only for the cap to punish him, electrocute him, once for hours. But death by bullets would be quick.

But what if I survive? What if they take me back? I will not go back. I refuse! Never again.

The equalizer walked closer, xer white armor clanking. Xe stood before KB209. An ID was written on the equalizer's chest: T2150

"Why are you outside after curfew, citizen?" T2150's voice emerged distorted and deep through xer helmet. "Do you know what happens to traitors?"

"I'm sorry," KB209 said. "I'm a teacher. I serve in a truthhall. I love the Father. Please, mux, don't take me to reeducation. I love the Father! I love equality! I ..." He could say no more. He trembled.

The equalizer stared at KB209's hand. The glove was still speckled with dog's blood.

"I recognize you," T2150 said. "From earlier this evening. I nearly shot you along with that dog."

"That filthy cur!" KB209 said.

The equalizer tilted xer head. "Why are you wandering out here? Getting close to dogs. Ignoring curfew. Are you a Zionite spy?" Xe gripped KB209, xer hands like vices. "What is your identification?"

"KB209," he told him. "A teacher at Truthhall Y6W. Resident of Apartment Block—"

"KB209?" The equalizer said. "By the Father! You were my teacher! When I was only a child!"

He trembled. "I'm sure you were an excellent pupil."

"You—KB209 xerself!" The equalizer released him. "My Father. You taught me all about the great martyrs. About W754U. And YB786. And G45I, who informed on his own family. You inspired me, mux! It's thanks to you that I became an equalizer, that I didn't end up in the mines." He took a step back, shuddered, and inhaled sharply. "Of course, all professions are equal. I'm no better than anyone, least of all miners. My apologies. I just mean, mux—you filled me with such hatred, such patriotism, that I knew I would join the Equapol. That I would fight the traitors and Zionites—like the heroes in your stories."

KB209 allowed himself a shaky breath. "Yes, well ... I apologize too. It's been a busy day inspiring more pupils. I'll be sure to never break curfew again, mux."

T2150 nodded. "See that you don't, comrade. I'll overlook your treachery this time." Xe tilted xer head. "If you can pay the service fee, that is."

Both relief and dread flooded KB209. A bribe. It would be costly. It would mean several nights without dinner. Maybe no heat this winter. But it would mean freedom.

Freedom? No, maybe not *freedom*. Not here. Not in this city. But it would mean avoiding a return to that cold, snowy camp.

He paid the bribe.

He hurried onward, and he returned home.

There was a shiny, state-of-the-art elevator, full of brass buttons and glass bulbs. But the electricity ran only an hour a day, and the elevator was just sitting there, cold and still. Even during the Electric Hour the elevator did not move. True patriots would not waste electricity. Not with the war going on. But they all boasted that in Isonomia, there was an elevator in every building, a lamp on every street corner.

KB209 climbed the stairs in darkness. He made his way toward the fifty-eighth floor. Of course, every floor was the fifty-eighth. All other numbers were unequal, each lying of its worth, claiming to be larger than the others. All other numbers were inventions of the Zionites.

"Fifty-eighth floor," KB209 counted, out of breath. He climbed onward. "Fifty-eighth floor." He wiped sweat off his brow, struggling up another flight. "Fifty-eight ..." He paused for air, then climbed one more floor. "Ah, the fifty-eighth floor. Here we are."

His legs throbbed. The bolts in his legs, screwed into his shortened bones, seemed to twist and crack his fibulae. His pulse pounded in his ears. It made the ringing from his mindcap even louder, each note a hammer.

He paused outside apartment 58.

I should have run.

Where did the dog come from?

I should have run to a field of roses.

I should have run into the muzzle of a gun.

But he knew: He would never make it that far. Not to the roses nor the gun. This city was a maze, and he was a mouse. And in this maze, there was no way out.

He entered his apartment.

It was a humble home. One room. There were no windows. There was no bathroom; KB209 shared the communal washroom on the fifty-eighth floor. There was a kitchenette, and a pot of cabbage soup was simmering, filling the room with its acidic miasma. Tomorrow, there wouldn't even be cabbage soup. No dinner at all. Not after paying that bribe.

A framed painting of the Father dominated the room, covering one wall. Candles shone on the floor, illuminating the artwork. The same portrait hung in every apartment. It featured the Father, in his golden robes and mask, astride a stallion, a saber raised in his hand. Zionite corpses lay beneath his steed. Three words appeared in the portrait upon a flowing banner: *Patriotism. Hatred. Equality.*

KB209's mate sat on a metal chair, staring at the portrait.

In the privacy of home, his mate had removed her mask. Even so, UV502 appeared genderless. Her face was gaunt, deeply lined, lipless. Her eyes were sunken, gazing blankly from wrinkly dens. Her head was hairless—no eyebrows, no eyelashes, barely any stubble around the metal mindcap bolted into the skull. She was naked, scars where her nipples and genitals had been. Scars on her legs where the Party had lengthened the bones with rods.

KB209 chose to think of her as female. Perhaps some relic of the old ways of thinking. In truth, he did not know her birth gender.

UV502 did not move as KB209 entered the apartment. She stared at the portrait of the Father. Not blinking. Face expressionless but eyes enraptured.

"Good evening," KB209 said.

Finally, a movement. UV502's fingers twitched, and then her hands clasped together.

"Thank you, Father," she whispered, barely audible. "The birds fly high. Thank you. Praise you."

KB209 stared at the television set in the corner. A small black and white box. During the Electric Hour, the box sometimes showed reels from the war. The White Army marching. The guns of Isonomia pounding the Zionites. The Father leading the troops onward, lauding their sacrifice. KB209 enjoyed those hours. But mostly the box was dead. So they stared at the portrait.

He removed his mask. There were no mirrors, but KB209 caught a blurry reflection in the dark television box. An aging face. Lined. Weary. Deep grooves framed the mouth. His skin was ashen. A disgusting face, he thought. Shameful. A face to be hidden.

He took a bowl of cabbage soup. He sat on the only other piece of furniture: a second metal chair. With his mate, he stared at the large painting.

They stared in silence for long moments.

"Splendid painting," KB209 finally said.

UV502 did not react.

KB209 tilted his head, squinting, examining the painting from a new angle.

"The way the artist captured the fluttering golden cape," he said. "Have you ever noticed how the sunlight hits the folds in the fabric? Quite uncanny, really. That's not easy to do, you know. One of my comrades at the rally, just a tier down, knows a little about painting. Xe says that—"

"The birds flew extra high today," UV502 said, staring blankly at the portrait. "I could hear them, Father. They were singing for you. Thank you, Father. For protecting us. Thank you for the birds."

KB209 turned to look at his mate. She had been assigned to him long ago. He wasn't sure how many years it had been. There were no calendars in Isonomia. Had it been decades already?

They had paired KB209 and UV502 at random. Allowing comrades to choose their own mates was oppressive. That was something the barbaric Zionites did. How could one choose a mate, judge a mate based on unfair traits like beauty, intelligence, personality? That oppressed those who lacked such qualities. The very concept of choosing a mate was disgusting. It was how animals mated.

So the Love Lottery had paired KB209 and UV502. He still remembered their wedding long ago, standing in the arena with hundreds of other assigned couples, praising the Father. He remembered coming to this apartment, seeing his home for the first time. They had stared at the portrait that night too.

He stared at the painting. The Father on his horse. Sword raised.

He turned back toward UV502.

"A child was ripped apart at work today," he said. "The other children tore right into xer."

His mate said nothing. She kept staring.

"I almost got shot today," KB209 said.

UV502 did not react.

For another long moment, they sat in silence, facing the portrait.

It was like this most nights. Quiet in their concrete box. The ringing loud in his ears. KB209 had tolerated these evenings for years. For decades. The endless hours of silent staring.

He wanted to talk to her, damn it. To hear UV502 tell him about her day at work. He didn't even know what work she did. After all these years, he didn't know. He wanted to make eye contact, even for just a second, like the eye contact he had made with the woman at the rally. He wanted even a second of intimacy, of connection.

He wanted to make love to his mate. She had no signs of gender, any organs of her sex removed, but he could have held her. Just held her in his arms. Felt the beating of her heart. Felt a connection to a living, breathing person.

And if he *did* want to make actual love—to have sex like animals—why should he not? Could they not find a way to perform the deed? He was one of the few uncut. He had been born before they castrated males. Sometimes the need grew so strong, screaming inside him, as powerful as the ringing in his ears. The ancient primal need to procreate. To love. To create life. Not life grown in a test tube but a womb. To hold a child and know the child was his blood.

They tore the girl apart. She could have been mine.

He thought of red nail polish.

He thought of LE905.

Bigots, bigots! she had screamed. *Kill the Zionites!*

But her toes sang of rebellion. Of breaking free.

The candles faded to flickering stubs. Shadows covered the portrait. UV502 knelt for her prayers. KB209 repeated them with his mate, knowing that if he did not, the mindcap would force it.

"Thank you, Father, for all you have given us," they prayed. "Thank you for the meals you place on our table. Thank you for the Party Police and the White Army that you lead. Thank you for smiting our enemies. Thank you for protecting us. Blessed be the Father, benevolent lord of Isonomia. Amen."

They pulled down the wall bed. They lay on the musty mattress. The last of the candles guttered out.

KB209 tried to ignore the bedbugs, the mold, the snoring of his mate. In the night, the ringing was so loud. He turned over in bed once, stared at the lump beside him. Wanting to hold her. To feel her warmth. Daring not.

Finally he screwed his eyes shut. He wanted to sink into slumber, to find freedom in his dreams, to explore meadows of red flowers, to find the place the dog had come from. But instead, when he finally slept, he became a mouse in a labyrinth. He scurried through the stone corridors, cats in pursuit. He tried to find a way out, but got more and more lost, until finally he approached a group of children, hoping to find protection among them. But the giant children lifted him, crushed him, ripped him apart, hung him on a pole and shocked him over and over.

Shostakovitch blared from speakers outside.

KB209 bolted up in bed.

It was a cold gray dawn. His ears rang. He rose from bed, saw his face reflected in the dark television. Ashen. Wrinkled. Defeated. He put on his mask, and he stepped outside. He marched with the crowd, step by step, heading back to toil for his Father.

CHAPTER FOUR

Fifty-seven hours passed. Toil, home, sleep, toil. And on the fifty-eighth hour, KB209 walked back toward the arena. The next rally was to be held. And he hoped to see her again.

As the thousands of comrades marched down the road, BOT76 leaned closer to KB209.

"I bet he'll be there today," BOT76 said. "In the flesh. The Father himself!"

"You say that every time," KB209 said.

"And someday it'll be true." BOT76 nodded vigorously. "You'll see, comrade. He visits a different arena every rally, you know. Today is our turn."

Both comrades fell silent as an equalizer marched by. The crowds kept moving, flowing down the labyrinthine streets between gray walls and towers. They reached Arena T671. The concrete dome loomed, draped with quelis banners.

As KB209 passed through the checkpoint, his fingers tingled. He barely felt the pain in his legs. An equalizer patted him down, and he thought of seeing her. Of LE905. Let the others dream of seeing the Father. KB209 came to see another soul. A treasonous thought, he knew. The mindcap reinforced the knowledge with a bolt. But not a thought he could ignore.

He entered the arena and walked with the others, climbing the stairs to his assigned tier.

She was there.

She was in her spot, waiting.

LE905 raised her eyes, and she made eye contact.

For the briefest of seconds, for the longest of eternities, they gazed into each other's eyes. His eyes sunken, weary, filled with ghosts. Hers brilliant blue like the rivers of Zion.

Then she looked down at her lap, ripping her eyes away like skin off muscle.

BOT76 shoved xer way forward.

"Oi there, LE!" xe said. "You look splendid today. I mean—we all do! Hell, that's the whole point, ain't it?" BOT76 sat down beside her. "So, LE, you reckon the Father will show up today?"

KB209 had to nudge his comrade aside. "BOT76, your spot is over there." He pointed at the slab of concrete.

"Yes, of course, of course!" BOT76 said. "Sorry about that. Hard to stay focused with our lovely new comrade here." Xe winked at LE905.

"Focus less on me, more on the rally, comrade," LE905 said. "Socialization may be done within the home with your mate, or once a year at Victory Day during the assigned hours. We are here to for a rally, not comradery."

KB209 took his spot beside her. She glanced at him again. For another electric moment—eye contact. And she winked. He knew he would replay that instant forever in his mind, shocks be damned.

Shostakovitch began to play. The rally began.

Today was a special day. The music did not come from the speakers. An actual marching band played in the arena, wearing White Army uniforms. The trumpets blared and the drums beat and the soldiers marched. Dancers followed, playing timbrels and waving ribbons. Soldiers carried the standards of Isonomia— golden quelii perched atop rods.

The performance was impeccable. Every performer moved in perfect unison. The marching was so precise KB209 almost thought the soldiers were automatons, that gears moved beneath their robes. Every soldier—the exact same height, same width, same movements. Same dead eyes.

KB209 had seen the White Army parades before. But they were rare, normally gracing the arenas only on Victory Day.

Something big must be coming, he thought. *Maybe BOT76 is right. Maybe today is when the Father visits.*

The marching band left the arena.

New soldiers stepped in. They were dragging chained prisoners.

Prisoners without equagarb. Naked and shameful. Prisoners openly displaying bodies, faces, hair—all their sinful parts. Revealing their age. Their skin color. Even their gender. Unmodified bodies, still with genitals, with breasts. Like animals.

The comrades booed.

"Sinful!" shouted a man.

"Disgusting pigs!" cried another.

"Shame, shame!" LE905 shouted.

KB209 shouted with them. Knowing he had to. As he cried out his rage, he squinted, struggling to see more details. The prisoners had been tortured. Bruises covered their faces, and the scars of whippings striped their backs. Blood, dust, and excrement caked them. The soldiers paraded the prisoners across the arena. While the prisoners were wretched, the soldiers were glorious. Their armor was polished, perfect, no scratch or speck of dust marring the white plates.

One of the soldiers stepped forward, and KB209 shivered. His heart nearly stopped.

This soldier wore finer armor than the others—purest white, almost blinding. Serrated blades rose from xer helmet, blood-red, forming a macabre crown.

This was no mere soldier. It was a general. An actual general, one of only a handful in Isonomia.

Comrades in the crowd gasped. They saluted, raising their fists.

"By the Father!" BOT76 whispered. "That's General EQL61! The White General! The great hero who leads the campaign in Zion." Awe filled BOT76's voice, and xe raised xer fist in salute. "It's not the Father, but—blimey, splendid guest! An honor!"

KB209 saluted with the crowd. The general spun in a circle, staring at the audience around the stadium.

"Behold, comrades!" EQL61 cried into a megaphone. "Behold the Zionites, our prisoners of war!"

The crowd booed louder.

"Zionite pigs!"

"Oppressors!"

"Capitalists!"

Comrades began tossing their shoes. Fervor filled their eyes. The shoes pelted the Zionites. The shoes were fabric, the soles rubber. They could not inflict injury, but throwing a shoe was the ultimate insult.

KB209 added his shoes to the barrage, missing the prisoners by several tiers. Beside him, LE905 tossed her own shoes.

He looked at her feet.

Again—her toenails were painted.

They were painted blue today. Shimmering, beautiful blue. The same blue as her eyes. The blue of sky and sea, blue from a long-lost era before the ash of war and smog of industry. The blue of rebellion in a world of gray.

He looked away hurriedly, heart racing. If an equalizer saw her toes, saw KB209 admiring them …

She'd be executed, and I'd be executed as a collaborator. He shivered. *This is rebellion.*

He knew what he must do. He must alert the Equapol! He must cry out—a traitor, a traitor!

Yet he could not bring the words to his lips. Peter the martyr had informed on his own father. And he, KB209, couldn't even turn in a stranger?

His pulse pounded in his ears. His body shook. He forced himself to look forward, to ignore her toes.

I never saw them. I never saw a thing.

In the arena, General EQL61 spoke into xer megaphone again.

"Our brave warriors of the White Army advanced deep into the enemy territory. With sacrifice and honor, they ran through the machine gun fire of the Zionite menace. Many ran into the mine fields, sacrificing their lives to clear a path for their comrades. Soldiers lay down upon barbed wire, dying on the steel to allow their comrades to charge across their backs. With courage, honor, and burning hatred, our heroes smote the Zionites, winning a great battle."

The crowd cheered. Fists rose across the arena.

"The war continues!" EQL61 said. "The wretched Bialik has vowed to keep fighting. Even as we speak, he musters more Zionite rats for his army of vermin. Still he plots to bring his depravity to pure Isonomia. To force upon us his wretched inequality. Gender!" The general spat. "Wealth and poverty!" Xe snickered. "Gold and trifles and women dressed as whores. But we will not be diseased! We will remain pure! The forces of equalism will smite the Zionites!"

"Smite them good!" BOT76 cried.

"Kill every last one of the rats!" LE905 screamed, hopping with her rage, fists clenched.

"Our warriors have captured these Zionites." The general gestured at the naked prisoners. "These rats plotted to invade our city. To pillage and rape and murder. We will bring them to justice!"

The soldiers lifted motorized shovels. For long moments, as the crowd watched, the soldiers dug pits in the sandy arena. They tossed in the prisoners, then began to refill the holes. Shovel by shovel, they buried the Zionites up to their necks.

Finally the work was complete. The soldiers left the arena. The Zionites remained, their heads sticking out from the sand.

The bruised heads whipped from side to side. The buried Zionites screamed, but they were gagged. The screams were muffled. Pathetic. Maybe they were trying to curse Isonomia. Maybe to beg.

From high in the bleachers, KB209 stared at the heads. He had never seen Zionites in real life. Here they were—the monsters. The demons. The foul enemy from the east. The rats who wanted to destroy everything the Father had built. He remembered seeing the reels, seeing Bialik live in splendor, guzzling wine and devouring food, while his own people hungered in the shantytowns.

Were these Zionites among those who hungered? KB209 wondered.

An electric shock from his mindcap told him: No. These were the Zionite oppressors. Those who stole food and treasure and decency. The enemy of equalism.

KB209 felt lucky that he lived in Isonomia. That he had an apartment of his own. A good mate. A job that earned him cabbage soup most days. All this glory—the Zionites wanted to steal!

"Thieves!" he shouted at the heads, and the mindcap rewarded him with a reduction in pain. "Imperialist pigs!"

Soldiers moved along the bleachers, handing out sacks of stones. A sack to each citizen. KB209 accepted his. He stared at the stones within, and he understood.

"Pigs!" BOT79 cried, hurling the first stone.

Others in the crowd joined xer.

"Murderers! Capitalists! Scum!"

The stones flew. Hundreds. Then thousands of stones. Most missed. But some hit the Zionite heads. Blood splattered the sand. The Zionites screamed, begged, but the stones still flew. Skulls cracked.

KB209 couldn't help but remember the girl at school, ripped apart. He looked down at his lap, wanting to see anything but this bloodshed. But his glove too was bloodied. It was still stained with the dog's blood.

"Zionite rats!" LE905 screamed, tossing stones.

KB209's mindcap began to buzz. He heard the voice in his head.

Fight for your Father, comrade! Fight or be punished.

KB209 threw his stones. But he threw them wide. He missed.

"You wretched scum!" LE905 shouted, hurling her last few stones.

KB209 looked at her. Her eyes were wide with hatred, her body tense, her cries loud. But he saw that her stones too were missing. They landed harmlessly in the sand. He remembered how at the last rally, her shoe had hit the image of Bialik directly in the eye.

LE905 knew how to aim when she wanted to.

She's missing on purpose, KB209 thought, shock filling him.

He thought back to the stories he taught at the truthhall. Stories of heroes and martyrs who informed on traitors.

There were many traitors. And some, comrades whispered, were organized.

There was an underground rebellion in Isonomia. It was a secret everyone knew. It was why the equalizers were everywhere. Why the curfew was enforced. Some claimed the rebels were helping the Zionites. Or that they were Zionites in disguise. Others claimed the rebels were Isonomians with no ties to Zion, that they were bigots who rejected equalism, who hated the Father, who wanted to return to the old days of decadence.

KB209 stared at LE905.

Are you more than just a rebellious soul? Are you one of them? Part of the underground rebellion?

Again the temptation rose to turn her in.

Her stones missed on purpose! He could tell the Equapol.

But what if the police scanned his mindcap, accessed his memories? If they learned his stones too had purposefully missed? That he had stared at her toenails, that he had harbored rebellious thoughts?

He kept silent. He was afraid.

Finally the Zionites were all dead. Their shattered heads lay on the sand like rotten fruit.

The monitors descended, and the same old reel played. A reel of the Father speaking of the glories of Isonomia. Then a reel of the wretchedness of the enemy. And at last, an image of Bialik, the great Satan.

The rally ended with cries of hatred. The citizens trailed out of the arena. Across the city, other arenas expelled their comrades. The millions moved along the streets, heading back to their toil.

Another cycle before the next rally.

But this time was different.

This time a mystery named LE905 was here. And KB209 was going to unravel it.

CHAPTER FIVE

"Well, that was something, wasn't it?" BOT97 said, slinging an arm around KB209. "Splendid rally! Best one in years. I am popped up! I think I hit one of the bastards. Right in the eye. You saw it, didn't you?"

They were marching down the street, leaving the arena behind. Countless comrades, flowing for miles down the asphalt canyons.

"I saw it," KB209 said. He shuddered to remember the stones tearing the flesh. Cracking the skulls. The brains on the sand.

BOT97 turned toward LE905, who was walking with xer. "And you, LE! Wonderful hate! Splendid hate! I've never seen anyone so full of hate. I bet KB209 wishes you were one of xer pupils. It's xer job to teach hatred, you know. You'd be xer star pupil."

"There are no star pupils," KB209 said. "They're all equal."

"Of course, of course." BOT97 yawned. "By the Father, I need a pop-me-up. What say we visit a milkbar before toil? We have a few moments. We deserve a drink."

"I'll pass," KB209 said. "You go ahead."

"Come on!" BOT97 nudged him. "We should celebrate! The White Army winning a battle and all."

KB209 refused again, more firmly this time, citing plenty of work at the truthhall. BOT97 found another few comrades to join xer. They headed down a road toward a milkbar, singing an old victory song.

KB209 found himself walking alone with LE905.

She looked at him. Again—that beautiful moment of eye contact. It was the third time. And it was more beautiful, more exhilarating, more warm and wonderful than ever.

The words slipped out of KB209's mouth before he could control himself.

"Actually, I *could* use a cup of milk," he said. "There's a quieter bar three blocks away. Would you join me, LE905?"

Oddly, once the words had passed his lips, KB209 felt remarkably calm. His pulse slowed. His trembling eased. It felt almost instinctive. An ancient ritual, as comforting and true as a nearly-forgotten song of childhood. A genetic memory embedded deep within him, the whispers of lost generations, preserved despite the metal and electricity and concrete, enduring in a place nobody could touch. He was asking a girl out on a date. It was rebellious, unthinkable, and as natural as rain.

"I can't," LE905 said. "I work in the laundromat on 58th street, and we're behind on the washing. Big shipment of bloody uniforms came in from the war this morning."

KB209 deflated. "Oh. All right. I shouldn't have presumed. I'm sorry."

His chest felt empty. His belly filled with ice. She had refused him. And the feeling of rejection stung, perhaps as ancient, as innate, and as powerful as the ritual of courting.

She looked into his eyes. He thought she was smiling behind her mask. He had never seen anyone smile, had never smiled himself, yet somehow he knew what it meant. Another truth embedded deep within his very being. A truth about what it meant to be human.

"How about after my shift?" she said. "I'll be done at sunset. With time enough before curfew. Will you meet me then? Outside the laundromat?"

His heart lifted.

During his hours of toil that day, KB209 could hardly focus. He taught his class. He tried his best to whip them into a frenzy. Again, only half the pupils reached red levels of hatred. Again the principal fumed and threatened. But the day passed in a haze, and he thought of blue eyes.

It was dark when KB209 trudged along the streets, leaving the truthhall behind.

But this time, he did not wander aimlessly, lost like a mouse in a maze, dreaming of escape. He did not return home, dejected, shoulders slumped. He walked with a straight spine, shoulders squared, barely feeling the pain in his mutilated legs. He walked to the laundromat.

She was waiting for him.

"Hello, LE905."

On a whim, he reached his hand for her to hold. He realized the glove was still bloodstained, pulled it back, and held out his other hand instead. She took it. Her fingers were graceful, naturally shaped. His had been surgically shortened, like his toes and legs. His hand always felt clumsy, and it was difficult to manipulate tools, and he felt deformed and ugly beside her. But of course, that was treasonous, for they were equal, as all comrades were equal.

Hand in hand, they walked through the concrete labyrinth. They reached the milkbar.

It was bustling at this time of day. The toil shifts were changing, and many comrades came to drink. The milkmaids sat behind panes of glass, tubes attached to their nipples, giving forth nourishment. There were no more cows or goats, of course. Bialik had stolen them all. Crops struggled in the dry, ashen land, and barely any sunlight pierced the eternal smog—the curse of the Zionites. But Isonomians were proud and worked hard. Everyone toiled for equality, and the milkmaids did their part.

The milk was free. The Father was kind, and he allowed every comrade a ration of milk per day. It would help sustain KB209 until he could afford more cabbage.

They ordered two cups. KB209 had his milk fermented, but LE905 ordered hers sweetened. They sat at a bar before a portrait of the Father, and they drank for long moments in silence.

KB209 drank slowly through his straw, savoring the beverage. He found the silence oddly comforting. At home, with his mate, the silence disturbed him. But sitting here with LE905— even in the silence, this was bliss.

He looked at her. She was staring at the portrait, sipping slowly.

"Do you ever wonder what he looks like?" she said. "The Father, that is. In the portraits, he's always wearing a golden mask. Do you think he's handsome? I wonder sometimes."

"I never wondered," KB209 said.

I wonder what you *look like,* he thought, looking at her white mask. *I know you have blue eyes. And painted toenails. What is the shape of your cheeks? Are your lips full and red, or are they thin like mine? Is your skin wrinkled and pale or flushed with life?*

"I suppose it's rather a silly thought." LE905 lowered her head. "To wonder how the Father looks. How anyone looks, really. We're all equal, after all. That's the whole damn point." She glanced at KB209. "But still, sometimes a girl gets curious. Too curious for my own good, I suppose."

He frowned. "A girl?"

LE905 gasped. She covered her voicebox. "I mean—a person! Oh, forgive me!" She trembled and glanced around. "You won't tell anyone, will you?"

He wondered why her mindcap had not shocked her. Perhaps it had, but she was hiding her pain, her tolerance higher than his.

"Not a soul." He smiled thinly behind his mask. "But yes, sometimes I wonder about people. What they look like. That's why the Father gave us masks. To keep our animal instincts at bay."

She stared back at the portrait. "My mate takes his mask off at home sometimes. Can I be honest? Sometimes I wish he'd leave it on. Oh, it sounds terrible, I know! But … he's old. He's so old, KB. His skin is scabby and covered in boils. When he kisses me, sometimes I cringe. I know I'm supposed to be a loyal wife. I know it's my duty. The Father chose him for me. But sometimes, I just can't help but feel that—" She covered her voicebox again. "There I've gone and done it again! Said too much. I'm horrible. I don't know why I'm telling you these things." She looked at him. "I feel too comfortable with you, as if I've known you for years, and it scares me."

He looked at her in silence. He had thought her a rebel of the underground. But it seemed more likely that she was simply rebellious by nature. Very young. Filled with curiosity and fire. He knew of such inclinations in young people. It was his task, after all, to recognize such passions and shape them into hatred. Whoever had taught LE905 had failed her.

Or perhaps I'm the one who fails my pupils. Perhaps she had a teacher far greater than I am.

A forbidden thought. He endured the shock in silence, gritting his teeth.

He held his glass of milk, not drinking. He faced the portrait, but his eyes gazed at some distant murky land. He spoke softly.

"Sometimes at night, I lie in bed by my mate. And I look at her. And I don't know who she is. I see an old person. A person like a corpse. Somebody who died long ago, whose body still lives but whose soul gave up. A wrinkled, pale old corpse. I don't know her. I think of her as female. But I don't know her gender. Or her name. Or her soul. I don't know what her dreams are. I've never talked to her. Not really. We've exchanged some words. Meaningless. Cold. I lie in bed, and even though her body is beside me, I feel so alone. They say that you feel the most alone in a crowd, but that's wrong. You feel the most alone in bed next to somebody who doesn't know who you are. Who doesn't love you. Who is like the corpse of a stranger. That is true loneliness, the kind that penetrates your soul like an icy blade." He blinked, the trance ending, and looked at LE905. "And now I've said too much."

She placed her hand on his. "You speak beautifully. That's exactly how I feel." She sighed. "At least tonight my mate won't be there. The White Army sent him off to the war. Even though he's old, they sent him." She laughed bitterly. "Maybe he volunteered to get away from me."

"You mean xe?" KB209 said.

"I mean he." LE905 nodded. "I know his gender. At least, the gender he was born with. He's cut. Castrated." She twisted uncomfortably. "He was born before the Father mandated all newborn boys be castrated. My mate volunteered. He castrated himself as a youth. For equality." She snorted. "Saved me from having to endure him in bed. That's a blessing."

KB209 frowned. Surely those words were treasonous!

"Your mindcap," he said softly. "Didn't it shock you? When you spoke those words. Didn't it hurt very much?"

She took a deep drink of milk, emptying her cup, then stood up. She looked at him.

"KB209, walk me home."

They walked through the dark streets. KB209 knew he should run home. Curfew was near, and the police were out. His mindcap was buzzing, hitting him with low-voltage bolts, prompting him to change course. He ignored it all. He would walk LE905 home, and let the world burn.

They walked through the labyrinth as the sun set, casting red light between the concrete towers. The light was almost gone when they reached her building, indistinguishable from the thousands of others—raw concrete walls stained with rivulets of rust and decades of smog. The towering mural of the Father was the only section of the building maintained, meticulously painted and repainted to golden glory.

They paused at the doorway, and LE905 gasped and covered her voicebox.

"Curfew is almost here!" she said. "You'll never make it back home. I'm so sorry!"

"I can run," KB209 said. "Bribe the police if they stop me."

He was lying. He was out of credits. If they caught him now ... He didn't want to think about that.

"No." LE905 shook her head. "Too risky." She thought for a moment, then her eyes widened. "Come up with me! I know it's brazen, but—spend the night. My mate is off at the war. Nobody will know."

KB209's insides shook. Should he?

His mate would likely not even notice his absence.

He nodded. His heart beat a little faster.

They entered the apartment building. Dust and ash covered the lobby. A man sat in the corner, bearded, not even wearing a mask or robe. He was devouring a cooked dog, sinking yellow teeth into the flesh.

"Whore, whore!" the old man shouted, pointing at LE905. "Show me your tits, slut!"

The man's mindcap buzzed. He screamed. He clawed at the bolts, struggling to tear the metal cap loose, then fell down. He writhed on the floor as the mindcap kept pounding him with electricity.

LE905 grabbed KB209's hand. She pulled him toward the staircase.

"He's been here forever," she said. "Ignore him. We all do."

He frowned. "Why hasn't the police arrested him?"

"We let him stay. He takes care of the rats and stray dogs."

As they entered the stairwell, KB209 looked over his shoulder. The bearded man grinned at him, teeth rotten, half of them gone.

"Freedom," the man said. "This is freedom."

He grabbed one of the bolts in his skull. He began to pull. Then screamed again.

KB209 quickly climbed the stairs, following LE905, leaving the wretch behind.

Following a long climb, they reached her apartment on the fifty-eighth floor. The doorway was rusty iron, and there was a bullet hole above the lintel. She opened three locks, and they stepped inside.

KB209 stared in shock.

He could barely breathe. His heart pounded.

"By the Father," he whispered.

The apartment was built to spec—a concrete cube, windowless, a cell like all the others in the city.

But it was nothing like where KB209 lived. LE905 had transformed her box into a place of treason.

It's beautiful, he thought. *It's so beautiful.*

A portrait of the Father was mandatory in every apartment, and one hung here too. KB209 could make out the picture frame. But LE905 had draped the towering portrait with a tapestry. The fabric exploded with colors. Circles within circles. Colors KB209 barely recognized. Blue. Red. Purple. Yellow. Other colors he could not name—maybe green?

Paintings on canvas covered the other walls, vibrant with more colors. One painting depicted many birds flying between trees. They were not crows like in the city. Birds of vibrant gold, blue, and red, creatures of breathtaking beauty. Another painting featured a rearing feline, mane golden, rising from grass under blue sky. KB209 had never seen blue sky before. Other paintings were of animals he didn't recognize.

"I painted them," LE905 said. "Those are parrots. And that one is a lion. See this painting? Those are gazelles. They have them in Zion. I saw them once."

His eyes widened. "You've been to Zion?"

"A long time ago," she said. "With my husband. He's a senior officer, and he let me join him on a campaign. We saw all these animals in the wilderness. The plants too. Trees and flowers. The smells of them! Beautiful smells. Zion is where I got the paints too." She giggled. "I stole the fabric from the laundromat."

KB209's mindcap was crackling. Just seeing these paintings unleashed bolts. He winced. His head spun.

"Oh, I forgot!" LE905 said. "I'm so sorry. Hang on."

She approached a wooden cabinet. KB209 thought it was wood, at least. He had never seen wooden furniture before. LE209 took out a tiny electronic device. It was no larger than a grain of corn. She attached the device to KB209's mindcap. It snapped into place, fitting into a groove at the back.

At once, the pain vanished.

The electrical bolts stopped.

The ringing in his ears—that damn, cursed ringing, designed to reduce his intelligence to an average 100—stopped.

For the first time in years. In decades. It was gone.

KB209 blinked, looking around. Hearing … silence. Beautiful silence.

Tears filled his eyes.

I feel human. This is what humans should feel like.

And suddenly he was weeping.

"Oh dear!" LE905 embraced him. "KB209, are you all right? I'm sorry. I should have explained! My husband gets these devices from the White Army. They're called scramblers. We use them when visiting Zion, when we're overwhelmed with their colors and sinful ways. They deactivate our mindcaps' punishment modes. My own mindcap has a scrambler built in."

He couldn't stop the tears. "The ringing is gone. I can think. I can hear. I can see colors without pain."

His deformed legs wobbled. LE905 held him, led him toward a couch. She had an actual couch, upholstered in actual fabric, not just metal chairs. They sat down. For long moments, KB209 simply breathed, calming himself, learning to hear and see the world in a new way. A world without pain. With color and beauty.

"I never knew colors could be like this," he whispered.

Anger filled LE905's eyes. "I think it's horrible how these mindcaps do this. To civilians, that is. Ringing in their ears. Punishing their thoughts. The officers don't have to endure this. Why should teachers? The whole thing is wrong."

KB209 trembled. "They'll hear us. Please, be quiet. The police will hear. The Father will hear!"

"Nobody can hear you here. You're safe." She placed her gloved hand on his thigh. "You poor thing. You're all shaken up. This is all very new, I know. Give me a moment. I'll make some tea. Tea always calms the nerves."

She put on a kettle, and KB209 watched in astonishment as she placed tea leaves—actual leaves—into two porcelain mugs. The truthhalls sometimes offered teachers flavored hot water, made from chemical powder. He had never seen real tea leaves. Had never, he realized, seen any leaves at all, only in the reels from Zion.

LE905 poured hot water over the leaves, and the aroma filled the room. A smell of rustling fields. Of wind through meadows. Of mist fading from a warm dawn under a sky with no smog. The gold and green smells of the east. Of a place called Zion. A place that was real—here in this room.

He accepted a cup. He sipped. He understood then the loathsomeness of cabbage soup, fermented breast milk, and powdered drinks. The tea flavors filled his mouth, as vibrant as the colors on the walls. He was not merely experiencing tea. He was experiencing a sunlit world of life and growing things. A world of sin, of inequality—but of wonder.

"No wonder Bialik steals so much," he said. "No wonder he oppresses his people for such treasures. They are wonderful."

LE905 signed. "Do you think Bialik is really a thief? Really the man we see in the reels?"

"Of course!" KB209 said. "He's monstrous. A hunchbacked vampire! But ..." He hesitated. "But sometimes, I wonder. I admit it. The mindcap shocks me. But I wonder." He shook his head. "For the first time, I can think clearly. I can smell and taste and see."

"Then there's something else I want you to see," LE905 said.

She removed her mask. And then removed her robes. She stood naked before him, revealed in all her sinful beauty.

She was young. Surprisingly young. KB209 didn't know how to accurately judge people's ages. But LE905 had no wrinkles. Her face didn't have the tired, ashen hue of those who had toiled for many years. She was beautiful, the cheeks pink, the lips full. She wore a metal mindcap like everyone, and she shaved her head around it, but he could see golden stubble. It looked as soft and pure as the grasslands of Zion.

Her body was slender, her skin a pale shade of gold. The Party had not disfigured her. She still had her breasts. Small.

Tender. Their humble size had saved them. There was no scarring between her legs either, only golden peach fuzz.

The Father was always portrayed golden too. But here was a true golden idol. True beauty. Not the beauty of authority—but of freedom.

"You're so beautiful," KB209 whispered, and tears flowed again.

She reached for his mask. "Let me see you."

He recoiled. "You don't want to see me. I'm ugly."

Her eyes softened. Gently, she removed his mask. Her eyes widened, and she smiled.

"Oh, Mux KB! You're quite handsome."

He looked away. "I'm old."

She laughed. "Oh my! But darling—you can't be older than in your forties. Younger than my assigned mate."

"I'm fifty-eight years old," he said.

She laughed again, and her eyes sparkled. "Aren't we all?"

She pulled him up from the couch, and she removed his robe. They stood naked together. KB209 looked down at his body. The legs—sawed and stitched back together, shortening him to 5'8". The toes and fingers—filed down. The skin—beginning to sag. The ribs—poking against his skin. Perhaps he wasn't old. But he felt ancient. He had lived for so long in the maze.

LE905 looked into his eyes and stroked his cheek. "You're a beautiful man. You're more than a number. Call me Ellie. And I'll call you Kay. Let us have names in here. Let us be loved. Let us live like the heathens."

KB209 wanted to flee. To run back to the familiar. But he didn't move. He was afraid. But he stayed.

"I've never made love to a woman," he said.

"I've made love to many men," Ellie said. "I'll guide you."

They made love. And he didn't need much guidance.
Something in him awoke. Something that had been sleeping all his
life. Something primal, a memory from his ancestors. He made
love to her on the rug, and she moaned beneath him. Her breasts
pressed against his chest, and her legs wrapped around him, and
she buried her face against his neck.

It was fast. He moved faster and faster until he climaxed
inside her, then collapsed, trembling, breathing heavily, afraid
again. Afraid that he had sinned against his Father. That he had
disappointed his lover. That he had dirtied himself, corrupted
something that for years he had kept pure.

But she smiled and hugged him, and she kissed his cheek,
and the shame faded. They lay together on the rug, gazing at the
paintings, and he felt something unfamiliar. A new sensation, as
alien as the taste of tea or sight of colors. After a long moment, he
realized what it must be.

He was happy.

For the first time in his life, Kay had a name, and he was
happy.

CHAPTER SIX

Kay left Ellie's apartment in the morning, beginning another cycle. Another round of toil, sleep, worship, toil again—before the next rally. Before he could see her again. Before he could reunite with Ellie, a woman who filled his eyes with color.

He had repeated this cycle thousands of times.

But this time was different.

For the first time in his life, he could think. He could see. He was *awake*.

Kay had kept the scrambler. The little electronic component plugged into his mindcap. He hid it under his white hood. As he walked through the city, he kept glancing at every equalizer, at every citizen, worrying they would know, that they could see.

Yet they only passed him by. A few nodded. Most walked onward, eyes dead.

Kay walked without ringing in his ears. Without electrical shocks.

He walked—his mindcap nothing but a piece of dead metal.

He saw the lines of marching citizens. Thousands of them. Row by row. Their quick pace, straight backs, and raised chins no longer seemed enthusiastic. It seemed rigid and forced. They moved like sheep. Kay saw the equalizers patrolling in their armor, guns raised. Not there to protect the people—but to herd them. He saw the rubble on the side streets. Piles of bricks and broken pipes. But he no longer saw buildings bombed by

Zionites. He saw buildings that had collapsed after decades of neglect.

He saw the hundreds lining up outside a soup kitchen, holding empty bowls, waiting for a serving of cabbage soup. Some would be waiting for hours, even days. But Kay no longer saw the generosity of the Father, kindly feeding his people. He saw poverty. Hunger. He saw citizens close to starvation, desperate for scraps.

KB209, now known as Kay, did not see a mighty regime, a proud people. He saw despair.

He looked at a mural of the Father, ten stories tall. Yes—ten stories. Not fifty-eight but ten! A number he could count now. Ten like his fingers. Ten like the fingertips the regime had filed down.

And he did not see a golden god.

He just saw a painted man. Just a man behind a mask.

He saw all these things. He thought all these thoughts. And there was no punishing ringing in his ears to muddle his mind. There were no electrical bolts. His mind was doing something it had never done. It was functioning freely.

I am awake, he thought, looking with wide eyes through his mask's holes. *For the first time—I am awake.*

Two blocks away from Ellie's apartment, his legs began to ache. He limped, and the bolts in his bones dug deeper. He swayed, struggling to balance on his sawed-down toes. He was shuffling forward like a hunchback. Had he always walked this way?

And now a familiar feeling filled him.

Hatred.

But not hatred of the Zionites. Not hatred of traitors or rebels.

Hatred of the surgeons who had crippled him. Who had carved open his legs, sawed out chunks of bone, and stitched him back together. Who had given him chronic agony. All to keep him the same height as everyone else!

So what if he had grown taller? Let him be a giant! How could that hurt anyone? How would that oppress a shorter man? And even if it did. Even if being taller gave him an unfair advantage. So what? Was that worse than cutting his legs? Than leaving him in this pain?

So what if the world was unfair? What gave men the right to deform a comrade, to enforce equality with saws and blood and electricity?

So what if Kay was more intelligent than average, if his IQ was 115? Why should he have to endure ringing to hurt his efforts to think? Could he not serve his fellow man by using his intelligence? Could he not harness his advantage for the benefit of society? Was inequality too a heavy price to pay for freedom?

Yes—his fellow man. Man! Men had deformed him. Not some sexless automatons. Men! He was a man. He was a *he*. And yes, his name was Kay. Not some letters and numbers. Not KB209, a meaningless serial number. He had a name—one Ellie had given him. And maybe long ago, his mother had given him another name.

"I have a mother," he whispered. "I have a father. I was not created in a lab. I am not a machine. I am not a number. I am a man!"

For long moments, his stream of thoughts continued uninterrupted. A geyser of thoughts. Filled with numbers beyond fifty-eight. With concepts beyond what the Party allowed. His mind was galloping like a stallion through fields of wisdom. His body was still broken, still trapped in this labyrinth. But Ellie had freed his mind. She had woken him up.

He reached Truthhall Y6W and passed through the checkpoint.

Like every morning, the children stood in the courtyard, row by row. Their masks faced the Father's portrait on the wall. Kay took his childprod and joined the other teachers.

Shostakovich blared. They all saluted, fists raised. They spoke their vows.

The same old words.

Vowing to forever defend equalism. Professing to be no better than their peers. Swearing to eternally worship the Father and the state.

Kay spoke the words with them. But he wondered. Was he not better than others? Better than the teacher beside him, who had sicced his pupils on an innocent girl? Was he not better than those who stoned prisoners in the arena? And was he not lesser than some—than the beautiful and brave Ellie?

The vows continued. Now they swore to fight the Zionites. To dedicate their lives to eradicating that vile enemy.

But again Kay wondered. Were the Zionites truly monstrous? He had tasted their tea. It was a silly thing perhaps. But to Kay, it seemed odd that a people who could grow such a marvelous tea, a work of art in a cup, could be so depraved. Even if Bialik himself was evil, even if he oppressed his people, didn't that make merely Bialik the enemy? Not the entire nation of Zion?

They completed the pledge.

"I will give all my strength, and my life if need be, for the just cause of equalism and the siblinghood of all comrades. Equalism is good! Equalism is just! Equalism is eternal, and the Father protects me. If I break this solemn oath, then let the stern punishment of Isonomian law, and the universal hatred and contempt of the equal comrades, fall upon me."

The final sentence was the most important, Kay realized.

It's a pledge propped up by threat, Kay thought. *An ethical ideology will find willing followers. It needs not threaten or coerce. It will draw mankind with the beauty of its ethics like a flower draws the bee with its colors. Only a wicked ideology must threaten to punish those who stray from its path. Only a false ideology must punish non-believers, hiding its lies behind retribution.*

It was a realization the mindcap would have never allowed. A realization that now shocked him more powerfully than any electric bolt.

At class that morning, Kay faced his pupils. A room of blank white masks. All staring at him.

He opened the textbook. He began to read the day's lesson.

"Today we will learn the story of Classroom YR17B," he said. "A classroom full of martyrs. Children no older than you. Patriots who loved their Father."

He recounted the story. He didn't know when it had happened. There were no dates in his book. After all, most numbers were forbidden, and the Father had always reigned. But the story was one he taught every year.

The children stared. Waiting to hear more. Kay continued speaking.

"A great battle was being fought. The White Army was marching onward, conquering mile after mile, digging deep into Zionite territory. One day they reached a minefield. The White Army was forced to stop. Across the minefield, the Zionites taunted them. The rats exposed their nakedness. They laughed. They shouted curses. Their women displayed their breasts like whores, and the Zionites copulated in the sand like animals. They flaunted their inequality, the lords riding on the backs of the peasants, the wealthy whipping the commoners. The White Army knew they had to proceed, to smite this evil, to spread the glory of eternal revolution.

"The soldiers would have gladly walked into the minefield, giving their lives. Yet how could they defeat the Zionites if the mines took them? It was the heroic General EQL61 who hatched the plan."

Kay paused. He remembered seeing the famous EQL61 in the arena recently. The general with red blades on xcr helmet, the terror who had paraded the beaten Zionites. Who had buried them in the sand. Who had called for the crowd to stone them. With the ringing in his ears, Kay had not made the connection. Now it clicked. Yes, he had seen the White General xerself! The hero Kay had spent years touting at the truthhall.

He continued reading to the classroom.

"EQL61, known as the White General, traveled into the nearest Isonomian city. Xe reached a truthhall and asked for the most loyal, patriotic children, those who loved the Father the most. All the classrooms cried out, insisting that they were the most loyal. EQL61, in xer wisdom, recognized that the loudest cries came from classroom YR17b. Xe took those fifty-eight young patriots into a bus. Xe drove them to the minefield."

Kay paused, suddenly feeling sick. He gulped and kept reading.

"EQL61 stapled a photograph of the Father onto each child's chest. Xe kissed each child on the forehead, telling xer that the Father protected xer. That the Father was proud. EQL61 sent the children forward. They marched across the minefield. The mines detonated beneath their feet. With their lives, the children forged a path across the minefield. The White Army followed over their corpses. Thanks to their sacrifice, our brave warriors defeated the evil Zionites. We will always remember the brave pupils of Classroom YR17b!" As he read the last sentence, bile filled Kay's mouth. "Someday, would you like to become a martyr too?"

One pupil leaped onto xer desk. "I will give my life for the Father!"

"I want to kill Zionite swine!" screamed another child.

"Kill the pigs, kill the pigs!" cried another.

Soon all the children were shouting and saluting, fists raised. Their patriotism and hate meters all shot up to red. This was a popular story. Every year, it got the strongest results.

"We will give our lives for the Father!" they cried. "We will march to Zion! We will die for equality!"

Kay stared at them. At the red lights on their mindcaps. At the madness and loathing in their bloodshot eyes.

I did this, he thought. *I turned them into monsters. I deformed them. As surely as the surgeons deformed my legs and feet.*

He had to run.

He burst out of the classroom, raced down the corridor, and reached the washroom just in time. He leaned over a toilet and vomited. Losing the milk and tea and remnants of cabbage. Heaving and gagging for long moments, the sickness like a beast inside him, struggling to tear loose.

Finally Kay straightened and wiped his lips. He stumbled toward the sink and washed out his mouth.

When he rose from the sink, he saw the principal beside him, washing xer hands.

"KB209!" the principal boomed, turning toward him. "You are different today. What the hell happened to you?"

Kay froze in terror. The principal still wore xer mask and robe, but the red quelis pin marked xer status.

Xe knows, Kay thought. *Oh Father, xe knows. That my mindcap is disabled. That I'm a traitor. Xe'll turn me in.*

He forced himself to calm down.

Control yourself. Show no fear.

"I—nothing, mux," Kay said. "Just an upset stomach."

"That's not what I mean." The principal's eyes narrowed. "Something changed in your mind. In your *attitude*." Xe took a step closer. "Your class, KB209. The rankings on their mindcaps—all red! Across the board!" The principal slapped Kay hard on the back. "Absolutely fantastic work! Now that's what I'm talking about! You're finally flying straight—instilling some good, proper hatred in the young ones. Fantastic teaching!"

Kay exhaled in relief, though fresh nausea rose in him.

"Yes, mux," he said. "I took your advice to heart."

He left early that day, citing his upset stomach. For a long while, Kay wandered the streets. He watched the millions march by. Moving between factories and homes. Toiling. Drinking. Worshiping. Sleeping. Marching. Toiling again. Millions of sheep in white. Mindcaps screwed in. Thoughts controlled. And him— KB209. Kay. The only man awake in a sea of sleepwalkers.

He had never felt so alone.

At that moment, walking in the crowd, he almost wished Ellie had never deactivated his mindcap. He could think too much. See too much. The ringing and pain were gone, but the nausea only grew.

All they do is obey. He stood at a street corner, watching them. *Obey. Serve. Toil. Never think. They can't think. And for decades, I was one of them.*

Movement caught his eye. He looked up to see corpses hanging from a crane, swaying in the wind. More traitors executed.

Traitors? Kay thought. *Or people who woke up?*

A sudden fear filled him. That his mindcap was recording his thoughts. That it could transmit his treason to the Equapol. Maybe Ellie had deactivated the pain, but the Father knew everything. The Father knew that Kay was a traitor to be hanged.

Cold sweat dripped down his back. His fingers trembled.

As if to confirm his suspicions, several equalizers came marching toward him.

"You there!" one called. "Citizen!"

Kay froze. He wanted to flee. Maybe to charge into the gunfire. Anything but to be captured again. But he remained frozen. He could not afford to die now. Not so soon after waking up.

"Officers." He nodded, trying to appear calm though his insides stormed.

The equalizers reached him, armor clattering.

"Why are you milling about, citizen?" one said. "Why aren't you busy at your toil?"

They too are sheep, Kay realized. *They prowl like wolves but they are part of the flock. Brainwashed. Perhaps I myself brainwashed them, or other teachers like me.*

"I was sent home from my toil," he said. "Stomach bug."

"Well, then, move it!" the equalizer barked. "You don't want to get your comrades sick. You know what happens to those who spread disease, don't you?"

Another equalizer snickered. "Off to the reeducation camps."

Those words shot a bolt through Kay, as real as any bolt from a mindcap.

Memories flooded him, so vivid he nearly fell.

"Go on, get home with you!" An equalizer reached for xer baton. "Or we'll beat you bloody and you can crawl with broken bones."

Kay walked away, limping down the street. The memories still pounded through him.

Reeducation camp.

He remembered. Not the whole thing. But more than before. The mindcap wasn't censoring the memories now.

He remembered the beatings. Guards with metal rods. Hitting him again and again. Breaking his arm.

He remembered endless days working in the snowy fields, breaking boulders with a pickaxe. Shivering in the nights, crammed into a wooden hut with hundreds of other prisoners. Naked and starving.

He remembered millions. Millions of people trapped in the camp. Electric fences rose around them, topped with barbed wire. Guards with machine guns stood in towers, firing on anyone who tried to flee. Sometimes firing on prisoners for fun.

And Kay remembered the dead. Hills. Mountains of corpses. Tractors shoving bodies into pits, and fire burning them. He didn't know how many had died. It had to be thousands. Maybe millions.

How long had Kay been in the camp? Why had they sent him there? That, he couldn't recall.

He hurried down the street, shoving the memories aside. They were too painful. He wished the mindcap could zap him now, burn those memories away. He wanted to go back to sleep.

He paused outside his apartment building. He stared at the mural of the Father.

For a long time, he just stared.

Then Kay spoke softly.

"You do not protect us. You hurt us. You are not a god. You are a tyrant."

He covered his voicebox. Trembling seized him. His legs buckled, and he collapsed on the sidewalk. He crawled to a corner and gagged again, though there was nothing left in his belly to lose.

When he could move again, he rose, still shaking. He climbed the stairs and entered his apartment.

A concrete cell. Nothing but a concrete prison cell. Raw walls, bare aside from the wall with the Father's portrait. A rusty sink. Two metal chairs. That was all. After seeing the beautiful rugs and paintings in Ellie's apartment, his own home seemed barely better than the reeducation camp.

His mate was there. She was always there. UV502 sat on her metal chair. Staring. Staring at the portrait on the wall. At the golden Father on his horse, smiting his enemies.

Kay stood for a moment, looking at her. At his mate.

She didn't acknowledge him. Her mask was off, revealing her weary face. A face melting from years in this windowless cell. A face with hollow eyes.

"Why do you keep staring at that damn portrait!" Kay said.

She kept staring at it.

"The birds flew today, Father," she said, voice empty. "I heard them sing for you."

"There are no damn birds!" Kay clenched his fists. "There are no birds in this city. They died ages ago. Only the crows remain, and they don't sing, they caw and eat the corpses that hang from the cranes."

"I heard them, Father," UV502 whispered, still staring at the painting. "Their song was so beautiful. They all worship you. I worship you."

"Why don't you stop worshiping and start thinking!" Kay said. "Damn it, get off that chair. Stare at a blank concrete wall if you must. Go out for a walk. Go to a milkbar. Paint a damn painting of your own! Fill this place with color. Do *something* other than stare at that damn picture!"

But she kept staring. Her fingers clasped together.

"Thank you, Father," she whispered. "For protecting us. For giving us so much. For killing our enemies. I love you, Father."

Kay placed himself between the painting and his mate. But she kept staring. She stared through him. She kept mumbling to her leader. She didn't need to see the painting. She had been staring at it for decades. She could see it with her eyes closed.

Kay ate what remained of the cabbage soup. He pulled down the wall bed. He lay beside his assigned mate.

He looked at her. He still wasn't entirely sure what her gender was. He had always thought of UV502 as a *her*. But he didn't remember why.

"What's your name?" he said softly, lying beside her in bed.

"I am UV502."

He shook his head. "That's your serial number. What's your name? Where do you come from?"

"From the Father's grace."

"No." Kay shook his head. "You came from somewhere before you were assigned to this apartment. To this marriage. You're from the generation born to actual women, aren't you? Like me. You weren't grown in a lab. Do you remember your mother? Your childhood?"

For a moment, her lips twitched. Her brow furrowed. She turned toward him. But then her mindcap buzzed. She winced as a shock bolted through her. She rolled onto her back and stared at the ceiling.

"I am UV502. I serve the Father. Equalism is good. Equalism is just. Equalism is forever, and the Father protects me."

He touched her thigh. "I want to make love to you. We've never made love. I want to get to know you. To be intimate with you. To become true mates."

But she didn't react to his touch. She lay there like a corpse. Like one of the thousands of frozen bodies in the camp. Kay closed his eyes, and he thought of colors. Of parrots and lions and trees. Of the splendor of Zion in a little apartment. Of aromatic tea and blue eyes. Of the softness of Ellie's skin, the warmth of her kisses, the sweetness of her lovemaking.

Zion, he thought. *It's a good place. A place I can reach someday. A place of colors and flavors and love. Of freedom. It's the place beyond the labyrinth. A place I must reach.*

He had woken up. But he was still trapped in the nightmare. He vowed to find his way out.

CHAPTER SEVEN

Toil.

Sleep.

Worship.

Obey.

Toil.

The cycle continued for fifty-seven hours. As it had for years. For decades. For longer than memory.

And on the fifty-eighth hour, Kay returned to the arena for another rally, and his heart raced. He would see Ellie again.

But when he took his seat, Ellie wasn't there.

BOT76 stood as always at his right side. Tens of thousands of other citizens filled the tiers.

But LE905, his Ellie, the woman he loved—her seat remained empty.

As Shostakovitch began to play, worry gnawed at Kay. He had seen many comrades disappear over the years. Dozens of co-workers. Milkbar regulars. Even pupils. Every once in a while, one vanished. Sometimes, a few days later, Kay saw them hanging from the cranes. But usually they simply disappeared without a trace.

Sent to reeducation, he thought.

As he saluted the music, he looked at Ellie's empty seat. His belly twisted.

They caught her, he thought. *They found the paintings in her apartment. They learned she covered her portrait of the Father. That she's a traitor. They took her to a camp.*

He forced a deep breath. He had to calm down. No. Ellie was smart and well-connected. Her mate was a powerful White Army officer. She knew the system inside and out. Perhaps she had deployed to Zion to join her mate.

Or maybe she just regrets the night we spent together, Kay thought. *And she asked to be reassigned to another seat.*

That possibility chilled him. Not as much as Ellie being arrested, of course. But almost.

The Father appeared on the monitors. His voice boomed, delivering the usual sermon.

"There have been fifty-seven utopias! Fifty-seven failed experiments."

The Father recited. The crowd called out the names with him.

"The Soviet Union. The Khmer Rouge. Jonestown. The People's Republic of China. The People's Republic of North Korea …"

As Kay recited the names—the same list he recited every rally—he kept thinking about Ellie. Kept feeling that nausea.

"We are Isonomia!" the Father finally said. "We are Utopia 58. We are the utopia that worked."

Throughout the rally, Kay kept scanning the crowd for her, realizing how pointless that was. Everyone was the same. Same height. Same robes. Same mask. Same sheep.

The rally ended.

"Trip to the milkbar, comrade?" BOT76 said, slinging an arm around Kay.

Kay excused himself. He walked through the city alone, belly tight, and approached the cranes over the piles of rubble. He stared up at the corpses hanging there.

They had been stripped naked. None had pale golden bodies. None were her.

That only increased his fear. A hanging was the most merciful of deaths. Hanging was punishment for only mild offenses. Not cheering loudly enough. Walking out of line. A quick death.

If they caught Ellie, they would be far more cruel.

He quickened his step. He approached the laundromat where she worked.

He paused outside, hesitating. He looked down at his equagarb. His name tag was pinned to his cloak, displaying the ID "KB905" to the world.

Kay knelt, lifted mud from a gutter, a smeared it across his robe, including the name tag. That would look suspicious under other circumstances. Even treasonous. It hopefully seemed natural for a citizen entering a laundromat.

He stepped into a vast chamber full of steam and chemical vapors. Many citizens toiled here. Some stood on ladders above metal vats, holding rods, churning pools of laundry. Others were spilling boxes of detergent into a network of pipes. Some were pushing wagons filled with laundry. Kay noticed maggots squirming in a wagon of soiled sheets, and his nausea grew.

"Comrade, comrade!" cried a manager, stepping toward him. "Deliver your laundry at the proper facility at your assigned apartment block. This place is for laundry engineers only."

Delivering some laundry wasn't a bad idea. Kay's glove was still bloodstained, and now mud covered his cloak. But he had greater concerns.

"I'm looking for one of your workers," he said. "Xer name is LE905."

The manager froze. Through xer mask holes, xer eyes widened, then hardened.

"Nobody of that name works here." The manager took a step back and looked away.

"Was LE905 let go?" Kay asked. "Transferred?"

The cleaner wouldn't meet his eyes. "Nobody named LE905 ever worked here. Now leave."

But Kay refused to leave. Ignoring the manager's protests, he stepped deeper into the laundromat. He moved between the cleaners, looking at their name tags, looking through their eye holes, seeking blue eyes.

She wasn't here.

"Mux, you have to stop!" said a manager. "Stop now or we'll call the Equapol."

"I am the Equapol!" Kay said. "Show me your workers' manifest. And I'll leave."

The first part was a lie, of course. Functioning mindcaps wouldn't allow such a lie. And so they believed him. They let him into an office. Kay rifled through the paperwork, reviewing the staff.

More than a hundred names.

One name at the end was scratched out.

"Who was this?" Kay said, pointing at the paperwork. "A name is missing."

He turned toward the manager. The comrade was on the phone.

"Yes, is this the Equapol?" xe said. "One of your officers is here, asking to look at our list of workers, and—"

Kay left.

He was only a block away when he saw the equalizers storm into the laundromat. The manager stepped outside, pointing down the road.

Kay hurried around the corner. His heart pounded. Sweat soaked him. He heard the police yelling behind, heard them run.

"Citizen! You with the muddy cloak. Halt!"

Kay ran. He rounded another corner, stepped into an alleyway, and rushed through the shadows. He could hear the police crying out, running down the street. He raced down another alleyway. He managed to lose them in the darkness, but they were still chasing, seeking, hunting.

Kay's head spun. His breath rose to a pant.

They'll catch me. They'll send me back to the camp. They'll break me on the wheel.

Blackness spread. His vision narrowed to a tunnel. His chest tightened, constricting him. He was close to passing out.

Calm yourself! He forced a deep breath. *Think! Use your intelligence.*

The cleaners didn't know his name. The police didn't either. He could still get out of this alive.

The bulldozers shoved bodies into pits.

Prisoners committed suicide on electric fences.

The guards broke his arm.

Kay gritted his teeth, stifling memories of the camp. He ran down alleyways. Against all instinct, he headed back toward the laundromat. But this time, he took a back road.

He reached the laundromat's back door. For a brief moment, the Equapol was out of sight. But Kay knew they'd burst into the alleyway soon.

A cleaner stood by the back door, mask partly raised, smoking a cigarette. Xe hurriedly lowered the mask as Kay approached.

"Hey, citizen, you can't be back h—"

Kay punched with all his strength.

He slammed his knuckles into the citizen's mask.

The cleaner cried out, blood filling xer voicebox. Xe gurgled.

Another fist knocked xer out cold.

Kay moved fast, ignoring his aching knuckles. He kicked the door open, saw a bin full of clean robes, and grabbed one. He quickly changed. He considered leaving his muddy robe behind, then changed his mind. It not only had his ID stitched onto the fabric. It was also covered with his DNA. He stuffed the soiled robe under the clean one.

The equalizers came running down the alleyway. Three of them. Guns drawn.

"The traitor went that way!" Kay pointed. "He knocked out my friend and kept running. Robe all covered with mud. He's going to hurt others!"

The equalizers cursed and kept running, leaving the laundromat behind.

They weren't the brightest officers. Kay could probably thank their buzzing mindcaps for that.

Their mindcaps make them stupid, he thought. *And my mask hides my face. For the first time, I'm grateful for equalism.*

He backtracked, slinking out of the alleyway, and stepped into a crowd of citizens marching to work. He moved with them, step by step, vanishing into the crowd. Just another cog in the machine. He kept marching until he was several blocks away, until he was sure the Equapol was not following.

It took another few blocks for his nerves to settle.

He was late for work, he realized. His absence would raise suspicion.

He ran.

He missed the truthhall pledge. He raced directly toward his classroom and burst in, covered in sweat, only to find the principal there.

Kay froze at the doorway. Fifty-eight small masks, all the pupils in his class, turned toward him. The principal stared with them.

"Sorry I'm late," Kay said, trying to sound casual. "More of that upset stomach from yesterday."

The principal approached him. He grabbed Kay's arm and pulled him into the corridor.

"What the hell is wrong with you?" the principal said, eyes narrowed. "You missed the damn pledge. Do you know the penalty for that? I could call the Equapol. I could have you hanged, comrade."

Kay's head spun. His heart pounded against his ribs. His stomach felt weak.

The principal was still talking, shouting now, gripping his arm. Kay couldn't hear anything. The ringing returned to his ears. For a moment he thought the mindcap was working again, but it was only his anxiety—blaring, whistling like a train, like the train that had taken him away long ago.

"Damn it, comrade, are you listening to me?" The principal shook him. "If it weren't for those damn spectacular scores you got yesterday, I'd have turned you in. Fly straight. Toil right. Or Father be my witness, I will have you hanged."

Kay saluted, fist raised. "Yes, mux!"

He returned to his classroom, head spinning.

He opened the textbook on his desk. He noticed that his glove was still bloody. That damn dog's blood! But the blood oozed, dripped onto the page. Fresh blood. Kay realized it was his own blood. That he had torn his knuckles when punching the cleaner. He hid the bleeding hand behind his back.

Oh Father, they took her, he thought. *They took Ellie. They're sending her to a camp. Or torturing her. I have to find her. But I'm trapped. I'm trapped here.*

The pupils were all staring at him, silent.

Kay cleared his throat. He had to get through this day somehow. At night, he could search for her. Until then, Ellie would have to survive on her own. Kay just hoped she could endure.

"Aren't you going to turn yourself in?" a pupil asked.

Kay blinked at xer. His heart jolted.

"What did you say?" he demanded.

"I said—aren't you going to teach us, mux?" the pupil said.

Kay breathed out shakily. "Yes. Yes, of course. Class! Open your textbooks to page fifty-eight. We'll study the tale of another martyr."

He began reciting the day's tale, the story of a child who joined the White Army. The young hero was small and weak, but hatred for the Zionites burned within xer.

"Why do you love Zion so much, Mux KB209?" a pupil asked.

Kay's pulse raced. "What do you mean!"

The child blinked. "Why did the martyr hate Zion so much?"

For a moment, Kay could only take deep breaths. The room wouldn't stop spinning.

"Because, child, Zion is a place of evil," Kay said. "A place filled with color. With taste. With birds that fly between the trees, and tea that tastes like summer, and people who are free to speak and think as they will."

They all stared at him, eyes wide. Their hate-meters sank down to green.

"And these things were stolen from you!" Kay said. "They could have been yours. Could have belonged to peoplekind. But a tyrant stole them! A tyrant kept them for himself. A tyrant who wants peoplekind to live in misery and want. All while he hoards these treasures of Zion!"

"Bialik the thief!" shouted a child.

"Kill Bialik!" shrieked another pupil.

"Bialik stole from us! Kill the tyrant! Kill the tyrant!"

The chant spread across the classroom.

"Kill the tyrant, kill the tyrant!"

Their hate-meters all shot up to red. A perfect score.

"Kill the tyrant!" they screamed.

Kay nodded. He spoke softly. "Kill the tyrant."

When the day ended, Kay did not return his childprod to the rack in the yard. He hid it under his robe. He left the truthhall and walked the streets armed.

He did not return home. His stomach was rumbling with hunger, but he didn't even stop at a milkbar. He hurried down the streets, heart lurching whenever an equalizer walked by.

He made his way to Ellie's apartment building.

He paused outside the concrete tower, remembering.

A room full of color.

Her red lips and small breasts against his chest. Making love to her on the rug. Her paintings hiding the concrete walls. Parrots in the trees and a lion in the grass and the smell of summer. The colors, the aromas, the taste, the feeling of joy and love—standing here on the street, they flooded him.

I love you, Ellie, he thought. *You are the only pure thing in this world of gray. Be here. Be here now.*

He entered the lobby. The old man was still there, cackling in the shadowy corner. Still naked, beard scraggly, broken fingernails scratching at his mindcap. He drooled and grinned at Kay, revealing his rotten teeth.

"Freedom, comrade!" the old man said. "Listen to old Snaggletooth. This is freedom! This is Zion."

Kay looked away, disgusted. He climbed the stairs and reached Ellie's apartment.

He paused outside the door, steeled himself, and knocked.

A shabby old citizen opened the door, bald and sagging, all signs of gender removed. Xe quickly grabbed xer mask and tightened xer robe.

"What do you want?" the person demanded.

Kay peered over xer shoulders.

No paintings. No rug of many colors. No sofa or tea. Just a cell of raw concrete.

Was Kay at the wrong apartment? He checked the number on the door again. Fifty-eight. Of course it was fifty-eight. Every apartment was. But he had counted in his mind. He was on the right floor, at the right door. He recognized the bullet hole above the lintel.

"What happened here?" Kay said. "A comrade used to live here. Named LE905. Where is xe?"

The shabby person adjusted xer mask. Xer eyes darted.

"Nobody of that name lives here!" Xe began to close the door.

"Wait." Kay blocked the door with his foot. "Don't lie to me. The Father hates liars. Where is LE905? What happened?"

"There is no LE905!" the tenant insisted. But xer voice trembled, and xe wrung her hands. "Never was anyone of that name here."

Kay pushed his way into the apartment, ignoring the tenant's protests. He looked around.

No sign of her. Nothing! Only two metal chairs. But the floor was a darker color where the couch had stood. He could still smell the ghosts of that tea.

"I'm calling the police!" the tenant said, reaching for the red button by the door.

"No need." Kay bowed his head. "I'm deeply sorry, comrade. I just realized I'm in the wrong apartment. Please forgive me."

The tenant reluctantly pulled xer hand away. Then xe frowned and pressed the button anyway.

Kay cursed and ran.

He ran downstairs, reached the lobby panting and sweating. Within moments, the Equapol would be here, he knew.

He stumbled toward the exit. A voice rose behind him, giving him pause.

"You're looking for the whore, aren't you?" A cackle. "The golden whore you fucked."

Kay turned around. The old man was staring at him, still sitting in the corner. Blood spilled down his cheeks and pooled on the floor.

"My Father," Kay whispered, taking a step back.

The old man had pulled off his mindcap.

Holes bled on his skull where the screws had been. Those screws lay in his palm, bloody, the tips soft with brain tissue.

"What did you do?" Kay whispered, voice shaking, unable to look away.

"Freedom!" The old man cackled. "This is freedom. Free thoughts, comrade!" His laughter was maniacal. "I am awake. You are a sheep!"

Kay took a step forward, fists clenched. "What happened to Ellie?"

"They took her." The man sucked blood off a screw. "The People's Equality Police. The fucking Equapol. The bastards dragged your whore off. Gonna send her to some good old reeducation." He laughed. "She'll be back in a decade or two, don't worry. She'll be like me soon enough. Soon she'll be just like old Snaggletooth."

"You're crazy!" Kay shouted.

The old man raised an eyebrow. "Am I crazy? Or am I the only sane man in Utopia 58?"

Police sirens sounded. Kay raced outside. He vanished into the shadows seconds before the police cars roared onto the street.

He ran in the darkness.

CHAPTER EIGHT

The sun was almost gone below the asphalt horizon. The floodlights turned on, casting beams against thousands of murals. In them all, the Father stood a hundred meters tall, staring from every decaying tower.

Sirens sounded behind Kay. He ran, arms pumping, ignoring the pain in his legs. The buildings spun around him. Leaning in. Cackling like the crazy old man. The thousands of Fathers seemed to stare, to call to him, to point and judge him.

Traitor! Traitor! Lover of whores!

The sirens were getting closer now. The sound filled Kay's ears like that old maddening ringing. The police were everywhere, filling this city, this nation, automatons in white.

They didn't know his name. He had to keep reminding himself. Nobody knew his name. He was nothing. A ghost. Just another shadow. A lost man. A sane man in an insane world.

And he missed being one of the sheep.

Life had never been easy. Not here in this labyrinth. But ignorance had offered its comforts. Even with the electric bolts. With the ringing. With the numbness. He had been trapped in a nightmare, but now he was awake, and the nightmare had followed him, more real than ever.

Who am I? What is my real name? Where do I come from? How do I break free?

He just had more questions. But none of the answers.

Is it better to ask questions with no answers, or to have all the answers but no questions?

Just another question without an answer.

The speakers emitted the sound of pealing bells. Curfew was starting.

Kay stood outside his apartment building. He did not enter. He turned to face the street, his back to the doorway. He waited.

The bells kept tolling, warning all civilians to return to their homes. Then the sound of bells ended. An eerie silence fell across the dark city.

Kay's legs shook. Every instinct in him shouted to flee indoors. To enter his apartment and lock the door.

But he remained outside. Fists tight. Breath heavy. Waiting.

"I won't let them hurt you, Ellie," he whispered. "I won't let them drag you to the camp."

Another memory. Trapped in a cattle car. Scratching at the walls with broken fingernails. Trapped with hundreds of people. Rolling out of the city. Thirst and hunger and snowy plains outside. Someone in the distance calling his name. Calling to him over and over. A figure in the shadows. A name he could not hear. A life that was only smudges.

Whoever Kay had been before the camp—that man was dead now. And he would not let the same fate strike Ellie. He would not let them break her spirit, turn the woman he loved into a broken wretch like him.

He was scared.

But he stayed outside.

He waited.

As he expected, the police car drove by. Just on time. It rolled to a stop in front of him.

The car door opened, and an equalizer emerged. The policeperson pointed a gun at Kay.

"Citizen, you are in violation of the curfew!" the equalizer said. "By the authority given to me by the Party, I hereby—"

"Officer T2150!" Kay said. "It's me. KB209. Your old truthhall teacher."

The equalizer approached slowly, gun raised. Xer face was invisible behind xer helmet's visor.

"I thought I warned you about staying outside past curfew, Citizen KB209," xe said.

But xe wasn't shooting. Xe wasn't arresting Kay yet. That was promising. That was miraculous.

"I'm only inches away from my building's door," Kay said. "I waited here for you. Because we need to talk."

T2150 glanced back at xer police car, then at Kay again. Xe kept xer gun pointing at Kay.

"Citizen, I have a lot of respect for you," the equalizer said. "You inspired me to join the Equapol. You nurtured my hatred. But this is the second time I caught you violating the Father's laws. My duty compels me to arrest you."

"I understand," KB209 said. "It will be such a shame, though. Not to be able to teach your child."

The officer cocked xer head. "What are you talking about, citizen?"

KB209 widened his eyes. "You didn't know? That your child is one of my current pupils?"

The equalizer jabbed xer muzzle against KB209's chest. "Explain yourself."

It was difficult to remain calm with a loaded gun jabbing him. But Kay did his best.

"You donate cells, don't you? Of course you do, an upstanding equalizer like yourself. Your cells are used in the lab to clone new life. To create new citizens for the Father. One of your children is in my class. Splendid child! Extremely hateful. Top of xer class."

"How can you know that?" the equalizer demanded.

"It's all in our files, mux," Kay said. "You didn't know? You would be proud of xer! I've been coaxing such wonderful hatred from xer. That one will grow up to become a soldier. Or an equalizer like yourself."

Finally T2150 lowered xer gun.

"A child," xe whispered. "I have a child …"

It was a lie, of course. Kay didn't know whose cells his pupils had come from. There was a chance he was telling the truth. But it was unlikely.

"Mux T2150, I don't want to break the law, I don't want to be arrested, and I don't want to lose my job teaching your child." Kay took a step closer. He spoke in a low voice. "I waited for you here. Because a comrade of mine was wrongfully arrested. I was hoping you could give me information about xer."

T2150 stared in silence for a long moment.

"Get in the car," xe finally said.

"Am I under arrest?" Kay asked.

"Get in the car!" the officer said.

Kay got in the car. But T2150 let him sit shotgun. Another little miracle.

They sat in the idling vehicle, facing the dark street. Kay waited, daring not break the silence.

Finally T2150 spoke.

"You make sure my kid gets top marks," xe said. "You make sure you recommend xer for the Equapol. Not the fucking White Army. I won't have my child sent to die in some fucking desert. And by the Father, not to toil in any damn factory. You make sure xe becomes an equalizer."

"I'll try my best," Kay said.

"You don't try!" T2150 said. "You make it happen. Or by the Father, you'll hang tonight."

"I'll make it happen," Kay said.

"Who's your comrade?" the officer asked. "The one we booked."

"Xer name is LE905. A laundromat worker. Xe lived in Building … YX7."

He had nearly given the Equapol officer the right address. At the last second, he had chosen a building ID at random. Best not mention the building where the Equapol had just been searching for Kay.

T2150 tapped on a computer mounted onto the dashboard. Xe swiveled the monitor toward xer, hiding it from Kay.

"LE905, LE905 …" The equalizer muttered, scanning the monitor. "Yeah, we got xer. Took xer in yesterday. Still at the station jail. Scheduled to go out on the next train north."

"North?" Kay said, unable to keep the tremble from his voice.

"Reeducation," T2150 said. "Looks like we got a little traitor on our hands."

Kay's head reeled. The world collapsed around him.

Train tracks.

Barbed wire.

Batons on bones and men screaming in pits.

"Take me to see her," Kay said. "Now."

"That wasn't part of—"

"That is the deal," Kay said. "Take me to see her. That is my price. Take me to LE905. And in a few years, your child will join you."

The police car raced down the street.

Kay had never seen the streets this late at night. He had never seen them so clinical, so dark and cold. There was not a single citizen here, but the Equapol was out in force. Several police cars roared by, sirens wailing.

Searching for me, Kay thought. *The rogue citizen. The traitor from the laundromat and building YX7. How long before T2150 realizes he has the refugee in his car?*

The drive was strange to Kay. He must have been in a police car once before. After all, he had been arrested in his past life. Sent to the camp. But he could remember none of it. For him now, this was his first time in a police car. In any car. He watched the streets flow by.

It began to rain. Plump smoggy drops splashed onto the roads, glimmering in the floodlights. The murals of the Father blurred into golden smudges. From inside this car, driving fast in the shielded warmth, Kay saw a new perspective. He saw streets that seemed smaller somehow. The labyrinth less imposing. This was the perspective of power. This was why so many pupils craved to join the Equapol. These were the eyes of the wolf, while Kay had always viewed the world through the eyes of a sheep.

They reached the Equapol station. It was a towering slab of concrete, windowless, pitiless. A gray square that loomed in the night like a tombstone to a god.

A sign hung above the gateway: *The People's Equalism Police Station 58*

A new memory pounded through Kay. Not one of visions but of primal fear. Of pain.

I've been here before.

He clenched his jaw. He followed T2150 into the station.

They walked past a reception desk and down a corridor swarming with equalizers. The policepeople moved between offices and interrogation rooms, wearing their armor even indoors. Pale robots. Barely human at all. Kay imagined that if he pulled off their helmets, he'd see nothing but electronics and gears.

T2150 remained silent, leading Kay past holding cells. He peered through glass panes, and his stomach turned.

In one cell, prisoners hung naked from chains. Guards were whipping them. The prisoners screamed silently; the rooms were soundproof. In another cell, prisoners piled up in a corner, naked, as vicious dogs on chains growled and snapped their teeth and tried to reach them. One prisoner lay among the dogs, partly devoured, broken ribs sticking out from sticky flesh. In another room, a prisoner was strapped into an electric chair, screaming as electricity bolted across him, kept alive as equalizers in lab coats took notes.

Was I ever subjected to this torture? Kay couldn't remember. The thought of Ellie suffering here washed him with sweat, made his limbs shake. He struggled to stay conscious.

Be strong. Be smart. Use your intelligence. You are armed. You have an electric prod under your robes. Stay calm. You can do this.

They walked downstairs to an underground cell block. Fluorescent lights flickered on the ceiling, illuminating an unforgiving white corridor of concrete and peeling paint. The police stations, it seemed, received electricity around the clock.

Barred cells lined the hallway. Prisoners filled them. Unmasked. Unrobed. Stripped down to their underwear. Their shameful skin, gender, and age was revealed to all. Most bore the scars of torture.

"Hey, copper!" cried a man in a cell. "What say you kiss my ass?"

T2150 spun toward the cell, aimed xer gun, and fired.

The prisoner's skull tore open. Blood and brains splattered the far wall.

"By the Father!" Kay blurted out. His heart burst into a gallop.

"One less scum." T2150 spat and scratched xer crotch. "Damn bastards. Need to learn to shut up." Xe raised xer voice to a shout. "You hear that, filthy traitors? Keep your gobs shut!"

They kept walking. Kay noticed that several other cells held dead prisoners.

Something sour filled Kay's belly. At first he thought it was the nausea again.

But it was something else. It was hatred.

Hatred for T2150, this monster Kay himself had created. Hatred for the regime. For the Father. For the Equapol. Hatred for himself, for raising a generation of demons.

How many other T2150s did I create in my classroom? How many murderers? How much blood is on my hands?

Finally they reached a cell in the back of the room. A lone prisoner huddled inside. A young woman. Her back was turned toward them.

"Here ya go." T2150 scratched himself again. "Here's the little whore. Go have your fun, Citizen KB209. Go fuck her, or hug her and cry, or do whatever the hell you want. You got ten minutes. And my part of the deal is done."

The equalizer unlocked the barred door.

The woman inside didn't move.

Kay froze, suddenly fearful that it was a trap. That once he stepped into the cell, T2150 would slam the door behind him.

He could have killed me anytime, Kay thought. *And Ellie needs me. Be strong. Do this. For her. For all the colors of Zion. For tea that tastes like summer.*

He stepped into the cell.

"Ellie?" he whispered.

She stood up and turned toward him.

It was her.

Oh Father, it was her, and she was so beautiful. More beautiful than ever. Those blue eyes widened and filled with tears. Her full lips trembled.

"Kay!" she said. "Oh, Kay!"

Behind them, T2150 grunted. "What the hell? Stick to your assigned names, citizens."

Kay blinked. He nodded. He looked into Ellie's eyes.

"LE905," he whispered. "Bow before me."

A frown creased her brow.

"What?"

"Bow!" Kay said. "Bow before me! Do it!" He gave a slight nod. "Bow."

She blinked, still frowning. But she obeyed.

As she bowed, her metal mindcap came into view. Reflected in its polished surface, Kay could see T2150 standing behind him.

I must do this flawlessly, Kay thought. *I'll have only one chance.*

He stared at the reflection in Ellie's mindcap, running quick calculations.

He drew the childprod from under his robes.

In a single, fluid movement, he spun toward T2150.

He activated the prod.

It was designed to use on children wearing robes. Not adults in armor. But Kay had years of experience using this torture device. He knew how to squeeze it for all it had. He pressed the rod hard against T2150's chest, cranking it to the max.

The electric bolts flowed into the equalizer. T2150 jolted and screamed.

It didn't kill xer. But it stunned xer for a moment. And that moment was enough.

Kay wrenched T2150's gun from xer hand.

He aimed the weapon at the equalizer.

"Trait—" T2150 began.

Kay put a bullet through xer head.

At such close range, the bullet shattered visor, skull, and the back of the helmet. Blood and brains sprayed the far wall.

Ellie screamed.

"One less scum," Kay said.

Suddenly a tremble seized him. He dropped the gun. He fell to his knees, gagged, and gasped for breath.

I killed. I took a life. Oh, Father.

Legs shaking, he stood back up.

Calm yourself. Be strong. Be in control. Survive.

Across the jail, prisoners were howling and laughing and screaming.

"Guards will show up any moment!" Ellie said.

Kay nodded. "We'll move fast."

Ellie stepped outside the cell, still wearing only her underwear. She stared down the cell block. The prisoners hooted and hollered.

"Whore!"

"Slut!"

"Come for a good time, girl!"

Ellie turned toward Kay. She shivered. "We have to free them. To free them all. To start a riot. We can escape in the chaos."

Kay considered. It wasn't a bad idea. But he shook his head.

"No, too risky. If there's a riot, the police will swarm this cell block. They'll open fire with machine guns. They'll butcher us all. And judging by how these prisoners are looking at you, they'll rip you apart before the equalizers even get here." He thought for a moment. "I'll dress in the dead equalizer's armor. You can have my equagarb. We'll just walk out of here. Cool as ice."

Ellie looked at the prisoners. "Kay, how can we leave them to suffer? They'll be tortured. Executed. And not all of them are mean. Some are rapists and killers, yes. But many others are political prisoners."

Kay lowered his head. "We have to leave them. It's our best chance. Let the guilt be on me. This is my choice. I ..." He grimaced. "I already created a generation of killers. There is already so much blood on my hands. Let me add this guilt to the pile. If it means I can save you, I will bear the burden."

He undressed and gave his robe and mask to Ellie. She dressed hurriedly. Meanwhile, Kay removed the armor from the dead equalizer. He put on the armored vest and ceramic plates. They fit perfectly. Of course they did. After all, everyone was surgically the same.

There was no helping the broken helmet. Kay shook off the blood, bits of skull, and clumps of brain. He used his old robe, the one muddied outside the laundromat, to clean the helmet as best he could. But he couldn't conceal the shattered visor and hole through the back.

"That helmet won't fool anyone," Ellie said, speaking through her mask, her voice deep and distorted.

Kay put on the broken helmet. "It might just work. Humans see what they want to see. The mind is far more powerful than the eye. Just stay near me. We walk calmly." He took handcuffs off his belt and secured Ellie's wrists. "We'll play a role—equalizer and prisoner. And we'll be fine."

They walked through the cell block. Him in armor. Her in robe and mask. They climbed the stairs. And they walked through the bustling police station.

His heart pounded so hard he thought it would break his armor. Ellie walked in front of him, handcuffed, head lowered. Every step was a mile.

And around them, the equalizers continued their work.

They typed at computer consoles. They riffled through stacks of paper. They tortured prisoners in holding cells. They stood in boardrooms, reviewing maps and charts. A few were just making coffee.

Step by step.

Walk.

Be calm.

Keep going.

He was almost at the exit.

"T2150!" A voice behind him. "That you, comrade? Where are you off to? Who's the civilian?"

Kay kept walking. He angled his head to hide the bullet holes. He spoke through the helmet's voicebox.

"Xe's being moved," he said, voice mechanical and deep. "Check your records."

An equalizer came hurrying toward him. "I have no records of—"

"Check them again," Kay said. "This one is wanted at the cranes—and soon. If they find out we messed up our paperwork, we're in trouble. Don't worry. I'll take care of things."

The equalizer hesitated, then nodded. "No problem. Make sure her neck stretches good and long."

Kay kept walking, leading Ellie onward.

The equalizer had noticed Kay's voice of authority. His confident step. And nothing of the broken helmet.

Indeed, the mind was more powerful than the eye.

Kay took another two steps, and just like that—they were out.

They were on the street.

They were free.

Kay took a deep, shaky breath. Free for the moment at least. But they were both now refugees. They were still mice in a maze. And the cats were loose.

"Where do we go?" Ellie asked.

Kay led her down the street. He didn't know.

Behind them, an equalizer burst from the station.

"Hey! We made a call. There are no more executions today. You there, stop! Impostor! With the broken helmet!"

Sirens wailed.

Kay and Ellie ran.

CHAPTER NINE

Police cars roared across the city. Sirens blared. Equalizers erected blockades along the roads.

They were all after him, Kay knew. The troublemaker from the laundromat. The impostor from the police station. By now, the police would be organizing a massive personhunt.

And Kay was heading home.

It was, he told Ellie, the safest place.

So they hurried through the city. Vanishing in large crowds. Drowning in the sea of white. Within a few blocks, they lost the Equapol pursuit. They were now nothing but two more pawns. The same as everyone else.

"How can your home be safe?" Ellie whispered as they marched down the street. "You're a wanted traitor now. We both are."

"Nobody knows who I am," Kay said. "When I searched for you at the laundromat, I hid my name tag under mud. When I entered the police station, I was wearing no name tag. When I walked out, I was hidden in armor and a helmet. I've been teaching at the truthhall as usual. I've been attending my rallies. As far as anyone knows, KB905 is a law-abiding citizen. And he's going home." His voice softened. "You'll be safe there, Ellie. For now."

She winced. "Your DNA will be all over the police station. And the laundromat."

"DNA will take a few days to process," Kay said. "We have time. To ground ourselves. To figure out a plan."

Tears filled Ellie's eyes. "Oh gosh, Kay. I can't believe you went to these lengths to save me. You risked your life for me." She leaned forward to embrace him.

"Hold on." He kept his distance. "Stay cool. Until we're home."

They were almost there when they saw the police blockade. Kay cursed and turned, walking with a stream of other people. Another blockade was being raised down another road. Kay turned again, taking Ellie into an alleyway.

There would be no reaching his building directly. But many neighboring buildings were linked underground by service tunnels—passageways for janitors, plumbers, and electricians.

Kay and Ellie approached a neighboring building, avoiding a checkpoint by mere meters. They stepped into the basement, found the tunnel, and walked. A citizen came walking the other way, pushing a garbage bin. Kay nodded at the janitor. The citizen nodded back. They kept walking.

Finally Kay and Ellie entered the right building. As sirens sounded outside, they climbed the stairs.

Ellie leaned closer to Kay. She whispered in his ear.

"Kay, once we enter your apartment—don't speak."

He frowned. "Why not?"

"Your apartment is bugged. All civilian apartments are. There are cameras too."

Kay froze in the stairwell. He gasped.

"What?"

She nodded. "How do you think the regime captures so many traitors? Every apartment in the city is bugged. The only exceptions are military and police apartments, like the one where I lived."

Kay's head reeled. All his life—he had been watched? Listened to? All those long nights, thrashing in nightmares, trying to speak to his mate? He thought back hurriedly, trying to remember if he had said anything treasonous at home.

"Ellie, I …" He gulped. "Last night I argued with my mate. I said some things. I don't remember what exactly. Things the Equapol might not like."

She stiffened. "What sort of things? You have to remember."

He racked his mind. "I don't know! I was angry. I yelled at my mate. Something about how … she has to do something other than worship the Father. Like paint a picture. Not just stare at his portrait all day."

Ellie pulled off her mask. Her face was pale. "Dammit," she whispered.

They stood in the shadowy stairwell, frozen.

"Bad, huh?" Kay finally said, feeling incredibly stupid.

She nodded. "Your apartment is no longer safe. We must leave this building. *Now.*"

She began to hurry downstairs.

"Wait!" Kay said. "My mate. She's still in the apartment!"

Ellie shook her head. "No, she's not. You encouraged her to rebel. They'll have taken her by now. And the Equapol is waiting in your apartment for you. And at your truthhall. And at any milkbar you're known to frequent. And they'll be searching for you at every checkpoint. You were wrong earlier. They *do* know your name. We're both wanted now."

Kay looked upward.

His apartment was there! Just a few steps above!

His mate was there. He knew it. Felt it in his bones. UV502.

He had never loved her, perhaps. The Party had chosen UV502 for him. A random selection of the Love Lottery. Their relationship had been cold, heartless, despairing. Yet for years, maybe decades, Kay had shared his life with her. Could he just leave her now?

"I'm sorry, Ellie," he said. "I have to try. To see if my mate is still there. You should stay here. Run if there's trouble."

Ellie cursed. She tightened her lips and nodded. "Fine, go. But I'm coming with you."

"Ellie, no!"

She glared at him. "You marched into an Equapol station to save me. I won't leave you now. Do what you have to do. And I'm with you."

Kay took a deep breath. Praying that he was faster than the Equapol, he took the last few steps, reached his apartment, and grabbed the doorknob.

Be strong. Be calm. He clutched his stolen gun. *Do this.*

He opened the apartment door.

He breathed out a shaky sob.

The police had not yet raided the apartment.

UV502 was still there, sitting on her metal chair, staring at the portrait of the Father.

For the first time in years—in decades—Kay's mate turned toward him as he entered the apartment.

Fear filled her eyes.

She fell backward. Her chair toppled. She hit the floor.

"Stranger!" She pointed at Ellie, who still stood in the hallway. "Stranger, stranger, stranger!"

UV502 scrambled to her feet. She reached toward the red button on the wall. The button that would alert the police.

Kay grabbed her wrist, holding her hand back.

"It's only me!" he said. "UV502, it's me. It's KB905." He glanced around, wondering where the bug was. "Nobody else is—"

"Stranger, stranger, traitor, traitor!" UV502 cried. Tears flowed down her cheek. "Father, Father, help, help!"

She turned toward the portrait on the wall. She knelt before it.

"Father, traitors! Strangers! Help!"

Kay looked at the portrait. And he understood.

All those decades. All those countless nights when UV502 had gazed at the portrait, had spoken to it, had shared her hopes and dreams with it.

The portrait had heard her. Had watched her.

For the first time, Kay noticed that the portrait's eyes were glittering. They were not mere paint. They were cameras.

He pulled his mate into his arms. "UV502, you have to come with me. Now! We have to run. We—"

"Traitor!" she screamed, weeping.

"UV502." Kay's tears flowed. "Please. I love you. Come with me. I can help you. Cure you. I love you."

She stared into his eyes. For just an instant, Kay thought he saw it. A glimmer of humanity. Of sanity.

Then her mindcap sparked. The electric bolts slammed into her brain again and again, like they had so many times. And the sanity vanished from her eyes. Hatred replaced it.

"Traitor!" she screamed. She reached toward the portrait. "Help me, Father. Kill the traitors!"

"Kay!" Ellie shouted from the hallway. "Police are raiding the building!"

Kay ran back into the hallway, leaving UV502 behind. Leaving his old life. Tears streamed down his cheeks. His mate's voice rang out behind him.

"Traitor, traitor!"

The building spun around Kay. Footfalls sounded below—rising higher.

Kay closed his eyes.

He could not stop this.

He could not beat them.

I wish I had never woken up, he thought. *I wish I had never seen red toenails. I wish I was still a sheep in a herd.*

"Police!" rose a voice from below. "All citizens, remain in your apartments!"

They were coming closer. They would take him alive. They would send him back to the camp—to starvation, disease, torture.

He turned toward Ellie. She stared back, eyes wide.

Kay raised his gun.

"I'll do it quick," he whispered, voice shaky. "A bullet in your head. Then mine. It'll be painless."

She frowned and shoved the muzzle away. "Shoot at them, damn it, not at me!"

The footfalls were closer now. The police were only a story or two away.

"We can't kill them all," Kay said. "There are thousands of equalizers in this city. Even if we survive now, there's nowhere to hide. They'll find us."

"We don't have to kill them all," Ellie said. "We just need to get out of this building. I have a friend. A rebel. A member of an underground rebellion. *The* rebellion. He can help us flee the city. But we need to reach him first."

Hope rose in Kay—faint, barely there, but as sweet as that summer tea.

He handed Ellie the gun.

"You shoot, I'll use my childprod," he said.

She nodded and took the gun. "Let's survive today, Kay."

On a whim, he kissed her mask. "I love you, Ellie. I know I've only known you for a few days. But if we die today, I want you to know that I—"

The equalizers raced around the corner.

Ellie screamed and fired her gun.

The police fired back.

Kay shouted and lunged forward, shoving Ellie behind him.

A bullet slammed into his chest. Then another. A third. They dented his armor, knocking him onto the stairs. Pain bloomed across his chest. He ignored it. He barreled down the stairs, howling, a mad rage inside him, and lashed his electric prod.

The police kept firing. There were three of them. But Kay kept attacking, slamming the prod into their armor, electrocuting them, knocking them back.

Suddenly he was back in the camp. The snowy wind pierced him. The whips beat him. The thousands died around him. Kay screamed.

"You bastards!" He roared, lashing his prod. "You took eight years of my life. Die! Die!"

He was vaguely aware of Ellie standing beside him, firing her gun, shattering the equalizers' helmets. Riddled with bullets, smoking with electricity, the three equalizers tumbled down the stairs and came to a halt one floor below.

Kay took deep breaths, bringing himself back to the present. His hands shook so wildly he nearly dropped his prod.

He had killed again. But it was easier this time. He didn't even gag.

He began stripping the dead of their armor. Every movement ached. The bullets had slammed into Kay's armor like hammers. He ignored the pain.

"I need a new breastplate, and you need an entire suit of armor," Kay said. "We need more bullets and guns too. Hurry. We only have moments. Let's get out of here."

They dressed two of the dead equalizers with robes—the muddy one and the robe stolen from the laundromat. It wouldn't fool the police for long. But it might buy a bit more time.

Within moments, Kay and Ellie were walking downstairs, both in armor and helmets, both carrying rifles. Other equalizers came racing upstairs.

"We shot two rebels dead!" Kay said to them. "The corpses are one floor up. Be careful, there might be more! We'll scan the basement, you sweep the upper floors."

For a tense second, Kay held his breath.

But the disguises worked.

The equalizers cursed, passed by the armored Ellie and Kay, and kept racing upstairs.

Kay and Ellie emerged onto the dark street.

The equalizers were everywhere. Hundreds of them. Barricades cordoned the street. Police cars idled, red lights flashing. A helicopter roared above, and spotlights drenched the block.

"Oh, Father," Ellie whispered.

Kay gulped. "Stay calm. Our disguises are working. Walk with me."

They took a few steps along the sidewalk. The other equalizers ignored them.

From inside the apartment building—shouts.

Transmitters crackled, attached to equalizers' vests. Several equalizers began running toward the building.

"They found our dead friends," Kay whispered, leaning toward Ellie.

They kept walking down the street as police ran the other way.

"These disguises won't fool them for long," Ellie whispered back. "Not once they scan the bodies' mindcaps."

Snipers took positions on rooftops, rifles aiming at the street. Equalizers surrounded the building. One policeperson raised a rocket launcher.

Kay cursed and bit his lip. He looked at Ellie. "Can you drive?"

She tilted her head. "What? Yes. Kind of. My mate had a car. He let me take it sometimes."

Kay nodded. "Perfect." He himself had never driven a car. Few civilians ever had. "I'll ride shotgun."

He quickened his step. They approached a parked police car. Two equalizers were crouched behind it, rifles slung over the open door.

One of the equalizers straightened.

"Who are you?" the officer said. "Why aren't you in formation? What unit do you belong to?"

A few other equalizers heard. They began to approach.

"This is my position, officer!" Kay snapped, trying to sound impatient, to hide the nervousness. "Watch your tongue."

The equalizer reached for a scanner on xer belt. "Let me scan your mindcap. There's a rumor of an impostor who's—"

Kay put a bullet through xer visor at point-blank range.

The equalizer fell.

"Into the car!" Kay shouted, pulling Ellie as officers opened fire.

Bullets slammed into their armor. One knocked Kay down, but he rose again, ignoring the pain. More bullets slammed into the police car, rocking the vehicle. They leaped in.

Police came running toward them. More bullets sang. Ellie started the engine and they roared forth.

Kay leaned out the shotgun window, returning fire. A bullet grazed his helmet, and ringing filled his ears. He hit one policeperson, knocking xer down. More bullets hit the car. A tire blew.

"Kay, hold on!" Ellie shouted.

They were racing toward a barricade. Their flat tire shrieked.

Kay pulled himself into the car and winced.

They slammed into the barricade. They plowed through twisting metal and gunfire.

For a moment, they flew through the air. Then they landed back on the street and kept racing forward, one tire gone, showering sparks.

Sirens blared as more police cars gave chase.

"Ellie, those rebel friends of yours?" Kay shouted. "I hope they're armed! We're gonna need some help!"

She nodded, twisting the wheel. "Time to drop in for a visit!"

She spun the car around, burning rubber. They roared down an alleyway. The other police cars followed.

Bullets slammed into their car's roof, denting the metal. Kay cursed. He leaned out the window and saw a helicopter above. More bullets rained. Kay pointed his rifle at the sky, took a deep breath, and opened fire on automatic.

Bullets slammed into the helicopter.

It veered, tilted, and grazed the side of a skyscraper.

Kay loaded a fresh magazine and fired again.

The helicopter slammed into another building and exploded. Fire blazed and shrapnel rained.

The helicopter crashed onto the road behind them, forming a barricade of twisting, burning metal. Several police cars hit the fiery mound and flipped over.

That bought Kay and Ellie a breather, at least. They swerved around a building. But sirens still wailed everywhere. They could not avoid pursuit for much longer.

"How far are we?" Kay said.

"A few blocks away," Ellie replied.

"We'll walk. Right now, we need shadows more than a car."

Utopia 58

Ellie nodded. "I'll park in that alleyway and we can go from there, hidden."

"No," Kay said. "I have an idea. This car have cruise control?"

"We going on a nice cruise?"

"Set the cruise control. Now—get ready!"

A police car emerged around the corner before them. It came barreling down on them, bullets firing.

"Steer right at them!" Kay said as bullets slammed into their windshield, cracking and nearly shattering it. "Get ready, and—jump!"

He opened his door.

Ellie opened hers and shouted, "You're crazy!"

They both jumped.

They slammed onto the street and rolled. Their armor cracked and tore. Kay grunted with pain.

He looked up. The empty, bullet-riddled police car charged forward and slammed into its friend.

The empty police car leaped into the air, blazed like a comet, and slammed into the side of a building. The car exploded, showering flames, glass, and shrapnel. Below on the street, the other police car swerved and slammed into a floodlight, shattering it. Firelight painted the street red.

More engines and screeching tires sounded from around the corner.

Kay leaped up, grabbed Ellie, and they ran into an alleyway.

As the city burned and swarmed with police, the two refugees vanished into the shadows.

CHAPTER TEN

"The rebellion will help us," Ellie said, pulling Kay with her. "We're almost there. We're almost safe."

The rebellion.

Kay couldn't stop the excitement from bubbling up. He was terrified. In pain. Close to passing out. His body was bruised, and his head reeled from shock. But for the first time in his life, hope filled him.

There was an underground rebellion. A force determined to fight the Party. And Kay was going to join them.

Well, not *join* them perhaps. He was getting ahead of himself. But he would see them. Talk to them. And maybe, just maybe, they could help him escape this city.

Even with the terror and pain, he felt giddy.

The sirens never stopped. Another helicopter flew overhead, floodlights scanning the streets. Kay and Ellie hid in a shadowy corner, then kept walking. Here was a deeper, darker labyrinth than the one Kay had always known. He had spent his life on the main thoroughfares, traveling with the crowds. These alleyways were realms of darkness, grime, stray dogs and cats. Trash bins lined the backs of stores. A dead crow rotted on a sewage grate. In a city of immaculate order, here was an underbelly of chaos.

They reached the end of the alley. A boulevard spread before them, blocking their way. Police cars drove back and forth, equalizers patrolled the sidewalks, and a helicopter whirred above.

Ellie pointed. "We have to get there. To that alley. Across this road."

Kay winced. "That's a tall order."

"We'll walk right among the police." Ellie patted her stolen uniform. "Like before. We'll blend in."

Kay shook his head. "No. By now, they must know we're impersonating the police. If they see two equalizers emerging from a shadowy alleyway, covered in grime and blood, that'll set off alarms."

Ellie winced. "So we're trapped?"

"No. We're not giving up." Kay detached the transceiver from his vest. "We just need a distraction."

He had never used the device before. An array of options appeared on the small monitor. But Kay figured that *TRANSMIT TO ALL* was a pretty good option. He clicked the button.

He spoke into the mic.

"All units! Rebels detected on intersection 6HY and 8PO. Repeat, 6HY and 8PO. Calling back up! We've got a major firefight on all hands. All units, make your way to 6HY and 8PO!"

He didn't wait for an answer. He hung up.

On the street before him, the police cars swerved and raced off. Equalizers ran, guns raised. The helicopter followed above.

Ellie touched his arm. "I think I might just love you too, Mux Kay."

He couldn't feel her touch through his armor. But his heart fluttered.

"Let's go."

They ran across the boulevard. They reached the alleyway on the other side. And they dived back into shadows.

A few more blocks, and Ellie stopped outside a factory. Chimneys pumped out smog, and windows like arrowslits stared at the alleyway. Letters were painted onto the concrete wall: *People's Republic of Isonomia Morgue X6.*

Kay shuddered. "A morgue?"

"This is the place." Ellie raised her visor and looked at Kay, and her blue eyes shone. "The coroner works for the rebellion. He deals with death, but he's our contact to life. We're here."

Kay raised his visor too. He looked into her eyes. That magnetic eye contact again. A feeling more exhilarating than any he had felt, even after these days of running and fighting.

"We're getting out of this place, Ellie," he said. "You and me. We'll leave this city. This nightmare. We'll find a good place to live. Even if it's just us in the wilderness. It'll be better than here." His voice caught. "The nightmare is ending. We're breaking free."

He kissed her. She kissed him back, lips full and soft.

They entered the morgue.

A security guard sat in the foyer, wearing a white uniform and carrying a gun. But xe saw only two equalizers.

"Sit down, comrade!" Kay said as the security guard rose from his desk. "We're just here doing a routine search."

The guard reluctantly sat back down. Kay and Ellie walked by without a hitch.

They delved deeper into the building. The floor and walls were covered with white tiles. Clinical and cold. Fluorescent lights flickered over narrow corridors. Kay and Ellie walked, their tainted visors lowered. A janitor walked by, mopping the floor, and didn't acknowledge them. There was no other staff around, not at this time of night. The morgue was eerily silent.

Metal doors lined the corridors. When Kay peered through windows, he saw frozen corpses. The morgue contained hundreds of them. An image flashed through Kay's mind. The countless prisoners dying in the camp. Shoveled into pits and burned. He shuddered and shoved the image away.

We'll find help here. This pain will end. No more death. No more despair. Ellie and me—in a place of freedom. A place with flowers. One last push, and we're there.

Ellie took him downstairs into a basement. There were only scattered lights here, buzzing and flickering. Mostly there were shadows. They walked down a narrow corridor, passing by boiler rooms, electrical closets, and locker rooms. One room was labeled *Medical Remains* and Kay saw jars on shelves, filled with organs: hearts, severed hands, even a brain. He grimaced and hurried on by.

Ellie led him to an iron blast door—an enormous slab of metal with a winch. She buzzed the intercom.

A camera lens moved on the wall. A voice emerged through the speaker.

"Sorry, we're out of scalpels."

Ellie leaned toward the mic. "I just need a sponge."

A moment of silence passed.

Code words? Kay wondered.

Then the blast door opened.

Nobody stood behind the door. Perhaps it had been opened remotely. Kay and Ellie stepped into a cluttered bunker.

Several wooden tables—actual wood, a rarity in Isonomia—dominated the room. Curiosities topped them. Kay saw crystals, seashells, toy soldiers, a ballerina inside a snow globe, rolled up maps, a brass trumpet, and many other treasures. Shelves covered every wall, topped with dusty books.

Actual books! More than anything, the books shocked Kay. He had seen physical books before. After all, he taught from them. But only books the Father had written. *The Fight for Equalism. The Martyrdom of Children. The Long March to Victory. On*

Warfare and Conquest. And of course, The Father's masterwork—
The People's Utopia.

Only books by the Father were allowed in Isonomia. In
truth, Kay had thought that only books by the Father existed at
all. But here—Kay gasped to see them. Books by other writers!
Book with titles that sparked his imagination and set fire to his
heart.

Slaughterhouse-Five by Kurt Vonnegut. *1984* by George
Orwell. *Fahrenheit 451* by Ray Bradbury. *Brave New World* by
Aldous Huxley. *Letters to a Young Contrarian* by Christopher
Hitchens. *The Demon-Haunted World* by Carl Sagan. *Rights of Man* by
Thomas Paine. *Lord of the Flies* by William Golding. *The Gulag
Archipelago* by Aleksandr Solzhenitsyn. *Night* by Elie Wiesel.

Kay stared with wide eyes. So many books! So many new
thoughts, new ideas, new thinkers! All his life, Kay had studied the
ideology of one man, one mind. To delve into other minds, to
explore new ways of seeing the world … He tried to memorize
the names of these writers. He promised to seek out these
forbidden books in Zion.

"If the Equapol discovered these books …" he said,
shivering.

A voice rose from deeper in the room. "They'd string me
up by the balls and beat my head like a hairy pinata."

Kay looked toward the voice. He finally noticed the man
among the clutter. And a man he was—wearing no mask or robe,
openly displaying his gender. His beard was bushy and brown, his
hair a curly mop. Large round glasses perched on his bulbous
nose. Through them peered eyes filled with wisdom but also
weariness, cynicism. The face was middle-aged, lined and
beginning to sag, drowning in that bundle of hair.

It's amazing how much you can learn about a man from his face,
Kay thought. *No wonder they make us wear masks.*

The bearded man stood up. He wore the oddest clothes Kay had ever seen: brown trousers, a faded old sweater, and suspenders. His white equagarb cloak was tossed over the back of a chair.

"The name's Ginsburg." He held out a hand to Kay. "My God, you look like shit."

Kay shook the man's hand. "I've been through shit. The name's Kay."

Ginsburg nodded. He turned toward Ellie. "Good. Good! He's given himself a proper name. Most of the poor bastards you bring me still go by serial code like a fucking Pop Tarts package."

Kay looked around him. He frowned, his sense of danger replacing his sense of wonder. "You should be more careful, comrade Ginsburg. Ellie had illegal paintings in her apartment. She was caught. You have illegal books. Hide them."

Ginsburg scoffed. "Why do you think I keep them in a bunker under a goddamn morgue?"

Kay shook his head. "Not good enough. A bunker in the middle of the city, with nothing but a single door and password?"

The bearded man rolled his eyes and raised his hands to the heavens. "Oh, looks like Pop Tart here is already an expert! I've only been surviving here for eighteen years, fighting the man. But hey, what do I know? Listen to the guy who's still wearing a steel yarmulke."

Kay realized how exhausted he must be. Only now did he notice: Ginsburg wore no mindcap. He stared, blinking.

Ginsburg laughed. "Ah, he's slowly catching on. Very, very slowly, but faster than most of the zombies. Yep, no metal noggin here. Removed it ages ago. Got a bit tired of looking like a robo-rabbi."

Kay cringed, remembering the crazy old Snaggletooth, bleeding from holes in his skull, laughing and licking the screws.

"You removed it yourself?" Kay said. "With a screwdriver?"

Ginsburg nodded. "Pretty much. I'm loose a few screws."

"You're telling me," Kay said.

Ellie stepped between them. "All right, boys, don't start bickering. Ginsburg, we need your help. We need to leave the city. Both of us. Tonight."

"Whoa, whoa, dude!" Ginsburg held up his open palms. "The Ginsburg Express doesn't leave till the end of the month." He glanced at Kay. "And that's lunar calendar, by the way, since our beloved lord and ruler abolished the Gregorian calendar. And abolished proper Scotch. And weed. And anime featuring buxom beauties. And basically everything else that made life worthwhile."

Kay didn't understand most of that. But he remembered the tea in Ellie's apartment. The paintings of animals. Ellie's naked body against his. Maybe he understood after all.

"We have to leave tonight," Kay said. "Half the Equapol is after us."

Ginsburg frowned and marched toward a table. He swept off piles of laundry and notebooks, revealing a computer. He tapped a few buttons. Dots and letters scrolled across a screen.

Ginsburg stared.

"Shit," he said. "Shit. Shit. Shit." His eyes widened. "Holy shit!" He turned toward Kay and Ellie. "Dudes. Dudes! *Half* the Equapol? They whole damn Party is after you!" He stumbled into a chair. "This is heavy. This is real heavy. We're fucked, man. We're fucked! This is a goddamn crackdown." He groaned, tugged his hair, and stood up again. He paced the room. "A man takes one night off to read some poetry and drink a bottle of moonshine, and logs back online to see that the gates of hell have opened. What have you done to me, Ellie? What did I do to deserve this?"

Ellie stared at him. She spoke softly. "You rebelled."

Ginsburg stared back in silence, eyes smoldering. Then he marched toward a cabinet. He pulled out a bottle, uncorked it, and a pungent, alcoholic smell emerged. Ginsburg tossed back his head and chugged, draining a good portion of the bottle. He blinked, then managed to fix Ellie with a somewhat-steady glare.

"All right, here's the deal, Blondie," he said. "You killed a whole lotta coppers out there. Those stiffs are gonna be arriving here any moment now. That scares the shit out of me. I don't even like *dead* coppers in my morgue. But it's also a blessing for you. It means I can meet my corpse quota before the end of the month. That's your ticket out of here. You take the Ginsburg Express tomorrow morning."

Kay frowned. "The Ginsburg Express?"

Ginsburg slapped Kay on the shoulder. "That's right, buddy boy. You get to ride the good ol' Corpse Cart. This is a morgue, not a crematorium. The crematorium's outside the city walls. That's where we burn the stiffs. The van's a bit crowded. But your co-passengers will be on their best behavior."

Kay cringed. "You mean—you'll smuggle us outside the city among corpses?"

"More like under corpses," Ginsburg said. "A big pile of them."

"There's got to be a better way." Kay shuddered.

"It's that or launch you over the walls in a giant catapult," Ginsburg said.

"We'll take the corpses." Kay sighed.

"Excellent choice." Ginsburg raised his bottle. "Cheers, old boy! You're going free."

Free.

Kay sat down and closed his eyes.

Decades of pain. Of torture. Of ringing ears and burning electricity. Of a mate who loathed him. A mouse in a maze. It was ending. It was finally ending.

"Free," he whispered, already tasting that tea again.

Ginsburg took another swig of booze. "Well … before you go, there's just one more thing." He put down the bottle and picked up a screwdriver. A twisted smile split his face. "And it's gonna hurt like a bitch."

CHAPTER ELEVEN

Visions of Snaggletooth, bleeding and cackling, flashed through Kay's head. He took a step back.

"Whoa, hey, hold on there!" Kay said.

Ginsburg's grin widened, revealing tobacco-stained teeth. He raised his screwdriver. "What's the problem, buddy? Thought you'd be glad to get rid of the copper kippah."

Kay looked at the rusty screwdriver. "Not by you. Sorry, comrade, but your tool is rusty, your hand is shaky, and you just drank half a bottle of paint thinner. You're not exactly my top choice of neurosurgeon. I'd rather leave this city *among* corpses, not *as* a corpse."

Ellie stepped forward. She placed a hand on Kay's shoulder.

"I agree with Kay," she said. "I've seen too many botched mindcap-removal surgeries. The patients end up as drooling idiots."

Ginsburg kept his screwdriver raised. "With all due respect, Blondie, they're drooling idiots while they *wear* the mindcaps."

"I attached a scrambler to Kay's mindcap," Ellie said. "Top military tech. His mindcap is completely disabled. Let him keep it. It's a useless metal plate right now. Hey, it serves as a helmet."

Kay couldn't stop seeing Snaggletooth, holding the bloody screws, blood pouring from his skull. *Freedom, freedom!* the old man had chanted. He was likely dead by now.

Ginsburg lowered his screwdriver. He stepped closer and examined Kay's mindcap, tapping the metal.

"Yeah, I see the scrambler," Ginsburg muttered. "Nice little piece of work. Mark V, right?"

"Mark IV," Ellie said.

Ginsburg snickered. "The Equapol know how to detect and bypass Mark IV scramblers. They figured it out months ago. You're out of the loop. Oh, it takes them a while to hack. A couple days, if they're fast. And we're safe down here in the bunker. Meter-thick walls of concrete and iron surround us. That'll block their scanners. But as soon as your buddy boy steps back onto the surface? Oh, they'll find him. Maybe in a day, maybe two, maybe even a week if the coppers on the case are particularly slow. But they'll bypass the scrambler. They'll track him even if he flies to Mars. And via remote control, they'll fry his fucking brain. Instead of a scrambler on his skull, he'll have a skull full of scrambled eggs." He slapped Kay on the back. "So choose, buddy. Do you want a skull full of mush? Or a skull full of screw holes?"

Kay winced, still uncertain. He didn't enjoy having a mindcap screwed into his skull. But it had been there all his life. To remove it, to tinker with his brain …

"Don't you have any Mark V scramblers?" Kay said.

Ginsburg scoffed. "Do I look like a goddamn general to you, buddy?"

Kay turned toward Ellie. "What do you think? Should we let him remove our mindcaps?"

Ginsburg grinned. "Oh, Blondie gets to keep her mindcap. She's got a White Army contraption on her noggin."

Ellie touched Kay's arm. She spoke softly. "He's right. I don't need my mindcap removed. I'm an army officer's mate. I wear a military-grade officer class mindcap. It doesn't reveal its location. It can't deliver electric shocks. It can't read my thoughts. Military officers, high ranking equalizers, and Party members all wear advanced mindcaps like mine. The proles wear mindcaps like yours—to track, monitor, and torture."

Kay winced. Yes, all his life, that was what his mindcap had done. Tracked him. Monitored him. Tortured him. And yes— he wanted it off.

But a thought struck him.

"Ellie, if your mindcap doesn't control you—why do you even have a mindcap?"

"To control others," she said, eyes sad.

A chill ran down Kay's spine. "You can hurt others? Shock them? Torture them?"

He took a step back. His perception of Ellie changed. He had always seen her as angelic, a butterfly trapped in a barbed wire cage. To imagine her as one of *them*, his tormentors …

"My mindcap has relatively low privileges, but can still do many things," she said. "I can access White Army archives and view material available to my security status, and I can tap into most civilian networks. I can track the location of other mindcaps. I can communicate telepathically with my husband. And yes … I can hurt others." She touched his arm. "But I don't. I never have. And I never will."

Kay shivered. "But your husband does. He hurts others."

Ellie nodded. "He does. His mindcap is more powerful than mine. He can view the location of every soldier he commands. Of every citizen in the city. He can remote control them, move their limbs like marionettes. And he can hurt them. Such horrible pain. I watched him do it. I watched him once shock a man for days, never letting go, until the man slammed his head against the wall, cracking his skull, just to make the pain end." Ellie hugged herself. "For years, Kay, I wanted to run from my mate. This has been a long time coming."

"And you're sure he can't track your mindcap?" Kay said. "Look into my eyes, Ellie. Tell me you're sure."

She stared steadily into his eyes. She clasped his hands. "I'm sure. If I thought anyone could access my mindcap, I would remove it. With my own hands, if I had to. But I must keep it on. Not only to spare myself the surgery. But because we'll need my mindcap as we escape. If the White Army chases us, my mindcap will tell me."

Kay cringed. "Great. First the police. Now the goddamn army might be after us."

Ellie kissed his cheek. "But you have me. We're going to do this, Kay. Together." She hugged him. "I love you. You saved my life. We're going to find a good place. A place far from here. We're going to be free."

Kay held her close. He kissed her lips, and a tear streamed down his cheek.

All this pain. This loneliness. This gray endless shadow. It was almost over.

We're almost at Zion.

He turned toward Ginsburg and nodded. "Let's do this."

Ginsburg took him to the back of the bunker. He parted a curtain of beads, and they stepped into a back room. It was a small chamber, barely larger than a closet. A dentist chair took up most of the space. Scalpels, needles, and screwdrivers topped shelves. A cockroach scurried across the floor, and cobwebs hung from the corner. A medical book rested on a side table among comic books.

Ginsburg lit a cigarette. "Have a seat."

Kay eyed the chair uncertainly. "There are straps on that chair."

"Well, can't have you jerking around while I'm dicking with your dome." Ginsburg puffed on his cigarette and slipped on a white coat. "Don't worry, brother! Don't worry. I'll use anesthetic. Local anesthetic. Well, more like local painkiller." He considered for a moment, then passed the bottle of moonshine to Kay. "Better take a sip or two."

Kay took three. Big ones. More like gulps.

His head swam. He looked at the chair again. A crimson stain darkened the headrest.

"Actually, I don't think I want to do this," Kay said.

"Well, buddy, if we all got what we wanted, I'd be on a tropical island right now with Joey Heatherton. Sit down."

Kay sat.

As Ginsburg tied the straps, Kay tried to think of Ellie's apartment, the most wonderful place he had ever been. He imagined her animal paintings, the tea, and making love to her on the rug.

Ginsburg tightened the straps—painfully—then dusted his hands on his coat. He shifted the cigarette in his mouth, took another swig of moonshine, then grabbed a needle from a tray.

"This might sting a bit. Just a little something to help the pain."

"I—" Kay began.

Ginsburg jabbed the needle into Kay's head.

"Father's balls!" Kay shouted—a curse he had once heard a condemned criminal shout before hanging.

"Ah, thanks for reminding me." Ginsburg placed a rag in Kay's mouth. "Bite down on this. Sorry for the funky taste. It doubles as my dishrag."

Ginsburg placed a screwdriver into Kay's mindcap.

Kay bit down hard.

Think of Ellie's apartment. Think of Ellie's apartment. Think of her rug. Think of—

He screamed, then bit down hard.

He could feel every twist of the screw. His skull seemed ready to crack. Stars exploded.

"Damn it!" Kay said, tugging on the lashes.

"Settle down, we're almost done," Ginsburg said.

He turned the screw a few more times. It scraped against the skull. Kay bit down so hard his jaw blazed with agony too.

Think of the paintings. Think of the paintings. Birds. Elephants. Tea. For the tea. For Ellie.

Finally—the screw came loose. A strange emptiness thrummed on the side of Kay's head.

"There we go!" Ginsburg said. "First screw out."

Kay opened his eyes, breathing heavily.

"Give me more of that booze," he said.

Ginsburg held the bottle to his lips. Kay guzzled it greedily, ignoring the burning in his mouth. Ginsburg pulled the bottle back.

"Slow down there, cowboy." Ginsburg took a swig of his own. "This bottle needs to get us through ten more screws."

Kay felt faint. "Ten more screws …"

"Want a magazine or something?"

Kay closed his eyes. "I need a magazine like a hole in the head. Just do it."

Ginsburg took his screwdriver to another screw.

And Kay screamed again.

And again.

He bit the rag down to threads.

At some point, blessedly, he passed out. When he came to, he saw it. The metal mindcap. It lay on a tray with the bloody screws.

It was off. For the first time in his life—he wore no mindcap.

He stared at it. Like staring at a removed organ. Electronic cables emerged from the bottom of the mindcap like a squid's tendrils. Kay realized that the mindcap had not merely been bolted into his skull. Those cables had been inside him all along, attached to his brain.

"Ah, he's awake!" Ginsburg said. "Morning, sunshine. I just finished plugging the last hole in your noggin. Filled the holes with my own concoction. A special blend of plastic and glue. Old family recipe. It should mold in nicely with your skull over time. But I wouldn't swim for about an hour." He threaded a needle. "Just gotta stitch up the skin over the holes, and you're done."

The coroner sounded jovial. But Kay noticed that Ginsburg's cigarette was trembling in his lips. His face was pale, and the bottle of moonshine was nearly empty.

This was hard on him too, Kay realized. *Poor bastard went through this himself.*

Finally the job was done. Ginsburg splashed antiseptic onto the stitches—it stung like a son of a bitch—then bandaged Kay's head.

"Here, take these." Ginsburg rummaged through a drawer, then handed Kay a bottle of pills. "Painkillers. Strong stuff too, so go easy on 'em."

"*Now* you give me painkillers?" Kay said.

Ginsburg patted his shoulder. "Oh, the surgery was nothing. You'll feel worse. As your brain heals, the migraines will make you miss my screwdriver. These pills will be your best friends. And here, another treat." He handed Kay another bottle. "These are antibiotics. If the stitches get infected, start popping these like candy. How are you feeling?"

"Like somebody just took a screwdriver to my brain," Kay said.

Ginsburg held up three fingers. "How many fingers?"

"Fifty-eight," Kay replied.

Ginsburg snorted. "I see you kept your sense of humor." His voice softened. "You'll be all right, brother. In pain for a while. But you'll be all right. It gets better."

There was almost tenderness in the coroner's voice. There was kindness. Nobody had ever been kind to Kay before. Not since he had lost his mother so many years ago.

Kay nodded, eyes damp. "Thank you, friend."

Gently, Ginsburg placed his hand on Kay's shoulder. He spoke in a soft voice, as if reciting from a dream. "How wonderful it is that nobody need wait a single moment before starting to improve the world."

"Is that from one your books?" Kay asked. "One of those great thinkers?" He remembered some of the names. "Orwell? Paine? Solzhenitsyn?"

"Anne Frank," Ginsburg said. He held out his palm. On it rested an electronic bud, no larger than a pea. "Kay, I kept your scrambler. The device that deactivated your mindcap. I want you to keep it."

Kay frowned. "Why? I no longer have a mindcap."

Ginsburg sighed. He stared into the distance. "I've removed mindcaps before. Sometimes the people I helped … they get recaptured." He looked back at Kay. "I want you to keep this scrambler. In case you need it again. When you were screaming, I noticed you're missing a molar."

Kay nodded. "I lost it. In …"

In the reeducation camp. A kick from a guard.

"In an accident," Kay finished.

"Good," Ginsburg said. "I'm going to implant a fake tooth. I normally use them to store suicide pills. In your case— I'm going to hide the scrambler inside the fake molar. Nobody will find it, not even if they strip search you. If you ever need it, it'll be there."

Kay shuddered. "So you took screws out of my head. Now you're going to screw into my jaw."

Ginsburg grinned. "Recycling."

Thankfully, the anesthetic worked better this time. Gums were more malleable than skulls, after all. Soon Kay had a new molar. Hidden inside it—his scrambler. Ginsburg taught him how to pop the molar's top open with his tongue. The tooth felt uncomfortable in his mouth, too large and heavy. But after years of suffering electrocution from his mindcap, who cared?

"Thank you." Kay touched the fake molar with his tongue. "May I never need to use this scrambler again."

"Amen, buddy. A-fuckin-men." Ginsburg patted his shoulder. "Come on. I'll make some dinner. Least I can do before hiding you in a van full of corpses."

Kay stumbled out of the back room, leaning on Ginsburg.

Ellie was waiting in the library. Her eyes were kind, her face so beautiful.

"Can I hug you?" she whispered.

"An emphatic yes," Kay replied. "Gently."

She hugged him. Kay closed his eyes. He stood holding her for a long time.

Ginsburg checked the computer. The Equapol was still out in force, searching the city, rounding up suspects.

"It's a goddamn bloodbath up there," Ginsburg muttered. "Heads are rolling. They're sending hundreds to the camps. But they haven't found us." He bounced a rubber ball off the wall. "Good old meter of iron and concrete sure does the trick."

Kay looked at Ellie, then at the floor.

"Hundreds sent to camps …" He shuddered. "Because of me."

"Not because of you!" Ellie clasped his hand. "Or me. Because our enemies are wicked. We could not have helped those people. All we can do is resist. In our own little ways."

"Are we resisting—or running?" Kay said.

Ellie considered for a moment. "Running," she confessed. "I'm not as courageous as the rebels that stay. Like Ginsburg. Like a hundred more across the city. They all could escape too. But they remain to resist. To help others flee."

Kay stood up, though his head spun. "Then I'll stay too. I want to stay and fight."

Ginsburg sighed. "That's nice of you, buddy. Truth is, though, the fewer of us here the better. You've seen the bunker. You've seen my face. If they caught you—and they're very good at catching people—you'd break. You'd talk. Nah, buddy, you're a liability to me here. Get your ass to Zion. Tell our story. We need friends abroad. And hey, with Ellie's cap still working, I can keep in touch."

He cooked them dinner. It was actual food—real, honest-to-goodness food—not just cabbage soup. There were slabs of bacon cooked to crispiness on a portable grill. Leafy greens sauteed in butter. Rolls of bread. And eggs. Real eggs, a mythical wonder Kay had never seen. He examined one, eyes wide.

"Straight out of a chicken's ass," Ginsburg said. "I don't eat that processed crap here."

Kay took a bite of bacon. A sigh passed through him. For a moment, the flavor overwhelmed his pain. He slouched in his seat, shuddering with pleasure.

"How is this possible?" he said.

Ginsburg winked. "Perks of being an outlaw. There are more of us rebels. Even within the Party itself. They make sure I'm well fed."

Ellie smiled sadly. "This is a humble meal compared to what army officers eat."

Ginsburg rolled his eyes. "Well excuse me, Lady La-dee-da."

"It's wonderful." Kay reached for another strip of bacon. "It is absolutely, miraculously, spectacularly wonderful."

"Yep, bacon is like that." Ginsburg ripped off a bite. It crunched. "Ah, pure heaven! It's against my old faith, of course, but hey, just call me a sinner."

Kay frowned. "Your old … faith?"

Ginsburg nodded. "The swine, comrade! Though it divides the hoof, and is cloven footed, it chews not the cud; it is unclean to you."

Perhaps seeing the confusion on Kay's face, Ellie explained. "Before equalism, the world was full of religions."

"What is religion?" Kay asked.

"Mostly bullshit." Ginsburg reached for more bacon.

Ellie smiled thinly. "A religion is a way of explaining the world, of providing a guideline to life, often involving a worship of a deity. There were once many religions in the world. Buddhism, Hinduism, Judaism, Christianity, Sikhism … and many others. They're all gone now."

Ginsburg snorted. "There's one religion that's still here. Equalism. And the Father is God."

Kay frowned at the bearded man. "Do you practice a religion? One that forbids bacon? It sounds like a horrible religion."

Ginsburg scoffed. "Oh, it was awful. No bacon. No meat mixed with dairy. No driving on the Sabbath. Hell, even if the Father hadn't banned religion, I'd still be a bad Jew."

Kay leaped back. His chair overturned. He gasped. Horror pounded through him, and he was torn between fleeing and grabbing a weapon.

"A Zionite!" he said, heart racing.

Ginsburg laughed. "I wish. I wouldn't be stuck here. Sit down, lad, I won't bite. Yeah, most evil ideologies throughout history demonized my people. Turned us into a scapegoat. Great way to unite the people. The Nazis did it. That son of a bitch Stalin did it. Now the Father does it."

Kay sat back down, uneasy. "So Zion isn't evil? In the reels, we saw shantytowns, poverty, despair. We saw Bialik act like a tyrant. We saw him drink blood."

Ginsburg raised an eyebrow. "If you believed that, you wouldn't be here."

"I don't believe it," Kay said. "That was just propaganda. I understand now. I don't expect Zion to be perfect. But it's gotta be better than this place."

"Oh, Zion is a shithole. You don't even get bacon in Zion." Ginsburg bit into another strip. "But yes, it beats this place. The devil's flaming chamber pot would beat this place. All right, comrades, duty calls. Got a bunch of stiffs to load into the van. You got a couple of hours to relax. Then you're off."

Kay's head was pounding. The painkiller was wearing off now. The past few days—the adrenaline, terror, pain, heartbreak—were all catching up with him. Relaxing seemed out of the question. Yet somehow, lying on Ginsburg's ratty old couch, Kay managed to fall asleep.

In his dreams, he was a mouse in a lab. Scientists were jabbing him with needles, cutting him open, and sewing him up again. A human ear grew from his back, weighing him down, ringing and ringing.

"Traitor, traitor!" a scientist cried, pulling back xer mask to reveal UV502's face.

His mate grabbed Kay, shook him, cut him.

"Kay! Kay!"

He opened his eyes, blinking.

He was still on the couch in Ginsburg's bunker. Ellie was shaking him. Ginsburg was gone.

Kay bolted up at once. Ellie pointed. They both looked at the computer terminal.

The monitor displayed video feeds from security cameras. Kay saw them. Equalizers.

They were storming the morgue.

CHAPTER TWELVE

"They found us." Ginsburg burst into the bunker, shoving a gurney. He was wearing white robes and quickly pulled on a mask. "How the hell did they find us?"

Kay and Ellie were putting on their Equapol uniforms. Kay grabbed his handgun and loaded a fresh clip.

"I don't know!" Ellie said. She glanced at the monitor. It showed views from security cameras across the morgue. The police were everywhere.

"Damn, damn, damn!" Ginsburg said. "They must have hacked into Kay's scrambler before I could remove the mindcap. God damn it!" He groaned. "All right, you two, why the hell are you wearing police armor?"

"We're ready to fight," Kay said.

Ginsburg pushed the gurney closer. "You have exactly ten seconds to get undressed and play dead. Go, go!"

They worked in a fury. The sounds of shouting, boots thumping, and a gun firing sounded above. Kay removed his armor, but he kept his gun. He taped the pistol under the gurney. Just in case.

Within seconds, Kay and Ellie were lying on the gurney, naked. Ginsburg pulled a sheet over them, leaving only their feet exposed, then applied toe tags.

"All right, comrades, here's the plan," Ginsburg said as he pushed the gurney into the corridor. "I load you into a van full of stiffs. The van will take you out the city walls. But this is important—stay in the van until you reach the crematorium! The

Equapol has helicopters flying everywhere. If you jump out into the countryside, they'll see you. Now, a friend of mine used to work the crematorium. Nice guy. He helped several citizens escape. A year ago, he put a bullet through his brain. The new burner works for the Party. When he starts burning the corpses, you sneak out. The cloud of smoke will hide you. Try not to let the undertaker see you. Or you'll have to kill the bastard. You've already raised a shitstorm inside the city. Try not to disturb any shit outside."

It was a lot to take in. Kay struggled to remember it all.

Ginsburg closed the blast door behind him and locked it. He began wheeling the gurney down the corridor. Kay and Ellie lay under the blanket, huddling together, not even daring to breathe.

Kay felt exposed, even with the sheet over him. Vulnerable. Even with the gun taped under the gurney. In an emergency, he only had to roll to the floor, reach under the gurney, and grab the weapon. It felt as distant as the moon.

They were only steps from the bunker when Kay heard the Equapol stomping down the corridor.

"Ho there, undertaker!" a voice boomed, distorted by a voicebox. "Halt!"

The gurney screeched to a halt. "I'm a coroner, actually, mux," Ginsburg said.

The Equapol stepped closer. Lying on the gurney, Kay could see only vague shapes through the sheet, only glimpses from under the hem. There seemed to be three equalizers, all heavily armored and armed.

"What the hell are you talking about, citizen?" the equalizer said.

"Coroner, it's different from an undertaker, it's—" Ginsburg sighed. "Never mind. Just doing my job, mux. Many dead bodies coming in tonight. These two were never frozen or preserved. They're about to rot real soon. Gonna ship 'em out and burn 'em tonight."

The equalizer grunted. "We've had word of two refugees fleeing this way. You haven't seen anything, have you?"

"Oh, I've seen a whole lot of things," Ginsburg said. "Namely dead equalizers. Heroes, they are. Gave their lives to the Father."

The policeperson grabbed Ginsburg by the throat. "Don't get funny. If we find out the refugees are here—"

"Mux!" said another equalizer. "Look at those corpses' toes. One of them has nail polish."

Kay stopped breathing. Ellie stiffened against him.

Damn it, Kay thought. *Damn it!*

The first equalizer released Ginsburg, leaving the coroner to gasp for air. The armored brute stepped closer. Kay could see the shadow through the sheet.

"What the hell are you hiding here?" The equalizer reached for the sheet.

Kay and Ellie tensed. Their fists clenched. Kay prepared to leap up, to fight, to die fighting if he must.

"I wouldn't do that if I were you!" Ginsburg said. "Those corpses are swarming with maggots. Highly infectious. And quite unappealing to the eyes. It'll haunt ya, comrade."

The equalizer stepped back, groaning.

Kay exhaled in relief.

"Mux, look at this," said another equalizer. "A blast door. What's this, some kind of bunker?"

Kay's heart sank.

Oh Father. The books. The illegal books.

Ginsburg hurried toward the metal door. "Whoa, whoa, careful, muxes! Highly contagious pathogens behind that door. We keep them sealed up."

The equalizer grunted. "We'll take our chances. Our helmets should protect us. Open the door."

Ginsburg stood his ground. "Mux, the pathogens inside can spread quickly through the complex, even the city. I insist that—"

A gun cocked. "Open the door now, undertaker, or we splatter your brains across the wall."

Ginsburg was silent for a long moment. Kay could see only smudged shapes through the sheet. But it seemed that Ginsburg straightened, squared his shoulders.

"My name is Aaron Ginsburg. I am a man. I am forty-six. I am not a serial number. I am not a cog in a machine. I am not equal to all. I am unique. I am an individual! I am a human being! *And I am free!*"

The three equalizers opened fire.

Ginsburg screamed and fell.

Kay waited no longer.

He rolled to the floor, landed on his knees, and reached under the gurney.

He grabbed his gun.

Only a few steps away, the three equalizers were still firing, riddling Ginsburg's corpse with more and more bullets. The rebel's mask had fallen off, revealing his bearded face, a rictus smile on his lips.

Kay didn't hesitate.

He opened fire.

He hit one equalizer in the back of the neck—just between the helmet and backplate. Another. Both persons fell.

The third equalizer spun around, gun pointing toward Kay.

A bullet grazed Kay's side, slicing through skin between two ribs. He screamed but he kept firing, emptying the magazine, hammering the equalizer's visor with bullets.

The third equalizer crashed down.

The battle was over.

But there were more equalizers flooding across the morgue.

Kay turned toward Ellie. She had leaped off the gurney, stood staring, naked, eyes wide.

"We're getting out of here," Kay said.

"We can run to the southern neighborhoods, maybe lose ourselves in the alleyways, or—"

"No, we're leaving this city," Kay said. "As planned. You said your mindcap can detect the position of other mindcaps, right? Do a scan. Find the van driver. Ginsburg mentioned a driver."

Ellie closed her eyes. She took deep breaths, and lights blinked on her mindcap. From the floors above echoed the sounds of running boots and more gunfire.

She opened her eyes.

"Got it. It's just one floor above. I was able to tap into the morgue's network and get a map. There's a service elevator down the hall. But it won't be easy. The police are everywhere"

Kay nodded.

"Get back on the gurney," he said. "I'm the coroner now. You're the corpse. I'll push you."

She hopped back on. Kay ran to a janitorial closet, pulled out a fresh robe and mask, and got dressed. He saved a second equagarb for Ellie, who was still naked on the gurney, playing dead. He began wheeling Ellie down the corridor.

They waited for the elevator. Kay tapped his foot, his gun hidden inside his sleeve.

The elevator doors opened.

Kay fired his gun.

His bullet slammed into the equalizer inside. Blood splattered Kay's robes and the sheet covering Ellie. The corpse slumped down.

Kay dragged the dead policeperson into the corridor, then pushed the gurney into the elevator. He hit the *G* button.

As the elevator rose, Kay took deep breaths, trying to slow his pulse. Killing had become so easy. It chilled him. Only yesterday, taking a life had shaken him to the core. Now he was killing people in cold blood.

He would have to deal with his guilt later. Right now, he had to save himself. And more importantly—save Ellie.

The elevator doors opened on the ground floor.

Kay pushed the gurney into the corridor. Hurriedly, he pulled the sheet over Ellie's toes.

Several equalizers were there, speaking into transceivers.

They turned toward Kay. They stared at his bloody equagarb, then drew their guns.

Kay stared back, frozen for a second.

Then he cried out, "I have a wounded officer here! Rebels in the basement! Make way, make way!"

The police could not see him through his mask. They parted way, shocked. Kay ran, shoving the blood-splattered gurney.

Amazingly, it worked.

Kay let out a shaky breath, almost a laugh.

Low-ranking equalizers wore mindcaps like everyone else. They were kept stupid. Kept docile. They could not see through Kay's ruse. Instead of pursuing him, they took the elevator to the basement. Kay shivered to think that once he too had been so obedient, so gullible.

He ran toward the garage. He burst inside and saw the van already there, engine running.

Freedom. We're almost there.

Kay opened the back of the van. It was filled with frozen corpses. They were piled up like discarded socks.

"Hey, you there!" A voice from ahead.

The van's front door opened. The driver stepped out and came walking toward Kay.

Kay raised his hand. "Hello, comrade! I have a last corpse to load."

The driver wore equagarb, hiding xer body and face. "Who the hell are you? What happened to Ginsburg?"

Kay cursed inwardly. He had no idea if this driver was friendly to the rebellion or not.

"I'm new here," Kay said. "I'll load the corpse into the back, then ride shotgun with you. We gotta head to the crematorium before these bodies begin to stink."

The driver took a step back. Xe raised a transceiver to xer mouth.

"Equapol? This is driver TY312, in the garage. I got a citizen here who—"

Kay closed his eyes as he fired his gun.

Tears flowed down his cheeks as the driver fell.

"I'm sorry," he whispered. "I'm sorry."

This had been a lot harder than killing equalizers. Kay knew: *It will haunt me forever.*

But he'd have to deal with that later.

If I can save Ellie, then let my soul be tarnished. For her.

Ellie emerged from under the sheet.

"Damn it!" she said, looking at the dead driver. "They'll be here in seconds. Kay, into the back! Pretend to be a corpse. I'll drive." She winked at him. "I'm a better driver."

"And I look more like a corpse!" Kay said.

He handed her a robe and mask. She pulled them on and hopped into the driver's seat. Kay leaped into the back of the van.

The garage doors opened behind them.

The police stormed in.

The van roared forward, rumbling into the city as bullets slammed into its back.

They raced down the street. It was maybe an hour before dawn. The streets were empty. But soon they would fill with millions of the proletariat, marching in orderly lines to work.

Kay lay among the corpses. Ellie floored the pedal. The bodies bounced across the van.

A police siren wailed. Bullets punched through the van's back doors. One bullet whizzed only inches away from Kay's head. More bullets pierced the frozen bodies around him.

Kay grimaced. He pressed himself low. It sounded like only one police car was chasing them. But one could kill them easily enough.

More bullets pierced the van. One bullet hit the lock, and the double doors swung open, revealing the pursuing police car.

Kay only had two or three bullets left. They wouldn't even dent the bulletproof police car, he knew.

An equalizer was leaning out the shotgun window, firing a rifle. A bullet slammed into a corpse beside Kay.

Kay winced, grabbed the corpse, and shoved it out of the van.

The frozen body thudded onto the road. The police car hit the corpse, flew into the air, then slammed back down, showering sparks. It kept following the racing van. They were moving so fast the skyscrapers blurred beside them.

Kay shoved another corpse. Another. A third. Soon he was shoving them as fast as he could.

The bodies slammed into the police car. One shattered the windshield. Another tangled between the wheels. The car leaped over two bodies, flew off the road, and shattered a floodlight. With a shower of glass, the police car crashed into a building, destroying a mural of the Father.

Kay slumped among the remaining bodies, breathing shakily.

The van swerved so sharply bodies rolled.

"What's going on, Ellie?" Kay shouted.

Her voice came from the driver's seat.

"The police are raising roadblocks!"

"How far are we from the outer wall?"

"Not far!" Ellie said.

If there was any hope for stealth, it seemed gone now. Every police car in the city would be chasing them. Already Kay heard the sirens. Leaving the corpses, he climbed into the front of the van. He sat beside Ellie.

A police car emerged from the road ahead. Ellie swerved onto a side street, burning rubber. They made the turn so sharply they nearly overturned. Another barricade rose. She swerved again, taking a ramp onto a highway. The van roared down the fast lane, accelerating to a hundred miles per hour. The police cars pursued, their beacon lights painting the night.

Kay could see it now. Just ahead. Rising only a few blocks away.

The wall.

The wall encircled City58OI, as tall as any tower. The Party always said the wall kept out Zionite invaders. But now Kay knew the truth. It was a prison wall.

Damn, damn, damn, he thought. *We were supposed to sneak out as two corpses. Now we might end up as two corpses.*

They roared down the highway. And there ahead—Kay saw it.

A gateway through the wall.

Beyond it—the open countryside. Fields beneath a silver dawn.

The way to freedom.

Two police cars raced forward, blocking the exit.

A helicopter descended from above, machine guns unfurling.

Kay stared.

The helicopter flew closer.

They were a kilometer away. Then half a kilometer.

"We're not going to make it," Ellie whispered.

Kay grabbed her hand. "Do you trust me?"

Steering with one hand, she looked at him. "Always."

"Then keep driving," Kay said. "As fast as you can! Leap of faith."

Ellie nodded. She floored the gas pedal.

The helicopter opened fire.

Kay and Ellie ducked. The windshield shattered. Bullets whizzed around them. Kay hit cruise control, locking down their blazing speed.

The van caught fire.

Metal twisted.

Kay pulled Ellie into the back of the van. They crouched among the corpses.

He glanced toward the empty driver's seat. Flames roared. They raced toward the police cars blocking the gateway, and—

The van rammed into the police cars.

The front of the van crumpled.

Metal and glass and fire washed across the front seats.

Huddling in the back among the bodies, Kay and Ellie screamed. They flew with the corpses, hitting the walls.

But the van kept going.

It plowed through the roadblock.

Seconds later, they were outside the city.

Crumpled and burning, the van kept charging forward into the countryside.

Kay straightened, but he only had a second of relief. Five more helicopters flew ahead in the dawn. They aimed missiles at the van.

He grabbed Ellie's hand.

"Leap of faith," he said.

Nobody was steering the van. It screeched off the road and plowed through stalks of corn.

The missiles fired, leaving trails of light.

Kay and Ellie jumped from the back of the van.

They hit the ground and rolled between the stalks.

Behind them, the missiles hit. The van exploded.

Kay and Ellie rolled to a stop, bruised and battered and bleeding. They lay on their sides, groaning.

They had jumped from a moving vehicle only yesterday. But this time they weren't wearing armor. Everything hurt. The bandages had loosened around Kay's head. His legs screamed in agony. The bullet wound on his side thrummed. He had banged his hip hard on a stone, and slamming into the police cars had crushed his elbow. For a moment, he could only breathe.

"Are you alright, Ellie?" he rasped.

She pushed herself up, covered in cuts, and coughed. She nodded.

They gazed between the stalks of corn. Nothing much remained of the van. It was now a burning, twisted pile of metal. The helicopter hovered above. Police cars screeched to a halt. Bodies had spilled from the van, littering the highway and field, some of them burning, all of them mangled. The fire was spreading through the corn, raising black smoke that hid the dawn.

Kay and Ellie crawled, moving away from the crash. After a hundred meters, they had to stop, to lie down, to gasp for air and nurse their wounds.

"There were a hundred bodies in that van," Kay whispered. "Bodies now burnt beyond recognition. As far as the Equapol knows, we're among them."

"They'll run DNA tests," Ellie said. "They'll know we didn't die in the crash."

"Let them run their tests." Kay stroked her cheek. "By the time the results come in, we'll be in Zion."

Her eyes dampened. She embraced him.

"We're free," she whispered.

They held each other, weeping and laughing as the world burned.

CHAPTER THIRTEEN

Another helicopter flew overhead.

Kay and Ellie lay flat in the fields, hiding amid the corn.

The helicopter flew by.

Kay and Ellie crawled onward.

They dared not walk. Not with the helicopters flying by so often. Not with drones buzzing overhead. Not so close to the city walls. So they crawled through the fields, moving from corn to wheat, and kept crawling. Inching forward. Just putting more and more distance between them and City58OI.

"They know we escaped," Kay said as another drone flew overhead. "They're hunting us."

Ellie smiled grimly. "Don't take it personally. It's always like this out here. The Party grips every corner of Isonomia with an iron fist. There are no walls out here. So they fly drones and helicopters around the clock."

Kay's stomach twisted. "So we're not free after all." He grimaced. "When we fled the walls, I thought we were free. But it's just more surveillance. More danger."

She placed her hand on his back. "But we're making progress. We've come so far. We just have to keep going. All the way to the coast. And from there—a ship to Zion."

Kay looked at her. At this woman he had fought with, rebelled with, fallen in love with.

Who are you, Ellie?

He had known her for only a few days. That was all. Yet she had become the most important person in his life. Not just in this phase of his life. But in the entire story of his life.

And he knew almost nothing about her. Nothing of her life before their escape. Nothing of her struggles, dreams, fears. She was a stranger. And Kay wanted to spend the rest of his life getting to know her.

He tried to crawl a bit more. Then he collapsed. He lay on the ground, shaking. The pain returned, throbbing, pounding, burning. His body felt like a single giant wound. He couldn't even crawl any farther.

With the immediate danger gone, the old fight or flight instincts were trickling away. The adrenaline wore off. His mind filled instead with images, words, fear, grief.

It all suddenly hit him. Days of trauma. The fight outside the laundromat. The terror at the truthhall, seeing the ravening children tear their classmate apart. The agony of the electric shocks. The madness of his mate. The battle to free Ellie from prison, the flight to the morgue, the corpses all around him. The fire and blood and deaths.

So many deaths.

I killed so many men I lost count, Kay thought. *Not just equalizers either. A van driver. An innocent.*

In the calm of the fields, the weight of it all crushed him.

"You're trembling, Kay!" Ellie said, her eyes kind. "Let's rest for a while."

He smiled at her. With all the pain and fear, that was something new and blessed. The ability to smile.

"I'm happy," he said. "I'm in pain, and I'm terrified, and I'm weak. But I'm happier than I've ever been. Not just because I'm out of that damn city. Not just because that damn mindcap is off my head. Because I'm here with you."

They rested for a while. Then they crawled onward, hiding amid the wheat whenever a drone flew overhead.

In the evening, they saw a farm. They waited until darkness, then climbed over the fence. Ellie raided a mulberry tree, and Kay picked apples from an orchard. They found a chicken coop, and Kay dared sneak inside. He stole a dozen fresh eggs, then fled when the chickens began to raise a ruckus.

All farms in Isonomia were owned by the state. Kay didn't feel particularly guilty.

Carrying the food, Kay and Ellie retreated back into a cornfield. They huddled in the darkness and feasted. It was the best meal Kay had ever eaten—even better than the food in Ginsburg's bunker. Citizens in City58OI never ate fresh fruit. This was food grown for Party members, White Army officers, and equalizers. Kay had never tasted anything so sweet, healing, and fresh. They had no way to cook the eggs, so they ate them raw. This Kay found less appealing, but he was so weak, so famished—not just from the past few days, but from years of neglect. He downed the eggs greedily.

"I'd suggest stealing a chicken too," Kay said. "But I don't want to risk starting a cooking fire, not with those drones everywhere. And I'm not so desperate that I'd eat a chicken raw. Not yet."

Ellie laughed. A real laugh of true joy.

"There will be many roast chickens in Zion. All the chickens that we could eat!"

"And bacon," Kay said. "Lots of crispy, wonderful, magical bacon."

"And steak." Ellie licked her lips.

"I've never had steak."

"You'll love it!" Ellie closed her eyes and moaned. "A nice juicy T-bone steak, medium rare, with a baked potato. Oh, and prime rib! I think I like prime rib even more. With mashed potatoes and peas and gravy. Oh, I'm drooling already."

"I don't know what those things are," Kay said. "But I can't wait to try them. There's still so much of life I want to experience. All my life, I was a prisoner. Finally I'm free, and there's so much to explore, to learn, to understand. Not just about food. I want to see flowers and forests. To see mountains. To maybe someday get married, raise a family. To be a human. Just to be a real human."

"You've always been a real human."

Kay shook his head. "No. I was a machine. A twisted cyborg, sleepwalking through a nightmare. I only became a human today. And I have so much to learn."

"We'll learn together," Ellie said.

Kay gazed up at the night sky. He spoke softly. "All I know about Zion is what I saw in the reels. The propaganda at the rallies." He shuddered to remember the arena, that horrible place of concrete, rust, and death. "But I don't believe what I saw. Shantytowns? Poverty? An evil land where Bialik oppresses his people? I can't believe that's real. The Father lied to me all my life."

Ellie leaned against him. "Zion isn't perfect. There is some poverty. There is some hardship. But no, not nearly as bad as the reels show. And it's a hell of a lot better than Isonomia. We'll get there. We'll build a new life."

Kay rolled over toward her. "Are there others, Ellie? Other Isonomians who escaped? Who reached Zion?"

She nodded. "Ginsburg smuggles people out every month. I never fled, because I had an easier life than most in the city. What with being an officer's wife. And I wanted to stay and help. To recruit more rebels. To help Ginsburg and others like him."

Kay's eyes widened. "So you *were* a part of the rebellion? I mean, not just a supporter, but an actual member?"

Ellie nodded. "I was. And still am. There are friends out here too. In the countryside. Some hide on farms, others in the mountains. We'll find help along the way. Transportation to the sea. A friend to smuggle us onto a boat." She smiled. "We won't have to crawl and swim all the way to Zion."

Kay stroked her cheek. "There's so much I don't know about you. I thought the Equapol caught you because of the paintings in your apartment. I didn't know it was because you're a rebel."

She laughed weakly. "Hardly a high ranking one. I'm a pampered girl, that's all. A pampered girl who wanted adventure. As far as rebels go, I'm just a foot soldier. A hobbyist, really." She sighed. "I was naive. I thought it was all good fun, to be honest. Just my little way of rebelling against the system, of associating with intellectuals like Ginsburg, of proving—if only to myself—that I'm not like my husband."

"What is he like?" Kay asked.

Ellie shivered. "Cruel. He is so cruel. I saw him do things. Such horrible things. Order his troops to slaughter innocent Zionites, even mothers and children. I saw him activate the mindcaps of subordinates, electrocuting them for days, driving them to suicide. I saw him leave in the mornings with a tool box full of torture instruments, come back at night with the tools bloodied and dented." A tear rolled down his cheek. "That was my life, Kay. A life with a monster. That's why I had to prove I was different. Why I ran."

Kay held her hand. "Did he hurt you?"

"Me? Oh, no. He hurt thousands of others. But he loved me very much, I think. In his own twisted way. Fish love."

"Fish love?" Kay asked.

Ellie nodded. "A man can claim he loves fish. If he truly loved the fish, he'd return the fish to the water. But the man eats the fish. He loves only how the fish tastes. What the fish can do for him. My husband's love for me was fish love. He cared nothing about my ambitions, dreams, needs. He loved only what I gave him. I'm only twenty-four, do you know? And he's sixty. I was a trophy for him, that was all. A pretty little decoration. Shown off at dinner parties, then taken into his bed for his pleasure."

Kay frowned. "But—showing you off? Sex? Both are forbidden."

"Forbidden for the proletariat," Ellie said. "Not for the military. And not for the Party. Oh, they all take off their masks and helmets in private balls. And dine on fine meals. And enjoy endless sex. My husband slept with many women, not just me."

"So much for equality," Kay said.

"Has there ever been true equality in this world? Every utopian regime in history promised equality for its poor. And the masters hoarded the gold for themselves. It happened in the Soviet Union. In North Korea. In all the rest of them. Yes, the poor ended up equal—all equally hungry. The leaders grew rich and fat, sucking their nations dry. We live in Utopia 58, Kay. This has happened fifty-seven times before."

"You told me your husband was sent to fight in Zion," Kay asked. "What if we run into him?"

She touched his arm. "Kay, there's something I have to tell you about my husband. He travels back and forth between Isonomia and Zion. In fact, you saw him only recently. In the arena. His name is EQL61."

Those words hit Kay like a fist of iron.

"EQL61," he whispered. "The White General."

He remembered. Of course he remembered.

The general at the rally. The general who had buried Zionites up to their necks. Who had ordered the crowds to stone them.

And an older memory. A memory that had lain buried for so long.

A memory from the reeducation camp.

Of a general in white visiting that hell in the snow.

Of a monster inspecting Kay, scoffing at his protruding ribs, then whipping him for daring to look an officer in the eyes.

It was him, Kay realized. *The man who whipped me nearly to death. Who murdered countless prisoners.*

He was trembling. Struggling to remember. Even without his mindcap, so many memories were gone. How had he ended up in the reeducation camp? His life before that horrible place was a blank. But he remembered EQL61. He remembered the sting of that whip. The cruelty in those cold blue eyes.

"Why didn't you tell me until now?" Kay whispered.

She smiled. "You mean, during our escape from prison, battle with the police, bloodbath in the morgue, and flight through police barricades and missile-firing assault helicopters? I guess it was never the right time."

Kay couldn't help but laugh. "Fair enough."

She caressed his cheek. "Kay, are you strong enough to make love to me?"

"No," he said. "But I'm going to anyway."

And he did—with all the pain of his wounds, with all the fear. It was slower than the first time. More tender. More careful. And even better.

She fell asleep in his arms. And for the first time in his life, Kay slept without dreaming.

CHAPTER FOURTEEN

They were weak, hungry, and wounded when they stumbled between the trees and saw the monk.

Kay and Ellie had been traveling through the wilderness for days now. Crouching in cornfields or tall grass when drones buzzed overhead. Stealing food from farms, drinking morning dew, never finding enough, always hungry and thirsty. Growing weaker every day. Desperate to reach the coast.

Kay was taking the pills Ginsburg had given him. One bottle to dull the pain. The other to fight infections. But the pain lingered. His wounds were slow to heal, and the stitches on his head were raw and wet. The hunger constantly gnawed on him. But hunger had always been Kay's companion. At least that was one pain he was used to.

On some days, traveling through the countryside, they saw other cities. Kay had never seen other cities before. They looked just like City58OI. Towering concrete walls. Behind them—concrete skyscrapers. Cities of cement and rust and despair. Drones and helicopters filled their skies.

Prisons, Kay thought, looking at these monoliths. *Not cities. Massive prisons.*

They kept walking.

The days were hard. Long, grueling days of walking, crawling, suffering the agony in his mutilated legs. But the nights . . .

The nights were bliss.

When the darkness fell, the stars emerged. Kay had never seen stars from inside the city. Had never seen anything but a sky of smog. But out here, several days away, even the Party could not touch the stars. Millions of them shone overhead, a dizzying array of possibility.

Kay didn't know what the stars were. The Party taught that the stars were angels who shone for the Father, a million candles blazing in his honor. Kay no longer believed that. The stars seemed impossibly distant, and Kay imagined that they were worlds of their own. Worlds of plenty, with food and freedom and friends.

Every night, Ellie and he made love. Some nights she rode atop him, glowing in the moonlight, as he cupped her small breasts, and they moved together like a part of the cosmic dance, one with the night. On those nights, the stars shone for her, and she became a goddess of the sky.

On the fifth day after fleeing the city, they reached the mountains. They walked over the foothills, moving between the pines, collecting pine nuts and cracking them with rocks.

"The temple is near," Ellie said. "The monk will help us. He's a friend of the rebellion. He'll bring us to Zion."

On the sixth day, they saw him.

They were deep into the mountains now, many miles away from any city. The air was colder up here. The shadows deep. Mist hovered between the craggy trunks, and ravens cawed overhead.

The monk wore white robes, similar to those all citizens of Isonomia wore. A mindcap topped his head. But he wore no mask, brazenly displaying his gaunt, bronzed face. A wagon wheel amulet hung on a chain around his neck. Kay recognized it from Ginsburg's library—the symbol of Buddhism.

The monk didn't acknowledge them. He held two straw baskets, partly filled with mushrooms. He knelt, picked another mushroom, and added it a basket.

"Hello there, Tenzin!" Ellie said. She climbed over a mossy log and approached the monk.

Kay followed. He walked around the log instead of over it. His legs always hurt—ever since the surgery. Spending days in the wilderness made them blaze with new pain. He could barely bend his knees.

The monk ignored them. He hummed softly, scanning the ground.

"There's one." Kay pointed at a mushroom between the roots of a pine.

The monk looked up at him. His eyes were dark and hard.

"That one is poison," the monk said. "It would turn your insides into a bloody stew."

"So sort of like my old mate's cooking," Kay said.

The monk didn't even crack a smile. He looked at Ellie.

"He looks weak. He won't survive the journey."

"He's stronger than he looks, Tenzin," Ellie said. "He's a good fighter. He killed many equalizers."

Tenzin snickered. "Any brute can kill a man. The true warrior defeats his enemy with wisdom, not violence."

Kay felt anger rise. "When the Equapol was firing on us, they didn't seem very interested in philosophical debates. Preaching peace and love is fine out here in the forest. Won't exactly work when facing a squadron of equalizers armed to the teeth and howling for blood."

Tenzin raised his eyebrows. He put down his baskets and stepped closer to Kay. Amazingly, Tenzin was shorter than the required five-foot-eight standard across Isonomia. Somehow, he had managed to avoid the surgery that inserted metal rods into the legs of those too small. And yet, despite his short stature, and despite his advanced age, Tenzin seemed fearless.

"Do not preach to me of violence," the monk said. "For fifty years, I've been studying the ways of peace and war. I follow the wisdom of the Buddha, not of a zombie just freed from his mindcap." Tenzin tapped Kay's bandaged head—painfully. "I've done more to fight the Father than you can imagine."

Kay snickered. "Yeah, I wear no mindcap. I had mine removed. You still wear yours! Don't pretend to serve some ancient religion."

Tenzin pulled off his mindcap as easily as doffing a hat. "A little disguise, my friend." He pulled back his white cloak, revealing orange robes. "I am a follower of the Buddha. Not of this wretched evil called the Father. Who do you fight for?"

"All right, boys, enough." Ellie stepped between them. "This isn't a pissing contest. We're all on the same side. Tenzin, do you have room for two more? We want a way out. On your next ship."

Tenzin's eyes softened. He looked at Ellie and seemed to deflate. "You too, Ellie?" he said. "You're leaving for Zion?"

She nodded. "My time helping the rebellion in Isonomia is done. My cover is blown. The Equapol is after me. But I'll do my best to fight from abroad. It's time I join our brave brothers and sisters in the east." She took Kay's hand. "With Kay by my side."

Tenzin looked again at Kay, appraising him like a man judging a farm animal.

"He's too thin. Too old. Too wounded. The journey overseas will be hard. It'll kill him."

"I've suffered worse," Kay said.

"And it left you weak," Tenzin said.

"No, old man," Kay said softly. "I survived eight years in a reeducation camp. I can do anything."

The monk stared at him in silence. Something akin to compassion filled his dark eyes.

"Maybe you're right," Tenzin finally said. "Very well. There are a few more in the temple. Refugees from other cities. You'll join them. In a week, the ship leaves. You'll be on it. But first—help me gather mushrooms. We have a ship to fill with them."

Kay breathed out in relief, leaning down to pick a red mushroom. "Smuggled inside a ship of mushrooms? Beats the truck of corpses."

Tenzin slapped Kay's wrist, knocking down the red mushroom. "Not if you pick the poison ones."

They climbed the piny mountainside, pausing to pick mushrooms they found on the way. In the evening, they reached the mountaintop. Kay stood between two pines, breathing heavily, gazing at the landscape. From up here, he could see for miles. Several cities rose across the land like parasites—gray pustules of misery, belching up clouds of smog, filling rivers with their filth. City58OI, his old home, lay beyond the horizon.

Train tracks carved the land. A train was moving along the distant tracks, as narrow as a thread from here, raising a plume of smoke. It was heading north. Heading to the cold lands of desolation. Heading to a reeducation camp.

The train might be filled with citizens rounded up after my escape, Kay thought. *They might be headed to hell—because of me.*

Kay closed his eyes and clenched his fists.

Get in, you scum!

A voice in his memory. A baton cracking his back.

Himself—shoved into a train. Crammed in with hundreds of others, manacled, beaten.

Somewhere on the platform—a woman, crying out to him, reaching to him. Calling his name. His mother? His mate?

Kay did not know. She wore a mask, but he knew she was a woman, that she loved him. That he loved her.

"KB209!" she cried, tears in her eyes.

He blinked, snapping back to the present. He shuddered. Yes, he recognized that distant northbound train. The same train he had screamed in, bled in. He lowered his head.

"Be strong, my friends," he whispered. "Survive. I did. Survive and someday join me in Zion."

The monk led them toward a jutting peak of stone and soil. He parted a strand of curtains, revealing a cave. A wagon wheel was carved above the entrance, painted fading yellow. Belying the rustic appearance, a security camera peered between vines.

"Welcome to my temple," Tenzin said.

They entered a large, shadowy cave. Baskets, crates, and jars filled the cavern, all containing mushrooms. Thousands, maybe millions of mushrooms. A handful of other monks were here, labeling jars and crates. They openly wore orange robes, and had no masks or mindcaps. Yet a portrait of the Father hung on the wall. And masks and white robes hung on pegs, ready to don quickly. A monitor hung on a wall, displaying a checkerboard of video feeds—presumably from security cameras.

"Hey, who's the stiff?"

A girl bounced toward Kay. Her orange robes billowed, hanging loosely off her short, slender frame. She had short black hair, which she pushed back with a muddy hand. She peered at Kay with dark, intelligent eyes. After years of seeing only masks, Kay struggled to judge people's ages. But this girl seemed about the size of the children in his truthhall.

"You look like a proper stiff," the girl said. "Blimey. How many times have you been to hell and back?"

"Tilly!" barked another monk. A tall, burly man stepped forward. He had a thick red beard, a bald head, and impatient eyes that glared at the girl. "You're being rude, you little pipsqueak. Get back to work."

The girl—Tilly—placed her hands on her slender hips. She glared up at the larger man. And large he was—Kay had never seen anyone so tall. He must have stood nearly a foot taller than Kay.

This one has been on the run since childhood, Kay thought. *He avoided surgery to shorten his legs.*

Indeed, with his wild red beard, the man seemed a barbarian. A caveman. Almost another breed of human. Kay could imagine him growing up among wolves, hiding in caves from civilization.

"I'm not rude, Pat!" the girl said to the wild man. "I'm just inquisitive."

The beefy redhead—Pat—raised a fist. "I'm going to pound you into the floor, girl."

Tilly raised her chin. "I'm not a girl. I'm fifteen! I'm a woman now. You'll see. Once I'm in Zion, you'll learn. They don't tolerate dumb brutes like you in Zion."

Pat rumbled, and his red beard bristled. "If you weren't a girl, I would have put my fist through your face."

"Too bad you're actually a softie." Tilly poked the giant's ample belly. "Literally."

The two finally seemed to notice Ellie, who still stood at the cave entrance. Both the tiny Tilly and the burly Pat approached and gave Ellie long, crushing hugs.

"Good to see ya, El," the said the giant ginger.

Tilly hopped up and down. "Finally I'm not the only woman around."

"*Girl* not woman!" Pat rumbled. Tilly flipped him off.

That evening, Tenzin tended to the new arrivals' wounds. The monk was surprisingly gentle, belying his gruff demeanor. He replaced the bandage around Kay's head, cleaned the stitches, and applied soothing ointment. With the same tenderness, he treated the cuts and burns across the rest of Kay's body.

"Pain is temporary," the monk said. "Don't fear pain. Learn to live alongside pain. To accept it. Examine it. Don't let it claim you. Make it your ally."

"Pain feels more like an enemy than ally," Kay said.

"The true enemy is within oneself," Tenzin said. "To fight anyone else leads only to suffering. It is like a river, forever trying to overturn a watermill's wheel, finding no end to its struggle."

Kay frowned. "But don't you fight the Father?"

"I try only to bring balance and peace," said Tenzin. "To heal rather than hurt."

"Not even hurt the Father?" Kay said. "I would hurt him if I could. I would kill him. I would strangle him with my bare hands. He's evil."

Tenzin looked up from his work. "Evil? There are no evil people. Only people who do evil things."

"Semantics," said Kay.

"I do not wish death or pain to the Father," said Tenzin. "I wish him the same peace I seek in my own life. I wish peace and harmony for all beings."

Kay sighed. "I thought Ginsburg's faith was confusing. Wishing peace even to the Father? Embracing pain? Your ways are strange."

"All of life is suffering," Tenzin said. "And all suffering comes from wanting. We want an end to pain, so we suffer. We want to hurt an enemy, so we suffer anger and resentment. We want love, prosperity, joy. We become embittered when we don't achieve these goals, or when we achieve them only to later lose them. Wanting is suffering. I don't want pain to end. I don't want the Father dead. I don't want wealth or power. I want nothing. And so I have no suffering."

Kay thought for a moment. "Interesting thought. But you're still healing my wounds. Doesn't that mean you want me free from pain?"

Tenzin sighed. "I'm not as wise as the Buddha. Perhaps he could have embraced the pain of wounds, allowing his body to heal itself. But we are mere mortals. And so we keep wanting. And we keep suffering."

Kay left it at that, feeling that he had scored a point. He wanted to learn more about other ways of life. Be they religions, like Judaism and Buddhism, or other ideologies, alternatives to equalism. A new world was slowly revealing itself to Kay. Not only a world of trees and stars and mushrooms, things he had never seen before, but a world of thought. Of ideas.

At first, Kay had thought that his lack of material things— food, sex, comfort—had been his greatest deprivation. The treasures the Father had stolen from him. Kay had delighted in tasting tea, making love to a woman, seeing the night sky. But now he realized those were comparatively trivial. The Father had stolen far more from Kay, and from all other Isonomians. He had stolen ideas. Stolen thoughts. Stolen different ways of viewing the world.

Kay didn't know if Ginsburg, Tenzin, or anyone else had the right way of things. Perhaps their faiths were flawed too. But Kay imagined that all ideas deserved to be picked up, examined, and placed back on the shelf alongside other philosophies. It was not equality Kay craved. It was diversity. The diversity of experiences and ideas.

He wished he could have saved some of Ginsburg's books. He vowed that if he arrived in Zion alive, he would seek books there, would build a library of ideas from different thinkers. Each book would be free for all to examine, to contemplate, to enrich the lives of their readers. Some thoughts would be rejected.

Daniel Arenson

Others used to build rich civilizations. All would form a tapestry of philosophy.

I'm learning, and I'm growing, Kay thought. *Ideas are meant to be shared, never stifled. True freedom is the freedom to share our thoughts. Those who silence ideas are shackling humanity like a master shackles slaves.*

"Tenzin," he said, "I heard Ellie call this place the temple. Is this what temples used to look like?"

"Come, I'll show you," Tenzin said.

He guided Kay toward the back of the cave. Tenzin shoved aside crates of mushrooms, then removed the portrait of the Father from the cave wall. He pressed a bulging stone.

A hidden doorway opened, revealing a chamber.

They stepped inside. Kay's eyes widened.

"It's beautiful," he said softly.

A hundred candles burned, filling the back room with golden light. Murals of flowers, birds, and dancers covered the walls and ceiling. A stone statue stood in a ring of candles, eyes closed, face stoic. Its one hand was raised, thumb and index finger forming a circle. Two other monks were here, both only boys, kneeling on the floor. They were carefully spilling colorful sand from bronze holders, forming a meticulous work of art across the floor. Neither boy looked up from his work.

"They're creating a mandala," Tenzin said. "A spiritual symbol of the cosmos. They'll spend hundreds of hours creating this work of art, forming elaborate patterns of many colors. When they're done, they will blow the sand away."

"It seems too beautiful to destroy," Kay said, admiring the mandala. With only colored sand, the boys had depicted monks, animals, rivers, trees—the most beautiful work of art Kay could imagine.

"It is indeed beautiful, but beauty, like pain, is ephemeral. Nothing lasts in the cosmos. That is what the Buddha teaches us. Joy, beauty, love—they all flow away like so much colored sand.

166

But so does pain. So does evil. The Father too will flow away. And the cosmos will continue. An endless circular pattern. And when we monks are done creating this mandala, we will begin a new one. Different. Unique. Yet the same."

Kay noticed that the mandala had one ring depicting robed, masked figures. The prisoners of Isonomia.

This too will pass, Kay thought. *The Father will not rule forever. This hell too will end. And the cosmos will circle on and on. This is Utopia 58. This has happened fifty-seven times before. And it will happen again. From dark to light, from terror to hope—the wheel rolls on.*

They gathered for dinner in a third chamber. This cave was large and round, filled with candlelight and warmth. Twenty defectors came to eat—all people like Kay, citizens who had fled their cities. Tenzin and his two boys cooked a cauldron of stew, and the delicious smells of mutton, potatoes, and mushrooms filled the caves.

They feasted. After the long journey, Kay was famished. He downed three bowls of stew. The others ate with just as much gusto. Tiny Tilly, smallest of the bunch, out-ate them all. She devoured bowl after bowl, even defeating the mighty Pat.

"Leave some food for the rest of us!" the giant redhead grumbled.

Tilly poked his belly again. "You've been eating too much anyway. I need more food! I'm a growing girl."

Pat grumbled. "I thought you were a woman."

"I thought you were on a diet!" she said.

The two nearly came to blows. But later, Kay noticed that Pat secretly passed his last bowl of stew to Tilly, then watched with soft eyes as she ate.

Kay looked at the other refugees. An elderly couple was holding hands. Two men were swapping jokes and laughing. A toddler huddled in her mother's arms. Nobody wore masks or robes. Nobody had a mindcap. They were eating real food.

Displaying real emotion. They were all still in Isonomia, all still hiding—but they were free. They were humans, not machines. Doing what humans must have done for countless generations before the Father.

Kay hesitated, then slung his arm around Ellie. She nestled against him, and he kissed her forehead.

"I wish I could stay," Kay said softly. "Stay and fight for Isonomia. Stay and help others. Like Tenzin helps. Like Ginsburg helped. Like you help."

She looked up at him. She caressed his cheek. "I want you to come with me. I could not bear to see Zion without you."

"Stay with me here, Ellie," Kay said. "Fight with me! In the rebellion."

Ellie sighed. "A rebellion? Only a few people. Scattered. Weak."

"We'll make them strong."

A tear flowed down her cheek. "You're braver than I am. I was never a proper rebel. Just a silly girl on an adventure. Stay if you must. I'll respect your choice. But I can't stay with you. I've been to Zion before. As a general's wife. I'll never know peace until I'm there again."

"Then I'll go with you," Kay said. "But here is a promise. Even in Zion, I'll fight the Father. I'll do what I can to spread word of his evil. To free more people. To speak on behalf of every Isonomian still trapped in this prison."

"That I can help you with." She kissed him. "You're a brave man, Kay. And a good man. And I love you."

Tenzin ate only a few spoonfuls of stew. The slender monk rose to his feet.

"Friends!" he said. "These are dark times. Filled with suffering and want. Yet these times too shall pass. Tomorrow morning, I'll begin the long journey to the sea. I'll be taking my pontoon down the river, ferrying my mushrooms to the ocean port. The officers of the White Army, fighting in Zion, desire their delicacies. My mushrooms are among their greatest pleasures. I'll hide each of you inside a crate of mushrooms, and I'll load you onto the *Samsara*. She's a civilian ship, one of the few allowed to sail to Zion. The captain is a good friend of mine—and sympathetic to the rebellion. He'll take you safely to Zion." The severe old monk actually smiled. "Just try not to eat all the mushrooms on the way."

"No promises!" Tilly said.

Pat snickered. "With this hungry little devil, there'll be no mushrooms left when we arrive. Just a tiny girl with a giant belly."

"Hey!" Tilly bristled. "My belly is tiny and flat. Unlike yours!"

She tried to poke his gut, only for Pat to growl and shove her hand away.

Tenzin raised his hands. The monk's smile widened. "Peace, friends! In Zion, you'll have all the food that you wish. In Zion, you'll finally find peace with the world. And with yourselves. Peace begins within. Seek always to rid yourselves of anger, hatred, desire. Live for the moment, and you'll always be free. Remember these words in Zion, and remember that—"

A hole burst open in Tenzin's head.

Blood sprayed in a mist.

The monk fell dead.

Equalizers stormed into the cave, guns blazing.

CHAPTER FIFTEEN

The defectors screamed.

The police swarmed into the cave, bullets shrieking.

The assault tore through a toddler, and her mother screamed, only for bullets to take her down seconds later. An elderly woman fell, bleeding, dying. Her husband knelt above her, and bullets ripped through his head. Tenzin's sons tried to run, but the rifles mowed down the young monks.

Kay leaped behind the cauldron of stew, pulling Ellie with him. Bullets slammed into the pot, raising sparks. Kay cursed his carelessness. He had not taken his gun to dinner. The weapon was higher up in the cave system, resting among mushroom crates near the cave exit.

Instead of a gun, Kay grabbed the cauldron. It burned his palms. Kay screamed, but he wouldn't release the pot.

"Pat, help!" he cried.

The giant redhead had taken a bullet to the arm. But he still whipped into action. He understood.

The two men gripped the massive pot, lifted it overhead, and hurled it at the equalizers.

Several equalizers fell. The cauldron crushed one person. Stew flooded from the pot, spilling over other equalizers. They screamed, desperately trying to slap off the burning stew.

Kay ran, barreled into one policeperson, and knocked xer down. Pat plowed into two other equalizers. Howling, the giant began slamming their heads on the cave floor.

Kay leaped over puddles of blood and stew. He ran higher up the cave system and entered a circular cavern. From there, through a jagged opening in the stone wall, he had a view of the forest outside. He glimpsed more police among the trees.

How did they find us? How many are there?

He raced between the crates of mushrooms, found his gun, and rose firing.

At the cave opening, an equalizer fell.

Another equalizer returned fire. Kay knelt behind the crate. Wooden slats shattered and mushrooms spilled. Kay waited for the equalizer to reload, then rose from behind the crate, firing fast and hard. Bullets ripped into the equalizer's arm and hand. A shot through the neck finished the job.

But there were more equalizers outside. Kay could hear them clattering up the mountainside. Bullets flew through the cave entrance, and Kay took cover behind another crate.

Defectors came running from deeper in the caves. Ellie, Tilly, and a handful of others. No more than a dozen. They all took cover behind crates. The other refugees must all be dead.

But Ellie is alive, Kay thought. *Thank God, Buddha, or whoever else is up there. Ellie is alive.*

Pat crouched by Kay behind the crate. The giant ginger hefted a white Equapol rifle. "Got me a nice little prize."

Ellie and Tilly had grabbed Equapol rifles too. That meant four defectors with guns. All four were firing at the forest, holding back the police. The equalizers stood among the trees. They tried to enter the cave, but the hailstorm of bullets held them back.

"How the hell did they find us?" Ellie shouted over the roar of guns.

Tilly glowered. "They followed you here! You and your damn mindcap."

"My mindcap can't be tracked!" Ellie said. "It's a military-grade mindcap."

"Well, they must have hacked it!" Tilly said. "Or you left a trail a blind dog could follow."

"That doesn't make sense," Ellie snapped. "Dogs use their sense of smell for tracking, not sight."

"Then you must stink like a pig!" Tilly said.

"Enough!" Kay shouted, firing more shots at the enemy.

He couldn't see how many equalizers were out there. Quite a few, judging by how many bullets were whizzing into the cave. Another crate of mushrooms shattered. Morels spilled across the cave.

"We can't hold them all back!" Kay said. "Is there another way out of here?"

"There's a ventilation chimney deeper in the caves," Pat said. Blood was dripping from his arm, but the giant kept firing his gun. "The monks carved it. But it's pretty damn narrow. It's just used for getting rid of the cooking smoke. I don't think we'll fit."

"I'll fit!" Tilly said. "You're too fat." She reached over to poke his belly, then yanked her hand back as a police bullet flew.

Pat groaned. "The mouth on you!"

"We'll try the chimney," Kay said. "Pat, suck in your gut and you'll be fine. Lead us there."

The giant squeezed off another couple shots, then ran deeper into the caves. Other defectors followed. Kay and Ellie remained, fired a few parting bullets at the police, then ran after the others.

They tore off the painting of the Father, pressed the bulging stone, and the secret doorway opened. They ran into the back chamber, the little temple with the murals. The mandala still covered the floor, an intricate masterwork of colored sand. The statue of the Buddha sat as serenely as ever. A few bullets flew into the room. One refugee fell, a hole in her chest.

Once everyone was inside, Pat hit a hidden button. The stone door slammed shut, protecting the defectors from the bullets. But Kay knew it wouldn't keep the police out for long.

"There, the chimney." Pat pointed.

Kay looked. He saw a hole in the ceiling. The shaft rose through the mountain, leading to distant moonlight.

It was indeed a very tight squeeze.

Tilly climbed the Buddha's statue and balanced on its head. She swayed, windmilled her arms, then leaped up. She caught the hole's rim, pulled herself into the shaft, and began to climb.

"Come on, follow!" she said.

Kay winced, not sure he'd fit—let alone the giant Pat.

"Come on, Pat!" Tilly cried, halfway up the chimney. "You can do it. You're just like Santa already! Fat and red and bearded. Sadly, not particularly jolly."

"I'll show you jolly!" Pat shouted.

The stone door creaked open.

Bullets flew into the room.

Pat turned away from the chimney. He raced toward the door. A bullet hit his hand, and he bellowed. Blood spraying, the giant shoved the stone door, and it slammed shut. Pat roared, leaning against the door, struggling to keep it closed. The police pounded on it from outside.

"Go on, go!" Pat shouted at the others. "Into the chimney! I'll hold them back!"

Kay grabbed Ellie and hoisted her up. The slender woman wriggled into the chimney and climbed after Tilly. Kay stood below, helping the other defectors climb into the shaft. Ten were still alive, all small enough to fit. Kay peered up the chimney. Most of the rebels had emerged onto the mountaintop. A few were still inside the stone shaft, climbing.

"Go, Kay!" Pat shouted, leaning hard against the door. His face was red. His arm and hand bled. The police were banging against the door with a ram now. It jerked open, and Pat bellowed and shoved it shut again.

"Come with me!" Kay said. "You'll fit."

"Go, damn it!" the giant roared. "Go get your ass to Zion! Look after the little one. Don't let her be a smartass. She's a good kid."

Kat wanted to stay and fight. But Tilly needed him. Ellie needed him.

He climbed onto the Buddha statue, then leaped up, grabbed the chimney, and pulled himself in.

Below, Pat howled.

Kay heard the door bang open. Heard the police storm into the room. Heard bullets fly. When Kay looked down, he saw Pat fall, body riddled with bullets.

Kay climbed in a fury.

"The chimney!" a robotic voice called from below. "The traitors are escaping!"

Kay climbed faster. A hand grabbed him from above. Ellie hoisted him outside just as bullets flew. One bullet grazed Kay's robes, tearing the fabric. He stumbled out onto the mountainside, heaving.

"Pat!" Tilly shouted, tears flowing down her cheeks. "Pat, where are you?"

The girl leaned over the chimney, then pulled her head back. Bullets were flying from below.

Kay and Ellie dropped stones down the chimney. A climbing equalizer fell, slamming into xer comrades below. Other defectors rolled a boulder forward. They sealed the chimney shut.

"Pat!" Tilly screamed. She clawed at the boulder, weeping, trying to go back. Ellie had to grab the girl, to pull her away, to whisper soft comforts.

Kay looked from side to side. He kept waiting for police to burst from behind the trees. If they weren't already on the mountaintop, they'd be here soon.

"Where's the river?" Kay said. "Tenzin said there's a river. And a boat."

Sniffing, Tilly pointed. "There."

Kay stared. His heart sank.

He saw the river. It was kilometers away, snaking across the valley.

"Police!" rose a cry.

Equalizers came racing up the slope. Bullets whizzed and slammed into trunks. Moss and chips of bark flew. One defector screamed, clutching a wound.

"We'll never make it to the river!" Kay shouted.

"Yes we will," Tilly said. "Follow me!"

The girl ran toward a metal pole. At first Kay had mistaken it for a simple utility pole, one of several that rose across the mountain, cables running between them.

Now he realized: It was a zipline.

Tilly leaped up, grabbed a pulley, and began ziplining down the mountainside at breakneck speed.

Kay knelt behind a boulder, firing at the oncoming police. He hit one equalizer, knocking xer down. A bullet slammed into the boulder, chipping the stone.

"Everyone, follow Tilly down the zipline!" Kay shouted. "I'll cover you!"

There were several more pulleys available. Tenzin must have used them to deliver crates of mushrooms down to his boat. Today they delivered defectors. One by one, they zipped down toward the river.

Soon only Ellie and Kay remained on the mountaintop. Both crouched behind boulders, firing at the enemy, holding them off. More and more equalizers emerged from among the trees.

When Kay glanced behind him, he saw his fellow defectors reach the valley.

"Go, Ellie!" he shouted. "Join them! Hurry!"

She nodded. She leaped from behind the boulder, squeezed off a couple more shots, then grabbed a pulley. Even as she ziplined downward, Ellie kept firing up toward the mountaintop.

Kay wouldn't get a better chance.

He ran for it.

As he raced toward the last pulley, pain slammed into his shoulder. It nearly knocked him down.

He kept running. He could barely lift his arm. Blood flowed down his side. He grabbed a pulley and began to dive.

He rattled down the cable at terrifying speed. Pain blazed on his shoulder, and he nearly released the pulley. More bullets whistled around him.

Kay turned. He saw the police gathering around the top pole. Kay fired at them, and one officer fell. But then Kay's gun clicked, out of bullets.

The police fired more shots. Kay winced, expecting more hits.

Thankfully, the cable took him through a thick patch of oak and maple. The branches provided cover. Bullets slammed into the trees. The police above could no longer see him.

Instead, the police began shooting at the cable.

Kay groaned, pawing at his pockets for more magazines. But he couldn't reach them. Not while holding the pulley.

Bullets sparked against the cable above Kay.

Kay grimaced, ziplining at top speed toward the river. He was almost there. Ellie was already by the water. He—

The cable tore.

Kay tumbled through the air.

As he fell, another bullet slammed into him.

He crashed into a pine tree. Branches shattered. Wooden shards dug into his flesh.

He fell, smashed through more branches, and hit the ground hard.

He lay, bleeding, one bullet in his shoulder, another in his calf. He could barely breathe. His blood dampened the ground.

Birds sang above. Not the ugly caws of crows but a beautiful symphony of songbirds. Red flowers grew beside him. Anemones, he thought.

This is where the dog came from. He smiled softly. *It's so beautiful. A beautiful place to die.*

Behind him, he heard the river. He heard muffled voices, calling him. Muted gunshots.

He saw a face above him. A pale face, beautiful, framed by auburn hair. The face of his wife. Of Christine.

"Christine!" he whispered.

His wife.

She was UV502.

But younger. Before the mindcap had broken her. Before the Father had possessed her. Her eyes still full of light.

A woman from many years ago. From before the reeducation camp had wiped Kay's mind. A woman he loved. Pregnant. Pregnant …

The memory pounded through Kay. He had been in love before. He had a child … a child …

Kay trembled. He had to learn more. Had to find his child. Had to *live*.

He pushed himself up, groaning with pain.

"Kay!" A voice from the river. "Kay!"

He stumbled toward the voice. He saw her racing uphill. "Ellie!"

He limped toward her. She caught him before he could fall. He leaned against her, and they ran toward the river. More gunfire sounded in the distance.

The others were already in the boat. It was a pontoon, homemade by the looks of it, with a humming motor attached to a wooden hull. Tilly stood at the wheel.

"Come on!" the girl shouted, beckoning.

Leaning on Ellie, Kay stumbled into the boat. He collapsed on the deck, bleeding onto the scratched wooden slats. At once, Tilly hit the throttle, and the pontoon raced downriver.

Only a handful of defectors had survived the flight. They gathered around Kay. One man held cloth over his wounds. Ellie ran to fetch the boat's medical kit.

A child. Kay gazed at the sky. *I had a wife. I loved her. She was pregnant. I have a child.*

He looked at birds flying overhead. And he saw metal disks. Flying above. Chasing. Unfurling machine guns.

His heart nearly stopped.

Police drones.

CHAPTER SIXTEEN

The Equapol drones buzzed through the sky like angry wasps.

Bullets pierced the river around the pontoon.

Some hit the deck, carving holes through the wood.

"Take them down!" Ellie shouted, pointing at the drones. "Fire!"

She aimed upward, firing her pistol. Tilly released the pontoon's helm and joined her. Kay was the only other refugee still armed. Even as he lay on the deck, two bullets in him, he pawed for a fresh magazine. Loaded. Fired.

Two drones fell—one into the forest, the other into the water.

The third drone zipped forward, dodging the bullets, and opened fire.

One of the defectors—a young woman with platinum hair—screamed as bullets riddled her. She fell overboard and vanished underwater.

Tilly screamed.

"Karin!" Tears ran down her cheeks. "Karin, no!"

She tried to turn the pontoon around, but Ellie stopped her.

"She's already dead!" Ellie shouted. "Keep steering us forward!"

The last drone dived closer. Its guns aimed.

Kay fired.

His bullet slammed into the drone, knocking it aside. More bullets from Tilly and Ellie finished the job. The drone exploded, raining metal shards into the river.

The pontoon rumbled onward, carving a white wake through the river.

For a long moment—silence.

Kay wanted to pass out.

He wanted to sleep for years. He wanted to die.

But he forced himself to remain standing. Even with two bullets inside him. Even with so much blood loss. With so much fear.

He stared at the surviving defectors. Just a handful. They stood on the pontoon deck, covered in blood and burns.

"We took out the last drone," Kay said. "But they'll have sent word to the Equapol. More drones will come. Helicopters too. We have to ditch this pontoon. And sink it."

The others stared at him. Their eyes darkened. Nobody wanted to lose their ride. But they nodded.

They flowed down the river for another kilometer, just to put a little more distance between them and the battle. Then Tilly steered the pontoon toward the riverbank, lodging it in the reeds.

The survivors climbed onto the riverbank, trudging through reeds and algae. They stepped onto muddy soil. With trembling hands, Kay fired his gun, putting several holes into the pontoon. Grunting with the effort, he lifted a stick and shoved the pontoon back into the water. It flowed down the river, taking on water. Soon it would sink and vanish.

Blood trickled from under his bandages. Finally, standing on the riverbank, Kay allowed himself to pass out.

For a long time, he floated through shadows. He kept seeing Christine's face. Floating above him. Smiling. Kissing him. That rosy face with red lips and auburn hair. He placed his hand on her swelling baby, and he felt the child kick.

Christine stroked his cheek.

"You'll be alright, Kay. You're a tough bastard. You'll live."

He wept. Reaching to her. "They're taking me to the camp. I'll die."

"You're tough. You're the strongest man I know. You will live. It'll take more than two bullets to stop you."

But in his dream, more bullets flew, slamming into him again and again. The White General laughed, blades on his helmet, as Kay crawled over shattered glass, unable to sleep, unable to die.

CHAPTER SEVENTEEN

Kay opened his eyes, blinked, and groaned. His dreams faded. His haunting torments dispersed.

Instead, he saw Ellie leaning above him.

Kay coughed, blinked again, groaned.

"The drones!" he said. "The police! They—"

"We're safe for now," Ellie said. "We're hiding in the forest. We're safe."

Kay looked around him. He was lying on a pile of dry leaves. The forest rustled around him. He couldn't hear the river.

The memories solidified. Shooting the drones. Sinking the pontoon. Seeking shelter among the trees.

"How long was I out?"

"An hour, maybe two," Ellie said. "We moved you deeper into the forest. The trees will hide us from drones. The others set up camp by a nearby pond. I told them it's too dangerous by the water. There's not as much cover from trees there. But they insisted on fishing." She rolled her eyes.

Kay allowed himself to relax, if only for a moment. The pain sank in, and he looked at his wounds. Fresh bandages covered his shoulder and calf. Both wounds were throbbing.

"I got the bullets out," Ellie said. "You were lucky. Both were only flesh wounds. You'll live. But you lost a lot of blood. And you should keep taking your antibiotics." She rattled the bottle.

Kay nodded. "And painkillers. Thank you, Ellie. You saved my life."

"Me?" She snorted. "You saved us all back there. You covered us while we ziplined down."

"I remember you doing your fair share of shooting." He clasped her hand. "I'm glad you're alive, Ellie. I thought we were both goners."

She grinned. "We're tough bastards, aren't we? The worst is behind us. We just need to reach the ocean. We're still far. Hundreds of miles away. But if we find transportation, we can reach the coast in three days, four at most. We can steal a truck. Maybe another boat. Hell, if we have to, we'll walk. But sooner or later, we'll reach the ocean. We'll sail east. We'll be out of Isonomia." Her eyes shone. "On our way to Zion."

Boots thumped nearby. Dry leaves crunched. People cursed and argued in the forest.

Kay and Ellie both stiffened.

"Equapol?" Kay whispered, reaching for his gun.

A figure stomped between the trees. Tilly emerged from around an oak. Leaves filled her short brown hair.

"Ellie, you better get back to camp." The girl waved at Kay. "Hey, stiff, nice to see you back among the living. You better come too."

She vanished between the trees again.

Shouting rose, startling birds. Stomping feet. More cursing.

"Kay, stay here," Ellie said. "Rest."

Frowning, she walked between the oaks, heading toward the water.

"I'm coming too."

Kay shoved himself up, groaned, and gritted his teeth. He found his bottle of painkillers on the ground, and he swallowed two pills. He limped between the oaks, every step like another bullet.

The others had set up camp by a pond. Somebody had fashioned a fishing rod out of a branch, but it lay fallen on the grass. Kay collapsed by a patch of reeds, already regretting his decision to walk the short distance.

Clouds hid the sun, and it was drizzling. The forest formed green walls around the pond. Branches stretched over the water like knobby fingers. Kay shuddered, feeling trapped here, blind, once more caught in a labyrinth. He couldn't wait to reach the sea, to see open spaces around him again. He stared at the trees, seeking police. Nothing. No drones. No bullets. For the moment they seemed to be safe.

Safe, at least, from the Equapol. But Kay suddenly had other concerns.

The other defectors stood by the water, jaws right, staring with dark eyes. Their fists were clenched. They seemed ready to attack.

What the hell is going on? Kay thought.

Most of the defectors had died during the mad flight here. Only Kay, Ellie, and four others had survived.

One of those survivors stepped forward, sneering. He was a middle-aged man. Muscular, his temples silvering, his jaw wide. Tattoos coiled around his arms, covering them like sleeves, and more tattoos peeked from under his collar. His legs were unusually short under the knees—the telltale sign of a tall man surgically brought down to specs. Kay knew the pain.

His name is Adrian, Kay remembered. He had learned everyone's names back at the temple.

"It's time to talk about the capper," Adrian said. He turned to glare at Ellie.

Instinctively, Kay dragged himself forward. He placed himself between Ellie and the tattooed man.

"Her name is Ellie," Kay said. "And I don't like how you're looking at her."

Adrian bared his teeth. "For weeks, we hid in the monk's temple. Not a goddamn problem from anyone. Then you and the capper show up. And within hours—the Equapol arrived." Her pointed at Ellie. "They followed her mindcap."

Two other defectors stepped forward. They were twin sisters, about thirty years old. They had smooth black hair, olive-toned skin, and almond-shaped eyes. Kay remembered their names: Li and Lei. They looked identical, but one had a scar on her forehead.

"I say we rip off her mindcap!" shouted Li, pointing at Ellie. She was a slender thing, graceful, but her eyes burned with hatred.

"Yeah!" said Lei, the scarred sister. "The rest of us have no mindcaps. Only Ellie has one. Tear it off!"

Ellie took a step back. Her face paled.

Kay was thankful for Ginsburg's painkillers. They dulled the pain enough that he could stay standing. He placed himself between Ellie and the others.

"Listen to me!" Kay said. "I've been traveling with Ellie for a long time now. We can trust her. She's loyal to the rebellion. And …" He glanced at Ellie, then back at the others. "And she's a good friend. She didn't betray us."

Adrian growled. He stepped closer. He was the same height as Kay, but he seemed stronger. Those tattooed arms rippled with muscles. Kay wouldn't be winning any physical confrontation here, especially not with his wounds.

"How long have you known her?" Adrian said. "What is a long time?"

Kay sighed. "A couple of weeks," he confessed.

Adrian snickered. "And while you were fleeing to the temple—did the Equapol keep popping up?"

"Of course," Kay said. "They have drones everywhere. They have helicopters. Cameras. Satellites. They—"

"They were tracking her mindcap." Adrian nodded. "I knew it. Look, buddy, your little girlfriend might be loyal to the rebellion. Her heart might be in the right place. But that mindcap will lead the enemy right to us. We'll rip it off."

Kay cringed. He remembered Ginsburg performing the removal surgery. It was among the most painful experiences in Kay's life—and that was saying something. And Ginsburg had used local anesthetic and sanitized surgical tools. They had neither here.

"You'd have better luck removing her spleen out here," Kay said. "Removing her mindcap would kill her."

Adrian shrugged. "So?"

"So—no!" Kay said.

"Fine." Adrian snorted. "So we ditch her. Let her survive on her own. Or better yet—we drown her in the lake."

Wincing, Kay turned to look at Ellie. The twins held hands and glowered at everyone. Tilly was trembling, her eyes red. Adrian was cracking his knuckles, perhaps preparing to scalp Ellie with his bare hands.

Ellie stared back at them all.

"Do you know who my husband is?" she said.

They all stared at her, silent.

Finally Adrian sighed. "I suppose you're going to tell us?"

Ellie smiled thinly. "My husband is General EQL61. You might know him better as the White General."

Adrian scoffed. "Bullshit."

The twin sisters laughed. "As if!" they said in unison.

Ellie stared them down. "It's true. But hey, don't believe me. You also don't have to believe that I wear a military-grade mindcap, one that can't be tracked by the Equapol. Sure, call me a liar. Say I wear a civilian mindcap. Believe I'm leading the Equapol to you. But remember one thing, comrades. My husband fights in Zion. He leads armies in Zion. And when we arrive, you won't just be dealing with the Equapol. You're going to miss the Equapol. You'll be dealing with the wrath of the White Army, the greatest, most powerful military on Earth. You might just want an ally who knows how that military works. Who has a mindcap that can access military information. Who knows how the White General thinks. But if that's useless to you? Go ahead. Kill me now." She shrugged. "You'll only be killing yourselves."

Adrian and the twins stared, eyes wide in shock.

Kay looked at Ellie. And he was proud of her. Proud of how she stood up for herself, how she spoke so eloquently. But at the same time, this was a new side of her. He had always known Ellie to be sweet, kind, loving. Now he saw a new Ellie—someone fierce, even threatening.

She's stronger than I knew, Kay realized. *She's not just a trophy wife who wanted an adventure, a girl who bit off more than she could chew. She's not bird of paradise who finally escaped its cage. She's a lioness, intelligent and deadly. And I love her more than ever.*

Adrian finally overcame his paralysis. He stepped toward Ellie, fists raised.

"You are the White General's wife!" he hissed, eyes mad. "The man who crucified ten thousand citizens—our own people!—along the road to City58OI. The man who had his dogs devour prisoners in his palace, a show to entertain his guests. The man who murdered his own brothers, fearing competition for his rank. The White General—the monster. The butcher. If you're his wife, you must die!"

He lunged toward Ellie.

Kay leaped forward, bullet wounds and all, and slammed into Adrian.

Kay wasn't just wounded. After a lifetime of privation, he probably weighed half as much as Adrian. But Adrian too was weary. The blow was enough. Both men crashed down hard. They crushed reeds, tore up grass, and nearly tumbled into the pond.

The twins shrieked, mud splashing them. Tilly cursed and scampered back.

Lying in the mud, Adrian swung his fist. It connected with Kay's cheek. White light blazed. The wounds on his head screamed. Blinded, Kay grabbed the larger man. He managed to catch an ear. Adrian bellowed. Kay shoved down hard, slamming Adrian's head against the ground. Weak as he was, Kay summoned this strength. Ellie had saved his life countless times. He would fight for her—to the death if need be.

Adrian roared. He punched Kay in the shoulder—right in the bullet wound.

Kay screamed. He fell backward. Yet even as he tumbled, he kicked. He hit Adrian on the shin. He knew where to aim. He hit right where the surgeons had sawed and reattached the bones.

The tattooed man screamed so loudly birds fled the trees, and Kay was worried the Equapol would hear from miles away.

Both men rose to their feet, gasping for air, and raised their fists. The twins gathered around Adrian, their own fists raised. Ellie came to stand by Kay, eyes fierce, teeth bared. The two factions moved closer, prepared to spill more blood.

"Enough!" Tilly shouted.

The tiny girl—fifteen but small for her age—raced toward them. She placed herself between the combatants, hands on her hips. Her short hair was tangled, sticking out in every direction, and fire filled her dark eyes. Adrian tried to approach, but the girl shoved him back.

"I said enough!" Tilly repeated. "Don't you see this is what the Father wants? To turn us against one another! We're all in this together. As for Ellie? So what if her husband is a butcher. That doesn't mean she is! I was also mated. My mate was an army officer too. Not a general, but high ranking enough. A brute who murdered many people. I saw him kill them." Her eyes dampened. "They forced me to marry him when I was only fourteen. I lasted for a year. And I escaped. Because I'm nothing like that. Nothing like those monsters who call themselves soldiers. And neither is Ellie. Which is why she escaped too! Isn't it, Ellie?"

Ellie lowered her fists. She nodded. "Yes." Her voice was soft. "We both know what it's like. To be mated to a monster."

Tilly dried her eyes. She glared back at Adrian and the twins. "Ellie is telling the truth about her mindcap. Because I had to wear one too. All military mates have to. You can't track them! You can't electrocute or control the person who wears one. They're special mindcaps. Mindcaps used to control others. Ginsburg removed mine because I begged him. Because I couldn't stand it. But if Ellie kept hers? That's fine. That's good! We need somebody like her on our team. We need Ellie."

"It's too risky," Adrian said.

Tilly spat. "Too risky? Everything we've done so far is risky. It was risky going to the temple. It was risky escaping in the first place. It was risky coming here. Since when did risk bother you, Adrian? Without Ellie, we're dead. And my friend didn't die for that! Pat didn't give his life for us to die in this forest, or to turn on one another like animals." Tears flowed down Tilly's cheeks. "Pat was my best friend. And he died so we could escape. All of us. Ellie too. He died so we could survive and make it to Zion. Together. He'd want Ellie with us." She wiped her tears away. "Ellie is now under my protection. If anyone tries to harm her—you'll have to get past me first."

Ellie smiled and hugged the girl. "I'm proud to have you as my protector." She looked at the others. "I'm proud to fight with all of you. You have my loyalty. Always. Now let's survive the next few days. Let's get to Zion." Her eyes shone. "The promised land."

"A land of milk and honey," Tilly whispered, gazing east.

Adrian finally loosened his fists. He wiped blood off his cheek and stared east too. "A land of no pain."

The twins turned eastward. They whispered, barely audible. "A land where nobody can hurt us. Where nobody can use us. A land where our bodies will be our own."

Kay gazed east with them.

What did Zion mean to him? For days now, he had imagined Zion as a land of aromatic tea, of colorful birds and proud lions, of food and shelter and love. But it was more than that. More than just beauty for the senses.

"A land of ideas," he said. "Of books. Of words. Of thoughts. The freedom to speak and to listen. The freedom to think. That is true freedom."

Ellie slung an arm around him. "We'll be happy there. The road is still long. There will be many dangers along the way. The White Army still fights along the Zionite coast. But we'll get by them. We'll make our way to the heartland. To the promised land. To freedom."

CHAPTER EIGHTEEN

They trudged through the forest for hours, lost and hungry and afraid, before they found the cracked road.

It was empty. The asphalt was crumbling, and weeds pushed through the cracks. Once this highway must have been grand. Four lanes carved the forest. Kay could imagine that long ago, before the wars, many cars had driven here. Today he saw three of those cars rusting on one lane, several others on the roadside. The forest was claiming the vehicles, roots stretching into empty windows, wrapping around dead engines, crushing the cars like wooden fists. The cars seemed ancient, relics of a different era. Perhaps one that predated the Father.

What was life like before equalism? Kay wondered. *How long has the Party ruled us?*

He didn't know. According to the books, the Father had created the universe. But in the rallies, they spoke of previous utopias. Failed utopias. Civilizations before the Father. The contradiction was always ignored. The mindcaps punished anyone who contemplated it. There must have been a history before equalism, Kay realized. Maybe a rich, ancient history. And now only cracked asphalt and rust remained.

Smog hid the sky, but Kay could make out the white smudge of an afternoon sun. He looked at the other defectors.

"This road leads east." He pointed. "It'll take us to the coast."

The others looked back with hollow eyes. They were all wounded. All exhausted. Mud, burrs, and dry blood covered them. Adrian held his pistol drawn, fist clenching and unclenching around it. When a crow cawed above, the tattooed man jerked, raised the gun, then lowered it with a curse. Li and Lei were holding hands, trembling, and whispering to each other in a foreign language; Kay had learned it was called Cantonese, a tongue from an ancient land overseas. Little Tilly, the smallest in the group, leaned on a walking stick. A bullet had grazed her thigh during the mad flight down the river, slicing off a chunk of flesh. The bandages were red.

Ellie stepped onto the cracked highway. Even in her haggard state, she seemed beautiful and strong to Kay, a goddess of the wilderness. She stared west and east, then nodded.

"This is Highway 406," she said. "It leads to City897. A city on the eastern coast. A port city." She smiled. "Kay is right. This road will take us to the ocean. In City897, we can find a ship to Zion."

"Whoop dee doo," Adrian said. "All we have to do is cross a thousand goddamn miles, then steal an entire ship, and cross a few thousand goddamn miles more. All with the goddamn Equapol on our asses. What could go wrong?"

A rumble sounded in the west.

They all froze.

The road began to vibrate.

"Back into the forest!" Kay said. "Hide!"

They retreated and took cover behind the trees. The rumbling grew louder. Even the forest began to shake. Branches creaked and leaves fell. Birds fled.

Kay peeked between the leaves, watching them roll by. White Army vehicles. A massive truck took up three entire lanes, carrying tanks on its back. Several armacars followed—heavy armored vehicles, smaller than tanks but still damn mean, mounted with machine guns. Next rolled trucks, troops sitting in

192

the open carriers, rifles in their hands. One truck had words spray painted on the side: *We're going to Zion to exterminate the rats!*

The convoy rolled by, belching fumes, adding more cracks to the asphalt. The defectors waited in hiding until the military vanished in the distance.

Kay sighed. "Looks like we're not the only ones taking this journey."

Adrian scratched his crotch and spat. "Maybe we should have hitched a ride."

Kay thought for a moment. With the highway empty again, the birds returned. The damn crow was cawing again, eying the group suspiciously.

"Maybe we *can* hitch a ride," Kay finally said. "With the next civilian vehicle that rolls by. If this highway leads to the port, there will be trucks. Civilian trucks."

Adrian scoffed. "I was joking, buddy. If we hitchhike, we leave a trail. The driver would squeal." He hefted his gun. "But we can hijack a truck."

Another rumbling engine sounded. Kay glanced at the road. A tractor drove by. Too small and slow for the group. They remained hidden among the trees. They let the tractor pass.

"If we hijack a truck," Kay said, "what do we do with the driver?"

Adrian shrugged. "Put a bullet through his brain. Who cares?"

"I care," Kay said. "We're not murdering innocent people."

Adrian snorted. "There are no innocent equalists."

Kay glared at the larger man. "We're *not* murdering anyone."

Tilly rushed forward, placing herself between the two men. Anxiety filled her eyes. "Boys, boys! We can just … leave the driver here on the roadside. Alive. He can then walk or hitchhike back to a city."

The group all turned to Ellie. The general's wife cocked an eyebrow.

"Why are you all looking at me?" Ellie asked.

"You're our leader," Tilly said.

Adrian barked a laugh, but he didn't contradict the girl.

Ellie considered for a moment. "I agree with Adrian that we can't hitchhike. It's too dangerous. Any driver could be an informant. We'll hijack a truck. A civilian truck. We'll wear our masks. And I agree with Kay—no killing. We'll leave the driver on the roadside. Yes, it's taking a chance. I realize that. But I won't kill an innocent."

That seemed to settle the debate. The twins nodded. Adrian grumbled under his breath but didn't openly object. They all placed on their masks and drew their guns.

They waited.

For long time, the road remained empty.

Another tractor drove by. They let it pass.

Long moments passed in silence.

Kay remained still, watching the road, but the others became restless. The twins were whispering to each other again in their language. Tilly sat slumped against a tree, head lowered, drawing stick figures into the soil. Adrian drew a knife and began slashing at a branch, carving a spear, which seemed pointless to Kay. The brute already had a gun, but maybe he was bored.

Kay glanced at Ellie.

"Hey, Ellie," he said softly.

She looked at him. "Hey, Kay."

Kay swallowed a lump in his throat. "Kay, are you all right?"

"Of course I'm all right." She smiled. "You're the one who got shot twice and fell from a zipline."

He smiled bitterly. "And trust me, I can feel it. But I mean it—tell me if you need help. Maybe Tilly is right. Maybe you're leading this group. You know a hell of a lot more about the Party than we do. We'll all follow you—all the way to Zion. But remember, I'm here for you. You don't have to carry this burden alone."

She kissed his cheek. "Right now, Kay, I don't think you could carry a baby. But you're sweet. Thank you."

"Maybe if it's a baby chipmunk," Kay said. "The runt of the litter."

Another engine rumbled in the distance. Kay peeked onto the road and saw a bus driving toward them. He frowned. One rarely saw buses in Isonomia. Back in City58OI, people mostly walked. Only police and Party members owned cars. This bus was painted green, not the traditional Party white, and the paint was flaking and overrun with rust. What was a bus doing here? Delivering soldiers? Party members?

Whatever the case, it seemed a bad choice for hijacking. Kay would wait for a truck. Hopefully one filled with delicious food.

Adrian seemed to come to another conclusion. The tattooed man put on his mask, stepped onto the road, and raised his gun.

"Pull over!" Adrian shouted. "Stop this bus!"

"Damn it, Adrian!" Kay called from the trees. "There might be passengers!"

But Adrian ignored him. He stepped to the center of the road, aimed his gun, and waved the bus onto the roadside.

Cursing, Kay joined him, drawing his own pistol. The others quickly followed. Soon all six defectors were standing on the road, masked, pointing their guns at the bus. Kay worried the bus would keep driving, would mow them down. But when Adrian fired a warning shot, the bus slowed to a halt.

The defectors ran, guns raised, and surrounded the vehicle. Kay and Adrian stood at the front, aiming at the windshield. A driver sat inside, hiding behind a mask, hands raised.

"Out, out!" Adrian shouted. "Out of the bus!"

Ellie and the others stood alongside the bus, guns pointing at the windows.

"Everybody out!" Ellie shouted.

"Driver, open the doors!" Adrian said. He fired another warning shot, shattering a window. "Out of the bus or you all die!"

Trembling, the bus driver obeyed. He stepped onto the roadside. About a dozen other people stepped outside, all wearing robes and masks. Kay was too nervous to count them. All had quelis medallions hanging around their necks.

"Please, we're only commuters," said the driver. "Going to pick strawberries at the farm."

"Down, on your knees!" Adrian shouted. "Hands on your heads! Down! Face the trees!"

"Down or we kill every last one of you dogs!" Ellie screamed.

She truly seemed to be getting into character. At least, Kay hoped it was just acting, not an actual streak of viciousness.

Shaking, the farmers knelt, hands on their heads.

"Please, please," one whispered. "I'm only a farmer. I—"

Adrian kicked xer. "Shut up!"

Ellie stepped onto the bus, then peeked out a window. "It's all clear, guys. Let's go. Leave the farmers. They'll hitch a ride with the next bus."

Kay breathed out in relief. Good. He preferred it when Ellie wasn't screaming about killing.

The twins hopped onto the bus, holding hands, still chattering to each other in Chinese. Kay didn't understand their words, but he could tell they were terrified. Tilly, despite her size, took the driver's seat and gripped the wheel.

"Come on, boys!" The girl honked. "All aboard!"

Only Kay and Adrian were still on the road, guns aiming at the kneeling farmers.

"Go on, buddy," Adrian said to Kay. "I'll take care of them."

Kay frowned. "Come on, Adrian. Let's—"

Adrian aimed his gun at the back of one farmer's head.

Kay cursed, leaped toward Adrian, and shoved the gun aside.

The gun fired. The bullet hit the road. The farmer screamed. So did the twins, watching from inside the bus. The farmers begged and wept.

"What the hell?" Kay shouted.

Adrian aimed his gun at the farmers again. "I'm taking care of it. Get out of my way."

Kay grabbed Adrian's wrist, struggling to wrestle the gun free. Another bullet fired, hitting the trees. The twins were still screaming. Tilly and Ellie ran off the bus, shouting something. Kay barely heard over the ringing in his ears.

"Damn it, Adrian!" Kay finally managed to pull the gun free. He hurled it into the forest.

Adrian scowled and lunged at him, knocking Kay onto the asphalt.

"You tossed my gun away!" Adrian raised his fist, prepared to punch Kay in the face.

Ellie leaped onto the tattooed man, grabbed his wrist, pulled it back.

"Enough!" she said.

Kay pushed himself up, tried to leap at Adrian, but Tilly grabbed him. The twins stepped forward too, pulling the combatants apart, shrieking something in their language.

Sensing an opportunity, the farmers ran into the forest. Adrian cursed.

"They're getting away, dammit!" He rushed toward the forest, began scrounging among the bushes. "Where's my gun? Goddammit, they'll squeal!"

"They didn't see us!" Kay said. "We're wearing masks."

Adrian spun toward him, glaring. "And you think the Equapol won't connect the dots? Won't know it's us? You put us all in danger."

"We agreed!" Kay shouted. "We agreed not to murder!"

"I agreed to nothing." Adrian finally found his gun, but the farmers had vanished among the trees. When Adrian tried to chase them, the other defectors blocked him.

"Adrian!" Kay placed his hands on the burly man's chest. "Enough. Calm down."

Adrian bellowed. He raised his gun again, aiming it at Kay.

For a terrible instant, Kay was sure Adrian would kill him. They all stood frozen.

Adrian stared at Kay. His gun shook in his hands.

Kay stared into the muzzle. He would not back down.

Finally Adrian spat and tucked the gun into his belt.

"Not worth the bullet," he muttered.

Kay couldn't suppress a shudder. "Goddamn it, Adrian. You goddamn idiot. Why did you do this? You're part of a group now. Not a lone rebel."

"I was thinking about the group!" Adrian ripped off his mask, revealing a red, twisted face. "I was thinking about saving us! Saving the twins. And the girl. Even the goddamn capper. All of you. I would have killed for you. Killed the world for you! I wouldn't let anyone else die because I hesitated. Never again! I …" He grimaced and looked away. "Forget it."

They all stared at him in silence for a moment.

"Adrian …" Kay said.

The brute stared at the ground, at the fallen mask of one farmer. "My wife. My children. My whole family. I could have saved them. I didn't pull the trigger then. They died." His eyes dampened. "I swore to never hesitate again."

Kay took a long, deep breath. "I'm sorry, brother."

He put his hand on Adrian's shoulder. But Adrian shoved it away.

"Forget it. Forget what I said." Adrian spat and stepped into the bus. "Come on. All of you. Move your asses. We've got a long drive."

The twins were weeping and hugging each other. They climbed into the bus and sat at the back. Tilly took the wheel again.

Kay remained outside for a moment longer. He stared at one of Adrian's bullets, which was lodged in the asphalt.

He looked back at the bus.

One day, I'm going to have a serious problem with him, Kay thought. *He'll aim his gun at me again. And then I'll have to choose. I too will have to choose between hesitation and killing.*

Kay loosened his pistol in his belt. He stepped into the bus, keeping his hand on the gun.

CHAPTER NINETEEN

Kay was taking a shift at the wheel, driving the bus down the cracked asphalt, when he saw the crosses alongside the road.

The landscape here was barren and dry. Lifeless plains spread toward distant mountains. The only sign of life were the vultures flying above. A city rose on the horizon, a concrete cube. A power plant pumped out smog on a nearby hill, and a transformer station buzzed and crackled behind barbed wire fences, hundreds of electric giants sprouting cables like hair. They were a day from the coast.

Kay was almost falling asleep at the wheel when the first crosses appeared. At first, he mistook them for more electric towers. It was only once he passed the first one that he realized: These were wooden crosses. And humans hung from them.

He hit the brakes, and the bus screeched to a halt.

Behind him, the other defectors jolted in their seats, waking from slumber. Curses filled the bus.

"What the hell?" Adrian called, eyes still closed.

Kay stared at the nearest cross. Disgust filled his belly. Crows were picking at the corpse. The eyes were already gone.

Behind him, the others finally noticed.

"Sweet Jesus," whispered Lei, or perhaps it was Li.

"Goddamn." Adrian groaned. "Stinks."

Kay couldn't look away. That eyeless, skinless face stared at him. The matted black hair fluttered in the wind.

A wooden sign hung around the corpse's neck. The letters were too small and faded to read from here.

Kay frowned and opened the bus door. He began climbing out.

"Hey, hey!" Tilly cried after him. "Be careful, dude! You'll get sick."

Leaning back in his seat, Adrian scoffed. "Leave him behind. I'll drive."

Tilly smacked the tattooed brute.

Kay ignored them. He walked across the hot asphalt, approaching the cross. The stench of decay hit his nostrils. It was so powerful Kay had to bite down hard and struggle not to vomit. He slipped on his white mask, filtering some of the air through his voicebox, and stepped closer. The crows cawed and fluttered across the corpse, perhaps mistaking Kay for a competing scavenger. The dead man's eye sockets stared down, filled with maggots. The fingernails stretched out, yellow and cracked, seeming too long when growing from fingers shriveled with death. The corpse's belly had burst open, spilling its contents across the ground. Insects bustled inside the cavity.

This body is dead, but filled with more life than ever before, Kay thought.

He looked at the wooden sign that hung from the corpse. A chill filled him as he read the words.

You escaped me, KB905. You stole my mate. So I will keep killing until you bring her back. Enjoy these gifts of decay. Your corpse will be next. Yours, EQL61.

Ellie came to stand beside him. She read the words with him. Silently, they returned to the bus.

Kay drove onward.

The crosses lined the roadside. Hundreds, maybe thousands of them. Corpses after corpses. Around each hung the same sign. The crows feasted.

They drove in silence.

With every corpse they passed, Kay thought: *I need to turn myself in.*

And with every corpse, he saw his fate if he did.

He drove onward, feeling like a coward.

Ellie squeezed his knee. She looked at him, eyes soft. She didn't need to speak. In her blue eyes, Kay saw the answer.

Keep driving. Just keep driving.

They had driven a mile among the corpses when Adrian rose from his seat.

"I say we turn him in!" he said.

Kay hit the brakes. The bus screeched to a stop.

Tilly and the twins jolted forward, banged their foreheads against the seats in front of them. They cursed. Adrian clung to a pole, remaining standing.

Kay left the driver's seat. He marched down the aisle toward Adrian.

The two men squared off, staring into each other's eyes.

"This only works if we're together," Kay said, staring into the larger man's eyes. "Tearing us apart is what the Party wants. What these corpses are for."

Adrian spat—right on Kay's foot.

"Those were innocent people." Adrian gestured at the crosses. "Innocent men, women, children. They died because the general wants you. You and his wife! Their blood is on your hands, *comrade*." He spat that last word like an insult.

"You're angry." With an effort, Kay kept his voice calm. "Seeing these bodies is hard. It's hard for me too. But I'm not guilty of their deaths. I didn't kill them. The White General is the only one to blame."

Adrian stared outside. He stared at those lines of crosses. At those crows. A child hung from a nearby cross. The tattooed man's eyes reddened.

"One of those corpses could have been my wife," Adrian said, voice choked. "Others could have been my children. Children I had before the damn Father started growing us in labs." He spun back toward Kay, face turning red. "I can't let anymore die. If turning you in stops the killings—I'll do it."

"Boys, boys!" Tilly hopped forward. "Don't make me knock your heads together, you two great pillocks. Nobody is turning anyone in. We're all in this together, all right?"

"Even if thousands die?" Adrian said. "Even if that psychopath general keeps butchering people until he gets his trophy wife back?"

Tilly looked at him, then glanced at Kay and Ellie, and doubt filled her eyes. The twins stared from their seats. One of them cursed in Chinese.

Kay fixed his gaze on Adrian. "And what do you think will happen if you turn me in, Adrian? Do you think the White General will give you a trophy? Take you out for dinner? He'll nail you up with the rest of them. You're nothing but a rebel now. Same as me."

Adrian ground his teeth. His eyes burned. "Maybe he will. Maybe I deserve to die. Maybe I want to die. If it means an end to this horror." He pointed outside at the crosses.

"It won't mean an end to the horror," Kay said softly. "Even if he catches me. And Ellie. And you and every other rebel. The horror will go on and on. Because the Party is merciless. They will continue to torture and murder and mutilate so long as they exist. As they did before we rebelled. As they will do after we're gone. And for every person they murder, they will create a new one in a lab. And the torture will continue forever. Our only hope is to save ourselves. As cynical as that sounds. We must leave this land. We must get away from this place of death. It breaks my heart. But we cannot help these people."

Adrian looked away. Veins bulged on his neck. His eyes were red—but red with grief, no longer with anger.

"They murdered my family," he said, speaking to the floor. "The bastard equalists. The Equapol. The White Army. The Party. The Father. They're all the same damn thing." His voice cracked. "They murdered them in the rally as the crowd cheered. Because of me. Because I rebelled. Because I escaped the mine where they had me chained, digging for ore. They made me watch. They kept me alive as punishment, knowing that my life is worse than death. How can I escape again and let more people die?"

Kay placed a hand on the tattooed man's shoulder. He spoke softly. "Because if we turn back now, if we surrender—they win. They win and all these deaths were for nothing. We have to keep going. Together. We have to *beat them*."

Adrian nodded. He clutched Kay's shoulder. Tightly. Thankfully, not the shoulder with the bullet wound.

"I'm sorry, brother," Adrian said. "Forgive me."

Kay nodded. "You are forgiven. Not only for today. But for whatever happened in the past. Our lives are clean slates. Our lives will begin again in Zion."

Kay was returning to the driver's seat when he heard the groan.

A long, raspy sound.

A sound from outside.

Kay looked outside, and he saw him.

A man hanging from a cross. The man looked at him with one eye. He groaned again.

Kay ran outside. The others followed.

"We need a ladder!" Tilly shouted.

"We don't have one!" said one of the twins.

Adrian dropped to hands and knees below the cross. "Climb on my back! Hurry!"

"We need tools!" cried the other twin. "We need a wrench or something. Oh God!"

Everyone was near panic. The man on the cross groaned again. The crows had taken one of his eyes. His skin hung in tatters. His hands and feet were nailed to the wood.

Hands shaking, Kay found a box of tools in the bus's luggage compartment. He climbed onto Adrian's back.

The crucified man looked at him. One drooping eye peering from ruin. A look so weak it seemed to be gazing from the afterlife.

Kay took a deep breath.

Ginsburg removed the mindcap from my head. I can remove a man from a cross.

He placed a wrench around the nail in the man's left foot. He pulled it free.

The blood flowed. And Kay moved to the other foot. And to the hands. And he caught the man as he fell. They lay him down on the roadside. The man lay on the ground, groaning, coughing, trying to speak.

"We need water, bring water!" Tilly said.

"Kay!" said Ellie. "Kay, do you still have antibiotics?"

"He needs a tourniquet or something, dudes," Tilly said.

"He needs a goddamn miracle healer," said Adrian.

They were all talking at once. Kay drowned it out. He looked at the man. He had never seen a more wretched soul. Holes in his hands and feet. An infected eye socket. Lacerations across his body—the work of the crows. Thirst and exposure had done the rest.

They poured water into his mouth. They bandaged his wounds. The man passed out, breathing shallowly.

They brought him onto the bus. They laid him between the seats. They all stared at the unconscious man.

Tilly poked Kay in the ribs. "Finally somebody who looks worse than you, stiff."

"Tilly, hush."

Kay crushed some of his last painkiller and antibiotic pills, mixed them in water, and poured them into the man's mouth. It was all he could do now.

"You're wasting that medicine, you know." Adrian sat nearby, feet slung across the seat in front of him.

"He needs it," Kay said.

Adrian looked at the wounded man on the floor. "The poor bastard won't last the night. Wasting good meds on a lost cause."

"I won't just let him die," Kay said.

Adrian snorted. "You were perfectly willing to let thousands die so long as you could keep fleeing. What's one more poor bugger?"

Kay wanted to argue, to call Adrian heartless. But maybe the tattooed man was right. Maybe Kay was hypocritical. Maybe he was wasting medicine. Right now, Kay was so weary, in so much pain, that he was moving on instinct more than thought. He took two pills of his own, eying with concern the dwindling reserves.

"I'll take a shift at the wheel," Tilly said. She patted Kay on the shoulder. "Get some sleep, stiff. You need it."

Kay sat down and closed his eyes. The bus rumbled down the road.

I might die in my sleep, Kay knew. *The drones or helicopters might arrive any moment and lob a missile at us.*

But he was too weary to resist. He sank into a deep, dark pit, where he hung on a cross, and where crows with white masks ripped at his eyes. In his dream, the corpses climbed off their crosses. The dead shuffled through a concrete city, leaking rot. They stared with empty eye sockets through masks of skin. Kay fled them through the labyrinth, lost, seeking a way out. One of the crucified bodies clutched his ankle, fingernails cutting his skin. The creature coughed, gasped, tried to speak.

"Bloody hell!" a deep voice cried. Adrian's voice.

Kay's eyes snapped open.

He was back on the bus.

The wounded man from the cross was awake. He still lay on the floor, bandaged, cadaverous. His breath rattled through what remained of his chest. And he was clutching Kay's ankle.

"It's a goddamn zombie." Adrian watched the scene with a mixture of disgust and amusement.

The wounded man was trying to speak. Only hoarse gasps left his mouth. His one eye was wide, entreating.

Kay leaned down.

"What is it, friend?" Kay whispered.

Everyone gathered around them. Ellie and Adrian. The twins. Tilly pulled the bus over and joined the group.

The wounded man grabbed Kay's collar. He coughed, tried to speak again. Blood dripped from his mouth. Finally something resembling words left his throat.

"Xe … lied." He coughed again. "Don't … believe …" His grip tightened. "One of you … liar … danger …"

"Who lied?" Kay asked. "About what?"

The man kept coughing. More blood dripped. He tried to speak again, made a choking sound, then slumped.

His breath died.

Kay pried himself loose from the dead man's grip. They all stared at the body, silent for a moment.

"Told ya it's a waste of medicine," Adrian said.

Tilly punched him.

The twins, who were watching silently, finally spoke up.

"What's the lie?" said Li. Her dark, almond-shaped eyes narrowed.

"Who's the liar?" demanded Lei, her sister.

The group all glanced from one to another.

"Nobody here is a liar," Kay said.

Adrian scoffed. "Somebody is. You all heard the zombie. One of us here in the group is a traitor." He cracked his knuckles. "One of us is about to get their skull bashed open." He glanced knowingly at Ellie.

"Why are you looking at her?" Kay demanded. "Ellie is trustworthy."

"No she isn't!" the twins said in unison.

"She still wears a mindcap," added Li.

"She's a damn equalizer!" said Lei.

Tilly leaped toward Ellie, shielding the taller woman.

"Ellie is our friend!" the tiny girl said, eyes flashing. She pointed at the twins. "Maybe one of you is the liar."

The twins laughed.

"Us?" said Li. "We barely even said anything so far."

"Yeah, we haven't had a chance to lie!" said Lei.

Tilly's eyes narrowed, scrutinizing them. "Oh, you two have said a lot. In Chinese! That only makes you more suspect. What do we even know about you two? You're always huddling in the back, whispering, gossiping. I trust Ellie a hell of a lot more than you two."

The women seemed close to blows.

"You have no idea how we suffered!" Li shouted. Tears budded in her eyes.

Lei embraced her sister, glaring at the others. "We were comfort women."

"We served the Party," Li whispered. Her tears flowed. "Ministers. Equapol and White Army officers. We were there to serve them tea. To dance for them at their parties, naked and shameful. To crawl onto their laps and into their beds. To pleasure them. Endure them."

She began to sob, and Lei comforted her, stroking her sister's hair.

"We suffered as much as anyone," Lei said, glaring at Tilly, then at the others. "You can't imagine what we endured before we escaped. Never call us disloyal again, just because we're quiet, because we're shy. This is because we're hurt. Because we're broken." Her voice cracked. "We hate the Party more than anyone. We would die before going back. And before betraying anyone here."

"Somebody else is the traitor!" Li said, wiping her eyes. She stared directly at Tilly.

The girl gasped. "You don't think I—"

"Well, it's not us!" Li said.

Again, they seemed close to blows.

Kay stepped between them. He raised his hands.

"Whoa, whoa, hold on!" he said. "We don't know what the dead man meant. We don't even know what lie he referred to. He could have meant the Father. We know the Father's been lying to us all our lives. About Zionites being evil. About the Party being good. About everything." He looked at the body. "He probably just meant the Father and his lies."

"Bullshit," said Adrian. "He said it was one of us. I heard it. You all heard it. And who's been feeding us stories of Zion? Of a promised land?" He pointed at Ellie. "The freak in the mindcap. I bet Zion doesn't even exist. She's leading us into a trap."

Ellie snickered, rolled her eyes, but said nothing. Everyone else began shouting at once. Accusations flew back and forth. Tilly was hopping on the seats, shouting that Adrian must be the traitor because he was such a "huge, stinky butthead." The twins were now insisting that Tilly was the traitor. Adrian roared that he would crack everyone's skulls and be done with.

Finally Kay had enough.

"Can we bury the man first?" he bellowed.

They all fell silent. They stared at him.

"Blimey, the stiff knows how to shout?" Tilly said.

Kay was panting. His ears thrummed. "Enough, all of you! We can't keep doing this. We can't keep turning on one another. Let's bury this man. Show him some respect instead of tearing one another apart over his corpse."

They got off the bus. Weeds grew from cracks in the road, and naked trees rose from dry soil. A factory stood in the distance, filling the sky with smog. They were a hundred miles from the coast.

They stood in silence for a moment.

"Did anyone bring a shovel?" Tilly finally asked.

"Goddammit." Adrian spat.

They had no way to dig. Instead, they spent an hour collecting stones, and they buried the corpse under a cairn.

"It's not much," Kay said, looking at the pile of stones. "But it should keep away the crows and jackals."

"Phew." Adrian theatrically wiped his forehead. "Now only the worms and beetles will eat him up. I'm so relieved."

Kay glared at the man. "It's something, damn it. It means we did something. That we care. That we acknowledged his death."

They all stared in silence at the cairn. A cold wind blew through the black trees, scattering ash. A crow circled overhead, cawing, perhaps upset about its meal being buried.

Finally, it was Li who broke the silence.

"Is Zion real?" she said softly.

Lei embraced her. "If it's not real, we'll build it."

Kay looked at the twins. "Of course Zion is real."

For another moment—silence.

Then Adrian spoke. "We're chasing a goddamn dream. There's no Zion. That's the lie." He cursed and kicked a rock off the cairn. His voice rose to a howl. "A goddamn lie!"

"Hush!" said Tilly. "You'll alert the Equapol."

"Let 'em come!" Adrian said. "I'd rather die in battle than chase a lie. I—"

"Zion is real," Ellie said, her voice soft.

They all turned toward her. It was the first time the general's wife had spoken in hours.

"I've been there," she continued, voice even softer now. "With my husband on a campaign. It's not a paradise. It's not a land of milk and honey and endless comfort. It's a hard land. A land at war. A land that suffers from many problems. Poverty. Constant warfare. A harsh, hot climate with sandstorms and drought. But it's also a land of freedom. And of much beauty. There are vineyards that rustle under the sun, and golden dunes that roll into pink sunrise. There are blue waters that are unpolluted, safe to swim in, filled with fish. There are cities and markets where people walk unmasked." She slipped her hand into Kay's. "There are libraries full of books. It's a land that's real. A land like the old world. Like Isonomia used to be before the Father. A land that will be our home."

The twins embraced, and their eyes softened. For the first time, the pair looked at Ellie with something resembling hope, even affection.

But Adrian's eyes still simmered with hatred.

"How can we believe you?" he said. "You're a general's wife. What if you're lying?"

Tilly stepped forward. For once, he girl did not hop or shout. Her eyes were soft, her voice softer.

"She's not lying," the girl said. "My friend Pat was a soldier once. He fought in Zion." She wiped her eyes. "Before he died."

Adrian scoffed. "Thanks for clarifying. But I assumed he wasn't fighting as a zombie, eating Zionite brains."

Tilly glowered. "You know what I mean. Pat was there. He saw it. A desert land. A land of golden cities. Zion. He told me about it, and I trusted Pat. He was my best friend. And I trust Ellie too." She embraced the older woman.

Kay looked at them.

The twins—used as "comfort women" for the regime.

Tilly—mated to a cruel man at only fourteen.

Adrian—who had seen his family murdered.

He turned to look at Ellie. She stared back, those beautiful blue eyes gazing into his. Kay remembered the first time he had seen those blue eyes. They still made his heart soar.

And you, Ellie. The woman who fought by my side through fire and darkness. The bravest woman I know. We'll do this together. We'll find the promised land.

Kay looked at them all.

"We all have reasons to hate the Party," Kay said. "To dream of Zion. I trust every one of you. You are my comrades. More than anyone back in City58OI ever was. I believe in Zion. We don't know what the crucified man meant. He was dying, maybe delusional. He didn't know us. But I know you. I haven't known you for long. But I know you better than I've ever known anyone. We're in this together. We are family. Let's get back on the road."

They returned to the bus.

They drove down the road.

An hour later, they saw the ocean.

The gray vastness spread before them, polluted and cold and lifeless. But beyond it rose a golden dawn. Beyond it lay a home.

CHAPTER TWENTY

Kay stood on the shore, his bare feet on the tarry sand, gazing at the ocean.

It spread before him like a living thing. Moaning. Breathing. Reaching across the shore, vomiting glassy shards and plastic bags, then recoiling into its polluted depths. Endlessly gasping for air. This was an ocean like the crucified man. Ashen and dying. Maybe already dead, its breathing but an echo of past life.

Long ago, Ellie had told him, this had been called the Atlantic Ocean. Today it was simply called Ocean2E. Kay imagined that long ago, the Atlantic had been filled with wonders. Sea creatures of every color. Glittering castles on verdant islands. A lush place of life. Today Ocean2E was a sea of filth.

"Tilly said that in old books, the oceans are blue," Kay said. "City58OI was beside an ocean. A different ocean than this. A pool of pollution and stench. I hoped that in the east, we'd find blue waters. But there's only more filth. More grayness. The Father ruined the world."

Ellie stood beside him. The malodorous wind ruffled her robes. She sighed. "We ruined the world long before the Father. For centuries, we polluted. Fought wars. Destroyed. We were weak. So weak that the Father could easily take hold. This isn't his fault. The fault belongs to us all. To mankind."

Kay raised an eyebrow. "Don't you mean peoplekind?"

Ellie gave a little laugh. "Thank God my mindcap can't shock me, huh?"

Kay placed his hands on his hips, looking at the ocean. "So how do we cross it?"

The other defectors gathered around Kay and Ellie. The group looked north along the beach. The port city rose a few miles away.

City897 looked like any other Isonomian city. Concrete walls. Guard towers. A million despairing hostages. But in one important way, City897 was unique.

Here was the great eastern port of Isonomia. From here, ships sailed to Zion.

There was only one problem.

"We have no mushrooms," Kay said.

"How can you think of your belly at a time like this?" Tilly said.

"I'm not." Kay rolled his eyes. "I mean—we don't have crates of mushrooms. The crates we packed at Tenzin's place."

Tilly scoffed. "That *we* packed? Dude, I spent weeks working there—collecting mushrooms, stuffing them into jars, packing crates, listening to the monks lecture me on meditation and karma. You just spent an evening there, eating more mushrooms than you picked."

"Regardless," Kay said. "We have no excuse to reach Tenzin's ship, the one he uses to export mushrooms to White Army forces in Zion."

"The *Samsara*," Ellie said. "That was the ship's name. She'll be gone by now."

"You mean gone to Zion already?" Kay said, heart sinking.

"I mean gone," Ellie said.

Kay understood. Of course. Damn it! If the Equapol had attacked Tenzin's temple, they would have investigated him. Found out about his mushroom exporting business. Found his ship—and likely impounded it. Or sank it with everyone aboard.

"Damn it," Kay said.

The others muttered curses too. Adrian spat. They too understood.

"Great," Adrian said. "Just damn peachy. What are we supposed to do now? Swim to Zion? Ooh, I know! Let's collect all this trash on the beach and build a raft! A wonderful raft of garbage! Wouldn't that be lovely? Instead of disguising ourselves as mushroom exporters, we can pretend to be floating piles of filth!"

"All right, all right!" Kay said. "We get it. Look, nobody planned for this to happen. We'll find another ship."

Adrian scoffed. He pointed at the city. "The port's inside that prison. And I ain't entering. The place is crawling with Equapol. And worse—the goddamn army."

They all looked at the city again.

Many ships were sailing from and to the port, leaving churning wakes through the trash. Some were military vessels— metallic, triangular, bristly with cannons. But most were cargo freighters and tankers. Isonomia didn't just end here on this coast. The Father ruled many lands overseas. Vast continents beyond this gray ocean. Not all these ships were sailing to Zion, that land that still resisted equalism. The Father's arms stretched far, engulfing the globe. Even the oceans swarmed with his might.

"All those ships on the ocean," Kay said, watching them sail. "And all belong to the Father."

"Not all," Ellie said.

Adrian snorted. "There's one he doesn't own." He pointed at a chunk of driftwood. "Get to paddling, capper."

Ellie ignored him.

"I remember the tales my husband told," she said. "Years ago, when he was only a colonel, he served in the navy. His job was to hunt pirates."

"Yarr, mate?" Tilly said. "Peg leg? Hook? Eye patch? Those kinda guys?" She snarled. "Shiver me timbers, bring me my rum!"

Everyone stared at her.

Tilly shrugged. "What, I read it in a book!" She snorted. "Oh right, *you guys* never had a secret library of forbidden literature. Philistines."

Kay ignored the girl. He turned to Ellie.

"Do you know where we can find a pirate ship?"

"No," she said. "But I know where we can find pirates. The Blue Oyster Club. The most notorious bar along the coast."

Adrian groaned and kicked a dead crab. "Let me guess. It's inside the city." When Ellie nodded, he spat. "Just fantastic."

They began walking toward the city, feet scattering trash across the beach. Ellie walked at the lead, her step quick. Kay struggled to keep up. His legs were aching more than usual; the cold ocean air seemed to freeze the bolts in his bones. His other wounds were agony. But he knew the pain was almost over. He would endure a little longer.

"Ellie," he said, voice soft. "How are you?"

The others were a few steps behind, arguing among themselves. They could not hear.

Ellie looked at him. "Fine, Kay."

"Are you sure? Back along the road, we shared our stories. The twins—serving as comfort women. Tilly—mated to an older man. Adrian—losing his family. But you didn't share your story with the others. Ellie, I just want you to know—if you hurt, if you grieve, you can talk to me."

She slowed down. Her eyes softened. She held his hand.

"You're a good man, Kay. Better than I deserve."

"You deserve better than me," Kay said. "I'm old, broken, a stiff as Tilly calls me. I'm twice your age and look ten times older. You deserve everything good that still remains in this world."

She heaved a sigh. "You're right, Kay, I don't share a lot about my life. Maybe I feel guilty. For being EQL61's mate. I can see how the others look at me. Adrian. The twins. Even Tilly sometimes. They all stare at my mindcap. When they think I'm not looking, they stare. And I know what they think. That I'm still one of them. One of the Party." She snorted. "That I'm still loyal to my husband."

"Did he ever hurt you?" Kay said, gently.

"No." Her eyes dampened. "But he made me watch. When he hurt others. Those crosses along the highway? EQL61 nailed in those people himself. He swung the hammer, not his troops. He always insists on swinging the hammer himself. I've seen him torture people before. He once invited me to a feast. Many other officers came. He pulled out a Zionite on chains, and he carved the man alive." Her voice dropped to a hoarse whisper. "He just took a knife, and carved him like a roast boar. Piece by piece. The man screamed for so long, but they wouldn't let him die. They let the dogs eat, and they laughed, and …"

She could say no more. Her face was pale. She was trembling.

"Oh, Ellie." Kay stopped walking and embraced her. "I'm sorry. I'm so sorry you had to see that."

She held him, crying onto his shoulder. "I don't like talking about these things. Because they're so painful. Because I cry. Because I can't be weak now. I have to get everyone to Zion. We both do. We have to lead them, you and I. For just a while longer, we must be strong." She wiped her eyes. "I love you, Kay. I want to live with you forever in Zion. You're not a stiff. You're a good, strong, brave man."

"We'll get there," he said. "And the pain will end. It'll all be like a nightmare. Something we can forget. Well, maybe we'll never forget. But we'll move on. We'll drink aromatic tea. You'll paint your birds and lions. We'll live in a little house among trees."

She grinned through her tears. "Maybe we'll collect mushrooms. Oh, and apples! We'll grow apples and make cider. You'll like cider."

"I don't know what apples or cider are, but I love them already. And I love you."

She kissed him.

They walked onward.

They reached the walls of City897.

The companions put on their masks and robes. Ellie walked with her hood off, displaying her mindcap. The others hid their heads under hoods. They approached the checkpoint leading into the city.

Three security guards stood here, wearing armor and carrying assault rifles. Crenelated towers were emblazoned across their bulletproof vests. Below the logo appeared the words *Isonomian People Patrol*. The IPP took the jobs the Equapol and White Army didn't want. They guarded bridges, checkpoints, borders, and anything that required a warm body with a gun.

The IPP had a reputation for brutality. These brutes guarded the reeducation camps. Kay had seen them slaughter many comrades.

The guards stepped forward, guns pointing ahead. Two held German Shepherds on leashes. The dogs growled, tugging on their chains, teeth bared. The animals too wore mindcaps.

"Why are you here?" said a guard, voice emerging deep and distorted through xer voicebox.

"We're here to work," Kay said. "We're factory workers."

The guards took another step closer. The dogs barked madly, pawing the air and snapping their mighty jaws.

"Where are your transfer papers?" a guard demanded. "What city were you sent from?"

Ellie stepped forward. She stared at the guards and raised her chin.

"You don't need to see our papers," she said.

"What—?" The guard blinked and frowned. Xe aimed xer rifle at Ellie. "I'll splatter your damn brains across—"

Blue lights ignited on Ellie's mindcap.

The guard fell silent.

The other guards stepped closer, prepared to fire.

The lights on Ellie's mindcap shone brighter. These guards froze too.

The dogs gave a last few barks, then sat and whimpered.

"You don't need to see our papers," Ellie repeated, voice low and dangerous.

The guards stared at her. Their eyes widened. Their pupils dilated. One guard dropped xer rifle from shaking hands. Another wet xerself, and the piss dripped under xer armor and trickled along the ground.

The guard spoke with effort, as if an invisible fist were moving xer jaw.

"We ... don't need ... to see ... your papers."

Marionette strings seemed to tug them. The guards stepped aside.

The lights on Ellie's mindcap shone bright blue. Chin raised, she walked through the checkpoint and into the city. Kay and the others followed.

They walked down the street, leaving the guards behind.

Tilly hopped toward Ellie, eyes wide through her mask holes. "Holy hell, talk about Jedi mind tricks!"

Kay frowned. "Jedi what?"

The girl rolled her eyes. "Philistines, I tell you."

Ellie was silent. Her mindcap was still shining. Her eyes were narrowed, filled with pain. She limped, stumbled forward, nearly fell. Kay had to catch her.

"A little farther," she whispered.

They walked a few more steps, then turned around a corner. The checkpoint was now out of sight.

Ellie collapsed to the ground, breathing raggedly. Her mindcap shut down.

"Ellie!" Kay knelt beside her.

She took a deep breath and shuddered. "It hurts. I'm not very good at this."

Kay held her hand. "You were amazing."

"Bloody brilliant!" Tilly said, hopping around them.

A police car came rolling down the road. Ellie quickly rose. The companions arranged themselves in formation. They marched along the street, feet moving in perfect unison. The police car drove by and vanished around a corner.

Ellie breathed out in relief.

"My mindcap won't work on Equapol," she said. "I don't have a high enough privilege setting. But it can help against lowly IPP guards. And some White Army too, if they're low ranking enough." She winced. "It just hurts. A lot. I hope I don't have to use it often."

Kay turned and gave Adrian a look.

See?

Adrian snorted and rolled his eyes.

They marched onto a wider road. Thousands of citizens were marching here too. All wore their white robes and white masks. All were exactly 5'8". All stared forward, silent, obedient. Dozens of equalizers patrolled among them, keeping them in line.

Kay suddenly noticed a flaw in their plan.

Tilly.

The tiny girl stood out. She was shorter than the required 5'8".

She was only fifteen, of course. She had avoided leg-lengthening surgery due to her young age. Right now, she walked on her tiptoes, trying to blend in as best she could.

It would be impossible to pass her off as a child, Kay knew. Children never walked among adults. They lived in truthhalls until they were old enough to toil in the factories. Kay just hoped Tilly had strong toes.

Kay leaned toward Ellie. "Tilly's height might be a problem," he whispered.

Ellie nodded. "If anyone stops us, I'll pass her off as my mate. I'll pretend to be a White Army officer, and I have the mindcap to prove it. Officers can marry underage girls."

"Sick bastards," Kay muttered.

Ellie nodded. "They are. Now hush. We must proceed quietly."

The defectors joined the crowd of citizens. They marched along. The concrete towers rose around them, packed so closely together they formed canyon walls. Murals of the Father covered many building facades. A statue of the tyrant rose from a city square, gilded and glorious, one fist raised to the smoggy sky.

This place looked exactly like City58OI, Kay's old home. He guessed that every city across Isonomia, the thousands of them, was the same. As equal as their people.

Marching here brought back painful memories. Decades of despair in City58OI. Decades of marching and toiling like a zombie. Broken and hurting. The mindcap controlling him. Never truly awake. Never truly alive.

Kay looked around him. He looked at the thousands of poor souls with their dead eyes. He pitied them.

They are the living dead, he thought. *And I was like them for almost half a century.*

His wounds still hurt. But the memories hurt more. A deeper, colder pain.

Suddenly—an older memory.

That memory of his wife. Of Christine.

The memory was suddenly so real Kay nearly fell over.

Christine! Beautiful pale face. Green eyes. Auburn hair. Christine. Pregnant.

Their son.

A beautiful boy with auburn hair. A family.

"Christine, he isn't right," a younger Kay said. "There's something wrong with the boy. We have to …"

Kay groaned. No. No! It hurt too much. And he was on the train again. Crammed into the car. Naked. Beaten. With hundreds of others. And he was toiling in the reeducation camp. Breaking stones with a pickaxe. Crying in agony, bleeding in the snow. Eight years of pain and scars and beatings. And—

"Hey, stiff!" Tilly poked him. "Your marching is off. March right!"

Ellie turned toward them. She looked at Kay, concern in her eyes.

"Kay, are you okay?"

He nodded. A few equalizers were patrolling nearby, hands on their guns.

"I'm fine. March on. Be careful."

With effort, he shoved the memories away. The group kept marching with the proletariat. Staring forward. Stiff and proper. Just a few more citizens in a great prison.

But this time we're not prisoners, Kay thought. *This time we're breaking free. I will find the end of the maze. I will find my way out to a land of red flowers.*

CHAPTER TWENTY-ONE

They walked through City897, the great port city of the empire.

Ellie led the group around a military base, past a police station, around a truthhall, and alongside factories. They made their way toward the port. The ocean gushed ahead, a boneless gray beast, growling at its concrete master.

The companions walked along the boardwalk. Hundreds of ships and boats moored here. Many were cargo freighters, and workers in white masks toiled, loading and unloading crates. Cranes rose like giant metal birds, dipping down to grab shipping containers, then rising again, their catch in their beaks. Lumbering tankers were anchored farther out, rising like a city of metal on the watery horizon, their chimneys pumping. Smaller ships were moving back and forth between the docks and those behemoths. The tankers carried gasoline, coal, noxious gasses—the dreadnoughts that had polluted this ocean, that were still spewing their gray innards into what remained of the water.

Many of the ships were armed. IPP corvettes zipped back and forth, leaving churning wakes through the muck, guarding the port. Equapol had a few ships here too, motorboats mounted with heavy machine guns, assisting the People Patrol. Behind them loomed the warships of the White Army—beasts of bright steel, towering, armed with cannons. Gods of war.

There were no fishing boats. That industry had ended long ago. If any life remained within this ocean, it wasn't anything you wanted to eat.

Moldy buildings lined the boardwalk—refineries, warehouses, military barracks, and a couple of soup kitchens. Nestled between a smelter and shipyard, they saw it. A seedy concrete house, blackened with years of smog. A rusty fence surrounded the patio, topped with barbed wire. Letters were spray painted above the front door: *The Blue Oyster Club*.

"It looks lovely!" Tilly said. "That is—a lovely place to catch tetanus."

A stray cat hissed on the patio, fur bristling. Several emaciated kittens fled. A drunk man lay sleeping in the corner, his mask loose, revealing a bit of stubbly jaw. Unmasking even an inch of skin could land a man in a reeducation camp. Kay knelt and adjusted the drunkard's mask, then leaped back as the man growled, snapped his teeth, and spat.

"Hands off, copper!" the drunkard said, then passed out and began to snore.

A bouncer stood at the door, wearing plates of scavenged armor—a hodgepodge of military and police scraps, their symbols scraped off. A dozen weapons bristled across xer back and hung from xer waist, making the brute look like a mechanical porcupine. The bouncer stared with bloodshot eyes through xer mask.

"No finks allowed," xe rumbled. "Get lost."

Finks. Rats. Squealers. Snitches. There were many names for them. Those who informed on their fellow citizens. Those who were cozy with the Equapol.

Ellie stepped closer. She held out a few iron coins.

"We're here to hire a ship," she said. "We ain't no finks."

The bouncer grunted. "Prove it."

Kay glanced around, then stepped closer. He pulled back his hood, revealing his capless head.

His companions gasped. Adrian cursed.

"You'll send us all to a reeducation camp!" Tilly whispered. "Idiot!"

Kay pulled his hood back up. He stared into the bouncer's eyes.

"Now let's see if *you're* a fink," Kay said. "Or a friend."

It was a gamble. And it worked.

The bouncer nodded. He opened the door, stepped aside, and gestured into the club.

As they passed through the doorway, Ellie leaned toward Kay.

"That was stupid," she said. "I could have controlled his mindcap."

Kay smiled thinly. "Ellie? Did you hear how he spoke? That bouncer wasn't wearing a mindcap. I knew we could trust him."

Tilly whistled softly, bouncing behind them. "Not wearing a mindcap in the middle of a city swarming with Equapol? Dude's got balls of steel."

"As do we all." Kay glanced at Ellie, the only capped one in the group. "Well, maybe other than Ellie."

They entered the Blue Oyster Club's common room. The inside wasn't any nicer than the outside. Pipes were exposed across the walls, leaking rust down the raw concrete. Wires hung from the ceiling, and a few light bulbs buzzed and flickered. Flies bustled everywhere, and a cockroach scuttled across the cracked floor. The place might have once been a small warehouse. Instead of crates, the building now contained humans.

Humans without masks.

The sight shocked Kay. He knew that citizens sometimes removed their masks at home. Technically that too was illegal, but rarely enforced. But here? In a public place? To go maskless? Some of these people weren't even wearing the white equagarb robes, designed to hide one's gender, skin color, and age.

"No wonder the bouncer was careful," Kay muttered. "This is a hive of rebellion. Right in the middle of the city!"

Ellie smiled thinly. "Oh, the Equapol knows the Blue Oyster Club exists. So does the army. They let it operate. Good intelligence is gathered here. At least when the finks do make it in."

Kay stiffened. He glanced around. "So there might be informants here?"

Ellie nodded. She spoke softly. "There are, sometimes. My husband got a lot of intel from this place. Let's be extra cautious."

They walked between the tables. Kay glanced at the crowd, trying not to stare. A burly man sat at one table, skin as black as night. His bald head and muscular arms shone with golden tattoos: sea serpents, waves, and anchors. A wiry man with a thin, ratty goatee sat at another table, feeding grapes to a leashed monkey. Two men were arm-wrestling, their veins bulging, their faces red. A woman stood on a stage, wearing a metal bikini, swaying seductively. A snake with gold and silver scales curled around her neck. A few of the scales were missing, exposing the cables and gears inside. Most people here were nursing mugs of grog. A handful were smoking hookahs, and purple smoke filled the air, thick and pungent.

The companions chose a table in a shadowy corner. Grime covered the booth, and flies buzzed around the lamp. A human tooth was rotting in the ashtray. A framed portrait of the Father hung on the wall, the glass grimy, and somebody had drawn a mustache over the Father's golden mask. That comforted Kay. A little act of rebellion. A little scribble of hope.

A waitress approached, a cigarette dangling from her lips. Her mask perched atop her head, probably kept there to pull down quickly in case of a raid. Her white robe hung open, revealing scars where her breasts had been surgically removed to conform to genderless equality. Other scars, small and faded, covered her torso. Cigarette burns, Kay realized.

"What'll be?" she said, voice raspy, and sucked on her cigarette.

"Anything not festering with bacteria," Tilly said.

Adrian scoffed, sitting beside the girl. "Nothing can survive in the moonshine they serve in these places. It's deadlier than paint thinner." He looked at the waitress. "I'll have a pint. And keep the drinks coming until I pass out."

"Tea please," Li and Lei said in unison. Both twins were wincing, looking around in disgust.

"Very, very hot tea," Li added.

"Boiling," Lei said. "We want to see the bubbles."

"Tea so hot it could sanitize surgical tools," Li said.

As the others ordered their drinks, Ellie touched Kay's shoulder.

"You and I—let's head to the bar," she said.

They left the others. Kay kept his hand under his robes, gripping his pistol. Ellie walked with more confidence, head held high, though her hood was pulled up to hide her mindcap.

The pair passed by a table where a dozen gruff, burly men sat. They wore no masks, revealing bearded, tattooed faces, the skin like old leather. One man was slamming a knife between his fingers. A few others were missing limbs; they wore metal prosthetics covered with spikes, and one had an actual rifle instead of an arm. They were all filthy and smelled like the sea. One man was missing an eye, and a little red finch nested inside the socket. The group paused to stare as Ellie and Kay walked by. One of the brutes spat at them.

"Sailors," Ellie whispered to Kay.

"Pirates?" Kay asked.

"Yes, but don't call them that." Ellie winked. "They're a bit sensitive."

"Oh, they look sensitive," Kay said. He watched one man crack open a goat's head on a tray, then scoop out a spoonful of brains. Another man was gnawing on a bone with sharpened, reptilian teeth. The man playing with the knife stabbed his finger, nearly severing it. His friends roared with laughter, and the wounded pirate soon joined them.

Leaving the sordid group behind, Ellie and Kay approached the bar. Most of the stools were taken. A portly man was shouting something about tariffs. A scarred dwarf scoffed, puffed on his cigar, and flipped off the larger man. One sailor sat slumped over his drink, sucking grog through a straw. He was missing all four limbs, and his prosthetics were just rusty iron rods. A topless woman gave Kay a wink. She wore prosthetic breasts on a harness, perhaps replacing ones the Party had removed.

"Silver coin for a trick?" the woman said.

"He's taken," Ellie said, clutching Kay's arm and pulling him along.

Finally they reached the end of the bar. A woman sat here alone, holding a pewter mug. Tattoos covered her arms, depicting sailed ships battling krakens, and an anchor pendant hung around her neck. She seemed to be in her late thirties. But maybe she was younger, and a life at sea had hardened her face, carving crows' feet around her dark eyes. She wore no mindcap, and her hair was long and black and braided. One side of her head was shaved, tattooed with a raven perched atop a skull. A heavy pistol with a wooden handle hung from her hip.

Several barstools were vacant around the woman, as if the other patrons were giving her space. Kay and Ellie sat down beside her. The woman ignored them. She took another sip of her drink.

A bartender approached, his gut straining a filthy wife-beater. His walrus mustache covered his lips, crusty with crumbs. A mask perched atop his head, crooked and just as grimy as the rest of him.

"Ellie!" the bartender said. He seemed to be smiling under his mustache, but it was hard to tell. "Good to see you again, sweetheart. How long has it been? A couple years now, hasn't it? How is the painting going?"

"Three years," Ellie said. "You have an impressive memory, ST670. I haven't painted anything in a while. But I see you still have the piece I painted for you."

Kay saw it now. A painting hanging over the bar. It featured two monkeys, mother and cub, among the branches.

"Call me Stan," the bartender said. "None of that ID nonsense in the Blue Oyster Club. Here's a little place we let our hair down. Not that I have much." He barked a laugh and tapped his bald head. "Who's your friend?"

"Somebody I trust," Ellie said. "Will you bring us a couple of grogs? The good stuff."

Stan barked a laugh. "Ah, clever girl. Yeah, I serve the turpentine to the brutes back there. You deserve the classier stuff. Brewed in my own sink!"

Looking at the bartender's filthy hands, Kay would hate to see that sink. But right now, his nerves were fraying, and his wounds ached something fierce. Anything that could dull his senses would be welcomed.

The bartender slapped down two dirty mugs, then filled them with grog—hopefully powerful enough to kill the millions of microorganisms who had undoubtedly made those mugs their homes. Kay took a sip and winced. It burned through his mouth and nostrils. He swallowed with an effort and coughed.

"Careful with that, buddy." The voice came from the shadowy corner, faintly accented. "Stan's Sink has a reputation around here. Men have been known to drink the brew, then wake up the next morning with their limbs rotting off."

Kay turned to look at the woman. She was still staring forward, nursing her own mug. The brew in there was different—darker, greener.

"The name's Kay." He reached out his hand for her to shake. "And this is Ellie."

The tattooed woman looked at him, sizing him up. She didn't shake his hand. "You look like shit."

"Well, I feel like shit too," Kay said. "Over the past few days, I got brain surgery, got shot twice, fell down a mountain, and jumped out of a moving truck. The grog helps, though."

The woman snorted, some of her intensity fading. She shook his hand.

"Isabelle Rodriguez," she said. Her accent intensified, as if speaking her name reminded her of home.

"Are you the captain of those boys back there?" Kay gestured with his thumb toward the table of pirates. The brutes were now playing a game of dice. One rolled snake eyes, roared, and punched another man. Both pirates crashed to the floor, punches flying, as the others laughed.

Isabelle snickered. "What's it to you?"

Ellie leaned closer, joining the conversation. "We're looking for passage east. No questions asked. Me, my friend, and the four at the table in the corner. We'll work for our passage."

Isabelle fixed the younger woman with a long, hard look.

For a moment, everyone was silent. Then the captain scoffed and sipped her drink.

"I've seen the likes of you before." Isabelle wiped suds off her lips. "Escapees trying to defect to Zion. Nah. I don't deal with your kind anymore. Too much trouble."

"We'll pay," Ellie said.

Isabelle cocked an eyebrow. "You lot don't look like you've got two silvers between you."

That wasn't far from the truth. The group had pitched in, emptying their pockets of coins. It didn't add up to much.

"We have seven hundred and twelve credits," Kay said.

Isabelle whistled. "And *twelve*? I'll be rich enough to buy the Father's golden mask!"

Kay rolled his eyes. "All right, so it's not a fortune. But we're hard workers. We'll clean. Cook. Do whatever we need to on the ship."

"You're heading east anyway," Ellie said. "I checked the docking logs. And no offense, Isabelle, but your crew looks useless. Most are missing half their limbs. All seem to be missing half their brains. You could use a proper crew for a voyage." She gestured behind her. "See that table? That's our group. The girl is quick and hardworking. The twins can clean and cook. And see that big, tattooed brute? His name's Adrian, and he's a mule. Used to work in the mines. He'll do whatever physical work you need."

Isabelle stared toward the back table. The group was busy drinking and bickering. Adrian and Tilly were both guzzling grog. The twins were sipping their tea, looks of disgust on their faces. Tilly noticed Isabelle staring and whispered something to the others. They all fell silent.

Isabelle regarded the group for a moment longer, then looked back at Ellie.

"You the leader of this group, kiddo?"

Ellie nodded. "Yes."

Kay couldn't argue with that. They had never officially chosen a leader, but if they had one, it was Ellie.

"Here's the deal." Isabelle emptied her mug, then pushed it aside. "Sell me the twins. And I'll take the rest of you to Zion."

Kay gasped. He leaped off his barstool. "Sell you the twins?"

His voice was too loud. From the back table, the twins looked up in alarm. They shivered and clung to each other.

"That's right." Isabelle nodded. "They're the ones I want. They're pretty enough. They still got their tits. And they're goddamn twins. They can entertain my crew. My boys sometimes go for months on a journey without women to warm their beds. The twins will serve nicely."

Back at the table, the others seemed to hear. Tilly moved ahead of the twins protectively. Adrian grumbled and stood up, fists clenched.

"Absolutely not!" Kay said. "We're not slavers."

"Everyone in this world is a slaver or a slave," Isabelle said. "Tell you what. I'll lease the twins. In seven years, I'll give 'em back. By then, they'll be worn out anyway."

Ellie's face flushed. She leaped off the barstool. "How can you treat other women this way?"

"Sweetheart, there ain't no more women or men." Isabelle tapped Ellie's head. The mindcap rang. "Your kind turned us into robots. Don't blame me for playing the game you created. Here's my final offer. Lease me your twins for five years. That's the lowest I'll go. The rest of you get a first class trip to the beautiful and sunny land of Zion."

"No!" Kay and Ellie said in unison.

Isabelle shrugged and lit a cigarette. "Oh well. Good luck finding another ship. Now get lost, I intend to get properly drunk tonight, and you're killing my buzz." She slammed her fist against the bar. "Stan, another mug!"

Kay's heart sank. He looked at Ellie. She was pale, silent.

"Ellie ..." Kay touched her hand. "You're not actually considering this, are you?"

"Of course not!" Ellie said. But her eyes darted. Her fingers nervously tugged at her cloak.

Heavy footsteps thumped across the concrete floor. A shadow fell. Adrian squeezed between them at the bar. The large, tattooed man gave Isabelle a hard look.

"I'll do it," he said. "Buy me. Same terms. Five years." Adrian's eyes were dark. "I ain't bedding no goddamn dirty pirates. But I'll work hard. I'll fight for you. Kill for you. Serve you. And you take my friends to Zion."

"Adrian, no!" Kay grabbed the man's shoulder, pulling him back from the pirate captain. "What the hell? We're not giving up anyone. We're in this together. We—"

"Yeah, yeah, I heard all your nice speeches, buddy." Adrian's eyes remained stony. "But if this gets the rest of you to Zion, I'll do it."

Kay gasped, speechless. Ellie stared with wide eyes.

Isabelle Rodriquez passed her eyes over the broad man, scrutinizing him from head to toes. She reached out, squeezed Adrian's biceps, then reached into his mouth and examined his teeth.

"You're a strong one," she said appreciatively. "Older than I normally like. But healthy. You got surgery on your legs, though. They're too short below the knees. How do you handle them?"

"I don't mind the pain," Adrian said. "I've felt pain all my life. Learned to deal with it."

Kay's head spun. He couldn't let this happen! Adrian was gruff, yes. Adrian was hostile. Sometimes violent. But he was a friend. A brother.

"I'll go." Kay stepped forward. "Take me instead."

Isabelle laughed. "No offense, compadre, but you look like a gust of wind could blow you over. *Dios mio*, you need a sandwich more than a gig on a ship."

"I'm strong," Kay said, voice low. "I've killed. Many times."

Isabelle looked into his eyes. She nodded. "Aye, maybe you did. I'm not saying you're mentally weak. There's something hard and cold in your eyes. But on a ship? Hell, I don't just need another killer. Got plenty of those. I want a goddamn mule who can lift crates, swing a hammer, and last for days without food during a hard voyage." She slapped Adrian's shoulder. "I'll take this one. Five year term. And you got your trip."

Tilly and the twins leaped forward. They embraced Adrian. They shed tears.

Adrian engulfed them with his large arms.

"Hush now," he whispered. "No tears."

Tilly wept. "Adrian, don't do this. You need to come with us."

He stroked the girl's short dark hair. "Ah, Tilly. You're so young. You still got your life ahead of you. And you, Li and Lei. You've suffered enough. You deserve joy."

"And you don't?" the twins whispered.

Adrian lowered his head. "I lost so much. My wife. My children. What waits for me in Zion? Nothing but ghosts. You go ahead. Build us a home there. In a few years—I'll join you. It will be nothing at all."

The bearded pirates stepped forward. One of them grinned, revealing only three rotten teeth. A one-eyed pirate hissed, revealing a forked tongue, and his pet finch retreated deeper into his eye socket. Two pirates—one covered in piercings, the other in ritualistic scars—raised chains. A third pirate, a man with only one leg and no nose, lifted a metal collar.

They chained Adrian. He stood, head held high, letting the pirates secure the manacles. They closed the collar around his neck. He was a slave. But his shoulders were squared, his back straight.

Tilly gave a huge sob. She ran forward to hug him, but the pirates yanked the chain, tugging Adrian back.

"No!" Tilly cried, leaping forward to attack the bearded men.

Kay had to grab the girl, to hold her back. She struggled in his grip, then finally relented and wept against Kay's chest.

They all put on their masks and robes. Eight pirates. Five defectors. One slave.

They walked across the boardwalk. The place was swarming with police and military. One equalizer stopped the group, and Isabelle brandished a bundle of papers—forged, Kay assumed.

"Here's my trading license, mux," she said. "And a little something for your trouble." She tossed him a few coins.

They walked the rest of the way unmolested. Isabelle led them down a pier toward her ship. It was an ugly thing, a flat rectangle of metal, covered with barnacles. The freighter was rusting and aged, barely afloat. It had no weapons that Kay could see. He hoped that Isabelle kept her weapons, like her profession, well hidden from the law.

"Welcome to the *Phantom*," Isabelle said. "My home."

Another equalizer approached. Isabelle showed her papers again. She paid another bribe. And a few minutes later, just like that, they were off.

They were sailing the ocean.

They were leaving the mainland of Isonomia behind.

Kay stood on the deck, watching the port become smaller and smaller. The factories, the walls, the old pain—shrinking. Fading. Becoming nothing but a cloud of smog, and then sinking below the horizon.

He walked to the prow of the ship. He stood at the balustrade, gazing ahead. The ocean spread for thousands of miles, a churning gray stew of pollution and plastic. But across it, Kay knew, it awaited. A golden dawn. A land of light. Zion.

Ellie came to stand beside him. She placed an arm around his waist and kissed his cheek.

"We're going home," she said.

Kay lowered his head. That memory was still there. As murky as this sea, and just as deep and terrible.

I'm leaving my son behind.

CHAPTER TWENTY-TWO

The *Phantom* plowed through an ocean of trash. An old ship of metal and rope, shoving through floating plastic bags and bottles, chemical foam, and globs of tar. The ocean was ugly. It smelled of decay. But Kay knew that beyond it lay the pristine wilderness, that place with red flowers.

"Hey, doofus. Chow time."

Something hot and wet hit the back of Kay's head. He turned from the porthole and faced the galley. Tilly was holding a spoon like catapult, already loading it with more gruel.

"All right, all right!" Kay said. "Don't waste food. Sheesh."

"I ain't wasting nothing." Tilly shrugged. "A rat's already eating it."

Kay saw the rodent grab the morsel and scurry away. He shuddered.

The galley was a large metal room in the bowels of the *Phantom*. The others—defectors and pirates alike—were all seated at the dining table. At least, what served as the *Phantom*'s dining table—an upside-down rowing boat. Kay just hoped it wasn't the ship's lifeboat. A meal was steaming on an assortment of metal and plastic plates: lumpy gruel, fried minced meat, and some deep-fried green stuff that Kay didn't recognize. The meal didn't look or smell appetizing, but it wasn't the main draw. The pirates were already cracking open bottles of grog.

"Hold on, nobody drink or eat yet!" Isabelle said. The pirate captain rose from her seat. She raised a bottle. "First we say grace."

A few pirates rolled their eyes. One rolled his glass eye so far it popped out, and the others roared with laughter.

"Silence!" Isabelle snapped. "We don't eat without giving thanks."

The room settled down. Everyone lowered their heads. Isabelle spoke.

"We thank our lord Nemo for this bounty. May he continue to bless us with his generosity, kindness, and vision. Though the evil of Nemesis covers the ocean surface, our lord Nemo protects the depths. Someday we will join his embrace, and we will sail aboard the mighty *Nautilus* through clear waters. Amen."

"Amen!" the pirates cried out.

"Now let's drink!" shouted one and opened a bottle.

Everybody began chowing down and guzzling grog. But Tilly frowned. The girl looked over her plate at Isabelle.

"Nemo?" she said. "The *Nautilus*? I read about them. They're from a novel. *20,000 Leagues Under the Sea.*"

Isabelle gulped down grog, then lowered her empty bottle. "Not a novel, little one, but our holy book. The sacred scripture reveals the wisdom of Lord Nemo."

Tilly's jaw dropped. She tilted her head, closed her mouth, and frowned.

Kay placed a hand on the girl's shoulder.

"We all need something to believe in," he said.

"Our lord Nemo is more than consolation in the ruin of the world," Isabelle said. "He's real. He's our lord. We don't question the holy book. Blessed be Nemo!" Her eyes shone with tears, and her voice choked. "I know that someday, after I die in battle, after I sink through the polluted waters, his submarine will be waiting. He will carry me into the *Nautilus*. He will revive me, and I will rise again. I will explore the depths forever. Fighting at Nemo's side."

Tilly's eyes softened. She raised her bottle of grog. "I'll drink to that."

They all drank. Kay even tried some of the fried green stuff. It wasn't bad.

He contemplated Isabelle's beliefs. Maybe Captain Nemo was only a fictional character. But then again, maybe Zion was just a story too. And that was a story Kay believed in. Had to believe in.

When the world lies in ruin, when everything that we thought true falls apart, all we have are stories. Even the fictional stories can give us hope, teach us truths, bring order to chaos.

"Someday you'll sail with Nemo, and I'll be in Zion," Kay said. "But I don't want to be a warrior. I don't want to explore. I just want a place where I can think. Where I can read. Where words and books and thoughts aren't forbidden. I saw a library once. Back in Isonomia. A library of forbidden books, of dangerous ideas."

Isabelle raised an eyebrow. "Sounds like you want to explore too. You just want to explore books. A different sort of ocean. But exploration nonetheless."

Tilly stared at her plate. She had eaten little. "I've been to a forbidden library before. I read a lot of books." She looked up, and her eyes shone. "In Zion, I want to write books of my own. To become a writer. I don't know if I have much to say. I'm not as smart as Ellie. I'm not as experienced as Isabelle. But I'll write my thoughts. About what happened to us. About where we came from." She looked at the floor and her voice softened. "And I won't be anyone's mate. I'll be free. Free to just be Tilly. A writer. A girl."

Kay looked at her, and he felt something soft and warm inside him. He remembered what Tilly had told them. How she had fled an older, cruel mate.

In Zion, you can be a girl, Kay thought. *You can still enjoy a few years of childhood in the sun.*

The twins sat at the far end of the table. Both had been quiet so far, as they usually were. But now Li spoke softly.

"In Zion, we'll have a little garden." She dared not raise her eyes, and her voice shook. "We'll grow tea. We'll open a little teashop. Just a quiet little place for a few friends."

Lei hugged her sister. She too spoke, voice just as soft. "We had to serve tea to Party men. Ministers. Generals. Cruel men who beat us. Who laughed. Who took us into their beds." Her tears flowed. "So in Zion, we'll serve tea again. But serve it without our bodies. Without our souls. It will be tea that heals."

The sisters embraced, whispering to each other.

"I'd like to try that tea of yours," Kay said. "I had tea once in Ellie's apartment. I'll be a regular customer, if you'll have me." He turned toward Ellie, reached under the table, and held her hand. "What about you, Ellie? What is Zion to you?"

Ellie squeezed his hand. Her blue eyes looked at him, so beautiful.

"Freedom," she said. "Freedom to be my own woman. Not the wife of a general. Not a toy or trophy. My life might be harder there. I won't be married to a rich, powerful man. I won't have the same luxuries as in Isonomia." She looked at the twins. "Li and Lei served me tea before. At galas my husband took me to. Nobody will serve me in Zion. And that's what I want." She wiped her eyes. "To pour my own tea."

One of the pirates frowned and turned toward his friend—a bearded brute with wooden teeth. "Why are these people so obsessed with tea?"

The other pirate shoved him, scattering lice. "It's metaphorical, you moron."

The door to the galley opened.

Adrian shuffled in, chains clattering. Sweat glistened on his body, and he carried a mop and bucket.

Kay winced to see his proud friend reduced to this. A slave mopping the deck. Guilt flooded him.

I've been sitting here, eating and drinking while Adrian toiled alone, in chains.

"Adrian!" Kay said. "Sit down. Eat. Drink with us."

The dour man stared at the table. For a moment, he seemed ready to turn and leave. But then Adrian sat down with creaking joints, grabbed a bottle with one hand, food with the other. The twins hurried toward him, mopped sweat off his brow, and served him more food and drink.

Adrian gulped down a piece of meat.

"You all can keep talking about Zion," he muttered. "It won't hurt my feelings."

Kay winced. "You'll get there too, my friend. In five years, you'll join us."

Adrian grunted and stuffed more meat into his mouth. "Hell, you wanna know what Zion means to me?" He gave the others a hard look.

They all stared back, silent, uncertain.

Adrian continued. "It don't mean shit. Not without my wife and kids."

The twins stroked his hair, whispered comforting nothings into his ears.

"Adrian, I'm sorry," Kay said.

Adrian snorted. "Spare me. I don't need no goddamn pity. I'm happier here in chains. Hell, I'm freer on this ship than I ever was back in goddamn Isonomia."

Kay stepped around the table. He placed his hand on Adrian's shoulder. "There will be a new life waiting for you in Zion. And we're your family."

"We're your family!" the twins said.

"A huge, big, dysfunctional family!" Tilly said. "And family never gives up. Family waits." She playfully punched Adrian. "We'll wait for you, big boy. We'll do all the hard work, building a big old house, planting a bunch of crops, and then you'll just waltz in and enjoy it all for free." She winked.

The bearded, lice-ridden pirate pulled out a handkerchief, wiped away tears, and blew his nose. "That's so beautiful." He turned toward his friend with the wooden teeth. "Why don't you ever tell me we're like family?"

Wood-mouth shoved him, scattering more lice. "We *are* family, you moron. You're my cousin."

The bearded pirate frowned. "I thought I was your nephew."

"You're both!" Wood-mouth slapped the back of the bearded pirate's head. "Moron."

Isabelle cracked open another crate of bottles. They all drank more grog.

Kay nursed his bottle. He looked at the others.

Family, he thought.

He too had lost his true family. Had lost most of his memories of them.

Maybe what I want is more than just books, he thought. *I want my memories. I want a family. If my old family is gone, let this be a new one.*

Ellie leaned against him, smiling. Under the table, she placed her hand on his thigh. Kay placed his hand on hers.

This is good, he thought. *This is family. This is love. May this never die.*

Yet as he looked out the porthole again, he wondered.

Was Zion no more real than Captain Nemo? Were they chasing an old story, just a dream?

He didn't know. But he vowed he would chase that dream around the world. And if he never found the promised land, he would still have the journey.

One of the pirates suddenly screamed and leaped to his feet, dropping his cigar. His beard had caught fire. The other pirates all roared with laughter. Wood-mouth laughed so loudly his prosthetic teeth flew from his mouth, clattered to the floor, and slipped through a crack to the deck below. This elicited even more laughter.

Kay sighed.

And at least I only have one fake tooth.

CHAPTER TWENTY-THREE

The *Phantom* sailed onward, and Kay lay in his cabin, holding the love of his life in his arms.

"We're almost there, Ellie." He kissed her lips. "We're almost home."

They had been sailing the ocean for two days now. Kay had spent most of them here in his cabin. There was little to see above deck. Just greasy pirates, smoggy skies, and miles of polluted water. But here in his cabin—a little corner of paradise. The cabin was small. The bulkheads were rusty. A strange smell rose from the pipes. It was little more than a prison cell, no better than his apartment back in Isonomia.

But Ellie shared this cabin with him. And to Kay, it made this space sweeter than any religion's description of heaven.

She lay beside him on the cot, naked, her body golden and warm. She had shaved her head that morning around her mindcap, leaving only golden stubble. It did not diminish her beauty. To Kay, she was the purest thing in his life. No machine implants could change that.

"I'm happy here with you," Ellie said, yet she seemed sad. "I almost don't want to reach Zion."

Kay frowned. "Why not? What do you mean?"

Ellie looked away. "I worry. About danger. About the war. About losing you."

Kay placed his hand on her hip. "I understand. We've lived in danger for so long. We're still scared. I am too. But we've come so far. We'll cross this final mile. We'll make it there." He kissed her cheek. "Our land of milk and honey."

A soft smile touched Ellie's lips. "Of tea. The milk and honey needs to go into tea."

"Of colors. Of all the colors in the world. I'll build you a house with a view, and you'll paint every day. You'll fill our house with color and light."

Ellie embraced him, clinging desperately. Tears filled her eyes. "I love you, Kay. No matter what happens. In heaven or in hell. I love you."

They kissed. And they made love again. Slowly. Then faster. Matching the waves of the ocean. If at first their lovemaking had been awkward, it had become a dance, an exploration of forbidden fire. When they climaxed together, he looked into her eyes, and he told her that he loved her. They lay together, holding each other, rocking on the ocean, making their way home.

She fell asleep in his arms. Kay looked at her, marveling at her beauty, the perfect shape of her lips, a creation of godly proportions, a work of art in a world of chaotic despair.

He looked away.

He looked out the porthole.

I'm sorry, he thought. *For those I left behind. For those I forgot. I can barely remember you, my Christine, my wife. I can only remember UV502, the ghost you became. I cannot remember you, my son. Not even your name. Only the sweet, milky smell as I held you for the first time. I don't know if you're alive or dead, my family. I don't know who I was. I'm sorry. I'm sorry that I betrayed you. Goodbye.*

The *Phantom* sailed onward. At midnight, a bell rang. A voice called out.

Isabelle opened the cabin door.

"I need you on deck," said the tattooed captain.

Kay bolted up in bed. "Is it an attack?"

Isabelle smiled. "Come take a look. We can finally see the lights of Zion."

CHAPTER TWENTY-FOUR

The passengers stood on deck, gazing at those distant lights in the darkness.

The lights of Zion.

A storm was brewing. Winds buffeted the *Phantom*, rocking the rusty old freighter. The rain poured, the drops thick with ash, painful where they struck bare skin. Lightning flashed and thunder boomed. But everyone was above deck. Nobody wanted to miss this.

There, past the sheets of rain, past the shrieking wind— Zion.

The twins embraced. Tilly stood atop a stack of crates, laughing and weeping, ignoring the storm that threatened to blow her overboard. Kay and Ellie held hands.

Adrian did not join them. He was a pirate now. More accurately—a slave to pirates. His chains jangled as he labored, cleaning the deck. But Kay saw that once, furtively, the tattooed man stared at the lights, then quickly looked away and returned to his work.

The pirates ignored the view. They must have sailed here often. A handful sat on the balustrade, drinking grog, storm and all. One even stood on the *Phantom*'s dragon-shaped figurehead, pissing into the rain. They might have seen Zion a thousand times. But the view brought tears to Kay's eyes.

"Is this really it?" he said. He huddled with Ellie by some crates, seeking shelter from the rain and wind. "Is this really Zion? Ellie, you've seen it before. Are we here?"

"This is Zion," she said, and her voice seemed lost in memory, her eyes gazing upon some past journey.

Yes, she's been here before, Kay thought. *On a campaign of war. Does this place still hold sadness for her?*

"Ellie." He held her hand. "Are we in danger here? How can we avoid the front line?"

She looked into his eyes. Her smile was sad. "The front line is long, and it's drenched in blood. Many battles rage across Zion's coast. Even now. But we'll make our way past the war. I'll guide you. Once we reach Jerusalem, we'll be safe."

"Jerusalem?" he asked.

Ellie had spoken that word in wonder. Kay repeated it almost as a whisper, a secret prayer.

"An ancient city on a desert mountain," Ellie said. "A city of copper and gold, of old stones and new life. That is the heart of Zion. The holy city. A city no enemy can touch. I've never been there. But I know that my husband has never been able to capture it. So that's where we'll go. That's where we'll defy him. That's where we'll find our new home."

Kay nodded. He spoke the name of that city softly, savoring it like the aromatic tea, like her love.

"Jerusalem …"

Isabelle walked by, her hair slick with rain, her copper earrings jangling. She spat, then gulped from a bottle of grog.

"We'll be there before dawn," the pirate captain said. "Those lights are White Army. We'll be moving south in the darkness and rain, well hidden. We'll dock south from them, and you'll be on your own. Just remember that—"

She fell silent.

She frowned.

"What?" Kay said.

The captain hushed him. She tilted her head.

Kay heard it then.

A roar through the storm. A whirring above.

Kay had heard this sound before.

"Helicopters!" he shouted.

They emerged from the clouds like angels of death. Metallic beasts of shrieking fury. Painted white. Shards of gleaming bone in the rain. Three of them, diving through the storm, their rotor blades churning the clouds and scattering the rain in circular arcs like glistening galaxies.

They were beautiful. They were gods of vengeance.

Their hatches opened like mouths. Ropes unfurled toward the *Phantom* like tongues.

"Fire!" Isabelle shouted. "Fire, dammit!"

She pulled a pistol from her belt and fired skyward. Her crew knelt on the deck, firing rifles, pistols, even a flamethrower.

From above they descended. Coated in armor. A hundred soldiers or more. They were warriors of the White Army, but they wore black, ghosts in the night. They were climbing down the ropes, guns in hand, helmets hiding their faces.

The fusillade from below sparked against armor, doing little harm. The soldiers were only meters away from the *Phantom*'s deck now.

Kay narrowed his eyes, gun in hand. Instead of aiming at the soldiers, he fired at a rope.

His first two shots missed. The third tore through the rope, and several soldiers tumbled and crashed onto the deck.

Before they could rise, Kay fired again. Again. His blast knocked one soldier overboard, and the armored warrior vanished into the dark ocean.

A megaphone blared above.

"Lay down your weapons!" boomed a voice. "Resist and you will all die!"

Soldiers landed on the deck. They raised their rifles, advancing. The storm intensified. The wind shrieked and the ship tilted. The rain slammed down in a fury. Lighting flashed, illuminating the soldiers like shards of obsidian. In the split second of illumination, Kay saw the forms of warships in the ocean. Moving closer. Three hulking machines of metal.

He moved closer to Ellie. She stood at his side, clutching a pistol with both hands. The twins and Tilly moved in behind them, weaponless.

"Lay down your guns!" sounded the voice again.

Kay knew what laying down weapons meant. He had already spent eight years in a reeducation camp. This time, they would send him there for life.

So he fought.

He fought for Ellie.

For Zion.

He fought because he could not die now. Not so close to the promised land.

Around him, the others—defectors and pirates alike—fought with just as much fervor. Everyone who had a gun was firing. Bullets sparked against the soldiers' armor, knocking several down. Adrian had no gun, but he swung his chains like a whip, shattering a soldier's visor. Tilly and the twins were swinging oars. They ganged up on one soldier, slamming their oars down again and again, finally knocking their opponent overboard.

The soldiers abandoned their plan to arrest the dissidents.

They opened fire.

Bullets streamed through the darkness. Kay shoved Ellie down, protecting her with his body. A bullet grazed his arm, and he grunted. A pirate fell beside them, three holes in his chest. The twins were screaming. Blood flowed across the deck, mingling with the rainwater.

"Stop this!" Ellie shouted. "Stop this madness, soldiers!"

Nobody listened. The bullets still flew, carving lines of light through the storm. A pirate fell overboard, neck spraying blood. One of the twins fell to the deck, clutching a bullet wound. Her sister cried out, kneeling over her, trying to stop the bleeding.

No.

Kay stood up. He raised his gun.

I do not die today.

Three soldiers advanced toward him.

Kay loaded a fresh magazine, aimed, and fired.

His bullets shattered one soldier's visor. Broken teeth flew.

The second soldier fell, then the third—but not from Kay's bullets.

Isabelle rose from below deck, a mad grin stretching her cheeks. She was firing a machine gun, laughing, mowing soldiers down.

Her pirates rallied around her, blasting the enemy. One pirate fired a bazooka at the sky, and an explosion rocked a helicopter. Soldiers thumped onto the deck, some dead, others convulsing and screaming. Tilly ran, began beating the wounded soldiers with her oar.

Kay loaded another magazine. He was running low on ammo. Lightning flashed again, showing the three warships closer now. Surrounding the *Phantom*. More soldiers kept descending, guns blazing. A pirate fell, his face blown open. Wooden teeth scattered. Bullets tore the legs off a second pirate, and the man crashed down, screaming. The canary fled from his empty eye socket, vanishing into the storm.

"Soldiers, enough!" Ellie straightened and raised her arms. "I am LE905, mated to General EQL61! I command you—stop!"

The soldiers only laughed. They kept advancing. One of the warriors raised a megaphone. Xe spoke in a deep, distorted voice through xer helmet.

"Ah, the general's little trophy wife. We don't serve your husband. We're the White Navy. And we'll have our fun."

More bullets flew. More corpses thudded onto the deck—both soldiers and pirates.

Li howled—a torn, agonized sound. The sound of a heart breaking.

Kay spun toward the horrible noise. He stared and his own heart broke.

Li was holding her twin sister. Lei had several bullet wounds in her chest. Her eyes stared lifelessly.

"Lei!" Li wept, pulling her dead sister to her chest. "Lei, my sister!"

A bullet tore through Li's head, silencing her.

Both twins slumped onto the deck, holding each other in death.

Kay stared in shocked silence. The twins lay still, blood flowing.

More bullets flew. One slammed into Adrian, and he fell, bellowing, blood gushing from his hand. A massive wave tilted the freighter. Adrian slid across the deck, leaving a bloody trail, and disappeared behind a pile of crates.

The last surviving pirates began to flee. Some scurried below deck. Others jumped overboard and began to swim. Among the pirates, only Isabelle remained to fight. Her machine gun was out of ammo. The pirate captain was now firing her pistol, refusing to flee.

And still soldiers kept coming.

Kay knelt behind a few crates, pulling Ellie down with him. But she shook herself free. She rose and began walking across the deck—toward the bullets.

"Ellie!" Kay cried, trying to grab her. But bullets flashed between them, driving him back.

As Ellie walked through the storm, her mindcap ignited.

Blue lights shone on her head, a beacon in the darkness.

Bullets streaked around her, sparking on the deck around her feet. None hit. Perhaps the soldiers were missing on purpose, hesitant to kill a general's wife. But watching from behind the crate, it seemed to Kay that Ellie had become a godly figure, a being of light and miracles whom no weapon could hurt.

As she approached the soldiers, they began to fall.

The soldiers clutched their heads, screaming, writhing.

Ellie kept advancing. Gazing forward calmly. Her steps graceful.

More soldiers fell, dropping their guns. A few tore off their helmets, clawed at their mindcaps. The metal domes were buzzing, sparking with electricity, burning the men's heads.

Ellie was bleeding now. Blood poured from her nostrils. From her ears. But she kept walking. Her mindcap kept shining. All around her, the soldiers fell. One managed to rip off a chunk of his mindcap, scalping himself, screaming. Another soldier leaped into the water, only for the electricity to spark with more vigor.

"Blimey, she's killing them!" Tilly whispered. She knelt by Kay behind the crates, clutching her wounded leg.

Adrian joined them. A bullet had mangled his hand, taking three fingers. He stared at the scene, eyes hard.

Ellie reached the prow of the *Phantom*. Lightning flashed again and again, illuminating her form. Around her, the last soldiers had fallen. They lay trembling on the deck.

Before her rose the enemy warships.

"Leave this place!" Ellie shouted. "These are not your people to torment!"

Another bolt of lightning. The warships were closer now. Looming over the *Phantom*. Their cannons pointing at Ellie.

Kay tried to run to her again. Adrian grabbed him, pulled him back. Kay struggled to free himself, but Adrian held him fast, even using just one hand.

"Let her do her thing, brother," Adrian said, voice low and gruff. "We can't help her now."

The warships rose and fell in the storm. Hundreds of armored soldiers stood on their decks, guns in hand.

You can't shock them all, Ellie, Kay thought.

Already blood was streaming down Ellie's face. Kay knew how her power weakened her. He knew controlling so many other mindcaps could kill her.

"Turn back now!" Ellie shouted. "That is my order! The order of a general's wife!"

A sailor fired.

The bullet sparked onto the deck near Ellie's feet. Perhaps a warning shot. Maybe just a shot that missed. Kay tried to run to her again, but Adrian still held him back.

Ellie climbed over the balustrade circling the deck. She clung to the railing, took a deep breath, then stepped onto the *Phantom*'s figurehead. It thrust out from the prow—an iron dragon, slick with rain. Ellie walked along the figurehead like walking along a balance beam. She stopped on the dragon's head, alone in the rain. The ocean churned below her.

She raised her arms. Lightning flashed around her. She seemed a goddess risen from storm.

"I am LE905!" she cried. "I am the mate of EQL61! I will lead these people to Zion!"

Her mindcap exploded with light.

Electricity raced down her body and into the figurehead beneath her feet. The iron dragon lit up. Electricity crackled across the beast, filling the metal jaws, igniting the eyes, spreading luminous wings. The dragon roared out electric fury like dragonfire. The storm of lightning branched out, hitting dozens of soldiers on the enemy warships.

Soldiers fell.

Hundreds crashed down onto their decks.

Thunder boomed.

Across the distance, Ellie turned to look at Kay. As if by divine providence, the rain stopped. A beam of moonlight fell on Ellie, and she gave Kay a soft smile.

"I love you," she said.

Then blood was pouring from her eyes. And she fell.

She crashed into the ocean.

"Ellie!" Kay screamed.

He finally managed to tear himself free from Adrian. He ran, slipped on blood, rose and ran again. He reached the prow, leaped over the balustrade, and dived.

He slammed into the icy water.

He dived through plastic, froth, and oil. He sank into the murky blackness.

"Ellie!" he cried, voice emerging with a cloud of bubbles.

He kept his eyes open, even as the polluted water stung. He tried to see her, to catch a glimpse of her glowing mindcap. He saw nothing. Nothing but clouds of plastic bags, bottles, rusty cans.

"Ellie!" he shouted again. His lungs ached for air. He tasted the salty filth of the ocean. His arms pumped, and his legs kicked, and he swam deeper, reaching out in the darkness, feeling for her.

She wasn't there.

She was gone.

But Kay kept swimming deeper.

Then I'll die with you. I won't leave you, Ellie. I won't leave you!

His heart pounded. His eyes burned, blinded. His lungs were screaming for air. He was close to passing out.

Ellie! Ellie, where are you?

Something grabbed his foot.

A force yanked him upward.

Kay struggled against it, trying to swim deeper, but the grip was too strong. Somebody or something was pulling him up. Kay fought. But the force was relentless. He saw a figure in the dark water. A man. Tugging him upward.

After what seemed like an eternity, Kay burst through the surface of the ocean. He gasped, gulping air with a horrible raspy sound. He coughed in a fit.

Adrian was holding him, dragging him through the water.

"Ellie!" Kay shouted.

"Shut up!" Adrian said. "You almost got yourself—and me!—killed. Shut up and swim!"

Adrian was still bleeding from the ruin of one hand. But he was gripping Kay with the other hand, pulling him along. The warships were still there. A handful of survivors stood aboard the *Phantom*, huddling in the rain. The ship was listing, taking on water fast. Tilly stood on the deck alongside a few remaining pirates.

"Why are you saving me?" Kay said.

"You are my brother." Adrian gripped him more tightly. "Now shut up and live!"

They were swimming toward the *Phantom* when something scuttled beneath them, rippling the water.

Kay stared at his friends aboard the *Phantom*.

The shape stormed toward them like a shark, carving a path through the trash.

"Torpedo!" Kay shouted. "Jum—"

The torpedo hit the *Phantom*.

An explosion lit the night.

Metal shattered.

The *Phantom* cracked in two, the deck shattering.

"Tilly!" Kay cried.

The burning halves of the ship overturned. People, shards of metal, and crates splashed into the water. The *Phantom* blazed, a great pyre, its flames rising like a demon into the sky.

Kay and Adrian swam through the debris. Crates floated around them. Scattered fires burned across the water. Smoke filled the air, and they couldn't see more than a few feet ahead.

"Tilly!" Kay shouted again.

Adrian growled. "Shut up! You'll bring the soldiers right to us."

Kay grabbed the man. They floated through the pile of plastic bottles, bags, crates, and twisted metal. "We have to save Tilly! She's the last one of us alive."

"She's gone too!" Adrian said. "We can swim to the shore. Come on!"

"No." Kay wrenched himself free. "We lost the twins. We lost Ellie. We lost Ginsburg and Tenzin and Pat and so many others." His voice caught, and he took a shuddering breath. "We're not losing Tilly. We are not losing her!"

He swam away from Adrian. Away from the coast of Zion. He swam toward the burning hulk of the *Phantom*.

A machine gun roared. Bullets pierced the film of garbage. Kay dived underwater. He swam a few feet, rose again, gulped air, and looked around. He saw scraps of metal, burning crates, and mutilated corpses. More bullets flew. Kay sank again, and bullets pierced the water around him, tearing through the sea of trash.

He swam closer, rose for air, and found himself in an inferno. The flames rose everywhere. Burning wreckage surrounded him in a ring of hellfire. The shattered bulkheads of the *Phantom* rose from the water like a blazing city.

There, in the center, she floated.

Tilly.

She was clinging to a crate with one hand. Only that hand and her face emerged from the water. Her eyes were fluttering. She was slipping.

Kay swam.

Tilly let go, vanishing underwater.

Kay swam harder. Driving forward. Ignoring the pain. He passed through fire, dived underwater, reached down—and grabbed her wrist.

He rose for air, pulling Tilly up with him.

Her eyelids fluttered. She coughed up water, then gulped down air.

Kay exhaled in relief. His tears flowed.

Ellie is gone. But I saved a life. Oh God, I saved a life.

"Tilly, can you dive with me?" he said.

She looked into her eyes. She was bleeding. Her skin was ashen; he could see that even in the firelight. But she nodded.

They took deep breaths. They dived underwater, and Kay pulled Tilly under the fire and between the bulkheads. They rose for air. Dived again. Swam through the darkness and firelight. Kay glimpsed the warships moving, plowing through the wreckage of the *Phantom*. The mangled metal and crates rose and fell on the waves. The rain intensified, putting out the fires, and black smoke hovered over the water. Kay and Tilly coughed, blinded.

Another torpedo streamed underwater.

What remained of the *Phantom* exploded.

Fire blasted skyward. A great wave rose, lifting Kay and Tilly. From its crest, Kay could see figures in the distance. A handful of people clinging to crates. Then the wave crashed, and smoke rolled over the water, and metal shards rained around him, pattering against the trash.

Kay was weak. Bleeding. His lungs and eyes burned. Everything ached, and invisible claws seemed to grab him, to try pulling him underwater.

Kay wanted to sink.

To let the pain end.

To join Ellie in the depths.

Oh God. Oh Ellie. I can't go on. I can't go on without you.

But Tilly coughed, weak, maybe dying. Tilly needed him.

Kay swam. With all the strength left in him, he swam through the agony, through the hellfire, pulling Tilly along. He swam blindly, but he reached the other survivors.

There were so few. Adrian. Isabelle. Three other pirates. They clung to crates, barely alive, floating under the smoke.

That was all.

The twins—gone. Ellie—gone.

Kay pulled Tilly onto a crate. She lay there, coughing, bleeding.

And again, Kay wanted to sink.

There's no more point to life. Not without you, Ellie.

"Come on, we'll swim under the smoke," Adrian said. "We'll swim to shore. We can make it in the darkness. Hurry!"

And Kay knew he had a choice.

He could give up now. He could die. The pain would end. Or he could live.

He could live for her. For Ellie. He could make her sacrifice mean something.

Ellie's voice seemed to rise from the murk.

Don't let my death be in vain.

His family rose before him in the shadows.

Live for us. Don't let all this pain be for nothing.

Kay didn't know if he had the strength. If he had the will to live. But he would do it for them. Not for himself. For those he loved. For the fallen. And for the living who still needed him.

You led us, Ellie, and you sacrificed yourself for us, Kay thought. *I'm not a leader like you. But so long as I live, I will fight for others.*

He clung to a crate, and he paddled with his legs.

He drove himself forward.

The others swam with him. Their crates were broken, barely more than slats of wood. They were the boats that would take them to the promised land.

They swam through smoke, fire, and darkness. They emerged from the devastation and floated through the piles of garbage. Soon they were swimming in complete darkness. Smoke hid the sky, and the rain extinguished the fire. They navigated by the lights of the coast, moving south, moving away from those lights, staying hidden in the cloak of night.

Hours passed.

They kept swimming. They kept bleeding. They kept *living*.

The waves lifted them. In the dawn, the ocean cast them onto the shore.

The sun rose behind the smog and smoke. The survivors lay on a beach of tar and broken glass. They crawled, clinging to life, coughing, trembling. Rocks rose around them, and oily seagulls cawed. Chunks of twisted metal and bare bones littered the beach.

They had reached Zion. And it was beautiful.

Kay laid his head on the sand, closed his eyes, and wept for his loss.

CHAPTER TWENTY-FIVE

Run.

Run faster.

Hide.

Survive.

The survivors made their way across the hard, lifeless landscape of Zion. Three defectors from Isonomia, the last who still lived. Four pirates, their ship gone. They moved fast and hard, even as their wounds blazed, as their bodies begged to fall.

This land was swarming with the White Army.

This land meant death.

Kay had imagined a land of milk and honey. A land overflowing with life. What he found was a wasteland. An unforgiving desert. Craters pocked the land, their blackened centers filled with artillery shrapnel. Charred bones lay in the sand, tripping the survivors like skeletons reaching from the grave. Mangled machines lay everywhere, burnt, twisted. Most were unrecognizable. Some appeared to be the shells of jeeps, tanks, planes. Some hid skulls within their burnt hulls.

A rumble above.

Kay looked up and winced. He had spent his life under the smog of Isonomia. But the sky of Zion was so bright. Searing blue, the sun a blazing disk. He stared through the pain.

His heart almost stopped.

"Plane!" he said. "White Army! Hide!"

He ran. The others followed. Tilly was limping, fell, and cried out. Kay lifted her, ran with the girl in his arms. He ignored the agony in his shortened legs. The pirates drew their weapons, but Kay shook his head.

"Don't fight—hide!" Kay said. "In that old tank!"

They ran toward the twisted wreck. The metal was rusty, falling apart. Holes peppered the tank's hull. They climbed in, and Kay winced as rusty metal scraped his limbs.

They knelt inside the tank, hidden from the sky. Spiders fled from the eye sockets of skulls. The skeleton of a gunner fell apart, spilling bones, helmet, and rusty weapons.

The roar above intensified. The plane flew overhead. Kay had seen it clearly enough. A war plane. Painted white. Emblazoned with a red equal sign, a star in the middle. The quelis, symbol of Isonomia.

"Goddammit!" Adrian said, crouching inside the tank. He looked at a fresh cut on his arm, filled with rust, and spat. "I'm used to fleeing damn equalists in Isonomia. Not here in goddamn Zion."

The survivors huddled together, even after the plane's rumbling faded. Tilly was hugging her knees, staring blankly at the dented hull. Captain Isabelle was staring at the ground, eyes hard. The other pirates—three had survived the battle at sea—were passing around a bottle of grog. The spiders crept back into the skulls, already accustomed to their visitors.

Kay looked at the survivors. People who needed him.

Ellie is gone. A lump filed his throat. *I must lead them now.*

"This is the front line," Kay said. "The battlefield between Isonomia and Zion. So yes, it's ugly. It's dangerous. But we're almost through. Ellie told me before she died." He had to pause for a moment, to steel himself. "She was going to lead us to Jerusalem. A city on a mountain. A city of peace and light and gold. There's no war there. That's where we must go."

Adrian snickered. But it sounded almost like a sob. "Sounds awfully familiar, brother. Just a little farther. Cross one more hurdle. And we're in paradise. First it was Zion. Now it's Jerusalem. What's next? If you ask me, it's just more bullshit talk of utopias. And I've had enough of utopias for a lifetime." He gestured around him. "What if Zion is all like this? Just rusty metal and spiders and skulls."

"Ellie wouldn't have led us to a wasteland," Kay said.

Adrian rolled his eyes. "Your precious Ellie was full of shit."

Kay roared.

Before he could stop himself, he lunged at Adrian, barreled into the larger man, and slammed him against the tank hull.

"Take that back, you son of a bitch!" Kay shouted.

Adrian fought back, even with one mutilated hand. He shoved Kay, knocking him back. He delivered a punch to Kay's cheek. Not a powerful blow. But enough to ring Kay's head like a bell.

"Your love blinds you, brother!" Adrian said. "Ellie was nothing but a dreamer. Just a goddamn dreamer like you. But the dream is a nightmare."

Kay leaned back against the tank hull, his strength gone. Adrian slumped down too, breathing heavily, his mutilated hand bleeding again.

Kay looked at the others. They were all staring back. He saw the doubt in their eyes.

"What if Adrian is right?" Tilly whispered. A tear drew a white path down her grimy cheek. "What if this is all there is? Just a wasteland of craters and bones?"

"I don't believe that," Kay said. "We've seen White Army barracks on the shore. We've seen their warships. Their planes. Why would the White Army have so many forces in a wasteland? There's more to Zion than this. We'll make our way to Jerusalem.

Like Ellie wanted. We'll survive. Don't lose hope. We've come this far. We're almost home."

They emerged from the burnt tank. They kept traveling across the land. Seven ragged survivors. Covered in filth. Bandaged and bleeding.

Has there ever been a more pathetic group? Kay thought. Then he realized: Yes. Everyone back in Isonomia. Millions of souls in masks and robes, marching like robots.

We're wounded, filthy, hungry, pathetic. But we're free.

As he walked around another artillery crater, pain stabbed Kay.

My family is still behind.

A memory. A new memory flashed through him.

Sitting at a table. His beautiful Christine smiling. His son eating solid food for the first time. The smell of oatmeal. Not an apartment. Not a concrete cell in City58OI. A distant house. A home. Happy. Safe.

Since removing his mindcap several days ago, the memories had been getting stronger. But still maddeningly illusive.

In the afternoon, they climbed rocky hills, and they saw a military barracks in the distance. The banners of the White Army rose there. Their armacars rumbled across the desert, raising clouds of sand. Hundreds of their troops were marching down a desert road.

Kay led his group into a cave. They huddled in the shadows, waiting for night to fall before they moved again. A few cracked pots, rusty old guns, and skeletons shared the cave with them. They spent a cold, miserable few hours here, hungry and thirsty, nursing their wounds.

Kay's own wounds were infected. The hole on his shoulder was leaking pus, and he could barely move his arm. With shaking hands, he popped open his box of antibiotics. Only five pills remained.

"Hey, give me that!" One of the pirates advanced toward Kay, growling. His wild beard stuck out in every direction, and he was missing several teeth. He reached for the bottle with a grimy hand.

Kay pulled the bottle back. "Your wounds aren't that bad."

The pirate growled. "I need it. I got an itch in my crotch."

"That's not my problem." Kay rose to his feet. His head grazed the top of the cave. "We need to ration these pills."

Another pirate stepped forward. This time it was Captain Isabelle, and her hand rested on her pistol. "Does that mean only you get to take them, Ghost?" She had come to call Kay that due to his pale skin.

"Those who are most wounded," Kay said. "I have two bullet wounds. Cuts all over my body. Goddamn holes in my goddamn skull. I'm taking one of these." He looked around at the group. "And Adrian is taking one. He lost three fingers. And Tilly needs a pill. Her leg is bad."

"I don't need one," Adrian said. "Give mine to the girl."

"What about my crotch?" the bearded pirate demanded, lowering his breeches to reveal a malodorous infection.

"Ugh, cover that thing!" Isabelle said. "Nobody wants to see it."

"I don't need a pill either," Tilly said, but her face was pale, and she was trembling and clutching her wounded leg. A bullet had grazed her thigh back at the zipline. The wound was getting worse. Festering.

"You're taking one," Kay said. "Hell, you're taking them all, Tilly." He handed her the bottle. "One a day. You're the youngest. And you're the weakest. You need these most."

"I'm not weak!" the girl said, but her voice was reedy, and sweat beaded on her brow.

"I know." Kay wiped her forehead. "But it'll keep us dumb ugly brutes from fighting over these." He looked at the others. "Besides, one pill won't do nothing to an infection. If we share, it'll be a waste. But five pills—those might give somebody a fighting chance. So let's give Tilly that chance."

The pirates grumbled, but they backed down. Adrian sat in the shadows, muttering, staring at the stone wall. The three male pirates began to drink, gamble, and sing dirty limericks—at least until Isabelle hushed them with a flourish of her knife.

After the sun set, they dared emerge from the cave. They could still see the lights of the distant barracks, but the soldiers and jeeps were gone. Kay led the group across the hills. He had hoped for complete darkness, but a strange, shimmering disk shone above. It was silver, the size of the sun, its light soft. Was this some strange aircraft of the enemy's? Perhaps a great flare? Kay cowered before this celestial spotlight.

But Tilly stood straight, eyes wide with wonder. She tilted back, admiring the light above.

"The moon," she whispered. She turned toward the others and smiled shakily. "It's the moon."

Kay frowned. "What the hell is the moon?"

"I've read about it in my books," Tilly said. "You could never see it in Isonomia. Not with all the smog. Only pale smudges sometimes. The dimmest light. Nothing like this."

Kay straightened, some of his fear leaving him. He stared up at that luminous disk, frowning. "What is it?"

"I don't know," Tilly confessed. "I've read different accounts. One book said the moon is a man's face in the sky. Another book said it's made of cheese. I read one book that claimed it's a giant floating boulder, and that men once flew there and walked on it."

All those explanations sounded ridiculous to Kay.

"So long as it's not a weapon of the enemy," he said.

"It's not." Tilly gazed at the moon, tears sparkling in her eyes. "It's something good. Something beautiful. A sign of hope."

"It's a sign that we're too exposed, even in the night," Kay said. "But we have no choice. We move onward. To Jerusalem."

They walked, sticking to the shadows behind the hills, giving the barracks a wide berth. Kay tried to walk confidently, even with the pain in his legs. The others followed, tacitly accepting his leadership. Kay didn't reveal the truth: that he didn't know the way. None of them had been to Zion before. Even Isabelle had only seen the coast, never walked on Zionite soil.

But Kay knew they had to get deeper inland. Out of the front line. Away from the hordes of equalist soldiers.

Finally, Tilly broke the silence.

"Where are all the Zionites?" she said.

Kay stared at her in the moonlight. "Inland. It's dangerous for them here."

Tilly bit her lip, looking around. "But if this is the front line, where are the Zionite soldiers?"

"Maybe they're hiding inside burnt tanks and caves," Adrian quipped.

Kay said nothing.

They walked onward in silence.

In the night, they passed by several more barracks. Even in the moonlight, they could see the banners. Equalist banners.

They walked onward for hours.

"How far are we from Jerusalem?" Tilly asked. Her voice was weak and she was limping again.

"Close," Kay said.

Adrian grumbled. "Do you even know the way?"

Kay sighed. "No," he confessed. "But hold on! Listen to me. If we can find a Zionite unit, even just a single platoon, they can help us. They'll help defectors. They'll show us the way."

"But there aren't any Zionites here!" Tilly said. Suddenly she sounded very young. "We've been here for a day and night. We've crossed many miles. We haven't seen any Zionites other than skeletons. Kay—what if they lost the war? What if they're all dead?"

The others voiced their agreements. The pirates muttered something about scalping Kay and eating his flesh. Adrian was grumbling again, something about how Ellie had led them to a graveyard.

"They're not all dead!" Kay said. "Ellie would have known. She warned us that we have to get past the front line first. We'll find Jerusalem. Come on, friends. We're almost there."

The moon was low in the sky when they reached an old battlefield. Thousands of burnt vehicles littered the desert, spreading to the horizon. Tanks. Armored troop carriers. Crashed airplanes. Kay had never imagined an army could be this large. The wreckage seemed ancient. The vehicles were almost unrecognizable, just rusty, burnt husks of metal. There were skeletons too, their bones scattered, some barely more than dust. Thousands. Tens of thousands of skeletons. They lay everywhere, many half-buried in the sand, still wearing helmets, some still clutching old guns.

Kay could make out symbols on some of the rusty helmets.

Pomegranates. Symbols of Zion.

"What the hell happened here?" Adrian muttered, walking among the dead.

"My guess—and I'm not certain, this is just wild speculation—is that a battle was fought here," Kay said.

Adrian snorted. "Funny. I mean—why the hell didn't the Zionites bury their dead?" He kicked a skull. Centipedes fled from the sockets. "These bones are old. Years old. Hell, maybe centuries old."

"Show the dead more respect," Kay said.

Adrian swept his arms around him. "Lots of respect here, all right. Left to rot in the desert."

"They're dead," Tilly whispered.

Kay placed a hand on her shoulder. "I know, Tilly."

She sniffed. "I don't just mean these skeletons. I mean all the Zionites. They're all dead. We're too late. Zion lost the war. The entire nation was wiped out."

Kay wanted to contradict her. But he only bit his lip. His own doubt was creeping.

"We have to keep going," he said.

"Why?" Tilly insisted. "Why keep going? This land is dead! Zion lost!"

They were all looking at Kay. The pirates reached for their weapons, as if ready to kill Kay if he argued.

Kay took a deep breath.

"We have to keep going," he said, "because we have nowhere else to go. What else can we do? Return to the sea? We have no ship. Surrender to the White Army? They'll torture us."

"We'll sneak past them," Isabelle said. It was the first time the captain had spoken all night. "We'll steal a ship. Sail the ocean again. Get back to a good life of piracy." She muttered curses. "I had a good life before meeting you bastards."

"The coast is too dangerous," Kay said. "Stealing a ship from the White Army? What if they take us alive? They tried to take us alive on the *Phantom*. If they do—they'll torture us. Leave us to rot in a cell. Or worse—send us to a reeducation camp. So we keep going. Until Jerusalem. Until the very end."

"And if Jerusalem is a graveyard too?" Adrian said, voice low.

Kay looked at the moonlit horizon. "I still believe. That Jerusalem is real. Waiting for us. Full of life and hope. I still trust Ellie, and she believed." He turned back toward the others. "If you don't want to join me, you can attack the White Army. You have a few guns, a few blades. Maybe you'll kill one or two soldiers before they kill or capture you. But I'm going onward. And whoever still believes, still hopes—come with me."

They kept walking. Dawn rose in the east, and Kay walked toward the rising sun, wanting to head farther from the western shore. It was their second day without food and water, and Kay knew that very soon, thirst and hunger would become a serious threat. They had no choice but to keep going.

The battlefield stretched for miles. Hot winds rose with the dawn, blowing clouds of sand. Every gust buried some skeletons and revealed others. The sand stung the defectors' skin. They wrapped their shirts around their faces, struggling forward through the storm. As the sand blinded him, Kay missed the lightning storm at sea.

They passed by massive machines in the sand. Some were cannons, their bores large enough that men could climb inside. Others were gargantuan airplanes, some nearly as large as the *Phantom*. Time had done its work. Rust covered most of these machines of war. But Kay could make out logos on them. Some machines displayed the quelii of Isonomia, but most sported the pomegranates of Zion.

Kay had never seen machines of war this large. Not back in Isonomia. Not among the barracks along Zion's coast. Airplanes the size of cargo ships? Cannons the size of buildings? These seemed like weapons from a long-gone era.

We can no longer build machines this large, Kay thought. *Maybe the war impoverished both sides. We're fighting with our last scraps of cruelty.*

The wind intensified, raising demons of sand. They trudged onward, leaning forward, and passed by a rusty machine on caterpillar tracks. It rose several stories tall, its hull poked with holes. Cannons stuck out from the machine, attached to gears the size of apartments. The shells must have been the size of cars.

Great metal jaws thrust out from the behemoth, a decaying hellmouth built to devour mountains.

This seemed to Kay almost like the skeleton of some ancient metal monster, a beast that had tormented the world. A gust of wind blew back sand, revealing crushed skulls around the treads. Kay could imagine this great contraption plowing across the countryside, cracking the earth, crushing tanks and jeeps beneath it, mowing through enemy troops. He shuddered.

Rumbling sounded on the wind.

A smell of gasoline hit Kay's nostrils.

He turned toward the sound. In the distance, waves of sand were storming forward.

Vehicles. Moving fast.

Kay grabbed Adrian and pointed. The tattooed man nodded. The others joined them, staring at the approaching clouds.

"White Army," Kay said, looking around for a place to hide. "Into this big lumbering machine. We can squeeze through that hole."

They climbed into the behemoth, suffering more scrapes. A piece of metal bit Kay's thigh, filling the wound with rust. He ignored it and helped the others climb in.

On the inside, the machine was the size of a truthhall. Sand covered the deck, forming small dunes. The wind shrieked through holes in the hull, ruffling the dunes, revealing buried skeletons. Ladders clung to the hull, half their rungs missing. Chains dangled from a metal ceiling high above, and hatches led to gunnery stations. The remnants of a massive engine rusted in the sand, as large as a house, home to lizards and mice.

The rumbling engines grew louder outside. Sand flew through the holes in the behemoth's hull.

Then the engines outside died. The sand settled. The smell of gasoline wafted.

They're right outside, Kay knew. *Only meters away.*

The crew remained hidden inside the behemoth. They pressed themselves against the hull, kneeling under the holes. A few pirates drew guns, began to rise, but Isabelle waved them down. They all hid.

Metal creaked outside—opening doors? Boots thumped on sand. Low voices spoke. Kay only caught snippets, but enough to recognize his language. Here were Isonomians.

White Army.

"General!" A deep voice, distorted by a helmet. "No sign of the Zionites, mux. They must have all died at sea."

A figure blocked the hole in the hull. A shadow fell. An even deeper voice spoke.

"They are alive, Major. Do not doubt me. My wife was helping them. They survived the navy assault. They are here. In Zion. And we'll find them."

Kay crouched under the hole, listening. His heart lurched. He could barely breathe.

My wife?

Kay's head spun. Could it be?

He dared to raise his head slightly, to peek out the hole. He saw a man in white armor. There was no mistaking the red stars on his shoulders. His crown of serrated blades.

There he stood. Right outside. The man who had ordered Zionites stoned to death in the arena. The man who had tortured thousands, murdered millions. Ellie's husband.

EQL61. The White General.

Kay felt faint.

"Mux, we found no tracks," said the major. "They could not have made it this far. They—"

The general grabbed the major's throat. He began to squeeze.

"They are here, Major." EQL61 leaned closer, tightening his grip. A sickening *crunch* sounded. "They swam to shore. They survived. They are here—somewhere. We will catch them—and all the other Zionite rats that infest this land."

The major was gurgling, desperate for air. But EQL61 kept tightening his grip. Squeezing. Crushing. A loud *snap* sounded from inside the officer's neck.

EQL61 finally released his grip. The major slumped down—dead.

Inside the rusty behemoth, the survivors all crouched, frozen, not even daring to breathe.

Outside, the general turned toward the rest of his soldiers.

"I want those Zionites!" he shouted, voice unnaturally deep, distorted, booming through his helmet. "I want them alive. I want them in pain. And I want them before nightfall! The hunt is on, my soldiers. Let's catch some rats!"

Through a crack in the hull, Kay saw a hundred soldiers raising their fists in salute.

"Yes, mux!" they cried together.

The soldiers leaped into their armacars, laughing and cheering, boasting of how many Zionites they'd catch. The engines roared again. The convoy raced forward, raising a storm of sand.

The defectors remained inside their shelter, silent for long moments. Finally, when they were sure the White Army was gone, they rose and stretched.

"Goddammit!" Isabelle said. The pirate captain paced the sandy chamber. "I'm used to just fighting ships. Now the entire armored division of the White Army is after me. Led by none other than the White Goddamn General."

"I knew we should have killed the defectors," muttered one of her bearded pirates, giving Kay the hairy eyeball.

"They're not after *us*," Kay said. "You all heard the general. They're after Zionites."

Adrian laughed bitterly. He patted Kay on the shoulder. "Brother, we are the Zionites."

Kay frowned. "We're Isonomians. All of us are."

Adrian rolled his eyes. "Sure thing, bro. But those dudes? They were after us. That White Gobshite even spoke of Ellie helping us. To them, we're Zionites now. No longer comrades of the glorious People's Nation of Isonomia. Nothing but filthy Zionite rats to hunt."

Kay grimaced as he remembered the reeducation camp. That place in the far cold north. The day EQL61 had visited, had beaten Kay nearly to death.

He gripped his gun. His hand shook around it.

I'm going to kill you, White General, Kay vowed. *For how you hurt me. How you hurt Ellie. For what you did to this land. I'm a Zionite now. And you are my enemy. You will die.*

They climbed out from the behemoth, earning a few more scratches. The desert spread before them, strewn with the ghosts of past wars. Kay led the way. They walked under the blinding sun.

CHAPTER TWENTY-SIX

At dawn, they saw it on the horizon.

A city on a mountain, golden in the sunrise.

Kay fell to his knees, eyes damp. His wounds were infected. His legs were twisted and bleeding. But all the pain lifted from him. He wept.

"Jerusalem," he whispered. "We found it."

Adrian stepped up. He scratched himself and shrugged. "Looks like a dump."

"It's the holy city," Kay said.

"Looks more like holy shit."

Kay glared at the man. But looking at Adrian, his anger faded.

He's scared to get hurt, Kay thought. *Scared to cling to hope. But I still hope. It's all I have left.*

"Come on, we can be there within a few hours." Kay stared at the mountain, squinting in the sandy wind. "There are clouds of dust on the mountainside. Vehicles. They might be Zionites. But just in case it's White Army—we stay off the roads."

"Great!" Adrian said. "More walking between rusty scrap metal and thorny bushes. I think I have a few fibers of flesh left on my legs. This should take care of them."

The tattooed man began walking toward the mountain, beckoning for the others.

They all joined him. The pirates were passing around their last bottle of grog. Tilly was limping quietly, hugging herself, her last few pills jangling in the bottle.

As they walked closer, they encountered more devastation. These were civilian ruins. A burnt, hollowed-out building clung to the mountainside, filled with overturned metal tables and chairs. It had once been a tavern, Kay guessed. A temple clawed the sky with crumbling towers, its domes lying fallen on the hills, overgrown with weeds. A few old cars rusted on the roadsides, steering wheels peeking from ruins of rust, tires gone. Several desert wolves ran nearby, holding bones in their jaws. The animals paused, gave the humans yellow stares, then turned and loped away, seeking easier prey.

At least there was some life here. The desert faded as they reached higher altitude. Olive trees, pines, and tall grass grew over the ruins of homes, the husks of buses, and a cemetery. A hind leaped down the mountainside, its horns entangled in a rib cage.

A few times, airplanes flew above. The defectors knelt, hid in the bushes, and waited until the planes flew by. One time, they saw a convoy of armored vehicles rumbling up a hill. White vehicles. Red quelii painted on them. Again they hid, waiting for the enemy to pass.

In the afternoon, they were climbing a steep slope. They were near the mountaintop. From here, they couldn't see many details of Jerusalem. From some locations, Kay could see brick walls, golden in the sunlight. Defensive walls. Topped with battlements.

"The walls of Jerusalem still stand," he said. "The Zionites are under siege, but they're alive. They're there. Behind those walls, there's safety."

"They better also have an entire roast horse, because I could eat one," Adrian said.

They were all hungry. Desperately hungry. The thirst was worse. They had found a few murky puddles that morning, had lapped them up. That water now roiled in their bellies, sour and sickening. Kay would have given up a roast horse, or roast anything for that matter, for more antibiotics. It wasn't just his wounds that were infected. His insides rumbled, likely swarming with little bugs he wanted to douse in a shower of penicillin. The others too were weak with injury and disease. Adrian's hand was a mess, and Tilly's leg was still raw with pus. Both were covered in feverish sweat. Medicine had become as urgent as clean water.

We're dying, Kay knew.

"Just a little bit farther," he said. "Just a few more miles. And we're there."

They kept going.

They were only a mile from the walls when Tilly collapsed.

The girl fell onto the rocky ground, bloodying her face. A few of the pirates laughed. Kay and Adrian knelt by Tilly, rolled her over. She blinked up at them, then coughed, turned her head, and vomited.

"She's burning up," Kay said, feeling her forehead.

Tilly stared at him with glassy eyes. "I don't want to die," she whispered.

"You won't die!" Kay said. "You just have a bit of a fever. The antibiotics will kick in soon, and ..."

Tilly held out the bottle. She had not taken any of the five pills.

"For you, Kay," she whispered.

Kay inhaled sharply. "Dammit, Tilly! I told you to take them!"

"I thought I could make it," she whispered. "I want to see Zion, Kay. The real Zion."

Kay took a pill, placed it in her mouth, and worked her jaws with his hand. She gulped and shuddered.

"You'll see the real Zion, Tilly." Kay lifted her, carried her in his arms. "We're almost there."

They kept climbing the mountain. Kay's legs hurt walking at the best of times. Now every step was agony. But he kept trudging forward. Moving through the pain. Savoring the pain. Carrying Tilly, leading the others. Almost at the end of their journey. Almost home.

The sun was setting when they reached the walls of Jerusalem.

Kay fell to his knees, nearly dropping Tilly, and took deep breaths. The others gathered around him, seeking shelter in the shade of the walls.

Kay had never seen such walls. They were not concrete, not metal, but built of huge limestone bricks, each one the size of a boulder.

Tilly reached out. She touched a brick with shaky fingers.

"These walls are ancient," she whispered. "Built thousands of years ago. They did not fall in the war." She smiled and her tears fell. "It's real. Jerusalem is real."

Adrian approached slowly, touched the walls too, and awe filled his eyes. Even the pirates were silent, and Isabelle looked at Kay, wonder in her eyes.

"You were right," the captain whispered. "Goddamn it, Ghost, you actually brought us here."

Kay was silent.

He approached a gateway in the walls. An archway, craggy and ancient, gilded in the sunset. There were no doors. Only a welcoming path into the holy city. Kay paused, took a deep breath, and stepped into Jerusalem.

He walked down a cobbled road.

Ruins rose along the road. Cracked archways. The shell of a limestone church. Fallen columns with elaborate capitals. Weeds grew between flagstones and bricks, and trees poked through holes in roofs. A few birds chirped and fled.

Kay saw no people.

His companions walked behind him, guns raised, eyes darting. They walked down the road, silent, heading deeper into the city. Kay turned onto a cobbled alleyway, and they climbed a hill. On the hilltop, they found a well, a few palm trees, and an orphaned archway rising from piles of fallen bricks.

From up here, they could see the entire city.

They saw only ruins.

Miles and miles of crumbling stone ruins.

Tilly lowered her head.

Adrian howled, lifted a brick, and hurled it.

Kay just stood, staring. Eyes dry. Barely believing.

"I was a fool," he finally whispered. He turned toward the others. "Nothing but a fool."

Tilly embraced him. She laid her cheek against his chest.

From above—that old rumble.

Engines. Roaring. Shrieking. Shadows racing across the ground.

Kay didn't have to look up. He knew what it meant. Airplanes. White Army airplanes. Hunting them.

He lowered his head.

Let them hunt. Let them kill us. Our hope is gone.

Shadows passed over him.

Bombs whistled downward.

"Run!" Tilly screamed, pulling him.

Kay ran with her, too weak to resist.

A bomb exploded behind them. The shock wave knocked them down. Buildings crumbled. Chunks of rock pummeled Kay and dust rained.

More bombs shrieked.

Tilly was screaming something, covered in dust, her wounded leg trapped under fallen bricks.

There is no point. No reason to continue.

But Kay's body moved on its own. He shoved the bricks off Tilly, freeing her leg. He lifted her. As explosions bloomed around the ruins, he ran, holding the girl in his arms.

More planes soared from the north. White planes. The planes of the general.

More bombs fell. Ruins shattered. Temples collapsed. Fire raged across Jerusalem. Kay stood in the inferno, the city blazing around him, Tilly limp in his arms. He tilted his head back and closed his eyes. He knew he would die here. He would die in the holy city.

"Kay!" A voice through the hellfire. "Kay, over here, dammit! Move!"

Kay opened his eyes. Through the smoke, fire, and dust, he saw Adrian. The man stood on a hilltop, holding open a metal hatch.

Kay understood. A bomb shelter.

He ran between fallen bricks. More planes roared overhead, strafing the city. Bullets hit the ground around Kay's feet.

Adrian vanished into the bunker. Adrian leaped, pulled Tilly close to him, and dived into the shadows.

He fell and crashed onto the floor, dropping Tilly. If not for the thick layer of dust, he might have broken his legs. Belatedly, he realized there was a ladder. Adrian stood on it, shaking his head in disgust. He pulled the hatch shut, sealing the fire outside.

Kay knelt, catching his breath. A bomb exploded above. The bunker shook. Dust fell from the ceiling.

But the bunker held. Boom after boom above, and the world trembled. But they lived.

When the trembling eased, Kay got a better look around him. It was a large bunker, and doorways led to deeper chambers. Human and animal bones, military dog tags, and bullet casings littered the floor. Isabelle stood in the corner, holding a bloodstained cloth to her head. The other pirates hadn't made it.

"We'll be safe here for now," Adrian said and coughed. Dust and blood painted him gray and red.

"Until when?" Tilly said, struggling to her feet. Her leg was bent and bleeding. "Until we die of starvation down here?"

"We'll probably die of thirst first," Isabelle said. "Or disease."

Kay frowned, ignoring them. Several crates stood in a dusty corner, covered in cobwebs.

Wooden crates.

"Wood would have rotted over time," he said. "These crates aren't that old. Not like the skeletons and ruins above."

He approached them. The crates were bolted shut. Kay stepped back and raised his gun.

"Cover your ears!" he said.

The others complied. Kay fired, shattering a crate's lock. He wrenched off the top ... and sank to his knees.

"Oh God," he whispered. "Oh my God."

"What?" Adrian trudged forward, leaned over the crate, then stumbled back. "Goddamn."

Kay rubbed his eyes, disbelieving. He looked again. They were there. It was not an illusion. Adrian had seen them too.

Canned goods. Bottles of water. Weapons too. Pistols, rifles, magazines of bullets. Medical kits with bandages, needles, painkillers, antibiotics. A cornucopia. Tears ran down Kay's face.

"How can this be?" he whispered.

Tilly brushed cobwebs and dust off a crate, revealing a pomegranate symbol. "The Zionites." She blinked away tears. "They're real. Or were not long ago. Look at the expiration dates on these cans! These are only a year old."

Isabelle shoved the girl aside. "Out of the way!"

The pirate grabbed a can, slammed her knife into it, and sawed off the top. She held the can overhead, gulping down peaches.

Kay ignored the food for now. He went for the water first.
His hands shook as he opened a bottle and guzzled it down.
Adrian and Tilly were drinking too, letting the water pour down
their throats, splash over their faces, clear away the blood and
grime. They all returned for seconds, downing more bottles.

Only then did they feast. Isabelle used her knife, opening
more cans. There were peaches, so sweet the flavor exploded in
Kay's mouth. There was tuna in olive oil with slices of jalapenos.
There were stewed tomatoes, pineapple rings, corn—all the
bounty of the world. Kay had never tasted anything finer. He
washed it down with more water—along with sweet, sweet
painkillers and antibiotics.

"Enjoying the feast?"

The voice came from deeper in the bunker.

The companions leaped up and raised their weapons. Tilly
had noodles hanging from her mouth.

A man stood in the doorway. He wore rags, and his beard
was long and white. A rifle was slung across his back. He raised
his open palms, a sign of peace.

"Hold on there, cowboys! I ain't gonna harm ya. The
name's Nathan. I'm a friend."

Several other people emerged from the shadows behind
Nathan. A woman with sunken cheeks and frightened eyes. Two
children who clung to her. A couple of teenagers farther back,
guns on their hips.

"Who are you?" Kay demanded, keeping his gun aimed at
the strangers.

"Are you Zionites?" Tilly whispered. A flicker of hope
filled her eyes.

"We're like you, friends," Nathan said, smiling through his
bushy white beard. "Defectors from Isonomia. Come on, come
in!" He gestured to the doorway. "Don't just hang out in the
lobby. Join the group. There are more of us."

Kay frowned and glanced at his companions. They seemed just as uncertain. Were these friends or foes?

Kay made the call, lowering his gun.

"If they were enemies, they could have killed us while we were eating," Kay said. "Let's see what's going on here."

They walked deeper into the bunker, and their eyes widened.

People filled the bunker.

Dozens. Maybe even hundreds.

They were all just as ragged, filthy, and wounded as Kay and his group. A few had amputated limbs, the stumps bandaged. Some seemed to be dying. But many stood tall, holding weapons. There were more wooden crates here, also filled with munitions.

"What the hell is going on here?" Adrian said, voice echoing through the bunker.

Nathan shrugged. "You know as well as we do, friend. My family and I—we only arrived yesterday. Gunther, the big guy over there with one leg, he's been here for a week. He's the most experienced one among us. Hell, a few others only arrived an hour before you."

"Arrived from where?" Adrian demanded.

"From Isonomia, of course," Nathan said. "Like you, I imagine. Like all the other groups. We defected. We made our way to Zion. I smuggled my family and myself in a cargo ship. Others found their own transportation. We all took the underground. And when we got here?" Nathan sighed. "Ruins. A fallen city. A fallen land."

Kay stared at the crates. He touched one. The wood was new. He looked back at the others.

"But these crates. They have pomegranates symbols on them. Zionite crates. The Zionite army must have been here recently."

Nathan nodded. "That's our thinking too. We think the Zionite army abandoned Jerusalem a while back, probably no more than a year ago, and made its way south. We've been nursing our wounds, waiting to recover, then plan to follow. We figure other defectors must have come here before us, found the same ruins, and also left. We hope to find them too. Hell, there might be thousands of us in Zion."

A young man stepped forward, shirtless and starving, his ribs pressing against his skin. His eyes, sunken into a gaunt skull, burned with intensity.

"The others are in Masada," the cadaverous man said. "The great fortress in the desert. That's where we'll join the heroes!"

Scattered cheers and a few prayers rose from the crowd. Voices cried out.

"The heroes!"

"The heroes are in Masada."

"We'll find them. We'll live."

Kay had heard similar talk before. He himself had spoken such words over and over. He realized how hollow they sounded.

He glanced at Adrian. His friend's eyes were dark.

"I don't like this," Kay whispered.

Adrian nodded, his hand tight around his gun. "Me neither. The whole thing stinks like bullshit."

"Think it's a trap?" Kay said.

Adrian glanced at the others, then back at Kay. "If it is, these poor sons of bitches are inside the same trap."

"Where the hell did we end up, Adrian?"

Adrian slapped Kay's shoulder. "Zion, my friend. Welcome to the promised land. A land of shit and sand."

Kay gestured for Tilly and Isabelle. They huddled together, the last survivors of their group. Many had boarded the *Phantom* on Isomonia's coast. So few remained.

"All right, guys," Kay said. "Group meeting. What do we do?"

Tilly raised an eyebrow. "I thought you were our fearless leader?"

"Ellie was our fearless leader," Kay said. "I'm just a dumb defector with holes in his head. And right now, that head is open to ideas. Literally."

Adrian's eyes were hard. "We fight. To the death. No more running."

"To hell with that!" Isabelle said. "We head back to the ocean. We hijack a boat. I can muster a good raiding team here. We'll sail back to Isonomia."

"I ain't going back," Kay said.

"Me neither," said Tilly.

Adrian scoffed. "To hell with going back. You heard the general. We're Zionites now. This is where we make our stand." He looked at the other defectors, sighed, and looked back at the group. "They're mostly old, sick, dying. They're not much. But we can whip them into an army. We might just be able to defend this bunker. Maybe even find that fortress they're talking about. Masada."

Tilly lowered her head. "I don't believe that fortress even exists. Maybe only as a ruin. We've found nothing but ruins until now."

"We found these crates," Kay said. "That's evidence that there are Zionites—real Zionites—still here. We just have to find them. And join them. Maybe we'll die in battle, yes. But at least we'll have a fighting chance. I'd rather die trying than give up."

Tilly hugged him. "All right, Kay." She sniffed and rubbed her eyes. "I lost everybody that I ever loved. Ever trusted. I was born in a lab, do you know? Made from chemicals in a petri dish. I never had parents. Never had a family. I thought that Pat could be family. But he died. I loved Ellie. But she died. But I still have you, Kay. You're like a father. And I love you. And I trust you. And I'll follow you."

Tears stung Kay's eyes. He stroked the girl's hair. "I'll do whatever I can to protect you, Tilly. Always. We'll keep going, and we'll cling to hope, and—"

A boom shook the bunker.

At first, Kay mistook it for another bomb above. Then he realized: it was the bunker door blasting open.

A second later, he saw them storming into the bunker.

Soldiers in white armor.

Their guns blazed.

Isabelle screamed, bullets riddling her chest. The pirate captain fell, her pistol still holstered.

The gaunt young man fell nearby, bullets ripping out his neck. Other defectors collapsed, blood gushing.

Kay leaped aside, pulling Tilly with him. They knelt behind a crate. Bullets slammed into it, and jars shattered, spilling fruit and vegetables. Adrian managed to leap behind other crates, then rose again, firing his pistol.

The soldiers came racing deeper into the bunker, shouting, firing their guns. They mowed down defectors. Dozens of the ragged survivors fell.

"Kill the Zionites!" shouted an officer. "Kill them all!"

Kneeling behind the crate, Kay and Tilly fired their guns.

Across the bunker, others joined them. Nathan and his companions knelt behind other crates, firing pistols and rifles. Bullets streaked back and forth. People fell on both sides. Blood washed the floor.

More soldiers came storming in. Kay hit one in the visor, and the soldier fell, only for another to replace xer.

One soldier hurled a cannister. Kay flattened himself over Tilly, expecting the burst of a grenade.

Instead, foul smoke emerged from the cannister.

"Chemicals!" shouted Nathan. "Gas masks on!"

The old man pulled on a gas mask, struggling to tuck his beard into it. Others followed his lead.

"Do you have any spares?" Kay shouted, coughing. His eyes stung. He held his breath, backing away from the smoke. Another cannister landed nearby. More gas emerged. More bullets kept flying.

Nathan ran toward a crate and ripped off the top. He tossed gas masks toward Kay and his companions. Hands trembling, Kay placed on a gas mask and took a deep, raspy breath. He then helped Tilly pull on her own gas mask. They ran deeper into the bunker. Adrian ran close behind, cursing and firing over his shoulder. A bullet had pierced his arm, tearing through a tattoo, destroying a red dragon's head.

The soldiers chased them, their helmets filtering the gas. Gunshots echoed through the bunker. More defectors fell.

"Nathan, is there another way out?" Kay shouted. His voice emerged distorted from the gas mask, reminding him of his old voicebox.

"At the back!" the old man cried. "There's another hatch. But—"

More soldiers came racing from ahead, guns blazing.

Defectors fell, riddled with bullets.

Kay skidded to a halt. Soldiers in front of him. Soldiers behind.

Kay looked at Adrian. His friend nodded.

"Let's get 'em, buddy," Adrian said.

They both roared and charged together.

Guns boomed. The two men raised crates, blocking the barrage. They ran into the gunfire. Bullets shattered their crates, but they kept charging.

They barreled into the soldiers before them.

The soldiers fell. Adrian grabbed a rifle, howling, covered in blood. He slammed the butt down again and again, shattering a soldier's face. He bellowed, barely human anymore. Kay grabbed a rifle of his own, swung it, knocked a soldier back. He fired his pistol, tearing down a man. They fought onward, killing, plowing a way toward the hatch.

Kay stepped over bodies. He grabbed the ladder. He climbed with one hand, firing his pistol with the other, and burst back out into the ruins.

More soldiers were running toward them.

Kay knelt behind a fallen column and fired. More refugees emerged from the bunker, coughing, adjusting their gas masks. They too opened fire. Bullets flashed back and forth. Adrian hurled a grenade—he must have found it inside a crate—and an explosion rocked the ruins. White Army soldiers flew, torn apart. A severed foot landed beside Kay.

For a moment, silence fell across the battle.

The soldiers all lay dead.

Adrian was laughing, spinning around, bloody arms raised, as if challenging anyone else to attack. Tilly knelt, weeping. Other defectors gathered nearby, praying, crying, tending to wounds. So few had survived.

Kay stood still, tense, and loaded another magazine.

A horn sounded in the distance, shockingly loud, making him start.

Kay stared, narrowing his eyes in the desert sunlight.

He saw a man on a hill. A man in white armor, standing before the sun. Staring at Kay. A man with red stars on his shoulders. With a spiked helmet.

General EQL61.

Kay fired his gun. Perhaps due to the distance, his bullet sparked harmlessly against the general's armor.

The general raised his horn again. He blew once more—a jarring sound like a dying god.

A thousand soldiers, maybe more, emerged onto the hilltop around the White General.

The battalion howled and charged toward the defectors.

CHAPTER TWENTY-SEVEN

A thousand white demons came racing through the ruins, howling for death.

"Run!" Kay shouted.

He pulled Tilly to her feet. They ran, stumbling over bricks and bodies. The other defectors ran with them. The enemy howled. Guns boomed. Bullets whizzed by Kay's head. More defectors fell. The survivors kept running.

They swerved around the ruins of a church, shielded from the barrage of bullets. Only a few dozen defectors remained.

"Time to die in glory, brother," Adrian said, discharging an empty magazine. He slammed in a fresh one.

Kay took deep breaths, his heart pounding. He stared around, desperate for a way to escape.

On a hill a few blocks away, he saw hope. He pointed.

"A military barracks."

Fences rose around the base, topped with barbed wire. Behind them, Kay could make out armacars, a guard tower, and a concrete building. A faded red pomegranate was painted onto a wall.

"We need those armacars," Kay said. "They'll give us a fighting chance."

"We'll never make it that far," Adrian said.

Behind them, the enemy soldiers had almost caught up. Adrian fired at them, cursing. A soldier screamed and fell.

"Yes we will." Kay began to ran. "With me, Zion! Run!"

Adrian ran with him, firing over his shoulder at the enemy. The other defectors joined the flight.

They raced over ruins. Past burnt cars, a twisted bicycle, and uprooted tombstones. Over hills of bricks and under crumbling archways. Down ancient alleyways and up hillsides littered with skeletons.

Every block, more died.

The White Army bullets kept flying. More defectors fell, blood soaking the earth.

The survivors kept running. Carrying their wounded. The bullets flying around them. Into them. Tearing more down. They raced through a cemetery, and more fell among the tombstones.

"Run!" Kay shouted. "Onward!"

It was only a short distance. A quick sprint. It lasted for eternity.

When they reached the barracks, they were so few. Adrian and Tilly, both so wounded they could barely move. Old Nathan, blood in his beard. Thirty other defectors, maybe forty. No more.

But behind the barracks fence, Kay saw them.

Armacars. Heavy armored vehicles on caterpillar tracks, mounted with machine guns. Empty and waiting.

Hope.

"Adrian, your grenades!" Kay said.

"Fire in the hole!" Adrian said, hurling an explosive.

They flattened themselves. The explosion tore through the fence, and chunks of metal flew everywhere.

Kay rose. Shrapnel had scraped his hip, searing through flesh, cauterizing the wound. One more scar. Another cut closer to death.

He ran through the pain. He led the others onward.

They raced into the barracks, crossed the courtyard, and approached the armacars. They were similar to tanks, just slightly smaller, and their turrets sprouted machine guns instead of cannons. Inside the armacars, they found more crates of weapons and ammo.

"We have a guardian angel, I think," Adrian said, standing with Kay among the armacars. His left side was mangled—a bullet in the arm, three fingers missing, burn marks across the cheek.

We're all wounded, Kay thought. *Dying. But right now, we must flee.*

He had no time to contemplate the mysterious crates.

"Don't count our blessings yet," he said. "We still need to get out of Dodge."

Adrian raised an eyebrow. "Dodge?"

"An expression I picked up from Tilly. Dammit, Adrian, get into a car and drive with me!"

Kay hopped into one armacar and took the driver's seat. He pushed a lever. The engine roared. Monitors flickered to life around him, displaying views from all sides.

In one monitor, Kay saw the White Army soldiers storm into the abandoned Zionite base. Their rifles boomed.

Ten armacars burst through the fence, mowing down soldiers, and roared down the hillside.

Kay gripped the wheel. The armacar leaped over bricks and ripped out tombstones. Tilly sat beside him, bouncing in the seat. Several other defectors huddled in the armacar's hold, clinging to their seats. The other armacars rumbled around them, tearing through more ruins, crushing bricks and columns beneath their tracks.

The White Army would not let them get away without a fight. Troops rose on the hill behind, aimed grenade launchers, and fired.

Several grenades missed, exploding around the armacars. Shock waves thrummed through the desert. Kay gripped the wheel as even his mighty armacar tilted, nearly overturning.

Another grenade slammed into a nearby armacar, tearing through the armored hull. Fire spread and men screamed inside.

"Nathan, get into the gun turret!" Kay shouted.

The old man nodded, climbed a ladder, and rose into the open turret. Soon the machine gun was rattling. The other armacars joined the assault, pounding the White Army with bullets.

The remaining armacars rumbled down a cobbled road. Several White Army soldiers emerged before them, firing guns. Bullets sparked against the armored hulls. Kay shoved down the throttle, accelerating. The soldiers leaped aside. One man died under the treads with a sickening crunch. More equalists swarmed, hurling grenades. An explosion tore through a temple. Balustrades, a tower, and walls crumbled, covering the street with limestone. A cloud of dust rose. The armacars swerved around the ruins.

Kay saw it ahead. The city gates. He charged through the archway, crushing fallen bricks. Four other armacars followed.

They roared out of Jerusalem.

They rumbled down the mountainside, uprooting olive trees, shattering skeletons, crushing stones. Kay dared to hope they had escaped, that they were safe.

Then Nathan cried out from the gun turret.

"A helicopter! Helicopter abo—"

A missile shrieked.

An explosion shook the world, destroying an armacar beside Kay.

Another missile roared, and Kay tugged the wheel, jerking the vehicle aside. An explosion roared beside him, tearing up cedars.

"Nathan, shoot it down!" Kay shouted. "Shoot it down, dammit!"

He kept driving. Nathan fired the machine gun upward.

For a second—silence.

Kay kept driving.

Then, with a roar of spinning blades and twisting metal, the helicopter crashed down before them. An explosion rocked the mountainside, raising a cloud of smoke and shrapnel and fire.

Kay had no time to swerve. He winced, stiffened, and drove through the wreckage.

The armacar plowed through the mangled helicopter. A rotor blade detached and flew, slicing several trees in half. A dead pilot thumped into the armacar, slid down, and was crushed under the treads.

The three last armacars kept driving, roaring down the mountainside.

The desert spread before them, rolling into the horizon. A landscape of dunes, rocky hills, lifeless despair. And according to the tales—a fortress on a mountain. The last bastion of Zion.

The desert is where we'll find our salvation, Kay thought. *Or make our final stand.*

Rumbling engines and gunfire sounded behind them. Kay could hear it even over the roar of his armacar.

He looked into a monitor showing the view behind him. He saw them.

Hundreds of jeeps.

White Army vehicles.

Soldiers stood inside, holding rifles, machine guns, grenade launchers. Helicopters flew above. The army was storming down the mountainside, pursuing the defectors. Their banners fluttered. Their engines shook the world.

One soldier rose in a jeep and raised a megaphone. The voice boomed across the mountain.

"Hear me, KB209! I will capture you alive! You took my wife from me. Yours will not be a quick death. I am General EQL61. I will have my revenge!"

Kay gritted his teeth and shoved down the throttle, praying for more speed.

The three defector armacars reached the desert. They stormed across the dunes, and the enemy followed.

CHAPTER TWENTY-EIGHT

Three armacars.

A handful of survivors.

A last flicker of hope.

They stormed across the desert, raising clouds of sand. Behind them, moving closer and closer, the White Army followed.

Hundreds of jeeps and tanks. Helicopters. Drones. Thousands of troops. The White Army in all its glory. And at its lead—a man with a crown of spikes. A man all in white. The man who had tortured Kay once, who could not wait to torture him again. EQL61.

Kay gripped the wheel, anxious to fire his gun at the general again.

I hit you with a bullet once, Kay thought. *I can again. And next time I will finish the job.*

The armacars leaped over dunes, slammed down, and kept charging. Their machine guns kept firing, pounding the pursuing enemy. But they did little good. There were more White Army soldiers than defector bullets. If there was hope, it lay in Masada. The fortress beyond the horizon. Perhaps only a rumor. Perhaps a chance to finally find life in the desert.

The dunes gave way to rolling, rocky hills like dunes of stone. The armacars leaped and fell, leaped and fell, and Kay felt like he was back on the ocean, swaying in the storm.

In the distance, a canyon came into view. A limestone mesa rose beyond it, a monolith like a tombstone to a god. Kay could just make out a tower on its top.

Was that Masada? The last fortress?

A jet roared. A missile streaked overhead.

An explosion tore through the desert.

Kay swerved, dodging the resulting crater.

Another missile exploded before him.

He swerved again, skirting the pit.

EQL61 was still trying to take him alive. Kay would not allow it. Tilly sat beside him. He would not let the girl end up in a reeducation camp.

If need be, I'll put bullets through our heads, Kay thought. *But if I still can—I will save us. I will give Ellie's death meaning. I will give all our lives meaning.*

The enemy was catching up. The armacars were powerful, but they were heavy beasts. Each probably weighed fifty tons. The White Army jeeps were lighter, faster, and were getting nearer and nearer. Bullets slammed into the armacars, chipping away at the armor. The helicopters thundered above.

"Keep firing on them, Nathan!" Kay shouted.

"We're running low on ammo!" the old man replied from the gun turret. "We—"

Bullets hammered the armacar.

Nathan fell into the hold, chest torn open. Blood stained his once-white beard. The other defectors inside screamed.

Jeeps roared forth and flanked the armacar. Soldiers rose and leaped onto the armacar's roof.

"Drive!" Kay said, pulling Tilly's hands onto the steering wheel.

He leaped into the hold.

A soldier was climbing into the armacar. Kay fired his pistol, knocking the soldier down. At such close range, his bullets tore through the man's armor.

Kay scurried up the ladder, crawled through a hatch, and entered the gun turret. He clung to the machine gun, swaying. His legs were still inside the armacar. His head and torso were exposed to the desert air. The armacar rattled as it stormed across the dunes. Wind and sand whipped Kay.

The jeeps surrounded him. Bullets flew. Kay knelt, seeking protection inside the gun turret's circular barricade. He rose again and fired, taking out another soldier.

Boots thumped onto the armacar's roof. A soldier landed there, armored, sandy, and scratched.

"Hello, Zionite!" the soldier said. "My master wants you alive. I'll enjoy seeing your torture. Hearing your screams."

The soldier raised an electric prod. A bolt of electricity slammed into Kay.

He fell, screaming, convulsing.

He tried to fire his gun. The soldier stepped on his wrist, crushing it, and fired another electric bolt.

Kay screamed. He lay on the roof, kicking, twitching.

"Kay!" came Tilly's cry from inside. "Hold on!"

The armacar swerved madly. Tilly must have been spinning the steering wheel with all her might. The soldier wavered and fell, dropping the electric prod.

Kay rose, lifted his gun, and emptied a magazine into the soldier's head.

Before he could load another magazine, two more soldiers leaped onto the armacar.

Kay was out of bullets. The rest of the ammo was inside the armacar.

He knelt, grabbed the fallen prod, and fired at one soldier. The equalist screamed and fell, buzzing with electricity.

One soldier now remained on the armacar. His visor was cracked, revealing a wide, stubbly jaw and sharp teeth. The man advanced across the armacar roof, raising his own crackling prod.

Kay tried to fire his weapon, but the damn thing was recharging. Instead, Kay howled and lunged at his enemy.

An electric bolt slammed into his chest. But it wasn't enough to stop Kay's momentum. He slammed into the soldier.

The equalist windmilled his arms, then tumbled off the armacar. Yet as he fell, he grabbed Kay's ankle.

Kay fell, losing his gun. The pistol scuttled across the roof, then fell to the desert. His prod followed, vanishing into the storm of sand.

The soldier tugged him toward the ledge. Kay grabbed a metal rung on the hull, desperately clinging to the racing armacar. Below, the treadmills were churning, crushing boulders.

The soldier tightened his grip. He reached out another hand, grabbed Kay's other leg, began climbing.

Kay kicked. Again. Again. The soldier gripping him had lost his helmet. His face was scarred, bleeding, grinning maniacally.

Kay reached into his pocket. He found a remaining can of peaches.

He hurled it with all his strength. It slammed into the soldiers' nose, and blood spurted.

Kicking wildly, Kay finally dislodged the man. The soldier fell, and the caterpillar tracks caught him, coating the treads with blood and guts.

Kay climbed back onto the roof, breathing heavily. Other jeeps were assaulting the other armacars. More were moving in to flank Kay's own vehicle. He climbed back inside and slammed the hatch shut.

A handful of other defectors huddled in the hold, trembling. Three were children. Two more were elders with white hair.

"You're going to have to fight," Kay told them. "There are guns in that crate. If soldiers break in, shoot them. Do you understand?"

They nodded, shaking, and lifted guns. Kay grabbed a new pistol, replacing the lost one.

The hatch opened above.

A soldier leaped down.

The children and elders opened fire. The soldier slumped down dead.

Kay nodded. "Good. Keep that up."

He took the wheel back from Tilly. They were near the mesa now. The monolith rose from the desert, its cliffs craggy. It looked like a massive fossilized tree stump, as tall as a mountain, its top flat. Canyons plunged around it like a moat, providing extra defense.

A rickety bridge spanned the canyon. It was made of chains and metal slats, rusting, bent. It was a bridge to salvation.

Kay hit the brakes. The armacar screeched, billowing sand and smoke. It came to a halt only feet away from the canyon's ledge. The mesa soared ahead, casting a long shadow. The two other armacars—the last of the group—halted too. Adrian climbed out of one. More defectors joined him.

The White Army was only seconds behind.

"Onto the bridge!" Kay shouted, leaping out the hatch. "Run!"

"They'll shoot us down!" Adrian cried.

"They want us alive," Kay said. "Run!"

He herded the others onto the bridge. Tilly ran first. The children followed, then older defectors.

Bullets flew.

Two children screamed and fell off the bridge.

Another bullet took down an elder.

Kay cursed and fired back. Adrian fired at his side. The two men stood by the bridge, not yet crossing the canyon.

"I thought they wanted us alive!" Adrian said.

"I guess that means only me," Kay said. "Get onto that bridge! Protect the others! I'll cover you."

Adrian spat and ran onto the bridge. He ran with the last survivors, crossing the canyon.

Kay remained behind. He took a deep breath, then reentered his armacar.

He spun the massive vehicle around toward the charging enemy, restarted the engine, and stuck the butt of a rifle against the gas pedal.

The armacar charged toward the White Army.

Kay leaped into the hold, pulled the rings out of several grenades, then scurried up the ladder.

He jumped, landed awkwardly in the sand, and cried out in pain.

The armacar kept racing toward the enemy, grenades rattling inside.

Kay ran at a limp, heading back toward the bridge.

An explosion boomed behind him.

Kay dived down, landed on his face, and covered his head. Stones and sand pounded him.

When he rose again, he turned and saw the armacar on fire, still moving, barreling through the White Army. Jeeps spun and crashed. Soldiers screamed, the flames gripping them.

Kay ran onto the bridge. It swayed, the metal chains clanging. The canyon plunged below him, so deep he could barely see the bottom. Kay was bleeding. Burnt. Everything hurt. He ran onward, reached the far side, and joined Adrian and the others.

He still had one grenade. Kay hurled it onto the middle of the bridge, then covered his ears.

The explosion took out the bridge. It fell into the canyon in a twisting heap of rusty metal.

"Dude, you are a badass!" Tilly said. Light filled her eyes again, a hint of life after so many days of pain. "I'm sorry I ever called you a stiff."

The bridge had taken them to the base of the mesa. The stone monolith soared above them. A snake path, barely wide enough for a single person, zigzagged up the cliff.

It was a long way up.

Kay took the lead. Every step shot bolts of agony through his twisted, deformed legs. The path was so narrow his right foot kept slipping over the edge, sending pebbles cascading into the canyon. He kept climbing, and the others followed.

Across the canyon, the White Army vehicles screeched to a halt. Hundreds of armacars and jeeps lined the canyon ledge. Soldiers leaped out. A few opened fire.

Behind Kay, a white-haired defector screamed and tumbled off the mesa.

A child collapsed on the path, a bullet in his head, then slid into the depths.

Kay, Adrian, and Tilly spun toward the enemy. They opened fire. They took out a handful of soldiers. It was only a symbolic gesture. Thousands still remained. More and more kept flowing in across the desert. Helicopters hovered above them, and jets roared overhead.

"Where are the goddamn Zionites?" Adrian shouted, firing and climbing. "I thought there was help in the fort. Why aren't they helping?"

"The fort must be abandoned!" Tilly cried in fear.

"Maybe we'll find shelter there," Kay said. "Climb! Faster!"

They ran, bullets picking them out one by one. The path curved around the other side of the mesa, giving them temporary shelter. But already another army division was arriving from the east. Thousands more. The enemy surrounded the mesa, covering the desert. Tanks rolled forth, aiming their canons at the stone tower.

Kay knew there was only one reason he was still breathing. *EQL61 wants me alive.*

He was tempted to leap down. To crash into the canyon. To die on his own terms.

But he was almost there. Almost at the top. He had vowed to lead his people. Only a handful remained, but he would see them to the bloody end.

They kept running up the snake path. The White Army did not bombard them with artillery. But they took pot shots with bullets, laughing and cheering as they picked out more defectors. Body after body tumbled into the canyon. The defectors didn't bother firing back. They just ran, losing more and more people, their hope all but gone.

Finally, winded, bloodied, the last of them reached the top.

Kay.

Tilly.

Adrian.

They were all who remained.

Atop the mesa's plateau, they found nothing.

A few chunks of ancient wall, only four or five bricks tall. A few stubs of columns. A single tower that still rose, half its circular wall gone, exposing its innards to the desert. A few skeletons lay on sandy cobblestones. Some still had bits of flesh and hair clinging to them.

There was no shelter. There were no Zionites.

A single statue rose in the center of the plateau. A gilded statue of the Father. Upon its pedestal appeared words engraved in gold.

Equalism is good. Equalism is just. Equalism is forever, and the Father protects us.

Kay fell to his knees. He stared, barely able to breathe.

The golden statue stared down at him. Almost kind. Almost loving.

Kay lowered his head.

Zion. A mythical place of peace and light. A utopia. Just another utopia.

"I'm sorry," Kay whispered. "I'm sorry, Adrian. I'm sorry, Tilly. I'm sorry."

Rotor blades thudded above. Several military helicopters rose to hover over the mesa. Hatches opened. Ropes dangled down. Soldiers of the White Army emerged.

Adrian roared, raised his rifle, and opened fire. His bullets tore into several soldiers.

The White Army raised stun guns. Electric bolts slammed into Adrian.

He bellowed like a wounded beast. He fell, crackling with electricity, burning. He kept firing. More bolts knocked into him, knocking him onto his back. He convulsed. Even as soldiers grabbed him, Adrian still kicked, still roared, still fought. He tried to turn his rifle on himself, but soldiers wrenched it free.

Tilly rushed toward Kay. They stood side by side. Another helicopter opened its hatch above, and soldiers descended.

"For Zion!" Tilly shouted, raised her gun, and fired at the enemy.

Kay raised his pistol.

He looked at the girl. This sweet, brave soul. A slender little thing with short hair, with so much hope, with a kind heart.

"I'm sorry, Tilly," he whispered, and a tear rolled down his cheek.

As soldiers leaped down around her, Tilly looked at him. In that last instant, Kay saw that she understood. That she was thankful.

He fired a bullet into her head.

She fell.

Kay turned the gun on himself.

Electric bolts slammed into him, and he fell. He managed to pull the trigger, but the bullet missed, firing over his shoulder instead of into his head.

More bolts flew. Lightning slammed into Kay. Again and again. He convulsed, screaming. He lost his gun. There was nothing but pain.

And then—it ended.

The electricity died.

Kay lay on the ground, twitching, smoke rising from his burnt skin.

A shadow fell over him. A boot pressed down on his chest, nearly crushing his sternum. Kay gasped for air, found none.

EQL61 leaned down. He stared through the dark pane of his visor.

"Pathetic," the White General said. "You barely put up a fight. I was hoping for a better hunt. But your pain will be so sweet."

Kay saw his fallen gun nearly. He reached for it. The general kicked it away. The gun clattered across the plateau and fell into the canyon.

The general's foot rose again.

Kay looked into Tilly's dead eyes.

The general's boot slammed into his head, and white light exploded, and Kay sank into darkness.

CHAPTER TWENTY-NINE

When Kay woke up, he was chained, dangling from the ceiling in a brick cell.

Everything hurt.

How long was I unconscious?

Where am I?

He didn't know.

Blood stained the cell. A rat was gnawing a human rib cage in the corner. Kay's toes just grazed the floor. The chains tugged on his arms, nearly dislocating them. Sunlight entered through a small, barred window, barely more than a vent. A portrait of the Father hung on the wall.

Kay flailed, jerked on his chains, desperately trying to wrap them around his neck.

He tried to swallow his tongue, ended up coughing, breathing again.

He roared.

Finally, he hung limply, chin resting against his chest.

"Why did you kill me?" Tilly said, tears in her eyes.

"I'm sorry," Kay whispered.

"You led us all to die!" said the twins.

"I tried to save you."

Ellie stroked his cheek and kissed him. "I gave my life for nothing."

His wife and child stared. "Why did you abandon us?"

They spun around him. Accusing faces. Betrayed eyes. Fading. Fading into mist and shadows.

The door creaked open. A man stepped into the room. He wore a white military uniform but no armor. He had no mask. His face was hard, deep grooves around a thin mouth, cheeks sunken below jutting cheekbones. A gaunt, pinched face, carved from cruelty. The eyes were glittering shards of steel. Kay had never seen this face. But he recognized the man at once.

"EQL61," he said.

The general stepped forward.

He swung a fist into Kay's face.

Pain exploded. Blood flew. A tooth clattered onto the floor.

"You disappointed me, KB209." The general cracked his knuckles. "I was expecting a better hunt."

Kay gasped for air.

"What do you want?" he rasped and coughed, blood dripping. "Why won't you let me die?"

"And deprive me of my fun?" The general cocked an eyebrow. "I think not."

The fist swung again. This time into Kay's stomach. He vomited blood.

"Kill me," he managed, barely able to sound the words.

The general laughed. "I'm taking you home, my boy. It's time to return to Isonomia. It's time to pay for your crimes."

Soldiers stepped into the room. They pulled a sack over Kay's head. They unchained him, knocked him down, kicked him again and again. He went dark.

When he awoke, he was trapped inside a box. A coffin. The world was swaying, and engines rumbled. He was on a boat, maybe in a plane. He banged against his coffin walls. He tugged at his chains. Trying to die. To suffocate. Living onward. Exhausted, he slept again.

In his dreams, he was marching through a labyrinth of stone. A mouse on a chain. Anxious to make his way out. But everywhere he turned, he ran into walls, and a golden eye above watched him, searing him with electricity. He kept scurrying through the maze, growing more and more desperate. But he could not find his home of forests and flowers, and around the labyrinth spread a gray sea of pollution.

He woke up in another cell.

These walls were not limestone bricks but concrete. This air was not stifling hot but icy. The light through the window was gray, and he could see smoggy sky. In the distance, Shostakovitch was playing.

He was back in Isonomia.

He still hung from chains.

For a long time, Kay drifted in and out of consciousness. Guards brought him food and water. He spat it out. They beat him until he ate and drank. Then beat him again until he vomited. Then had doctors treat him, heal him, only so they could hurt him again. They left him on his chains. He slept.

Kay didn't know how many days passed before they brought her to him.

When she stepped into the cell, Kay was delirious. Maybe dying. Unable to tell the difference between dreams and reality. He only knew that wakefulness brought worse nightmares than sleep.

She stepped closer, hesitated, lowered her eyes and trembled.

"KB209?" she whispered.

Kay looked up. He looked at her lined face. At her sunken green eyes. At the auburn stubble growing around her mindcap.

It was her. She was here. Perhaps a reality. Perhaps only a dream.

"UV502," he said. "My mate. My wife." Tears burned. "My Christine."

She touched his cheek, then pulled her hand back as if bitten.

"You're bleeding," she said.

"Christine." He trembled in his chains. "Are you real? Are you really here?"

She nodded, and now her eyes too filled with tears. "They took me. I was worshiping the Father. I was a good comrade. I was good, KB209. But they took me. They said you were a Zionite. They hurt me." She let out a sob. "They hurt me so badly. They said I could go free if I talked to you."

Kay lowered his head and wept. They had tortured her. Tortured his wife. Because of him.

Finally he mustered the strength to raise his head, to look at her again. And he didn't see the wrinkled, bald, aging woman. He saw his young, beautiful bride. A woman with radiant skin and flowing auburn hair.

"Do you remember who you are?" he said. "Do you remember us?"

She was trembling violently. But she nodded.

"I am Christine." She touched his cheek, and her tears flowed. "But I don't remember your name."

"Kay," he whispered. "That's good enough."

She nodded. "Kay."

"Christine." He swung on his chains, trying to bring himself closer. The movement shot pain through his joints. "Christine—our son. Do you remember our son?"

Fear filled her eyes. She took a step back.

"No," she whispered, lips trembling.

"Christine, our son!" Kay swung toward her, tugging the chains. "Don't you remember? What happened to him?"

She shook her head wildly. "We have no son."

"Where is he?" Kay raised his voice, hoarse, desperate. "Christine, where is our son?"

She sniffed. "You don't remember?" she whispered.

"What happened to him? Oh God, Christine, tell me. Where is he?"

She stepped closer. She placed her hands on his cheeks. She stared into his eyes.

"You don't remember."

Kay shook his head. "They erased my memory. At the reeducation camp. For eight years, I suffered there. A slave. Tortured. Broken. Rebuilt. My mind wiped. I don't remember my name. I don't remember who we were. Only faded images. Echoes. Where is our son?"

Christine caressed his head, running her fingers through his hair. "We were farmers, Kay. We didn't live in this city. We lived among trees. There were red flowers in the spring. We didn't have much. A few vegetables. A little bit of corn. We paid our dues. We gave to the Party what we could. We were willing to go hungry to feed our soldiers. One day you spoke to me. In our barn. You said that ..." She trembled, took a deep breath. "You said that the Father took too much from us. That maybe we should give a little less."

"Flowers," Kay whispered. "Red flowers. Anemones. A red barn."

"Our son heard you, Kay. He heard your treason. So he ran. He ran to the Equapol." She was weeping now. "He informed. He turned you in. And they took you, Kay. The police came, and they took you from me. They put you in a train. And they sent you away for eight years. And when you came back, you were a broken man. You didn't even know my name. I didn't recognize you anymore. All I had was the Father. All I had was his love."

Kay stared, shock pounding through him.

"Peter," he whispered. "Our son was named Peter ..."

Christine nodded. "I couldn't forgive him. My son took everything from me. We had a rifle."

"Don't." Kay shook his head, closed his eyes. His voice cracked. "Don't tell me."

But Christine kept speaking. "I took that rifle. I went into his room when he slept."

"Christine, no—"

"I killed him, Kay." She sobbed. "I killed our son. For what he did. He was Peter. He was G45I, Martyr #58. You know his tale well."

Kay wept.

Yes, he knew that boy. He had taught that tale a thousand times in the truthhall. A thousand times, he had grieved.

"I have to go," Christine whispered. "The Father needs me. I did my duty." She kissed his forehead. "He needs you too, Kay. Worship the Father. He loves you. Equalism is good. Equalism is just. Equalism is forever, and the Father protects us."

"Christine ..." he whispered. "Kill me. Please."

She turned and left.

Kay remained in his cell, lowered his head, and waited for the darkness to take him.

CHAPTER THIRTY

Kay didn't know how long he stayed in this cell. Maybe it was weeks. Maybe years. There was no time here. No days or nights. Just forced feedings. Fever dreams. Memories and regret.

Sometimes they unchained him, let him sleep. Sometimes they hung him from the ceiling, beat him. Sometimes they healed him. Sometimes they interrogated him, asked him about Zion, about Bialik, and he told them what they wanted to hear.

After the passage of eras, they moved him.

They covered his head in a sack. Bound him in more chains. Took him in an armored truck. They dragged him down hallways. He could see the cracked concrete beneath his feet, stained with old blood. Neon lights flickered. They shoved him into another cell.

Here Kay languished. Maybe for days. Maybe for years. Alone and chained in the dark.

The door opened again.

Kay winced, expecting more soldiers, more beatings. Ready to beg for death again.

But it was not the general or his men.

A robed, masked figure entered the cell. The robes and mask were golden.

The figure stepped closer and stared at Kay.

It was the Father.

Kay stared at the golden idol. The being he had seen in paintings, murals, statues, and videos a million times. Now the

Father himself stood before him. Silent. Hand held out, a gesture of love.

Kay knew he should beg forgiveness. Should worship his god. Should swear his eternal loyalty. He knew that if he did this, he would go free.

He would return to the labyrinth.

He would be a sheep again.

He stared at the Father—and he spat. His spit landed on the Father's shoe.

The Father stared down at the shoe, then pulled it off, revealing toes with red nail polish.

Kay blinked.

The Father removed the golden mask and robe.

Kay stared, knowing this was a dream.

"Ellie," he whispered.

She smiled sadly. "Hello, Kay."

Kay tugged on his chains. The pain in his joints flared. Real. Agonizing. He was awake.

Ellie stood before him.

"Ellie!" he cried. "Ellie. Oh God, Ellie, you're alive!" He trembled. "You came to save us. Get me out of these chains. Adrian is somewhere here too. We can escape. We—"

Ellie raised an electric prod and slammed it into his sternum.

Kay screamed as electricity raced across him. He convulsed and his chains rattled.

Finally, after what seemed forever, she pulled the prod back. He gasped for air.

"Good," Ellie said. "Be quiet. For too long I listened to you speak."

He stared at her, silent for long moments.

His Ellie.

The woman he had met at the rally.

The woman who had led him to the ruins of Zion.

The woman he had fallen in love with.

The woman who had betrayed him.

"You're the Father," he whispered. "You've been the Father all along."

His heart felt empty. He could no longer feel pain.

Ellie smiled. "No. I'm not the Father." She tapped her chin. "At least—not the original one. Not even the only current one. There are many who don the costume."

Kay took a shuddering breath. He let his chin drop to his chest.

"A lie," he whispered. "It was all a lie."

Ellie shrugged. "What is a lie? What is the truth? Only what we determine. Only what the Party decides. What the citizens accept. Oh, the Father used to be real. We didn't make him up, if that's what you mean. But he died. Of old age. He was just a man, after all. He died over three hundred years ago. But, well … the sheep need a shepherd. The mob needs a leader." She stroked Kay's cheek. "The Father is eternal, Kay. And the Father protects us."

"And what of Zion?" he said, voice louder now, hoarse, and he tasted blood. "You led us there. Was it all a sham? Another lie? Just a circus to entertain your husband?"

"Oh, Zion too was once real," Ellie said. "We didn't invent it. For a long time, Zion was a great enemy. But we defeated it. Zion fell three centuries ago. The Father himself, the true Father, destroyed that land. But following that victory, Isonomia weakened. We grew complacent. Fat. Decadent. An army cannot exist without an enemy. Nor can an ideology. So we kept Zion alive. It gives my husband and his soldiers a purpose. It gives the people a scapegoat. It keeps Isonomia strong. There can be no nationalism without an enemy. There can be no order without chaos. There can be no subjugation without hope to crush. There can be no Isonomia without Zion." She kissed Kay's forehead. "And you, my sweet Zionite, were part of this noble goal."

Kay laughed mirthlessly. "So that's what you do. Recruit people for your show."

She nodded. "Me and others. We find rebels. Troublemakers. You tried to steal food from the Father. Even after years in a reeducation camp, you spoke against the Father in your apartment. We knew you would make a perfect rebel. Tilly. Adrian. The others. All had rebellious tendencies. Oh, we knew about you all years ago. We read your minds, you know. We record every thought. So I recruited you. Others like me recruit more defectors. I led my little group to Zion. To give my husband some playthings to hunt."

"But you fought with us!" Kay shouted. "You killed Equapol with me! You killed White Army sailors with me!"

She laughed. "Of course. That's part of the fun. Dealing with rebellions keeps the Equapol on its toes. Deaths cull the weak. The police need an enemy. As for the navy, well ..." She frowned. "They crossed me. You were toys for my husband. Not for them. The sailors tried to steal his fun. So I killed them. Next time, they will fight the enemies we find for them. Not the enemies I find for the White General."

Kay stared at her. Feeling so empty.

"All that I did," he whispered. "It was for nothing. All my struggles. My fights. My pain. The people I killed. The people I betrayed. For nothing."

Ellie's eyes softened. She caressed him and kissed his lips.

"You did it for Isonomia," she said. "You are a martyr."

"You kiss me," he said. "You kiss me like you did a hundred times before. Was that all fake too? Those nights of making love? Of sleeping embraced? Just part of the show?"

Ellie looked away, for the first time taken aback. Then she looked back into his eyes, and he saw something there. Something deep. Something resembling humanity.

"I do love you," she said. "In my own way. I enjoy sex. I enjoyed our time together. These are human needs. I have them too. I'm not proud of them. But I acknowledge them. I fulfill them when I can." She thought for a moment, then nodded. "Yes, Kay. I love you. That was all real. I knew you were somebody special. Somebody who could do great things. Just … not the things you thought."

He gave a bitter laugh. "What great things? Languish here in a prison cell?"

"Oh, my love …" She kissed him again. "You won't be here for much longer. I came to say goodbye. And to thank you." She walked toward the door, then looked back at him. "Goodbye, Kay. The Father will protect you."

Kay closed his eyes, despair flooding him.

So much pain.

So much hope.

For nothing.

He thought of his wife. Of his son. Of a forest and flowers. And he waited for the end.

CHAPTER THIRTY-ONE

They came for him as Shostakovitch played.

Kay could hear the music above. The same chords he had heard so many times. The music of his life. The music he had been born to. The music he would now die to.

The guards unchained him, dragged him from his cell. They didn't blindfold him this time. They put no sack over his head. He saw a concrete corridor. He saw the flickering lights. He saw many soldiers around him, hiding inside white armor.

They passed by another cell. Guards pulled out another prisoner. The man had a bruised, swollen face, one eye gone. He seemed barely alive.

"Kay?" the man said, voice hoarse. "You look like shit."

Kay's heart twisted. "Adrian."

His friend looked at him, his one remaining eye damp. "Brother."

The guards dragged them. They pulled several other prisoners out of cells. They were all dressed in rags. Tortured. Barely able to walk. The soldiers pulled them forward on chains, up a staircase, and through a hatch.

The prisoners emerged into the arena.

Concrete tiers rose around them. Fifty-eight thousand people roared. All in white robes. All wearing masks. The sound was deafening, and the music blared from the speakers. Equalism banners fluttered in the wind.

Kay knew this place. He had been here thousands of times. Arena T671.

The place where I met you, Ellie.

EQL61 was already here. He marched around the arena, holding a megaphone.

"Behold, comrades! Behold—captured Zionites!"

The crowd booed and howled with hatred. The masks spun around Kay. Twisted with fury. Condemning. Dripping malice. Fists rose. The arena shook.

The general continued speaking.

"We fought them long and hard in the desert. They murdered many of our people. But we won a great battle! We captured these wretched capitalists of the east. Servants of Bialik. Drinkers of blood! Bringers of disease! Sub-human Zionite rats!"

The crowd roared, tried to leap forward, to attack. They had become a mob, given to their bloodlust.

I was once one of them, Kay thought. *Coming here. Chanting. Hating. Wearing a mindcap.*

He looked at them. And he pitied them. And he realized that for all his pain, he was free, and they were not. They were the true victims, more than he could ever be again.

Because I tasted freedom, Kay thought. *Because I removed my mindcap, and I could think, and I could see. Because I woke up. And they are still asleep. They are still caught in the nightmare.*

In the middle of the arena, the soldiers had prepared hills of sand, and Kay thought of the golden dunes of Zion. The soldiers pulled the chains, dragging the prisoners onto the sandy mounds. They buried them there. Leaving only the heads exposed. Kay. Adrian. Ten others. A soldier laughed and spat on them. Another kicked a prisoner in the head. The soldiers retreated, smirking. The prisoners remained in the sand.

Across the theater, soldiers were moving along the tiers, handing out baskets of stones.

The White General raised his megaphone.

"For equalism! Stone the Zionites!"

The stones flew.

Most missed. Most never even reached the arena, landing instead among the tiers, hitting other citizens.

But hundreds of stones still reached the buried prisoners.

Stones tore through skin. Cracked skulls. Shattered faces.

They slammed into Kay's head. Blood poured. He saw stones pummel the prisoners around him. One took out Adrian's remaining eye. Kay tasted blood.

Many citizens, furious that the prisoners still lived, leaped from their seats. They bounded down the tiers, ran across the arena, and hurled stones from nearby. Kay lost a tooth. Somebody kicked his head. The crowd was everywhere. White masks. Screams. Hateful eyes.

And among them, Kay saw her.

A figure in the crowd.

Smaller than the others. A child.

He looked at her name tag. RT765. He recognized that ID.

One of his pupils. A girl.

She displayed no outward signs of gender. But when Kay looked into her eyes, he knew. A little girl.

As the stones flew, the girl stared through the holes of her mask, confused. Her mindcap shone. Its hate indicators were still orange, not yet fully red with rage. Very soon, Kay knew, the mindcap would shock her, would drive her mad with pain, turn her toward hatred.

But for a few seconds, she was awake. Curious.

Kay reached with his tongue toward his cheek. He felt it there. His prosthetic molar. The one Ginsburg had given him.

Kay pushed with his tongue, popping open the fake tooth. A small device spilled out. It swam in his bloody mouth.

The scrambler.

Kay spat it out. The little piece of metal landed on the sand.

The girl picked it up.

A stone flew. It took one of Kay's eyes.

He looked at the girl.

"Attach it to your mindcap," Kay said. "Slide it into the groove at the back."

The girl tilted her head. She attached the scrambler to her mindcap. Her indicators turned green. Her eyes widened. For the first time in her life, she was thinking clearly.

Another stone flew. Kay felt his skull crack. A boot kicked, tearing an ear.

With his one eye, Kay looked at the girl. He smiled at her.

He knew that his life had meaning. He knew that all this pain—his rebellion, his battles, his suffering—had served a purpose. He had never needed to find Zion. He had needed to find a girl. To find a rebel. To find a future leader.

He had indoctrinated thousands of children, brainwashed and twisted their minds. But at the end, he set one free. It was the greatest thing he had ever done.

"Build Zion," he told her.

She nodded. She understood.

More rocks flew. One hit his remaining eye. There was only darkness now, and the pain was fading.

And Kay saw them.

Green forests. Red flowers. Beyond them—his friends, waving to him from a golden city, calling him home.

The End

NOVELS BY DANIEL ARENSON

Earthrise:
Earth Alone
Earth Lost
Earth Rising
Earth Fire
Earth Shadows
Earth Valor
Earth Reborn
Earth Honor
Earth Eternal
Earth Machines
Earth Aflame
Earth Unleashed

Children of Earthrise:
The Heirs of Earth
A Memory of Earth
An Echo of Earth
The War for Earth
The Song of Earth
The Legacy of Earth

The Moth Saga:
Moth
Empires of Moth
Secrets of Moth
Daughter of Moth
Shadows of Moth
Legacy of Moth

Dragonfire Rain:
Blood of Dragons
Rage of Dragons
Flight of Dragons

Misfit Heroes:
Eye of the Wizard
Wand of the Witch

Kingdoms of Sand:
Kings of Ruin
Crowns of Rust
Thrones of Ash
Temples of Dust
Halls of Shadow
Echoes of Light

Alien Hunters:
Alien Hunters
Alien Sky
Alien Shadows

Standalones:
Firefly Island
Flaming Dove
The Gods of Dream
Utopia 58

KEEP IN TOUCH

www.DanielArenson.com
Daniel@DanielArenson.com
Facebook.com/DanielArenson
Twitter.com/DanielArenson

Made in the USA
Middletown, DE
22 August 2019